VOLUME 2 OF THE DON'T...

COMPLICATED MOONLIGHT

"I don't need to have all life's plans figured out to know I want your mouth on mine in this moment, Klive.
Please stop talking and kiss me."
- Kinsley Hayes

Lynessa Layne

USA TODAY BESTSELLING AUTHOR

Also by Lynessa Layne

The Don't Close Your Eyes Series

Killer Kiss – a novelette

Don't Close Your Eyes

Complicated Moonlight

Mad Love

Dangerous Games

Hostile Takeover

Target Acquired

Point Blank

Short Stories

The Getaway

Winter in Roatan

Whispers Through the Trees

The Crow's Nest

Magazine Articles

The Villains of Romantic Suspense

This is a work of fiction. Names, characters, places, businesses, social sites, organizations, locales, events and incidents are either products of the author's imagination or used fictitiously and used for entertainment purposes only. Any resemblance to actual persons, living or dead, or actual events is purely coincidental.

Copyright © 2021 Lynessa Layne

Copyright © 2022 Lynessa Layne

As adapted from original manuscript Copyright © 2014 Lynessa James

Fast Layne Independent Publishing - All rights reserved.

No part of this publication may be reproduced, distributed or transmitted in any form or by any means, including photocopying, recording or other electronic or mechanical methods without prior written permission of the publisher, except in the case of brief quotations embodied in critical reviews and certain other noncommercial uses permitted by copyright law. For permission requests, write to the publisher, addressed at authorlynessalayne@lynessalayne.com

ISBN 978-1-956848-15-1

Cover created by Lynessa Layne. Image courtesy of Shutterstock. All rights reserved.

Lynessa Layne does not own the rights to music titles mentioned. All musical references are for entertainment purposes only. Reader assumes all responsibility for legally obtaining content.

For Holly.
From accidental reader to unexpected best friend, I'm so blessed to have found you through the broken road that writing created. You've been there through the good, bad, ugly and awful. You were the voice of courage during dreadful discouragement, no fiction necessary. The things we've faced and overcome in our journeys are a remarkable testament to God's provision no matter the path we find ourselves on. I love you dearly and I'm so grateful you accidentally bought the wrong book.

Cast of Characters

- **Klive Henley King** – anti-villain./hero also known as Complicated Moonlight and Kinsley's pirate. Enforcer of crime syndicate, Nightshade, leading double life

- **Henley** – Klive's alter ego for pulling hit jobs and undercover stings

- **Kinsley Fallon Hayes** – Protagonist. Bartender, college student, renowned sprinter known as Micro Machine

- **Andy and Clairice Hayes** – Kinsley's parents

- **Ben** – Andy Hayes' co-worker, Klive's friend

- **Jase Michael Taylor** – Navy SEAL, Navy SEAL, lead singer of Rock-N-Awe, lifeguard, Kinsley's longtime crush

- **Tyndall Taylor** – Jase's little sister, Kinsley's best friend

- **Mike and Bianca Taylor** – Jase and Tyndall's parents

- **Rustin Keane** – Jase's childhood best friend, combat veteran, cop

- **Nightshade** – crime syndicate

- **Joey** – Klive's personal security detail, private investigator

- **Eric** – Klive's Nightshade lieutenant

- **Christophe** – Klive's private investigator, Joey's employer

- **Marcus** – Kinsley's manager, Nightshade member

- **Gustav & Jarrell** – bouncers at the bar Kinsley works at, Nightshade members

- **Bayleigh & Garrett** – Kinsley's co-workers

- **Constance Marie** – Kinsley's friend, Jase's co-lead for the band Rock-N-Awe

- **Antoine (Sweetness)** – Constance's cousin, Gustav's brother, Kinsley's hairstylist, military spec-ops, has worked with Jase

- **Inferno** – biker gang crime syndicate comprised of dishonest firefighters. Rivals of Nightshade.

- **Ray Castille** – Inferno's disgraced leader, Fire Marshal

- **Pat Connor** – Inferno biker

- **Sara Scott** – Kinsley's co-worker, Patrick Scott's widow

- **Adrian Miller** – Kinsley's art professor

- **Ian Walton** – Kinsley's personal trainer and track coach

- **Eliza, Lindsay, Julie** – Kinsley's track relay team

- **(Looney) Lucy** – Kinsley's track manager and biggest fan

- **Brayden** – who Kinsley dubs Frat Toy, has huge crush on her

- **Shay** – Kinsley's alternate/replacement on the track team

- **Nolan and Devon** – Jase's buddies from high school

- **Matt** – lifeguard who works with Jase

- **Angela Ansley** – Kinsley's high school nemesis

- **Detective William Bartlet** – worked Sara Scott's murder, saddled with training Rustin

- **Sheriff Ansley** – William Bartlet's boss, Angela Ansley's father

Character Point of View

♂ = Klive King

♀ = Kinsley Hayes

1 | ♂

Kinsley smiled over her shoulder as she skipped away with the exuberance of a giddy five-year-old. She held the rose like a girl ready to pluck the petals and ask whether *he loves me, he loves me not.* I kissed two of my fingers and waved, unable to help relishing her joy. *I caused that? What a feeling!*

When I turned from Kinsley, the man who'd stolen my freedom pilfered the fleeting happiness from my soul as he lumbered down the stands. A smirk of knowing lit his wholesome veneer as he stopped before me.

"Cheatham, how are you?" I asked but couldn't give a damn.

"Not as well as you appear to be, Klive, especially after last night …." He peered beyond my shoulder. "She's talented. Quite attractive. A little young, don't you think?"

"Hobbies always are." I smirked in kind.

"Rumor has it this is more than a hobby. You're breaking protocol." He shook his head as though we discussed some travesty, concerned empathy replacing the smirk. "Klive, I'd hate for the collateral damage to be on such a scale, but she'd make a great martyr. Track fans would gather on their social platforms to mourn their small-time icon while pledging war against whomever we pin the blame. She might draw more attention to her sport dead than she has alive. A great legacy."

My eyebrow lifted as I half-smiled. "You want to go there over a rumor? I don't think you want my trouble on your doorstep, Cheatham. There's mutiny in the ranks, and I am not inclined to allow disrespect a foothold. Perhaps you're the cause of it?"

He chuckled and relaxed his demeanor, shook his head, but I could tell his eyes were on her once more. "I see why you showed up. She has very pretty legs for being so tiny, doesn't she?"

Testing my temper. *Always testing!* I continued undeterred. "She's a server at a Nightshade bar. The second server within three weeks taking shit from Inferno. Either I draw the line that I won't put up with boundary-testing by those beneath us, or we risk looking weak and allowing them to overthrow. Up to you. What should it be? Unless that's your plan?"

"And what of your plan? I still own you for two more months. I'd hate to increase that sentence because you chose disobedience in the final stretch."

"Enough. If I want to get laid while defending my territory, 'tis nothing different from anyone else. Your threat implies a motive for causing the divide. In which case I have a right to defend myself and anyone else in the face of *your* mutiny."

"That a challenge, Klive? Remember who created you. Do you think you're the only *golden boy* at my disposal?" He tilted his head to see her better. "If you screw anything more than the girl, I'm removing the distraction. And if I'm not mistaken, her little friend looks awfully familiar ... haven't I met her before?"

My jaw clenched, but I thought of Jase Taylor and the damage he would do if he had any idea that his sister, Tyndall Taylor, was being threatened. Cheatham didn't know I had *golden boys*—hitmen—of my own.

He eyed my face and said, "Gotcha. Heed my warning. Best to stay away from the girl. I don't want a war within the underground.

Let them have their whores to pay their debts. That's an order. You violate, you know the penalty."

"No. She's not a whore. Their debts are their own."

"Oh, Klive, haven't you learned? Most women are whores for the right price. Inferno's debts will become yours if you say no to me ever again."

He passed me and jogged right up to Kinsley. I didn't have to hear to know he asked for a photo after having the gall to shake her father's hand like a friendly admirer of her gifted sprint. His phone rose before he pulled her close for a selfie just like several others had before him. Now Cheatham had her face as his way of marking her for any *golden boys* assigned to remove her.

Would they be so foolish to do so if they knew they'd have to go through me *to get to her?*

I jogged down the stands and mixed into the crowd departing the venue. My personal security detail, Joey, kept eyes on Kinsley. Eric, my Nightshade lieutenant, played a convenient body double as he wore what I was. He walked toward my vehicle without looking over his shoulder so I might study Cheatham's actions from the shadows. Beneath the stands, I unzipped the backpack Eric left for me, changed my shirt, pulled on a shaggy brunette wig, added a ball cap and a pair of sunglasses. I licked the back of a temporary tattoo and placed the symbol to the inside of my left wrist.

In truth, I wasn't as worried about Cheatham's threat as much as what he was setting into motion on my end. *What was his goal? Forcing me into more time?* Something more was afoot.

I fished for a set of keys in the bottom of the bag, then zipped the tines closed and pulled a strap over my shoulder.

From beneath the stands, I couldn't help spying Kinsley between the beams of metal. I crouched and crept closer until I was close enough to hear her conversation with her father.

"—will Jase think?"

"Daddy, Jase isn't my boyfriend, and the guy was just another fan. What's the big deal?"

"The big deal is your career vanishing because of a crush on an older man."

"My career *vanishing*?" She waved the rose I'd gifted her like a sword between them. "I just won every heat. What have I lost? You act like he's forty or something."

"What if he is? What then?"

"Daddy, what if he's just a fan and you're overreacting? Seriously. Just, next time maybe don't come. I'm out of here."

"What about Tyndall? I thought you were staying with her."

"She has her boyfriend now. Like most of my friends. Some are even—*gasp*—married with kids! And their lives aren't ruined because they gave up extracurricular activities for real life!"

I gave a silent whistle and turned my head, noticing a redhead sitting nearby cupping her mouth. *Kinsley's sister?*

Kinsley waved her father away and turned toward the locker rooms once more. Her father called out, "Don't you need a ride home? You never said where you were going!"

"I'm riding the bus with all the normal girls! And you're right, I didn't say."

"Kinsley Fallon!"

"Hayden Andrew Hayes." The redhead cursed his full name.

Damn! A tone like hers had to be from a wife.

"Oh, Clairice." Andrew Hayes wilted by her side as she wrapped arms around his broad shoulders. "My baby. Where's my baby girl?"

"Andy. Can you imagine what a fool you've made of yourself if she's telling the truth about the guy with the rose? It's not the first time someone's given her flowers after a win. Why this one? When will you realize she's not a baby anymore? She's an *adult*. Your baby girl, yes, but a grown woman. You said you'd give her space, but maybe that's easier said than done?"

He placed a hand over one of hers on his shoulder. "No, I know this guy, Claire. Ben invited him to lunch with us a few times to get his advice on difficult client relations. He knows his stuff, has a silver-tongued charisma when he isn't busy snubbing those beneath him, far too young to be so successful. It's dangerous for someone his age to hold so much power. The British accent makes it worse."

"You accuse Kinsley of crushing on an older man, now you say he's too young. Which is it?" she asked. "Did this man not work for this success? Was it just handed to him because of some social standing?"

He sighed. "From what I've gleaned, he's worked for every title and penny he's earned."

Well, thank you very much, Mr. Hayes. What the hell is bad about that?

"So, he's a successful, driven, powerful snob and you're afraid he's going to work at earning our daughter's attention by driving hours upstate to give her roses after showing her support at her track meet? And, by the way, he seems to have a knack for dealing with difficult people which we both know you've trained your little girl to be." She hummed while her husband frowned. "I think he deserves the benefit of the doubt, Andy. Kinsley hates snobs. Do you really think your partner at work would befriend a snob?"

Andrew Hayes gave a bitter laugh. "Ben *is* a snob."

His wife slapped his hand. "I don't know what's gotten into you, but Ben is perfectly kind. I'm sure whoever this man is may have something more than charisma and an accent going for him."

"Hell, Claire, he does. Remember my birth—"

"Andy, Claire?" Kinsley's friend, Tyndall, jogged back in from the parking lot and held her side. Kinsley's parents looked at her.

"I screwed up. I already sent Kinsley packing on the bus because I have a date later, but since you're in town, you mind grabbing a bite with me so we can catch up?"

"Please, Tyndall, if you wouldn't mind, we'd really enjoy your company," Claire told her.

"Yeah, not to be rude, but I could tell papa's kinda freaking out, so maybe I can allay your fears?" Tyndall offered.

Wow. I'd heard enough.

I walked out from under the beams beneath the stands and straightened the wig, so the hair fell somewhat over one eye. Eric's black 911 Porsche was front and center in the lot. Rather than heading for his car the way I should have, I found the barista who worked in the coffee shop in my building. The ultimate test. I cleared my accent and lowered my voice.

"Hey, it's Lucy, right?" I asked when she exited the locker room with a group of girls. They all gaped, one elbowed Lucy's ribs. I rolled my eyes behind the reflective glasses.

"Yes?" Lucy turned, excitement lighting her face at a male's attention singling her out among the throng.

"Is Micro Machine inside? I was hoping to get a picture with her before—"

"I'm not taking any more pictures today," Kinsley said as she emerged. The group of girls gasped; some blushed. She stared them down as she ignored me and passed them. "Sorry. Not feeling well." She paused to face me. "Lucy's not my handler. You'd do better to ask my coach if you're ever looking for me. Some people just claim to know me when they're just piggybacking the ass of the racehorse."

Damn! She was *very* angry. In ways I'd not even experienced on the lift when we'd first met!

What the hell caused such a dramatic shift from the bubbly girl I'd left on the track? Surely, not just the bit with her father?

"My mistake. I'm sorry. Yes, next time," I told her and waved, prepared to be on my way.

"Wait. Please, forgive me. Get your picture." Kinsley's bag fell off her shoulder to the ground. She walked up while I hurried to raise my phone and put my arm around her. When she leaned close and smiled, she inhaled. Her face inspected mine. After a couple snaps on my phone, she rushed to pick up her bag.

For the second time, I'd made the mistake of wearing the cologne she responded to like a drug.

"What kind of cologne do you wear?" Kinsley asked with no hint of flirtation or interest. "Smells nice. Would love to get some for my father."

Lucy hadn't recognized me, but did Kinsley?

Was this her passive anger turning on me with the daddy card, or was this the way she treated guys she wasn't interested in?

Did her kindness toward me mean she was interested the way her father feared?

"Sir?" she interrupted my internal questions. I realized she'd been crying. Her nose was pink, and she sniffled a couple of times.

"I can't recall," I told her.

"That sucks." She waved with cautious indifference.

"Hey, are you okay?"

"Yep. Seasonal allergies."

I nodded and allowed the distance to grow between us, but Cheatham could kiss my ass if he thought I'd stay away for long.

2 | ♀

What the hell just happened?

I rushed back inside the locker room to hide myself inside a stall, leaving my father in turmoil on the empty track. How did he think I felt?

Tears rushed to my eyes. I wasn't sure what bothered me most: the idea that Daddy thought I would play two men against one another, or that he accosted me in public over my accepting a gift from a fan? Sure, Klive King wasn't just any fan, but how would Daddy know? What about the other stuff fans had given? And what the hell was with Tyndall bailing on me for some guy she refused to talk about?

Tyndall texted while I pulled some toilet paper to swipe beneath my eyes. *Kins I hope ur ok. Was about to leave when I saw u run away from your dad. The boy can wait. Interference for my girl comes first. I told your parents u had to ride the bus, but that I'd like to have dinner with them to catch up. Get out of here!*

Breathing a sigh of relief, hot tears spilled down my cheeks. My best friend chose me. I blew my nose, then thumbed a huge thanks. *I owe you, Tyndall!*

Yup! she texted with about twenty party emojis. *Ur buying when I come 4 SB!*

Happy hour, whaaat! I thumbed. She texted that I was cheap, causing me to smile.

The main door squeaked and slammed.

"— see that guy?"

A group of girls giggled into the area to change and primp. I yanked my feet from the floor and pinned my shoes against the stall door. No way I was risking an opponent seeing me cry when I'd just kicked ass in all of my races.

"What guy?"

"The one who gave her the flower."

"A guy gave Micro Machine a flower?" *No! They were talking about me!*

"Did she beat him with it or tell him to keep it?"

"Ugh, pay attention."

"Her precious daddy looked ready to beat her with it."

Holy crap! These weren't opponents. They were teammates!

I leaned over to peek through the crack in the stall door, but couldn't see faces, just a mass of about seven bodies and ponytails blocking the sink and mirror area.

"Can I use your deodorant? I left mine at home."

"What did he look like?"

"Sure but wipe it off when you're done. Does my face look too fat with my hair up?"

"Who? Daddy or flower guy?"

"Really?"

"H.O.T. And your face looks fine, but you're breaking out."

I closed my eyes when they made dirty remarks concerning my father, then Klive. *Jesus, you hear this* .... My nails bit the flesh of my empty palm.

"Was it the same guy that left the roses on her bag for Valentine's? The stalker in the stands?"

"I thought Lucy left those for her," one teased. They all laughed while Lucy told them to hush. Hers was the only voice I really knew by heart. I wasn't in the habit of hanging with undergrads.

"Do we go to school with him?"

"No," Lucy interjected. "He's like thirtyish. You really don't know who he is?"

"No, who?"

"Y'all are cute. He's like a big deal in business or something. I know him because he buys coffee from *me* by request every morning before he goes to work," Lucy told them like she had an upper edge. "I'm his favorite barista because I make his order exactly how he likes." I rolled my eyes. I so wanted out of here. "You think he was hot today; you should see him in a suit. And he smells so expensive it's like I'm being fanned with money every time I hand him his order. His tips are great, so I guess I am." She giggled.

"Is *he* her boyfriend?"

"I thought she was a lesbian."

"Maybe she is a lesbian but turned straight for his money."

"I would, hee-hee."

"She's so butch sometimes."

"Butch or bitch?"

"Right? Maybe bisexual? I don't know what he sees in her. Someone should tell him to have a little fun with the holier-than-thou Bible-thumper to take the stick outta her ass and nose outta the air. She's gonna need to say her prayers if she has to go up against that trans-gender sprinter."

I gasped and squeezed the phone in my fist so I wouldn't yank the door open and start shit. Gossiping girls weren't worth a suspension from the team.

"Don't say that," Lucy jumped in. "Is that guy on the schedule? I think Walton is training her harder in case. She should be fine."

"Lucy! Shame on you! Pronouns!"

"Seriously, Lucy, you're blinded by celebrity. SHE is gonna kick Micro Machine's ass and knock her off that high horse. She can't win every relay forever."

"Ooh, speaking of kicking someone's ass, I wish you guys had been with me and Lucy last night!"

"Shay, don't. We don't know what happened," Lucy begged.

'Shay' continued without pause. "Last night, we went to the bar she works at. Let me tell you. To-tal HO. Sexy ho, but ho."

"More like whore."

"Stop," Lucy warned. "Her boss makes her dress that way. Our track uniforms show more, so back off. She's just being nice to people. She has to flirt to make tips."

"Luce! Quit coming to her defense all the time!"

"Micro Machine?"

"Ho?"

"Whore?"

"Do we even know her real name?"

"I think it's Kelsey or something, but she had a different name on her uniform last night when we ran into her. Probably the name she uses when she's in work mode, if you know what I mean." Several girls giggled. I withheld everything inside not to kick a bitch's ass. Tyndall texted again, but I smothered the vibration in the name of eavesdropping.

"Are you guys kidding me? She champions our team, and you don't know her real name?" Lucy asked.

"Everyone calls her Micro Machine and it's not like she's ever introduced herself or even hung out with any of us. Why would we know her real name?"

"Yeah, she's a snob. We undergrads are beneath her skill level."

"Ooh, yeah, don't get too close to her, you might slow her down."

Lucy sighed. "Can you blame her for keeping her distance if this is how you treat her?" *I know right? Damn.*

"It's not like we treat her this way to her face."

"Her name is *Kins-ley*," Lucy enunciated the syllables like they were stupid. "Maybe she's not a snob, but just perceptive. If she hadn't been at the bar, we wouldn't have gotten inside or had free drinks, so be grateful." At least Lucy was disgusted. "Shay's just jealous because she doesn't exist to Brayden every time Kins is around. Ironic because I'm pretty sure Kins doesn't know Brayden exists, so...."

"Bitch."

Lucy made a sound like she didn't care while I dug through my brain for anyone named Brayden.

"Aw, you guys got free drinks just for knowing her?" one whined. "Where does she work so I can throw her name, too?"

"Psh, I'm not telling you. You'll ruin it. She doesn't even know you exist either," Shay told another girl. "So, y'all know that biker that was on the news this morning?"

"The gang stuff out in Hillsborough?"

"Yeah. Well, last night we saw him before he died. In THE bar! Guess who he was sexually harassing?"

"Shut up."

"Totally. And now he's dead? And there's this guy who sings there. So hot! He walked up and almost got in a fight over her, then some other guy came and grabbed her like she was in trouble, then the one who works with Lucy stomps in and grabs her and she leaves."

"What? With the hot guy? She left with him?" one rushed, hanging on every word with the suddenly silent witches.

"I can't keep up with this."

"No. He stayed. She left with some other guy."

"I don't think we should be talking about this anymore," Lucy cut in. "Put your stuff up. Coach Walton is going to be pissed if we're late."

"Let him be pissed. He wasn't when Micro Machine took her time getting on the bus this morning. Maybe she was coming off the walk of shame with this guy's friend?"

"Y'all," Lucy said. "She rode with her dad this morning. He dropped her off." *Thank you!*

"Whatever, Luce. Let her finish."

"Yeah, let her finish," they all agreed and silenced Lucy.

"So, she leaves the bar, then the bouncers come and grab the biker but leave the friend he came with just sitting there. He's mad but looks ready to piss himself. The singer and the hot guy Lucy works with talk to him for a minute then they leave, too."

"And?"

"And what? He just sat there like he was grounded to the chair. That's all I know." Zippers closed. "I'm just saying, maybe the guy wasn't done by one of his own. Maybe the other two had something to do with it."

"Ugh. So lame. You listen to too much *Crime Junkie*."

"Oh, I know right? Makes me so paranoid, but what a great story, yeah? Slutty bartender pretending to be good girl bangs two guys who kill biker for touching her then blame it on a gang."

"You forgot track star," one giggled. "Good girl track star moonlighting as slutty bartender to pay her way through college—"

"Guys stop it. She's not like that."

"Like what? A bi-sexual Bible-thumper?" one teased.

"No, she's not paying for college because she's on scholarship."

"Partial scholarship."

"Ah, so still a bi-sexual Bible-thumper." They giggled while my eyes narrowed.

"Y'all suck," Lucy pouted.

"Lighten up, Lucy. We're just playing around. For real, though. Can you find out if they're together? Like *together* together. Or if she's sleeping with both of them? Since you know her so well. And him. And if they're not, maybe you still have a shot with her."

Lucy sighed, then picked up in her chipper bullshit like she'd never been upset. "I'll see what I can do. But, if they are together, they'd make a great couple since you think she's a lesbian and peeps think he's gay."

"Who? The singer or the hot one?"

"The hot one."

"Ha! Maybe they're the perfect cover for one another."

"Aw, Lucy, I don't blame you for having a crush on her. She's pretty. Great T&A. Just cop a feel where you can get it. Pretend it's an acci—"

With a slam, the door cut their conversation. My face fell into my palms, and I prayed for God to help me go outside and get on the bus with this group of traitors masquerading as teammates.

When I pushed through the exit, to my dismay the girls froze as they spoke to some jockstrap Bieber wannabe asking Lucy of my whereabouts like she was my handler. Ugh.

After glaring at the girls and calling some of their crap, I forced a photo with the fan. Hmm ... I'd never met anyone else who wore Klive's cologne, but I braved asking the name so I might buy a bottle and spray the pirate's coat in the faded fragrance.

"Smells nice. Would love to get some for my father," I told him so he wouldn't get his hopes up. He stared like he wasn't sure what I wanted. *C'mon, dude. Doesn't have to be a big deal.* Maybe I should tell him that I wanted to cuddle inside the crushed velvet coat of my ex-boyfriend, watch chick flicks and binge chocolate after cleaning a litter box for five cats.

"Sir?" I prodded, fighting my smartass impulse.

"I can't recall," he said.

Seriously? "That sucks," I told him. *Bye, Felicia. Who didn't remember their own cologne?*

"Hey, are you okay?" Bieber asked.

"Yep. Seasonal allergies." *Maybe I ought to straight up ask Klive what he wears that way I can spritz myself in his fragrance like a cat pisses on a post to inform others they are wasting their time? Poor guy. Wasn't his fault my apparent crush on an older man ruined college boys for me.*

In the distance, Coach Walton waved his arms. The girls ran for the bus. To be a bitch, I took off after them and passed them up to bound onto the bus and steal the seat beside the one I knew Walton would take.

The others boarded about five seconds later. I smiled at my reflection in the window to hide my angry gloating from them. Coach settled in beside me when the doors shut. As the bus moved, I felt his unwavering attention trying to grab mine, but I plugged earbuds and picked a playlist to drown everyone out.

Too bad sound didn't drown the pain of my best friend pulling away for someone who'd keep plucking her strings for as long as he wanted. She may have run interference for me, but the moment my parents finished dinner, I knew she'd be running for the arms of whatever-his-name-was and feeling absolved for doing something nice in the middle of her obsession.

Could she see it? Did she see and not care? No way Tyndall would become that callous. Something bothered her the way my issues bothered me; like I could run from Inferno, from the conflict of the way the rose felt beneath my nose, the pressure points my father kept prodding at, the idle gossip of two-faced mean girls.

Every crotch-rocket that passed the bus pulled my eyes as a magnetic hope for Klive's. Every Harley-style motorcycle sent automatic fear an Inferno biker would be straddling the hog with the intent to exact revenge on me. My hopes and fears simultaneously intensified with every blurred white line on the highway back to Tampa. Because back in Tampa, both Klive and Inferno took residence, and both scared me for reasons I didn't like thinking of.

3 | ♀

THE WINDOW SMEARED WITH the sweat that formed on my brow the closer we got to town. When I lifted my head, Coach Walton handed me a paper towel from his fast-food bag, then felt my forehead after I dabbed away the moisture. I refused to remove the earbuds as I jogged down the steps and dismissed his concern. Words were useless. Only when I stood on the pavement did I recall I was the only one without a ride. Well, hell. My car was still at the bar.

"Come on," Walton said after jerking one of my earbuds free. "You're clammy. Lovesick. And we need to discuss your right ankle, show-off. No more sprinting until Monday at practice."

His tone wasn't friendly, but he wasn't antagonizing either. He was different, too; irritable, tired.

All I said was, "Thank you. And I'm not lovesick, but my best friend is. Why do people get so stupid when they like someone? As if no one else exists?" I grumbled. "The rose was a gift from a fan. Don't worry."

"Like the mondo three dozen lavender roses? Or the dozen red ones left on your duffel bag at practice? I'm worried, but we won't rehash my concerns. You need to go home and rest for the remainder of the weekend. You're lucky I let you run. A stupid mistake on my part. And yeah, people are stupid when they're in love. The type of stupid that runs on adrenaline after injuring their ankle."

One of my eyes squinted, the other bugged in irritation. "I thought you said you weren't going to talk about this now. And you mean the kind of stupid that *allows* someone run on an injured ankle? I can't go home. You have to take me to my job so I can pick up my car. Then, I'll go home and rest."

"You mean the bar?"

A passive-aggressive jab. *Just breathe in for one. Two. Three. Out one. Two. Three.* I pulled the rose back to my nose so the scent might soothe my temper. "Yes. That's where I work. I could just walk the rest of the way on my bad ankle."

"Tempting thought. I'd hate to force you into extra ice baths." The corner of his mouth twitched as I stared for a moment, then rolled my eyes and shook my head.

"Thanks for the ride and letting me sit by you. For real."

He nodded. That was that until I hopped out in front of the bar, hoisting my bag back over my shoulder.

"Looks like a busy night," he exclaimed, eager to be the hell out of there. "Stay safe, Micro Machine. We'll assess the damage before I force ice baths, okay?"

"Ten-four."

We waved, then I greeted the bouncer holding the crowd away from the door. The line went around the side of the building, the music blared from inside, and I stood out like a nun in a whorehouse in my jeans and University tee next to the itty-bitty skirts and tops.

"Aw, look guys, someone ordered a schoolgirl for my birthday party!"

"Dream the dream, frat toy." I smiled at one of the idiots I remembered Jase passively threatening some weeks back. This flirt seemed to think pulling a girl's hair was still the way to win.

Well, Bayleigh and Tyndall would agree, but maybe that depended on the guy doing the pulling. "Gus, hold him out here a little extra, yeah?"

Gustav's laugh vibrated like the bass coming off the walls of the bar. "You know I'm s'posed to hold *you* out here after last night, too, right?"

I nodded and shot him the biggest innocent eyes I was capable of. He opened the door on another loud chuckle with a warning I'd better keep a low-profile.

"Just grabbing my keys, and I'm outta here. Scout's honor, sir."

Before he changed his mind, I rushed inside and was immediately aware of how short I was in my flip flops, as well as how vulnerable my toes were as I tried to navigate between chicks in heels of all heights and the men eager to hook-up by the end of the night. Bayleigh danced to *Super Bass* behind the bar as she rolled her hips, counted shot glasses and tossed bottles to Garrett. He twirled them over his wrists, flipped them behind his back or up in the air three at a time while idiots clamored for the spillage on purpose. That meant Marcus wasn't in, and I was glad since I was pretty sure he'd flip his crap if he'd known Gus allowed me in one night after I'd been harassed by Inferno.

An Inferno member who was now dead.

Could that seriously be real?

Someone who'd sat at one of my tables last night was now forever gone to never sit at another again.

Nausea stole the party vibes. Before I became a coward with my thoughts, I focused on weaseling in between people and ripping my duffel through the small gaps.

"Hey!"

"Watch it!" Women bitched at me as they stumbled sideways or spoiled for a fight. In this setting I dared them. At the rate I was going, why not? Shoving my foot up someone's ass was a better reason for my ankle injury than overreacting to some creep scaring me at the beach. Were those things connected?

As I finally squeezed behind the bar, Garrett denied and grabbed me by the elbow, which I effing hate. I jerked my arm away.

"I just came for my damn keys unless you're about to tell me you had my car towed?" I may as well of snapped my fingers and bobbed my head.

"You have a locker for a reason!" He shouted over the choir of drunk women singing along with Nicki Minaj only so many feet over.

"Peeps can pick locks," I argued. He gave me a deadpan, not buying my lame retort.

"Marcus's office. Bayleigh put them in there last night after you left."

"Then why give me crap about my locker?"

"How'd you get here?" he demanded.

"My coach drove me after my meet. Can I go now, dad?"

"Can you please go now, child?" His eyes darted to my appearance and around us like a protective brother. "Can't win," he said.

"I so did!" I grinned too big as Bayleigh rushed up to give me the quickest of hugs. "Gross, Bayleigh, you have boob sweat!" I whined as she bent low and embraced me.

"Thanks for cleaning me off," she teased, then told me to vamoose, but I didn't miss her worrisome expression. Curiosity for me and my well-being? Or did she maybe know too much about last night? Jeez. I was paranoid. Too suspicious of everyone in my life. After all, Patrick's own allies could've killed him in some bar brawl.

Marcus's office looked slightly different from two nights ago. Cleaner, but still crazy messy, so I searched for a bit before spotting my keys next to the security monitors. How could I resist? Or help wishing tall, dark and hot, Klive King, lurked somewhere ready to sneak up on me and lock us in here before locking his lips on mine. Shame. I couldn't even blame a buzz on these thoughts, but maybe there was something to be said of the atmosphere in the bar; the dirty dancing on the floor, standing room only between tables, the couple kissing in bar area. The only movement in the hall was the bar-back restocking fruit or empty liquor bottles.

A new song mixed with another. The bass got heavier, reverberating the planks beneath my feet. The crowd condensed to make more room for groups on the floor.

My fingers were just wrapping around my keys when I stopped breathing in conflicted shock. Not over Inferno this time.

Jase Taylor!

On the floor. Some slut dancing with him. His bestie, Rustin Keane, danced nearby with his own blow-up doll. Let's be honest, if any girl isn't you, they're all blow-up dolls, right? Because right now they weren't allowed to be human. I couldn't remember the last time I'd felt this type of jealousy.

"What the hell?" My keys curled in my grip, stabbing the flesh of my palm as I stormed into the hallway and through the back door so I wouldn't charge onto the dance floor and make a fool of myself.

4 | ♀

BY THE TIME I pulled into my driveway, I'd driven myself crazy with memories of Jase's hands and skin all over mine while he'd professed to care about me. *To get in my pants? Not even twenty-four hours ago. Now his hands and skin stamped whoever she was!*

I felt cheap.

How could I believe a single word he'd told me? How could I be mad at the woman who had no idea I existed? Did Jase even remember I existed without my being right in front of him?

He wanted to play games?

I WON games!

I tossed my track duffel so hard, the bag hit the bed, rolled to the other side and tumbled to the floor. I didn't give a crap.

I trudged straight to my curling iron and let that baby heat up to the temperature of the ensemble I yanked from my closet. A second later, the ripped tags to a leather mini and a slinky halter top hit the trash can. Tyndall was great about buying things she thought would look cute on me that Daddy would honor kill me for owning. Daddy wasn't home to see me march out in a pair of heels made to punish men.

Tonight, Jase was on the naughty list. That dog was an afterthought as this bitch parked across the street and strode across the pavement toward the front of the building like a Bond-girl bad ass who didn't wait in line.

"Whoa." My badass faltered. *Speaking of Bond girls, this car was made for one.* I slowed to drool like a dude over the finest damn Ferrari I'd ever seen parked in the front spot Marcus reserved for some VIP. The black paint shone like silk in the moonlight. I glanced past the black beauty. The entire row near the sidewalk gleamed like an exotic dealership ad; Lamborghini, Porsche, Bugatti, two Maseratis, three black Escalades, Tesla, two Mercedes, but the car parked between the last two caught my breath. The engine block protruding from the hood. I hadn't seen that car since high school, because muscle of that magnitude was only brought out to play for special occasions.

Why would this be a special occasion? Who the hell was in the bar?

"Now, hold up, Kins. It was one thing to grab your keys, but this? Marcus said you shouldn't be here—"

"Save it, Jarrell," I told one of the bouncers. "Jase shouldn't be here, either. After all, *he* was the one instigating a fight with those Inferno bikers. I was just serving their drinks. And if I'm not here, I'm going somewhere else. At least here you can keep eyes on me, yeah?"

Our head bouncer, Gustav, cursed while I cut the line and pulled the door for myself before either of them had the chance to stop me. According to the most recent news reports, Patrick's threat had been removed in a tragic gang rivalry last night, right? What was I afraid of?

Nothing, I thought, as I walked into bumping club music and paused to assess the crowd for the high rollers driving those cars. My perusal halted on Jase at a table with several men, but each came with a woman draped around them like necklaces. Pretty, shiny, cubic zirconium impostors mixing with diamond divas.

COMPLICATED MOONLIGHT

He didn't see me. I couldn't *unsee* the redhead dragging her nails over the dragon tat on his left arm.

Rustin shoved a brewski-bearing arm between her and Jase. I turned away when Rustin glanced up like he felt my stare. As I squeezed through the thick crowds, drama didn't seem the best idea. Bayleigh caught my eye with a huge flare of hers as she hefted a tray of shots. I tapped my lips and dangled my keys. She acknowledged me with a shake of her head and snagged them on her way past, giving me two fingers to signal two shots. I took what she offered, tossed them both, grateful for the liquid courage she knew I needed. She knew why I was here without my saying a word.

The liquor stung my esophagus, blazing a path to my stomach and blood stream. A guy moved past and grabbed my waist. I slapped the shit out of his hand.

"Don't!" I warned.

"Bitch." He yanked back.

I rolled my eyes and wormed between bodies finding common rhythms on the floor, groups around tables with drinks in their hands. I waved to those who grinned in surprise.

"Hey, sexy! Long time no see!" Delia, a young heiress from New York, bent to kiss each of my cheeks. "Let's dance!" She snatched my hand and draped our grip over her shoulder. A few in her crew came with as she led us to the dance floor. They became my camouflage as they created a natural barrier while we danced as guardians for one another against horny guys with groping hands.

"Who are we punishing?" Delia asked with a naughty smile and gestured to my appearance. "Hold on. Don't tell me. The singer? Jase?"

I nodded and tapped my lips, so she'd share in my secret.

"So much for that serenade. Happy to oblige," she said at my ear over the music. One of her bangle-drenched arms slithered over her head as she rolled her hips to the beat. Her hand holding mine turned me beneath her arm to pull my back to her chest. We fell in sync while she guided my hand to the back of her neck. She wasn't a lesbian but loved making everyone wonder. She was very pretty, enjoyed dancing in flashy dresses, and enjoyed torturing men even more.

Last spring, while tending bar, I'd intervened on a sexual harassment issue she'd had. Ever since, we'd found great company on my rare nights off work. From then on, we played safety for each other when we were in the same place at the same time.

"You've been spied. The singer's watching," she told me. I grinned and swiveled down low while she held my hands over my head. I worked back to standing then turned to face her rogue smile. We bit our lips and she waved her women around us to block his brief view.

After another song, Delia asked, "Want to have some drinks with us?"

"I'd love to, thanks," I told her. Delia's friends played with my hair, asked whether the curls were natural.

One chick popped the strap where my halter came together at my back. "Dangerous," she teased.

"Exactly, she's here for torture," Delia told them. "Why else would she be in rare form? Although, I think it suits her."

"Ha!" I laughed. "Thanks, but no thanks. I'm gonna catch a draft if I keep this up much longer."

"Not if we find the right warm body to keep you from catching a cold," she said.

Delia raised a shot glass and proposed a toast to exacting vengeance. We each lifted shots of rum from the tray in the center of the table and clinked the glasses together.

"Speaking of warm bodies." Delia's eyes shot to the side. While I tossed the shot, I glanced in the direction she indicated and saw none other than the guy I'd dubbed 'Frat Toy'. Beside him stood a bitch I'd now recognize anywhere.

"Oh, Delia, don't you know I'm trying to avoid drama?"

"Clearly," she joked. "I can get away with this because this is who I am." She placed a hand to her shimmery blue dress. "But, if you don't take the upper hand on your look now, I'm afraid those Basic bitches are gonna pitch this to Insta."

I shook my head in bitter remembrance of everything those girls said about me in the bathroom only hours ago. Their group was dressed more provocatively than I was, yet *I* was the ho?

I took Delia's advice and squeezed between guys huddled around several pitchers of beer at the next table.

"Ah, Frat Toy. We have to quit meeting like this." I grinned at the one idiot who'd be stupid enough to drop everything for a chance I'd never given him. He choked on a swig he'd lifted to his lips.

The tart by his side gasped. "Micro Machine?!"

"It's Shay, right?" I asked. Her face flushed. "Love that dress. It'd take what? Two inches to climb beneath it. Might be a problem for some of these guys, though." I winked.

"Ooh, damn!" The frat boys laughed at my dig.

Shay's buzz sobered when I said, "As evidenced by my skirt, I prefer at least six inches."

The undergrads blatantly gaped, having never seen me in this capacity. I had no more doubt that Lucy was a lesbian as she chewed my clothes off with her mothy eyes.

I re-focused on the guy Shay huddled closest to and took a lucky guess. "Brayden?"

Frat Toy nodded and gave blind knuckles to one of his buddies, never taking eyes off me. Flattering. I couldn't resist rubbing salt all over that wounded face of Shay's.

"Didn't someone order a schoolgirl for your birthday?" I joked, calling his crap from the line earlier.

"Oh, shit." One of the guys cursed and leaned against the table enough to jostle the drinks and pitchers.

"Wanna dance?" I asked Brayden. He checked his surroundings then gestured to himself in question. "Yes?" I shouted over the music.

He nodded and asked Shay to hold his drink, grasped my hand, and pulled me to the floor before I changed my mind. I avoided eye-contact with anyone else, acutely aware that I'd drawn attention. Not because I was me, but some because I was. Delia once told me, times like these, names no longer existed, and everything became all about product display. Who had the most appealing apples or biggest banana? These men could care less who I was. They took stock of the way my legs glowed under the sheen of baby oil gel, the black eyeshadow heavy over my cat eyes, the way my hair spiraled between my cleavage and down my almost bare back. The peek of midriff when I'd roll my hips or raise my arms.

The way Brayden looked at me, no doubt he was one of few who held my name and face higher than my body parts, although he wasn't immune from the allure. When he reached for my waist, I shook my head, a little smirk over my glossed lips. Intrigue fanned the heat in his brown irises.

"No touching. We dance. I keep my hands to myself; you keep yours to yourself. Got it?" I instructed and placed my hands on my own waist while my body moved to the new song, fingers traveling to my hips, dragging over the skin of my belly, up, up, up, lifting over my head. Belly dancing met with Latin flare as the music vibrated through the soles of my high heels.

Brayden's hands fisted, eyes locked on the calculated isolation and sway of my curves, before he obeyed and fell into the rhythm.

"Not bad," I complimented his natural ability.

"Not fake," he said, gesturing to his 'tan'. "I'll prove it."

"Huh?" I asked, unable to make his words out over the volume and rattle of bass. He broke the rules and grabbed my hand and waist to salsa properly and began testing whether I could hang. The more I kept up, the further he pushed, determined to make me stumble in a turn so he might swoop in and capture me.

"*Guera*, who taught you how to dance?"

"My slave-driver mother forced every dance class she could," I shouted over the song and focused on footwork.

"Tell her thank you," he teased, making me laugh.

Okay, so this was a lot of fun. More fun than I expected to have, considering I'd come bent on revenge. I saw what Shay saw in this guy. Didn't keep me from resenting the glimpses of her evil eye from the sidelines. Brayden cheered as I messed up.

He caught me and manipulated me into a dip. Shay's eyes glazed. Guilt gripped my gut.

No! I wasn't going to feel bad for a bitch who'd trashed me only so many hours ago for no reason.

After another song of him showing off, I had the sneaking suspicion she didn't even know much about the man dancing with me, nor did his friends because they watched us like a spectator sport while he intensified the turns, pulled me against him, rolled our hips in unison, shoved me away while holding to my fingers, turned me in circles all over the small areas he saw between couples grinding against one another.

My abs hurt from giggling almost as much as from how they constantly whittled with the Spanish lyrics. Brayden sang along in an accent he claimed straight from Mexico.

"Illegal?" I jested.

He laughed over the music and said, "You are! We should deport you for holding out. Who knew Micro Machine could do something other than run away?"

"Oh smooth!" My fist covered my smile at his return dig. At that moment I realized I needed to slow my roll before I risked injuring my ankle or leading him somewhere I wasn't interested in going. Coach would've murdered me for wearing heels. Funny how the adrenaline and endorphins stole all pain and rational memory. Okay, and maybe all the alcohol....

"Want to break for a bit?" I asked. "I mean, you have a line of partners waiting if not." True story. Some of them made me insecure because I was just a little white girl and they the Latin locals eyeing me like I'd claimed a piece of their culture. Jeez.

"*Si*," he said. "*Necesito un trago.*"

I shook my head when he translated.

"Brayden, I definitely know how to translate someone needing a drink." I grinned over my shoulder as we pressed through the crowd to the bar. When we got up to the stools, none were available, which was just as well since I didn't want to draw Garrett's attention.

Brayden leaned in between groups and paid for a couple of hurricanes.

5 | ♀

He nodded and handed me my drink, taking a huge 'sip' of his own like the liquor was water. I was so thirsty; I did the same till we were both down to ice cubes. I peeled the damp strands of hair away from my sweaty skin, gathering the curled mass to pull the spirals over my chest allowing my back to breathe. A wet patch covered the front of his shirt. His black hair hung damp about his forehead. Frat Toy was kind of handsome now that I let myself notice. His personality wasn't bad either. I learned he was a paramedic studying infectious diseases and had a passion for vaccinating children in impoverished countries.

"So, you want to be a type of doctor without borders?"

"Exactly. That's the dream." He filled our break with altruistic causes I couldn't help feeling drawn to. He asked about my psychology program and how I wanted to help children.

"I know my calling is based on the things I've seen growing up," he said. "But I can't help wondering if yours is? Sorry if that's too invasive."

"Not at all. I started out wanting to be a counselor, but shifted to nutrition, specifically aimed on childhood diabetes. Coach has drilled nutrition for so long, I figure I can keep the habit going beyond track. So much of our foods are tainted with unnecessary sugars, we are facing a fifty percent increase in diabetes as a whole—" I cut myself off. "I'm sorry. Get me off the pulpit." I smiled.

"By all means, keep going."

"What it really comes down to? I want to teach parents and their children as a way to also reduce the overall depression and suicide rates in tomorrow's adults through better health now. My original career goals still tie into my new ones. To those who much is given, much is expected, and everyday I'm aware of the opportunities I've been blessed with. Can't allow this to go to waste or into a box of something I did once."

"Biblical," he observed. "To those much is given."

"Yes," I gushed, impressed he understood the reference. "The spiritual well-being is tied into the physical and mental— Wow, stop me before I offend you. Want to talk politics next?"

His head tossed back on a laugh. "Sure, and after we threaten to kill each other over how to fix the world's problems, want to pull our phones out and text the rest of the conversation while we stand here together?"

"Oh my gosh, right?"

The easier our conversation, the guiltier I felt over Shay, and the more I realized the responsibility of knowing better. She was younger, envious. I had a flash of memory where she'd tried out for the relay team but was told she'd needed more training.

"Hey, Brayden, are you and Shay talking?"

"Shay?" He shrugged. "Thought she was on the other team. She hangs with Lucy's crew."

Bayleigh whistled and gestured me over with her chin. "Need a refill? This is from him." She pushed a Tequila Sunrise my way while my heart plummeted to my toes in fear of Jase. I didn't want him cornering Brayden for something I'd invited. "What's wrong?" Bayleigh asked.

"Is this from Jase?" I asked.

"Psh. No, but I happen to know he's seeing red."

"Nice. Which one?"

"Ha! You think I'm talking about the redhead at that table? She's here with someone else, but I think she's a prostitute because she's making the rounds, ya know?" Our noses shriveled. "Screw him, Kins. I'm talking about Complicated Moonlight in the flesh, babes. No hat. No male-pattern-baldness. All safe." She beamed like I'd won the lottery. I leaned over the bar to peer down the way with a huge grin at the one guy I knew Jase to be insecure about based on his mini rant from last night. "Hey, Brayden," I tugged his attention from scoping Shay with different eyes. "You mind if I catch up with an old friend while you go please, please, *please* ask Shay to dance?"

"Really? I swear if she humiliates me because you're wrong, you owe me and my pride a dance."

I laughed and held my hand out. "Deal. I'll even throw in a drink on me."

"All right, Micro Machine. Here goes nothin'." He shook my hand, then ordered another round of what Shay held.

I leaned in beside him and asked, "Bayleigh, bump this up, will ya?"

She chuckled and poured more tequila into my juice and grenadine after she passed Brayden his order. He tipped her, we clinked drinks, then parted ways. Sunrise-in-hand, I breezed toward the personal bubble that Klive King somehow maintained for himself in this mayhem.

"Thanks for the drink, sir."

His eyes held a self-satisfied knowing as he turned sideways to greet me. "You're welcome." He chewed a cherry stem and held his glass. Cherries on ice. I took a few healthy swigs of my sunrise, thirsty for so many reasons.

"No booze?" I asked him.

"What?" he shouted and waved me closer. I swallowed, trying to keep myself calm as his legs parted for me to stand in the small space he'd allowed. Now, he had no personal space and neither did I. His free hand remained on his thigh, but we had so little room, my thighs pressed against his, which meant my bare skin brushed against his hand.

Without thinking, I tugged the stem from between his lips, unable to take my eyes off them. "What, no knot?"

"It's for your own good." He winked and delivered the most devilish grin that twisted my tummy and had me sucking too much from the stir-straw in my mouth. "I have it on good authority you're on the watch list," he said.

"That so? Marcus tell you that?"

"Nah, common sense did. What are you doing here?"

I snickered and shook my head. "I'm dancing. What're you doing here?"

"Watching."

I sucked the rest of my drink down and set the plastic cup beside his glass. My vision was happy fuzzy with my mood. "You gonna tell on me?" I bit the stolen cherry stem.

His eyes followed the motion, jaw muscle flinching. "Don't need to."

"Am I in trouble?"

"You're causing it."

My head tilted. "For whom exactly, Klive?"

All play fell from his face. His hand snaked around my waist as fast as a viper. I gasped as he pulled me against his torso, my hands landing on his shoulders.

"Who told you my bloody name?" he said against my ear.

Adrenaline rushed through every vein.

"You just did," my speech rushed on a gush of wind.

"Clever girl."

His fingers relaxed and tip-toed ever so softly up the skin of my back.

"Oh," I breathed even as I felt like I couldn't. My back arched in response. In these heels and how he sat, his hair tickled my nose with the scent of shampoo. The heat of his temple branded my cheek. Fear and attraction collided with the alcohol I'd chugged; his breath brushing below my lobe, the soft whisper of his fingers on skin that was never touched, that testy attitude. So many dormant places on my body lit. I should've fought the way I pressed against him, but I pretended his hold was my stability, my fingers digging.

His fingers stopped at the clasp of my halter in the middle of my back. He caressed the spot like a threat I nearly wilted beneath.

"Now, my sweet, who really told you?"

My response was weak and compliant at the dip in his tone of voice; simultaneously sexual and scary.

"I wasn't positive until you confirmed. Last night my boyfriend was bitching about 'Klive' coming to take care of business like he didn't have it under control. Since you introduced Eric on your own, I used deductive reasoning."

He pulled back enough to assess my face with a dark calm to his ice gray eyes. "So, is he your boyfriend now?" *No! Alcohol blunder!* "Because at the track you said he wasn't. I'm just trying to keep up."

My tongue traveled against my cheek as I felt a real fear at displeasing him. "No, we aren't together. I referred to him that way to clarify who I was talking about. In case you haven't noticed, Jase is here with everyone else."

"And how does that make you feel?"

I narrowed my eyes at his dig and mixed messages, conflicted with how I hated that his playful side vanished because of my misstep, but pissed that he had a problem with me at all.

I shrugged as if Jase's junk didn't bother me. "He's his own man."

Klive King nodded, the unrelenting gaze picking apart my feelings. *Did he want to hurt them? What was his damage? Where was the playful pirate who teased, flirted and calmed the chaos even as he created his own inside me at every meeting?*

"Perhaps Jase's sidekick, then? Or the boy you were dancing with. Hard to keep up on who's making headway when it seems everyone has."

My jaw dropped. He tipped my mouth shut. "It's nothing personal, love. I believe I've gotten the wrong impression of you, is all. I thought you weren't easy, didn't date strangers, or dress like a ho, but you're your own woman. Who am I to stop you?" His hand on my back splayed before he released me, almost shoved me, so he could stand and pull his wallet to toss cash on the bar making this feel like a transaction.

I couldn't breathe.

What the hell?

"For your information, *Mr. King*, no one is making headway, including you."

"Whatever makes you feel better, kid."

I gaped like he'd slapped me. My hand rose to slap the hell out of him, but he snatched my wrist in motion and suspended my hand between us. "Uh, uh, uh." He tsked.

"You asshole." I spat the stem I'd knotted in his face, then glared at the eyes that hours earlier had made everything glow in front of Tyndall. Gone was everything in his for me, too, and that hurt the most, like feelings were optional.

I yanked my hand from his grasp and shoved against his chest for space, but I couldn't get any. Couldn't get enough air. Couldn't make the spinning stop on the emotional spiral. What had changed from the track to now? *I hated this day!*

COMPLICATED MOONLIGHT

I weaved toward the hallway, stumbling in my heels and stabilizing against the wall. I couldn't push outside the back door fast enough. As soon as I tripped onto the gravel my guts poured from my body. Someone cursed and jogged over to grab my hair, but I sobbed and begged them to leave me alone.

"Kins, it's Brayden. I'm not going to hurt you. Just get it all out, okay?"

"I'm sorry," I rasped, puked some more, then continued. "I hate throwing up so much. It hurts so bad." I hated that I heard giggling from somewhere.

"Hey! Put your damn phones away!" a man shouted.

"You heard him!" Jarrell's voice shouted from behind me. "Erase that shit, now or else I'll make sure you never enter this place again." He knelt beside me. "Kinsley, you okay?"

"I'm sorry, Jarrell." I sniffled and sobbed as he wiped my mouth and cheeks with the bottom of his shirt. "Don't do that. You shouldn't do that." My voice broke on my hoarse protests and another bout of sobbing.

"Is she okay?" Brayden asked. "Kinsley, you okay?"

"She's okay, boy." Jarrell took my legs from under me and carried me to an SUV. "Too much to drink. She mixed her alcohols and doesn't drink much as it is. Did your friends delete that shit?"

"Yes, I made sure."

"You promise? Because I have ways of finding liars and setting them straight."

"Whoa, man, I promise. Where are you taking her?"

"I don't answer to you, boy. Watch out." Jarrell laid me onto a leather seat, pushed my legs inside and shut a solid door, heavy like my daddy's BMW doors. Jarrell got into the driver's seat and said something, but I tucked my knees into my chest and cried silent tears on the leather cooling my cheek.

"This is the worst day, Jarrell. Why are men so mean?"

The vehicle pulled off the lot and smoothed over the pavement where he picked up speed.

"Shhh. I'm sorry, Kins. Try to take a nap."

Next words I heard were, "Yeah. She got sick. I'm pulling into her driveway now. She's okay. Yes, Boss, will do."

He got out of his SUV. I pushed myself to sitting and scooted to him when he opened the door. I gripped his extended hand. He wrapped a stabilizing arm around my waist as I insisted on walking. Thank God my father's car wasn't in the driveway and parents weren't home. Jarrell carried me up the stairs.

"Where's your house key, baby girl?" He set me on my feet.

Crap! No way I was telling him I'd left them at work.

"It's inside the globe for the porch light."

He stared at me for a moment, then reached up and unscrewed the lamp, unlocked the door, handed the key over. "That needs to change, Kins. No one should be able to find a way in that easily. Lock up behind me and lay on your side when you sleep. Got it?"

"Yes. I'm so sorry." My lower lip trembled. "Thank you for making sure I got home safely, Jarrell. You're a good man."

"You're a good woman, Kins. That's why this shouldn't happen again."

"Yes, sir." After the door shut, I locked the deadbolt, pulled the chain, then slid to the floor.

Jarrell's voice carried through the hollow steel. "Queen Bee back in the hive."

6 | ♀

Knock. Knock. Knock.

Nuh, uh. Nope. Just a dream. I drifted back inside the current, floating and happy in the sunlight of a beautiful beach day. The tide carried my weight like a pool float as I stared at the bluest of skies without a care for sharks or seaweed tangling between my toes. A loud boom, boom, boom of thunder jerked me out of serenity. Dark clouds stole the clear skies. The water beneath me went gray; as gray as Klive King's eyes in the midst of anger. Waves swelled as the riptide sucked me below the surface. I begged him not be mad, to rescue me before I drifted out to sea—

Boom. Boom. Boom.

"Please, I'm sorry." I mumbled against the cushion beneath my cheek.

Boom! Boom! Boom!

The door.

The door! Crap!

I kicked at the throw blanket I'd twisted myself in and flung myself off the couch in clumsy motion to get to the front door, neglecting the peep hole, jerking the knob open to a dim sky of similar gray to the dream. I rubbed a crusty eye, and focused on …

"Jase?"

"Damn." He whistled. "Morning, beautiful. You okay?"

"I'm fine."

"Affirmative."

One of his hands propped on the door frame, the other extended a Dunkin' Donuts cup that my autopilot seized.

"May I come in?" he asked.

"Why?" I grumbled, trying to clear the fog. "What time is it?"

"A little after six a.m." He sidestepped my groggy mood to cross the threshold. I shut the door behind us while he looked at the tousled blanket and couch cushions on the floor, leaned back to peer down the hall. "You alone?"

"Why wouldn't I be?"

"Well, after you left last night, I wasn't sure. Not to mention, well...." He gestured. "Not that I'm complaining. Just don't spill your coffee this time." He winked.

I looked down at my halter top and gauzy panties. Instead of getting them in a twist, I was glad the top wasn't guilty of a wardrobe malfunction in this perv's presence.

"What do you want, Jase?"

"To know what you were doing at the bar when I thought you were gonna stay with my sister after your meet."

"Really?"

"No." He smiled, but there was something soft and sweet where he'd normally have the joy of an inside joke lighting his eyes. "I was there when I shouldn't have been either. Had to know if Inferno would have the balls to show again, and if so, couldn't stand letting the staff take care of it on their own since I was part of the problem. Jarrell said he drove you home last night and some frat boy was poking around ya. I'm assuming the one who'd glued himself to you on the dance floor?"

"Oh, you wanna play?" I threw an exasperated hand toward him. "Should I ask if you were poking any of the hookers you had glued to you while I was busy winning relays?"

He leaned back against the arm of the couch. "Nah. It's not like that, Kins. Not poking anyone." I scoffed at the absurdity.

"For real," he insisted. "After how intense things got with us Friday night— well, Saturday morning— I was trying to distract myself and give us both some oxygen. I spent yesterday thinking about what you want over what I want but decided what you want ties into what I want, too. Does that even make sense?" He shook his head like that might organize the mixed-up contents. "Look, first off, let me just say last night you were so hot, I was afraid I'd melt if I came near you. Second, if I had anything to do with Alpha Beta Asshat working you on the floor, I'm sorry."

I fought a grin at his name-calling and maintained a serious facade. "It wasn't like that. We have mutual friends. He cheered me up."

"Stop, Kins. You know how I know this thing with him is nothing? Because I know you, and if I was shot down on Friday night, frat boy was probably vaporized before he even danced with you."

I shook my head and drew patterns in the carpet with my toe.

"Hey, I came by because I'd like to take you out for breakfast. Afterward, I can take you to pick up your car so you don't have to deal with your dad. Tyndall said he gave you a hard time yesterday at the track about moving too fast. I told her, duh, she's supposed to be fast. What's his problem?"

I snorted and wrapped my arms over my chest.

"All jokes aside, last thing I'm sure you want to do is try and pretend everything is okay at the holy house of hypocrites on Sunday morning. Not to mention ask for a ride to get your car because you were too drunk to drive."

"They're not a house of hypocrites, Jase. They're human. Fallible. Imperfect."

"Uh, huh. I'll believe that when they wake up and realize it. You down?"

I rolled my eyes, then met his. "I'm down."

"Yes!" He punched a triumphant fist overhead, then pulled his fist down to his chest. Silly idiot. "Get dressed. Don't put on makeup or anything. Maybe just clean the smudges from what's left of last night's and throw on something comfortable. You have ten minutes. Go. Before pops wakes up and finds me in here with his half-naked daughter," he ordered.

I nodded and went to my room. His gentle play and valid points about my father coaxed me to accept his offer, but tension coiled between my shoulder blades at his mention of Tyndall. Didn't sound like she'd told him about me and Klive, which was great since there *was no* me and Klive to worry about anymore.

Shouldn't that be Klive and me?

That douche bag. I wished I never knew his name, but wondered what the problem was about my knowing his name that upset him? Wait. *Was this about accidentally calling Jase my boyfriend?* Any idiot could've seen we weren't together last night, so why the harsh reaction?

And what was up my intense reaction to his insults?

While I shucked the slinky top and slutty panties, I hated to admit Klive made a very sore point about the things I'd told him on our first meeting in the elevator. Was Klive *disappointed* in me?

The idea hurt worse than his insults and the way he'd frowned down at me with nothing in his eyes. He'd never looked at me that way, not even as a stranger when he'd known nothing about me.

Ugh! I didn't want to think about him! How come when other people got tanked, they forgot things, but I wasn't offered the same luxury of forgetting the razor-sharp cuts Complicated Moonlight had carved into my memory? Not fair.

At the five-minute mark, toothbrush-in-mouth, I walked into my flip-flops wearing cut-off shorts and a tank, then pulled my hair into a sloppy bun. Jase stood and popped his hands in that snap-clap thing guys do when they're bored. At the kitchen sink, I rinsed and spit, downed some water and ibuprofen, and we went outside to the light of sunrise cresting the horizon. I peered over the dew-covered railing of the patio at my daddy's Beemer dotted with humidity droplets in the driveway. The main house slept dark and quiet, thank the Lord. I locked the door, remembered Jarrell's warning about my key.

"Hey, where's your truck?" I asked. "Did someone drop you off here?"

"Would you believe me if I told you I walked?" he asked. The aviator sunglasses propped on Jase's head came over his eyes causing his hair to fall over the reflective lenses. He pushed a hand through his fresh tresses and waggled his brows like a man with adventure on the mind. My belly tingled at a look like that aimed my way, not to mention how hot he was in those sunglasses.

"Okay, should I change to tennis shoes to jog to breakfast, crazy?"

He laughed while his flip-flop footfalls steered us out to the street. "May I?" he asked and held his empty hand out to mine.

I chewed my lip and shook my head. "Nuh, uh. I'm still mad at you."

"Mad at me? For what? The inflatables?"

"Inflatables?" I couldn't help but laugh.

"Yeah, bubbles for brains and boobs. Kins, seriously? If you get to be mad about them, then I get to be mad about the frat pack making advances."

I shook my head again, but sighed and shoved my hand between us, leaving my fingers open. He looked down and batted at them the way a cat would.

"What is this? A toy?"

"All right, mister. Take it or leave it. Last chance."

His bear paw snagged my kitten claws and swung our hands back and forth, up and down, as we strode along like the few other morning walkers. Two weeks ago, I'd have never thought I'd be in any affectionate capacity with this man.

"Will you tell me where we're going?" I asked.

"It's a surprise."

"Of course, it is."

We crested a small hill one street over and half-a-mile away where none other than *the* dream car slept beside a curb like a sleek black panther ready to wake up and roar. I gaped at him with an awed smile of pure ridiculousness. His mirrored my glee, even though he was the driver.

"Jase. Jase. I don't even know ... I'm getting in there?" I pointed with hesitation.

He grinned like a giddy boy. "You're getting in there. I'm getting in there. *We* are getting in there. Together."

"But we're not *together* together."

"Driving a hard bargain, baby? Just for that I may have to drive you crazy." He released my hand to rub his palms together before pulling a set of keys attached to a pair of dice from his cargo shorts.

An old lady watering her roses looked up and waved at Jase. "I kept a sharp eye on your pride and joy, young man. That's a fine Charger. I remember when my boyfriend had one of those, but that was back when they were new. 1970, right?"

"Yes, ma'am," Jase confirmed with an impressed nod.

"A lot of room in that backseat. Shame they just don't make 'em that way anymore," she told him with a wink.

Yikes! I cringed imagining how many girls had been in Jase's backseat, but was too amused by the imagery of this Maggie

Smith look-a-like getting frisky with someone back in the day. Jase pulled his aviators down the tip of his nose to flare his eyes at me. I did the same, then he grinned at her.

"Thank you, ma'am, but I wouldn't know. Been saving this backseat for someone special." He charmed her under his spell.

I giggled and told him, "Well, I'll say prayers God one day brings her your way."

"Oh, Lord love a duck. Son, you're gonna have your work ahead of you. Good thing, because I know her father." The lady waved, then turned back to the smattering of yellow and red blooms.

"Shameless," I murmured under my breath as he opened the door for me like a perfect gentleman.

"You heard the lady; she knows your dad. Appearances are everything."

"You kids have fun," she said.

"Yes, ma'am."

"Don't forget," she told him. "We made a deal."

"Oh, believe me, I'm good for it," he told her.

Once I was seated, Jase closed the door and trotted around the car, saying something to her I couldn't articulate. He pulled his door open and hopped inside the black and white leather interior. The shifter was a chrome stick with a black and white billiards ball labeled 01. I traced the numbers with my index finger.

"My homage to the ghost of General Lee," he offered when he saw me looking. "Made it myself."

"Wow."

In reverent awe, I took stock of the meticulous detailing throughout the space, finally landing on the windshield. The chrome engine block protruded from the center of the glossy black hood. Where last night I hovered like a vulture at the sight of this car, now soft hummingbirds stole my breath. I swallowed, willing them to cease the incessant fluttering. I had a testosterone reaction to a sexy car, but nuclear reactive estrogen as I looked up to see way too much deviant excitement lighting his face.

"Oh, hell, what's that look for, Jase? I ain't getting in that backseat with you, sir."

"Aw, not even to appease an old lady?" He popped his bottom lip like a pouty idiot, then pinched my knee to make me laugh. I slapped his hand from my leg. "Roll the window down to fully appreciate the thrill, baby."

I did as he said while he did the same on his side.

"You ready for this, Daisy Duke?"

"For what?" I asked. He bit his lip through a wicked smile, turned the key. The whole car shook and vibrated beneath us. Beginning guitar riffs sounded from an AC/DC eight-track over the stereo. *Shoot to Thrill* had nothin' on the volume of the engine he revved loud enough to wake up half the neighborhood! "Oh my gosh, Jase Taylor, do you want to die?!" I cried in panic and jerked my head toward the lady in her garden. She was *clapping*. Jase tossed his head on nothing less than pure glee, gripped the 01 ball, then squealed the tires as he punched the gas and clutch, shifted gears, and tore away from the curb like something out of *Dukes of Hazzard*!

I twisted to sit correctly in my seat, double-checking my seat belt.

"I'm settling a score for her!" he shouted over the music. He downshifted as we came to a stop sign, then turned right and revved the beastly engine all over again. "I bet she can still hear that," he said. My jaw dropped. "What?" he asked. "She told me to do it in exchange for watching my car. Said her neighbor's cats have been pissing on her roses and killing them. An eye for an eye." He winked, then focused on the road and keeping control as he pretended to lose control while he flew past the unmanned guard station at the front of the neighborhood. Thank God for green lights, because a couple of cars idled in wait as Jase shot through the intersection and fishtailed onto the main drag through the left turn.

"Whooooa!" I squealed and held to whatever I could grab which happened to be his right bicep and the door. His flesh flexed beneath my fingers while he moved the stick and kept the adrenaline thrumming as the highway underpass loomed empty a block away. He seemed like he didn't even register my hand on his arm. I tried not to panic as he warned me to hold on for his favorite part.

"Clear on right?"

"What?" I looked to my right, but *why would there be anyone there if it was an on-ramp and we were at an empty intersection?* "Clear. Yes. But the light's *red*!"

"I know! Hold on to that fine ass! Plant City PD might be all over us in a minute!"

He ran the light, hit the clutch, pulled the brake and sent us into a set of donuts, smearing black circles over all the lanes under the highway. The engine roared and echoed beneath the concrete bridge overhead. Rubber-burned smoke filtered into my nostrils while my body caught in the most exhilarating g-forces. I did as he'd commanded, laughing and squealing the whole time, and held as we whirled until he slung the car onto the highway ramp toward the beach.

"Holy bloody hell, Jase Michael Taylor, you are *crazy*!"

"Heard that. Better not be going British on me, baby!"

My chest rose and fell. He was right. I'd said bloody. Klive's word. *Damn Klive!*

I wanted to ream Jase's ass for all that terror, but I was too excited, too lit, and my cheeks hurt from how big I smiled. He looked over his shoulder while he crossed the lanes to get to the fast one on the left, shifted into cruising once he was at a comfortable ten-miles-per-hour over the speed limit, then glanced nervously at me. He pulled a double take. His grin spread to match mine.

"You have the best smile," he breathed.

"Ditto," I blurted, face flushing. "Thanks for not killing us back there, and now I'll have to make sure my mom's cat isn't getting out at night to piss on her bushes."

He tossed his head on a laugh, released the stick shift, rested his hand on the back of my headrest. His thumb brushed my hair. "Hungry? Hungover? Happy?"

"All of the above?" I offered.

"Well, even though you just binged on all those donuts back there, I took the liberty of making breakfast, so I hope you didn't ruin your appetite."

"You're an idiot, Jase."

"You love it. Admit it."

I did, but no way I was saying anything pertaining to the L-word to anyone.

7 | ♀

I FANNED MY FINGERS through the most serene of breezes. Jase exited the highway and aimed for the beach.

My hair whipped loose from the bun while his tresses tossed about his glasses, his elbow propped on the door, fingers wrapped around the steering wheel. The other hand relaxed over the ball of the shifter. Every now and then I'd trace his veins with my eyes, seeing this man differently as our dynamic expanded to hold more intimacy. He had the advantage of hidden glances I could only suspect with the prickle of skin I'd swear he touched with his mind. The glasses reflected nothing but my image when he turned his head.

Jase smiled through AC/DC lyrics he belted with that sexy rasp I loved. My reflection smiled, crazy hair like dancing flames flying around the light caramel color of my face. The girl in the mirrors didn't project insecurity. She appeared as someone I wanted to be, not too mature, not too young. Somewhere in a confused middle my mind tight-roped day in and out, but she sat confident and controlled for the moment. The kind of girl who handled the kind of man staring at her.

He drove us through St. Pete, over the drawbridge, and down a winding road leading to a national park. A manned guard in a ranger uniform came out and Jase handed him his military ID. The man waved us through. We parked in an empty lot near an overgrown old bunker built for World War II. The car shut off. Without the droning engine, loud music, and the pressure of the wind, my ears felt stuffed full of nests of cotton housing distant chirping birds.

"Don't forget to roll up your window, sweet Kins." We grabbed the knobs on the doors to manually close the windows, then got out and pushed our locks down. "Weird not using a remote, huh?"

I nodded while he unlocked the trunk and produced an actual basket with a blanket.

"Want me to carry something?" I asked.

"No. I've got this. And if your hands are full, you can't hold mine."

"Player."

"Who's playing?" He slammed the trunk closed and grabbed my hand. We trudged up a hill full of grass and sand with the sound of water not seen until we reached the top overlooking a beach. "What'cha think? Here or down there?"

"Here. This way we don't eat *sand*wiches."

He chuckled at my pun and jostled what remained of my bun. "Here, help me with the blanket." I did, then sat on the spot he patted before he jumped down beside me and dug through the basket on his lap. I leaned back on my hands, legs stretched in front of me. "This is for you." He pulled a cheap bottle of pink champagne, orange juice, and a plastic flute. I winced and slapped his stomach when he put them on my legs. Goosebumps broke over my legs at the chill.

"This is sweet, but alcohol is the last thing I want right now."

"I have it on good authority that this is your favorite drink on Sunday before church."

"What?" I leaned back to look at him better. He grabbed the champagne, ignored my guilty embarrassment, and pried the bottle open. When the cork shot into some trees with the sound and force of a bullet, the birds scattered.

"Oh, shit," he said. We covered our mouths and scanned the bunker like kids in trouble.

"Isn't there a no glass containers rule here?" I whispered and ducked should anyone come looking.

"There's also a no hunting rule." His eyes bugged, big, round and smiling. "C'mon, goodie-two-shoes. Hold the cup."

I took the stemware and held the plastic up while he made me a mimosa in the fractions I instructed to my liking. Where the acidic orange juice stung my raw throat, the fizzy bubbles and alcohol soothed the ache of last night's idiocy.

"Were you outside last night? When I got sick?"

He finished pouring himself one, too, and leaned back on his free hand, the other tipping a sip to his lips. Jase stared at the calm ocean water lapping at the shore below. "I was. Want me to kick his ass?"

"Whose?"

"Really?" He peered at me the way he'd done the shore, but again, my own image stared back, this time pink embers lit her cheeks. Embarrassment.

"The frat boy?"

"No. The man."

Oh, boy. Jase may be offering more than he could back up with that one. I chewed my lower lip. "You saw that, too.... It was my fault. He called me out for my attire and behavior, and it hurt my pride, my feelings. Had I been sober, I doubt I would've gotten so upset or offended, but he was right."

"Well, I thought you were beautiful, and you're an *amazing* dancer."

"Thank you."

"For real, Kins. That wasn't all stripper pole, baby, which let's be honest, that's all these club rub downs on the dance floor are. A stripper contest or audition for the next porn star in someone's bed. You make me wish I didn't have so much first-hand knowledge or participation."

"You make me wish that, too, Jase," I whispered, unable to look at him as I might reveal the ultimate vulnerability where he was concerned. "Last night I wasn't myself. Hell, lately I'm not myself." I took a long gulp of my drink.

"I know who I am and who I wish I was," he said. "But the line between the two seems zigzagged or erased. Like I can't find it in places, so I revert to what I know. What about you, Kinsley? Who are you? Where are you going?"

Tears welled in my eyes. "I don't know, Jase. I thought I did. We both know that's not me."

He sat up and took my chin, so I had to see myself in his glasses. He lifted them onto his head, shoving his hair back from his face. The honey of his irises glowed golden in the morning light.

"Know who you are? You're the girl across the hall laughing with my sister, pink cheeks caught looking at me looking at you, trying to hide it from Tyndall. We had that in common. But you're also the girl you go to church for and pray forgiveness after stumbling all over yourself in the house of God. I think I broke every single commandment anytime I went with my family and saw you there. I'm too big a hypocrite to enter those doors, and until I figure out how to get a grip or make this righteous, I won't go."

"Jase." I didn't know how to respond, how to calm the heartbeat pounding in my chest and ears, how to tame the conflicting emotions of being the one to cause someone to leave the church and how he wrapped that in a hidden compliment.

"Kins, you're the conviction of Biblical scripture rolled into the sin on the pages. You're *Song of Solomon* and the Virgin Mary at once. I've traced the red letters of Jesus' words trying to find the things in them that make you who you are, but all I see are the things I'll never be."

"Stop." I placed a finger to his lips. His hand found my elbow. Calloused fingers drifted up the skin of my forearm until he took my hand and kissed my palm. My eyes closed. The blanket tickled my back as his unshaven whiskers tortured the skin around my mouth while his lips opened and caressed mine, our tongues meeting and dancing. I don't know what happened to the plastic flutes, champagne, or orange juice, only that they played a part in the buzz of this release. He dragged the elastic hair tie from my hair, and I knocked the glasses from his as I speared my fingers through his soft brown tresses. How long had I wanted to ruffle his hair and now my grip held clumps, much like his on mine.

"Ahem."

We startled and knocked heads before ripping apart, our chests heaving while we sought the source of interruption.

"Got a complaint of a shot fired in this area. Since you two are the only ones up here ...." The ranger trailed off. His eyes left us to look at the mess we'd made of our picnic. Mine followed the same path. I wasn't sure how long we'd made out, or how we'd bunched the blanket so bad, but my face was certainly on fire as Jase explained. The ranger nodded, spoke into the walkie on his shoulder, then said, "Well, kids, I hate to do this, but you're in violation of our no glass policy, and you're responsible for any litter, which means I'm gonna have to ask you to find that cork. Don't want any harm done to the birds or animals that call this home."

I cupped a laugh that burst without warning, then rushed to clear my throat and say, "Yes, sir. We will."

"No, ma'am. I mean now."

Jase sighed and stood to offer me a helping hand. The ranger took up the champagne bottle. My cheeks burned the same shade as the fluid sloshing at the bottom. We trudged to the wooded area Jase shot the cork into and ten minutes later I held the trophy like the big winner.

"Great job, young lady. Now, who gets the prize?" The ranger displayed a ticket pad.

"Oh, c'mon, man. You're gonna give us a ticket?"

The ranger nodded. "We take the environment very seriously here, Mr ....?"

"Keane. Rustin Keane," Jase told him. My laughing eyes shot to the lorikeets chattering in the trees.

The ranger peeled the ticket from the pad. "You have a great rest of your day. Oh, and if you didn't realize, you're gonna need to leave the park. Two-week suspension. Do you need an escort?"

"Damn, sir. No. We'll clean up and clear out," Jase told him. The ranger tipped his hat and gave a kind smile like he hadn't just ruined everything.

As soon as he was gone, we burst into laughter as we folded the blanket and repacked the basket.

"I can't believe you sold Rustin out like that."

"Why not?" he asked. "Rusty would've done the same to me. Aren't corks biodegradable?"

"One hundred percent, but coming from that cheap champagne? Probably synthetic, so we can't hold it against him."

"I thought you liked cheap champagne."

"I do. Guess that makes me a cheap date and you a lucky man," I teased.

"Definitely a lucky man if you're my date."

"Aw!" I angled my face for a quick peck of his sweet lips.

We walked back to the car. When we drove through the gate, Jase made the engine roar on purpose. I shook my head in disapproval but smiled out the window.

We ended up parking beneath a low bridge beside the water's edge of Tampa Bay. Several fishermen wore waders in the aquamarine water catching sun and fish. We propped the trunk open and spread the blanket, then climbed inside to sit criss-cross-applesauce. The basket opened between us, and Jase passed me a plate covered in aluminum foil. When I peeled the foil back, steam escaped from a platter of miniature red velvet pancakes.

"Oh, Jase! How did you know about these?"

"How do I know about anything? Tyndall is a great negotiator. In return for the intel on your mimosas and daddy's pancakes, I had to agree to let her drive my car when she comes to visit."

I winced. "That's a hefty price. Why these pancakes?"

"Because she said you never fight with your father and that he always makes these when you're upset. Didn't take a genius to see how shitty yesterday must've been for you."

"That is the sweetest ...." I leaned up on my knees to cup his cheeks and kiss him over the basket. No tongue. A few sweet pulls of his lips. I sat back. "You get mad points for today. But, I am sorry about that ticket."

"Meh, I'm not. Rusty might be, but he knows peeps down at the station who can pull strings for him." He produced a tub of homemade cream cheese dip and smothered a folded pancake before consuming the breakfast dessert. "Now, that's good junk food right there." He was right, and I felt a pang of guilt about consuming sweets twice in one weekend.

"What do you mean about Rustin?"

Jase's lips lifted at the corner. He gestured I dip my pancake. I did and hummed.

"Very yummy. Did you make these?"

"With my mom this morning. Last night she called your mom for the recipe but didn't tell her I wanted to cook for you. And Rusty is a cop, Kins. Didn't he tell you?"

I slapped my forehead in recollection. "Duh, yes, he did. I forgot. He turned on the red and blue lights when we left the bar after Patrick harassed me. I still need to call Sara and check on her, but I just can't bring myself to face her after her ex was so rude to me. Part of me feels responsible, but I know it's just that I feel guilty for what happened before he met his demise. I don't know what to say, ya know?"

Jase coughed on the soda he drank. "You have nothing to feel guilty about." He regarded the water, then refocused on me.

"Patrick Scott got himself killed. Know how?"

"You know?"

"Duh. Station talk. Rustin tells me everything."

"Then, yes, I'd love to know."

"There are actually two Patricks in Inferno so one of them goes by Pat. Before Friday night, Pat Connor was looking for Patrick Scott to clear up some confusion that made its way to his doorstep because of their names. News won't say, but Rusty says that Patrick Scott got in deep with drugs and was dealing but loved his own product too much.

"The boss doesn't give stuff for free. Patrick Scott couldn't or didn't pay. Since he's part of Inferno, Patrick Scott's debt fell on the whole gang which was why Pat Connor's been hunting. You watch surveillance, Patrick Scott was in the parking lot *before* they sat at your table. Pat Connor happened upon him waiting for Sara.

"After we kicked both their asses for what happened with you, my bet is Connor was done taking shit for Scott. Killed him to solve all his problems. Sad. I know they have a son together. Dumb reason to die. The kid is probably better off without a dad like that in his life. I know Sara is."

The pancakes didn't taste as good as they had seconds before.

"Whoa, Kins, your face is pale. Too much to drink before eating?"

I nodded, thinking again of everything I'd told Klive King about Sara's husband when I thought *he* was the Pat I'd been nervous over. *Patrick Scott wasn't my Rusty Nail, Pat Connor was!*

"Here, baby. Drink this." Jase handed me a Sprite and took an ice pack from the basket to put on the inside of my elbow. "I'm sorry. Never knew you were such a lightweight. I really screwed up my homemade date, huh?"

My eyes yanked up to his and I shook my head. "Not at all. This is the best, Jase. If anyone screwed it up, it's me. Guess you should've packed Bloody Mary mix," I joked.

"Well, girl, you ready to hit the highway before the church crowds let out and clutter the roads?"

Jase climbed out of the trunk. When I stood, he held to my waist. I placed my hands on his shoulders as he gazed up at me.

"That water sure is pretty, but this is the best view."

My lips spread into a bright smile.

"Be my girlfriend, Kins. Like a legit couple. *Together* together." *Oh!*

My smile faltered from shock. My lips lacked words.

Finally, "I'm flattered, but can I think about it, Jase? Tyndall is my best friend, and I just don't want to rush into anything that might make her mad at me. You have no idea how many girls used to pretend to be her friend to get close to you. It was one of her biggest pet-peeves."

"Damn." He glanced away, licked his lips, seemed ashamed. "You're right, I had no idea. That's pretty messed up." He sighed and looked back into my eyes. "Baby, we are well beyond high school. You aren't spending the night with my sister to spy on her brother." His eyes left mine to travel over my breasts, down to my hips, then back again. "I wouldn't be opposed to a sleepover with you now, sans little sister. I might not be able to braid your hair or paint your nails, but I can hold your ponytail and curl your toes."

Hot damn! I released a breath. "Jase Taylor, you need to behave." I couldn't help my grin, though.

"Kins, you can think about it. All of it." He winked like a naughty player. "Tyndall's kinda known and teased me about you for years. If you talk to her, she might be proud I finally had the balls to make a move." His fingers dug into my waist, tickling involuntary giggling from me when he lifted me like a child from the trunk. "Let's go get that car and get you home before your father thinks someone kidnapped you."

8 | ♀

WE PARALLEL PARKED AT the curb beside the funky shops and restaurants just beginning to flip their open signs. For a beat, I sat and looked down the street at the building I worked in. Something about coming here in the fresh light of day made the parking lot and sidewalk smaller than the expansive bustle of late afternoon and night. Not only the bar, but the entire area dragged lazy like they, too, nursed a slow-fading hangover.

"Weird seeing the bar in the morning, huh?" he asked.

"Yeah. Doesn't even look like the same place."

What's done in the dark always comes to the light. In this cast, I saw the stucco structure for an otherwise hollow square of cinder block and mud with walls and a liquor license. The *people* inside the building made the atmosphere and events, gave the business the opportunity to thrive or dive. The business returned the favor, but at the core, this was a place to congregate, just like a church. The patrons sought fellowship, music, worship, every bit as much as those in a building topped with a steeple or brandishing a clever sign by the road with a Christian joke like 'cross training inside'. Humans used different tools for the same patterns of behavior.

I peeked at one of their gods in the bucket seat beside mine, realizing I was guilty of worshiping him same as the other patrons did. I realized I needed to tread with caution the feelings developing for Jase and evaluate the ones I'd always had. Did I want him because everyone else did? Because he was easy to want? Easy to fall for? This guy asked *me* to be his girlfriend.

He interrupted my inner war. "Why does Inferno drink here if they have their own bar in the boonies with no one else to bother them?"

I hummed, zoned out for that moment on his point. "Maybe it was Sara? And now that Patrick's paid his debt and Pat Connor's no longer hunting him or Sara, we won't see them as often? Or maybe that's wishful thinking."

"Or maybe they love the drama," he observed.

"Good point." My unseeing eyes traveled to my Honda Civic parked across the street from the bar. "Can I ask you something, Jase?"

"Shoot."

"Tyndall loves this car. Everyone loves this car. She said you only bring it out for special occasions. Last night I couldn't help noticing your Charger in line with several exotics. What was the special occasion?" I turned my gaze on him to find him staring at me. He lifted his hand to the headrest behind me and shifted his body to face mine.

"Last night wasn't the special occasion. The parking was coincidental. You spend so much time working on the inside and parking in the back that you rarely see the front or who's parking there. We get exotics in the lot all the time, but only when the spots on the paved street fill up first. The special occasion was this morning. I'm saying I brought my sexy black woman to meet my beautiful white mistress."

And like that, the heavy cloud lifted with our laughter.

"I must say the two of you get along better than expected. We should do this again sometime," he said, lips lifting at the corner while I melted.

"I'd love that," I gushed too fuzzy happy not to lean across to close the space between us. "I had the best time. Thank you for everything."

He cupped my cheek and dragged a thumb down the slope of my nose before leaning in to kiss me one gentle time. "Thank you, sweet Kins."

I softly sighed as I pulled away from the warmth of his smile and got out of his muscle car feeling altogether weak. I shut the door and leaned through the open window. "Bye, Jase."

"Bye, baby." He blew an air kiss.

I jogged across the street around the back to enter through the employee door, praying Marcus wasn't in the building. His office was closed, so I walked out to the floor and squatted behind the bar after greeting newbie, Fred, and a solo drinker perched on the end. "Fred, have you seen a set of car keys with—"

"Hey, piss ant, make me a Rusty Nail, will ya? And don't give me any bullshit about being out of Drambuie, or else I'll make a special trip to the liquor store and bring you one just to watch you do the job, got it?"

Shit! Pat Connor in the flesh like his ears had been ringing! The broom in Fred's hands froze mid-motion. I held to the small shelf beneath the bar searching for anything to use as a weapon.

Where the hell were my keys? Or the tiny paring knives?

"Kinsley. Kinsley. Kinsley." My eyes closed in dread.

Klive! Klive! Klive! My mind pressed his name like a panic button. Didn't matter how mad he'd made me. I knew no one else who put the fear of God into the asshole who ordered me to come out of hiding. Seeing nothing but nuts and napkins down here, I had no choice but to rise before the Inferno— sans vest— who scared me the way Klive King scared him.

"Well, darlin'. You're like whipped cream on my Sunday."

Nice double entendre. I glanced at Fred, who stood stock still, ready to piss his pants. I had two options: give in to fear or pretend. Opting for option two, I snapped at Fred and told him to resume his duties, then I grabbed a cup and made the biker a Rusty Nail but snagged a cherry before I pushed the drink across.

Be a bitch! Klive's voice instructed. *As long as you fight back, there's a chance you'll win.*

As he took the cup, I said, "Nope. Not finished."

"Huh?"

"Making your Sunday." I dropped the cherry in his drink with a cruel smile. His eyes narrowed before he seized my wrist and yanked me across the bar. The chunky wood punched my ribs, chopping the scream from my lungs. I struggled against him. His hand fisted the hair at my scalp, his other pinned my wrist behind my back. The nails of my free hand didn't scratch or dent his anger.

"You little bitch. You think you can play games with me? I was just about to ask Fred, here, if he'd heard any scuttlebutt about where Patrick Scott disappeared to before someone killed him. I'll ask you instead." *Oh shit!*

"The only Patrick I know of is you!"

The broom clattered to the floor while Fred disappeared. The guy drinking at the end of the bar was pulling his phone, but the biker saw. "You call the cops and I'll call my four friends waiting outside."

"Bullshit!" I called his bluff and clawed at his hand in my hair. "There was no one out there. And if you want information on your pathetic friend, why don't you watch the news?"

"The news does what it's told. And if you don't start doing the same, I'll haul you outside and let you decide whether I'm lying." His grip tightened and twisted. Several strands ripped free of my scalp, and he groaned at the sound of my whimper. "The best part is I don't need help taking care of you. In fact, Kinsley, I'd reserve a room at the Ramada to relish it for days."

Hell no. Tears stung my eyes while pure anger surged like power through my veins. Pain be damned, I'd rather have a bald spot than cave to my fear of this sick asshole! I spat in his face and slipped beneath his arm. His hand twisted in unnatural ways forcing him to release my wrist, the hold on my hair as I jerked away. As if daring Klive King to get me out of this one, my hand whipped so hard and fast across Pat's face, my nails splintered his pained howl.

"You stupid fool!" he snarled. "You're going to regret that!"

"No," I lowered my tone in ways I didn't recognize; the way Klive had lowered his on me last night. "*You* are going to regret that." My words spit from an adrenalized stupidity, my body trembling like a traitor to my mouth's confidence.

"That a promise? I don't see your singer or big bad bodyguard rushing to save you. You're here alone, which means if something happens to me, it's because of a call you made."

"No, it's because of the choice *you* made. No one forced your hand. You're responsible for your own actions just like Patrick Scott was responsible for his."

He licked the split skin at the corner of his mouth, then smiled like the Joker incarnate. "I taste blood in more ways than one, darlin' and that's 'cuz you have it all over your pretty little hands."

"I didn't have a hand in anything!" I shouted.

"You have a role in *everything*!" he countered, making me leap back against the bottles and rattle them on their shelves. When two of them crashed to the floor, my keys fell with them. Autopilot snatched them and ran for the hallway. I heard the heavy thud of a falling stool, his footfalls pounding the wooden planks while I slammed against the back door and flung through into the blinding light of day, sliding and skidding in flip-flops on the chunky gravel lot.

Over my shoulder, I watched Pat burst through the back door, but a figure I hadn't noticed stepped out and clotheslined him in the throat. Pat wheezed and slammed to his back on the sharp stones. Jase bent over him, fisted his shirt in both hands and thrust him up against the stucco wall. One punch, two punches, three punches to the gut, four to the face, and Jase released his hold. Pat's body crumpled to the ground, but not before Jase scraped his bloody face like a cheese grater over the harsh stucco exterior.

I stood unmoving, staring at the blood trail on the wall, willing my body to get the hell out of here, but I couldn't! Pat laid limp, unrecognizable on one side of his face. Jase had his phone to his ear as he cleaned the blood off of his fist with his tee shirt. "It's Kinsley. Pat screwed with the wrong girl. You need to send someone to collect him before I fucking finish the job myself!"

The man from this morning's romantic picnic was nothing like the monster in front of me. Pat's words haunted me to the extent that without thinking, I blocked his body and stood trembling before a blood-spattered Jase.

"Who are you talking to?" I demanded in that weird tone again.

"It's not your business, Kins. Go up front and get in my car."

"No."

"*No?*"

"Did I stutter?"

"Hold on, man." He pulled the phone over his chest and glared at me like I was in over my head. "Kinsley, I'm a very pissed off asshole right now, I'll admit to that, but I don't want to turn this on you, so I'm asking you as politely as I can to get in my fucking car so I can keep you safe."

"And what about him? Huh? What's going to happen to him if I leave and get in your car like an obedient little child?"

"Kinsley Hayes!" I jolted at the thunderclap of Marcus's anger as he rounded the building and shoved a finger in my face. "You heard the man, and I gave you strict orders to stay away from the bar which you clearly disobeyed!"

"Don't talk to me like this is my fault!"

"It *is* your fault! You're suspended indefinitely. If I so much as catch you trying to get inside as a patron or even as the damned janitor, I'll fire you for insubordination and call the police to have you arrested for trespassing! Is. That. CLEAR?"

My jaw trembled as I turned and ran through tears to my car. Thank God for a key fob otherwise I may have fumbled too much trying to get the door unlocked for all the shaking in my hands. I keyed the steering column as Jase called my name and jogged across the street, but I found the ignition, looked out the back window, threw the car in reverse, backing into the sleepy intersection. I shifted into drive and sped out to the highway.

Sometimes people find themselves in situations they didn't ask for. Klive's words jogged through my panic-fogged brain and I realized I'd just entered one of the worst, only now I didn't have him coming to my defense. How could I handle Jase doing so? Last night, Klive told me I was causing trouble. At the time, I'd assumed he was flirting, but now I wondered if he'd given a veiled warning.

9 | ♀

I DROVE WITHOUT A destination, considering my options. I didn't want to go home to my parents because my father would see right through me if I tried playing this off, especially after yesterday. Instead of driving home, I drove to the one place I'd been avoiding. The traffic onto Clearwater Beach didn't bother me. My head was too cluttered. I barely remembered the drive, to be honest.

Two hours had passed when I pulled into a spot several blocks from Sara's building. When I got out of my car, I put my phone in the center console, then opened the trunk. Piles of mail, schoolbooks, track sweats, toiletries shifted as I rifled through junk for my ball cap. Finally, I pulled the brim low over my forehead. No hiding my ponytail, but whatever.

Yesterday I'd shuddered at the idea of someone watching me. Now, I'd swear I felt eyes, and suspected plain-clothed men of being Inferno in disguise. Wait. That wasn't yesterday, that was Friday. Gosh, now my days were blurring.

The traffic and beach were so packed I realized what a suspicious fool I was. People came from all over the world to visit a continuous contender and sometimes winner of America's best beach.

As I trudged closer to the condo, I wished for tennis shoes to pretend to be a jogger rather than getting stuck behind groups who didn't understand the meaning of 'excuse me' as my needing past their loitering blockades. I wasn't feeling too polite or patient.

Thirty minutes later, I came to the hallway of Sara's condo and saw her locking the door. Relief and sadness mixed in my greeting when she called out to me first.

"What are you doing here, Little Red?"

"Please, Kinsley today," I told her in a very sobered tone. A tone out of character. "I came to check on you and offer my condolences. Are you okay?"

"Here, let's go back inside." She plugged the key into the door, but I placed a hand on hers.

"If you were leaving, I don't want to keep you. I've been praying. I'm really sorry."

"My parents have Noah. I was going to grab some ice cream and eat my emotions. Ironic that you show up here, you know, having coached me out of those behaviors. Feel like my sponsor has caught me red-handed," she joked.

"I'll go with you. Or for you. What flavor do you want? You want a gallon or a pint?" I asked.

Her face fell and took on the seriousness mine did. "I'd rather we go inside and talk than feed my emotions." She glanced both ways down the empty hallway. Unease expanded in my belly.

"Okay," I told her and waited for her to push the door open. She didn't have to tell me to come in. I walked inside as if we were the best of friends and her place was mine.

When the deadbolt locked, she sat on the couch and offered the chair across from her. For about ten minutes, she made small talk like we hadn't just seen one another two days ago. I remained silent and gave cordial responses as she needed to fill the space before breaking into the heavier subject matter.

Finally, "Kinsley, I'm a bad woman, because I feel nothing but relief. When the police called, I had to coach myself into pretending to be sad. Told myself to feel sad. Tried to conjure the way it felt to fall in love with him way back when. But I'm blank. Calm. If the cops hadn't told me gang violence was the cause of death, I was worried they'd make me a suspect for not caring. They haven't told me when they'll release his body, so I can't exactly plan his funeral yet, but I am already rehearsing my sad face. In truth, I know I'll cry when I see Noah grieve. My mom said he hasn't really reacted much either. I think he's confused."

I nodded. "That's normal. Everyone grieves in their own ways. You both might be this way for a while, but don't be surprised if he starts having melt downs in the weeks ahead or even getting in trouble at school. I'd find a child psychologist immediately and get the grief before it gets him. Maybe see a psychologist together. No prescriptions, just therapy and coping. Will help with your battered wife syndrome, too." I bit my lower lip and cursed myself. "I'm sorry. That was improper. I didn't mean to imply you had battered wife syndrome—"

"Kinsley. Please. You didn't hurt or upset me. It's a real thing. No one wants to see themselves as a battered wife, but this season of my life has been about hard honesty. Seeing what I never wanted to. I just never expected this to enter the picture."

"Grief is strange, Sara. You feel nothing now, but there are definitive phases for a reason. You might be working when suddenly reality slams into you and you burst into tears. I'm not trying to discourage you, just want you to realize if and when this happens, you're perfectly normal. I'd even go as far as thinking this is a state of shock. Shock can last months, believe it or not. Sara, if you ever need someone to crumble with, I'm here."

She swallowed a lump of sudden sorrow, her eyes shining with tears. "You have no idea how much that means. I know we aren't super close, but real friends just get it. I've been feeling so guilty, and hearing your assurance helps. Thank you." Sara released my hand to scrub tears from her cheeks as they fell. "How are you? Are you okay? You really don't need to be so bothered about me. I never have to worry about that man hurting me or my son ever again. God bless you; you just look like this is all your fault or something. You take the weight of other people's problems and carry them like you have to solve them. Please don't carry this."

I considered telling her about Pat assaulting me, but this was her pain. I wouldn't add any extra worries to her newfound freedom. The more I thought about everything, the more I realized I should leave her be. I stood after a little more small talk and excused myself to use the restroom. I paused. "Hey, Sara, did I drop a black business card when I was changing on Friday?"

Her brows dipped. "No. I haven't seen anything. You're welcome to look in the bathroom though."

I went through the bedroom. The sheets on her bed were a twisted mess. Clothing tossed on the floor. Lubricant sat on the nightstand. Yeesh. I blushed and averted my eyes onto my own business. When I closed the door and stood before the mirror, I was glad I'd thought of adding a baseball cap because I had a big red mark along my hairline on my forehead from Pat's hand. I pulled the cap back down as a shiver went through me. *Should I call Rustin and report what happened?* Klive's chastising words echoed in my mind; *expose roaches, they scatter.* Inferno didn't seem like a roach infestation. More like termites who could take your whole house down without you knowing. Was something bigger going on? Pat said I had a hand in everything. How could that be?

I washed my hands and peeked around the floors and counter to see if Klive's card was there, but no sign.

I left the restroom and gave Sara a firm goodbye hug. "I'm serious about my offer. Even if you just need to sit with someone while you cry, or we can throw dollar store ceramic plates at a wall together; something cathartic that doesn't involve exercise."

She grinned at that. I waved when we parted; she to grab that pint of ice cream. I walked the shoreline with my flip-flops in hand while watching the water lapping at my feet. Carefree kids and adults of all ages sunbathed or frolicked in the waves, played volleyball and football in the sand. Is this what I looked like before chaos? Careless, almost shallow, in my spoiled bubble of beautiful luxury? Bike rides in bikinis, paintball with my daddy, sandcastles and seashells ... *where was my boring life?* The one where my only worries consisted of relays, research papers, which shift I worked at the bar?

Was my date in Jase's car, his picnic, eating breakfast in his trunk *today*? Those events seemed like last week. Regular life slipped through my fingers.

I lifted my right palm to inspect this little weapon, recalling the pain of slapping Pat as hard as I could. I'd only ever slapped a handful of guys in my life and none to that degree. If I told Klive of my reaction, now my turbulence, would he be proud instead of disappointed the way he'd indicated last night? Would he look the way he had Friday night when Pat was hauled out of the bar? Why on Earth would anyone be stupid enough to come back for more? Why—

"Look out!"

I ducked, just as a bare torso in swim shorts dived in front of a football that almost hit my head.

"*Brayden?*"

He pulled the ball out of my air space and chucked the pigskin back to a group playing near the lifeguard stands. "Guilty as charged. Ironic running into you here. How are you feeling?"

I shrugged. "I'm okay. No hangover, so that's good."

He cursed and warned me as the ball flew toward us again. While he shifted, I crashed into him as we simultaneously leapt to catch the ball. He grabbed me while I grabbed the ball. Down we went. A modest bit of tension released before I realized he was holding me on the sand. I pushed up with an apology and extended my hand.

"You got room for one more?" I asked as he took my palm and pulled himself up. "I could use the distraction."

"Um, don't take this the wrong way, but none of the girls are playing."

"I see, so you're afraid I'll make you look bad?" I teased. His face fell like he'd just screwed up. I realized I'd opened a door to make him feel that way. *Abort!* "Hey, Brayden, no worries." I pulled the football to my shoulder and lined the shot, sailed the pigskin through the air in a beautiful spiral that would make my daddy proud. The guys ran in competition. I gave Brayden a polite smile. "Next time you let girls play, count me in. See ya around." I moved around him and continued my contemplation.

"Wait!" He jogged ahead to turn and walk backward in front of me.

I smiled and told him to watch out for a kid's sandcastle. He turned and stumbled over nothing while I snickered.

"That's messed up, Micro Machine. You've got a beautiful spiral. I'm intimidated. You win. Soccer is more my thing anyway." He stopped so I had to. "Please stay. Play. Even if none of the other girls play. Show them you're human?"

My head tilted at his plea. That's when I saw everything in the revealing light of day and sobriety. Brayden was the guy with the crush on the girl everyone hated. The guy exhausted with defending himself against their negativity. The guy who wanted them to see what he saw.

COMPLICATED MOONLIGHT

"As opposed to bionic?" I half-joked, lacking my normal humor. "Sorry, I'm a wretched actress."

He grinned, shy and sweet, at the sand. I wondered what life was like with a boring frat boy doing boring couple things. No danger, risk, attitude. Nate had been a normal frat boy who'd held my hand and picked flowers, studied with me, took me to movies, pretended to drop popcorn in my shirt so he could find kernels while I swatted him away. As simple as life with Nate was, therein was the problem. I wasn't simple. I was moody and felt like a curse to those who felt anything for me because I was horrible at reciprocation.

"Brayden, I really shouldn't stay. Not today. I'm avoiding responsibility, and I'm not supposed to be running. It's my fault for asking when I had no business doing so. But thanks. Maybe put in a word with your buddies because I don't mind their fear."

We shared a laugh, but there was no masking his disappointment.

"Kinsley, I'm not a chauvinistic jerk. I'm really sorry if I gave off that vibe. I'm sorry—"

"There's nothing to be sorry for. And you're safe. I'm not mad or upset. I'm being honest. How's Shay?"

His head tilted this time. He conceded with an impish shrug, blush in his cheeks. "You were right about her. Thank you," he said. Someone got laid.

"You should call her the day after, so she isn't wondering."

"Am I that obvious?" he asked.

"Nah, you're a guy." His face changed, and I rushed to tell him I was joking again. "Seriously, though, Shay is pretty fast. Might be a good ally on your team over there. I'll see ya around, okay?"

"Brayden!" one of his friends shouted. "Come on, man! You're holding the game!"

Thank God! I waved and stepped around him without looking back. A lump filled my throat as I thought of how I usually waved over my shoulder. That wave was for playing with Klive King when he was playing with me. Where was *that* guy? Where did he go on Sundays? I thought about going to the beach bar to see if he was there, but that was creepy stalking, and I wasn't that desperate. Yet.

Instead of the beach bar, I opted for a place I never went. Hooters. The original, back on the mainland.

"Kinsley Hayes, what do I owe the pleasure?" Constance asked me when I was seated and finished requesting her as my server. "Are you alone?"

"Yes, it's just me."

"Wow, this must be an emergency. You hate this place."

"No, I feel insecure and inadequately equipped in this place," I corrected, a small smile on my face as I looked at the voluptuous calendar girls prancing past with their butt cheeks and boobs bubbling from booty shorts and tiny tanks. Perfect hair, tons of flawless makeup. Not a plain Jane in the bunch. They carried themselves with the confidence of women who knew they were beautiful and lacked a single dorky day or period puffiness.

Constance put a hand on her curvy hip, her own face done up as beautiful as a Christie Barbie doll— that is, if Christie was covered in tattoos and sported a red and black weave.

"Girl, hush. They'd hire you in a second. You'd make way more in tips here than you do at the bar. Benefits package. Best of all, no live bands or boys who sing in them." Ruh, ro. She sensed boy trouble.

"Constance, are you trying to recruit me?" I joked to try and clear the air. "Doesn't look like y'all need any help. Besides, my daddy would murder me."

"Gonna have to get over those daddy issues if you're gonna be a part of the real world, babe."

"All right, you. Spare the lectures."

She had me follow her to the bar and sat me on a stool, placed a napkin and cutlery on the table, then asked my drink order. Water for me. "Of course. And would you like crab legs?" she asked. I nodded. She always brought me an order if she pulled a shift here before performing with Jase at the bar. "You sure you aren't running away from someone?"

I gasped and gave her the best confused look I could muster. She rolled her hazel eyes.

"I came to see if I could spend the night at your place since you're closer to my father's work. I want to have coffee with him tomorrow morning. As a surprise. Why would you ask if I was running away?"

"Jase has called twice and left me a text message about you. I can't answer while I'm working, but I did see his text. He wanted to know if I'd seen you. You want my phone? You can text him whatever you want since I'm assuming you aren't texting him right now."

"Thank you, Constance. I'll tell you later if you're cool with me staying. What time do you get off work?"

"Yes, you can stay. My shift ends at four, so I'll be done in time to eat with you if you'd like?"

"Sounds good."

"Kins." She leaned close to my ear. "You didn't sleep with him, did you?"

"No. I'd have told you."

"Whew." She straightened and pulled her phone to lay the bedazzled case on the table, then went to check on two other tables after plugging my order into the computer. I opened her phone and read Jase's text.

Constance, u seen or heard from Kins? Tryin 2 reach her. IMPORTANT.

I thumbed back: *No. At work. Can't talk.*

10 | ♂

I RAN MY HAND over the back of my neck and sighed.

"Hey, Klive, you're close. In another month this will be in the past. Try not to think too much." Joey sat at the drafting table in my home office. He peeled at twelve layers of velum diagrams as he inspected each grid for fine discrepancies, then laid each down to see how they lined up with the ones beneath. "This is your finest work. You'll retire a legend beyond the bodies you've dropped. A very rich legend." A layer fell atop another. He leaned in close to study city intersections for drops and pickups.

Getting closer, so much closer. Almost done.

I tapped the end of my graphite pencil to the sheet he searched. "We need to craft a diversion for this intersection here so red and orange don't notice they occupy the same turf. Their rivalry is too strong, and we don't need any more gang violence in the news. Bad for real estate and tourism. I don't want to impact the economy."

"You're right," Joey agreed. "Fly under the radar all the way. Tap each domino enough to knock the other in motion, then get 'em out before they realize they're one piece in a bigger design. We could cause a car accident. Stop traffic in all directions. Nothing too elaborate. Minor injuries. No children involved. Sanders enjoys the gritty stuff. He'd probably like a new car if you ask him to wreck his. He gets the itch to trade up every other year. And he loves showing new scars to women looking to lick his wounds." Joey glanced up with an evil grin. I nodded but didn't smile, so his diminished. "Bitchy Bonny on the brain?"

I shook my head, but he knew I wasn't refuting his question. I wondered how the mind could be so occupied by one person and still manage everything necessary to continue through life. "I really upset her last night, Joe. You saw, she threw up because she was crying so bad. She wasn't in the bar doing anything more than every other patron." I stood straight and sighed. "She was beautiful. Too beautiful for someone trying to avoid stirring trouble with bad men. I've never felt like a bigger fraud."

"She was teasing danger. Pretty obvious she enjoys risk, or else she wouldn't be wilting over you. She's a thrill-seeker."

"Wilting?" I scoffed. "There's a flowery word."

"It's apt. Klive, it's my job to watch her. You think I pay constant attention and fail to notice her emotional responses, her body language? Not the worst job I've had. You trying to make us all mad for your girl, so that we'll be so nuts for her, we all pull our guns if she's harmed?"

Shit called. "You sound like your brother."

"Yeah, well, he's smart, but so is your plan." He shook his head. "I should be watching her more today after what happened."

"She's with Taylor. He'd never let anything happen to her."

"Then relax. You do what you have to in the name of survival. You're trying to save both your lives. If insulting Kinsley pushes her back to safe distances, you did your job. Although, I think Cheatham's a dumbass if he thinks he's gonna put a number on either of your heads. You've worked too hard to build loyalties. A hit on you means mutiny, and he's not the one calling shots anymore. He'd start a bigger war than this small time Nightshade Inferno shit."

"We need him to believe he's calling the shots until my contract is fulfilled. This way, if he comes for me after my obligation was fulfilled, he'll look like a liar to everyone loyal beneath him. I'm done. I can taste the first vestiges of freedom already. Just do me a favor and double-check my work? This look right to you?" I lifted the top eleven layers and pointed to the key of positioning, times, dates, code names scheduled to pull off the largest delivery Nightshade would take part in to date. We weren't the suppliers; we were conductors in a massive orchestra of several major names who didn't realize they were part of a larger picture. Never tell the right hand what the left is doing.

Joey rubbed his shaved chin and loosened his tie from the collar of his starched button-down.

"Klive, you know you don't have to ask. I'm on your ass whether I'm assigned or not. You're not getting yourself killed on my watch, and that includes all your schemes. You may be looking at witness protection if you're found out, though."

"I've thought of the pros and cons for the better part of two years. If I don't try, I'll always wonder."

"Funny, I recall those very words about a certain female who's being shoved in the opposite direction."

"Dammit, Joey!" I lost my cool. "Make up your mind. What would you have me do? Claim her in the open and buck my boss' order because I'm too arrogant to follow a leader? I can't. Not yet. Do you think my mind isn't going mad with the way she looked at me last night? At taking orders like I'm still some bloody underling Cheatham controls? Maybe he's caught on and toying with me to see if my arrogance will give me away? Ever think of that? I want her, but I need to want her so bad that I can keep her alive even if it means watching her give herself away to someone else!" I snapped the graphite pencil between my fingers and flung them at the wall, but the small maneuver did nothing to curb the building frustration.

Joey's lips twitched. "Could always fake your own death since you're obviously in the mood for theatrics."

"Dammit. Where's the fun in that?"

He stood up and opened his arms.

"What the bloody hell are you doing, mate? I'm British. I don't do hugs."

His laughter rang through the office. "You're a bi-coastal, half-breed British American who chose that snobby accent over my Southern charm. I'm not offering a hug. I'm offering you to come at me before I go at you. Hit me. You need blood."

"I'm not hitting you."

"She's a slutty bitch with daddy issues who's gonna drop her panties for Taylor because you're too afraid of Cheatham, you pussy."

"Joseph Prince, I swear, if you don't walk out that bloody door...."

"This is fun." He laughed, then his smile dropped. "Come on, King! Cheatham's right! You're soft! NOW, PROVE HIM WRONG AND HIT ME!" Joey lunged. My fist swung to block the punch he threw at my face. I gripped his fist, but his other thrust toward my stomach. When I dodged, we wrestled to the floor, and I squeezed his throat in my hands. He went limp and stared at me, deadpan. I yanked my pressure-white fingers from his neck. He sucked air. "That's better," he said, breathing hard, "but you do suck at following directions. I told you to *hit* me."

So, I did. His face bucked to face the door. Blood dribbled past the tongue that darted over his lip. I stood and offered my hand.

"That's better," he said. "Now, let me check your work with the cork board, asshole."

Joey gripped my hand and pulled himself up, but clocked me across the face, grabbed my throat with one hand, yanked my head down, and kneed me in the stomach. He jerked the waste basket from beside my desk to shove my face over before my lunch spray-painted the trash inside. When the deed finished, he tossed the silk square from the pocket of his blazer to the floor near my hands.

Grime spit from my lips. "You're a fucking fool." I cleared my throat and spit again, then lifted to my feet.

He huffed and rifled through the drawer in the desk for thumbtacks and a spool of red yarn. "You made her puke last night. You needed absolved, so I'm doing you a favor. You made her suffer. You suffer in kind. Now, there's nothing left to feel guilty over. You can slip back into your skin to resume your role as the dick we take orders from. You told her to be mean. Now, *you* be ruthless, Klive. *Very* ruthless. Lead by example the way you always have."

I nodded. He tapped several keys on the open laptop on the desk adjacent to the drafting table. My phone vibrated in my pocket as the printer spewed pages. Joey opened a span of floor-to-ceiling drapes to expose my wall-length cork board. He grabbed the first sheet from the printer while I placed the phone to my ear.

"Taylor, is there something I can do for you?" I asked.

Joey looked at me over his shoulder. I worked my jaw to be sure he hadn't done real damage.

"As a matter of fact there is, asshole!" Jase shouted.

Joey tacked the page to the board when he saw my jaw clench. He paused while I listened to Jase's blistering rant about Pat Connor from Inferno.

"What you can do for me is get this sick fuck off my girl before I kill him with my bare hands!"

I swallowed and gripped the phone with white knuckles. The icy anger in my blood froze my voice. "You will have to be more specific." But he paused to shout at Kinsley to get to his car so he could keep her safe. His voice muffled like his hand covered the phone, but I didn't mistake her argument, nor Marcus's furious interruption.

"Oh, Joey." I called his attention with sadistic sarcasm. "Would you please be a dear and call Gustav and Jarrell? Head to the bar for a pick-up immediately. Call Marcus for details on your way. Time to be very mean."

"Gladly." He tacked his page to the board and checked the clip of the pistol holstered at his side. His blazer ripped away from the chair and wrapped around his shoulders as he shoved his arms inside and tucked his keys in his pocket. We jogged downstairs to the main level of my house. Joey had his phone to his ear, grabbing valuable details from Marcus while I waited longer than tolerable for Taylor to quit chasing Kinsley and speak.

I opened the door to my library, pulled a book, walked through the secret passage. Lights lit the stark white room. I dragged a stainless-steel slab with dangling shackles from a large storage closet.

"You there?" Jase huffed into the speaker.

I grunted while selecting implements from a wall of objects, tossed them on the nearby counter. Striking a match, I stared at the flame as the wick of a candle spit sparks before the fire danced atop like Kinsley's hair whipping in the breeze at the beach bar.

"I took her to the bar to get her car," he explained. "No bikes in the lot. All cool, right? Wrong! Pat Connor was inside. He put his fucking hands on her! If that new kid, Fred, hadn't run outside shitting his pants, who the hell knows what would've happened! I can't keep my animal in the cage, man! If you want my attention, prove it. Twice now he's fucked too closely, and there won't be a next time without me killing him and leaving you with the mess," Jase spat.

"Watch your tone, Taylor! Remember who you're talking to!" I commanded, closed my eyes, and counted back from ten. "Where is Kinsley?"

"She ran from me. Got in her car. Drove away. Who the hell knows where she's going."

I rubbed my chin, jaw tight as a vice. "Was. She. Hurt?"

He laughed, a maniacal lunacy. "No."

"No?"

"No, King, she's hurt. She was physically okay to run away from him. But, inside she *is* hurt, and when she's hurt *you* need to remember who *you're* talking to! You're gonna fix this, and I'm not joining this time, because you need to pay for what you did last night. *You* hurt her. *He* hurt her. I can't separate the two when all I see is pain I need to extinguish. Feel me? So, whatever you do had better live up to that reputation of yours, because anything less than an underground earthquake ain't good enough!"

The phone clicked. My previously clenched jaw fell open in nothing less than stunned outrage.

I closed my eyes against the blinding stark walls in thought of the ways I would go at Jase Taylor for speaking that way, how I'd punish Nightshade for that disrespect were he a member. I quaked like a mental patient trapped in a padded room tied into a strait jacket with insane inspiration. But Taylor wasn't the target. I opened my eyes with clarity and tapped Marcus's contact. He answered on the first ring. "Send me the footage from the cameras, then get rid of it."

"On the line with Chris as we speak, King. I overheard Taylor fill you in. Don't kill him. He's just—"

"Insane with anger," I supplied. "Taylor's safe *this* time."

"Taylor is exactly who you're looking for. You're getting who you want even if he pisses you off." Marcus clicked a mouse in the background. "Footage sent. The guys just arrived. I kept the package on ice in the cooler. They're about to load up and be on their way."

"Very well. Do me a favor while you've got him on ice?"

He listened to my instructions, agreed, then disconnected. I thumbed the email app on my phone and tapped play on the surveillance.

11 | ♂

REPLAY. STOP. REPLAY. STOP. **Replay**.

The surveillance videos played and replayed beneath my thumb. New evidence jumped out of the frames with each view. The 'bystander' drinking at the end of the bar nodded at Pat when he walked inside. His phone was in his hand all along. Who was he texting? If only I had an angle for that area to zoom in on his device. A van parked in a lot adjacent to the back parking lot of the bar; two grainy heads moved inside the vehicle; another smoked a cigarette outside the driver's side door as though waiting for someone.

When Pat yanked Kinsley's hair, I forced myself beyond my anger to rewind and study the man on the stool. As soon as Pat grabbed Kinsley, the man shook his head and started to call someone, but Pat shouted at him. I checked the time stamp on the phone call, then re-opened the footage of the parking lot. Zoomed in, the smoker pixilated, but I saw his hand held a cigarette to his lips. In his other, I caught the brief flash of sunlight glinting off glass. He raised the device, tilted his head, and lowered the phone back to his side.

Pause. Time. The minutes and seconds matched. I hit Marcus's contact again. "How did you know to go to the bar when you're off today?"

"Fred hit the silent alarm in my office before running outside. I got the call from the security company but refused officers on the scene."

I nodded as though he were in front of me. "What about the man inside the bar? The one on the stool?"

"You saw the video. He ran out the front as soon as Pat chased Kinsley out the back. Why?"

"I'll call you later. Joey's here with the package."

I disconnected just as Joey opened the passage ahead of Gustav and Jarrell. The men wrestled a large bag. The middle sagged and squirmed. I sighed in new contentment as I unzipped the bag and smiled at the prey struggling inside.

"Place him on the table. Keep the bag beneath him to catch the blood. Less clean-up."

"Mmmm! Mmmmm! Mmmmm!" His head thrashed as he cried against the black tape over his mouth. "Mmmm! Mmmmmmm!"

My men laid him on the slab and adjusted the edges of the bag around his frame. "Cut his bonds. Secure his hands and feet into the cuffs beneath the table." I peered down at Pat; his struggle futile against my bouncers. "Oh, Pat, if you calm down, I'll let you watch a little video." The phone came to life before his eyes.

"Mmmmmmm! Mmmmmm!"

"Quiet. You'll ruin my favorite part. Don't you just love cherries on your Sunday? Clever girl." I winced when he grabbed her hair and jerked her against the bar. "Now, that, right there. You couldn't just keep your hands to yourself, could you? She was being nice, making your order on her day off, going above and beyond, really, wouldn't you agree, Joe? Gus? Jarrell? Oh, wait, you guys haven't seen this yet, have you? How inconsiderate of me not to share."

The two bouncers towered behind Joey; their arms wrapped over their barrel chests. Dead pissed eyes. Joey jerked his chin toward my phone. I gave them the footage to view and chuckled to myself, evil intent swimming like glee through pools of blood in my mind while Patrick Connor struggled against the cuffs.

"A room at the Ramada to make it last for days?" Gustav growled. "Sounds like a request to make this last, King."

"He's makes a great point," I told Pat as I rubbed my bare chin in speculation. "Days, you told her? *Ooh!* You hear that? That solid smack? I *love* that part. Don't you just love a bitch who fights back?" I ripped the Gorilla tape from his mouth, relished the agony birthed by his volume and his terrified flinch. His chin pinched in my fingers; I jammed my thumb nail into the split Kinsley gave his lip. Blood traveled between the follicles of stubble. "That's *my* girl," I snarled. "She's right. She didn't make this call. You did. Now, we are going to have a little chat about your leader and whether Ray knows his gang is flagrantly trespassing all over my private property. Gustav, pull his pants off, please? Jarrell, grab the pliers."

"No! No! *NOOOOO!* No, no, no! I'll tell you what you want to know."

"I know you will. But we've made preparations. You see, Pat, I'm in the mood for two cherries on my Sunday. One for Kinsley. One for me. The real question is whether anyone's in the mood for a banana split. Guys?" I rubbed my chin again and looked around the room to my men. Pat's head swung in wild desperation, eyes bright and shining with tears, arms and legs yanking against the cuffs biting at the skin on his wrists and ankles, tightening with every movement.

"You see that?" Gus asked Pat. "That fear and panic you got? That the type you and your friends had in mind for our girl?"

"No, no, no, no! I swear I was just talking shit. I didn't have any friends involved."

"There's your first and last lie." I held a small branding iron to the candle's flame. Pat's eyes widened.

"No! Ray doesn't know! All he knows is Patrick Scott had debts and Ray kicked him out for bringing baggage." The handle of the small faucet turned beneath my free hand where I tested the hiss of the iron against the thin stream of water. I returned the iron to the flame. "Patrick wanted back in and offered his ex-wife as atonement, but Ray said she was a well-traveled highway. Said only fresh pavement would make him change his mind. A group of us knew where to find a virgin."

Gustav thrust his fist so hard against Pat's jaw, Patrick's teeth burst loose like marbles in his mouth. Joey grabbed Pat's hair to help him spit them out, but Jarrell knocked his hand away.

"Let him choke to death!" Jarrell shouted. Gustav jumped between Joey and Jarrell to keep them from taking their anger out on one another.

My hand rose. "Enough." I carried the branding iron and lifted Pat's head myself. The skin of his sweating temple sizzled beneath the glowing metal while he gagged on blood and sucked teeth down his throat. "You swallow them. Drink your blood and suffer the flavor of your mistake."

Sick wet sounds contracted through his windpipe and smothered the repeated "Nnnn" of his attempted plea. Gustav jerked Patrick's trousers and undergarments down to his ankles, exposing the thick rubber bands Marcus wrapped around this pig's bollocks.

As Pat's eyes clouded through swallows, I dropped his head, then dropped the used iron into a bowl of ammonia. The men's eyes roved over my hand tools, power tools, surgical tools, canes, brass knuckles, clamps, anything that might exact revenge and cause the earthquake my candidate requested. While I'd love to rip Pat's fingernails off, I focused on the message.

"I'm sorry, King," Pat finally sputtered.

"You neglected the full explanation. If Patrick Scott is dead, why on Earth does Ray still expect a virgin?"

Tears fell down the sides of his face and a puddle spread beneath his body over the bag. "Aw, man! Come on. I hate changing diapers!" Jarrell whined. Joey chuckled and tossed Jarrell a towel to shove beneath Patrick.

"What's the point in saying anything else if I'm just gonna die anyway?" Pat sobbed.

"Tell me and I won't kill you." I wasn't going to kill him anyway. Not yet.

"He sent someone to collect, but they were told the deal was off."

"By whom?!" My voice struck like lightning and thundered against the walls.

"I thought it was *you*!" he cried.

"You are damn right it was me!" Wasn't me. The only thought I had was Cheatham, which meant he was already moving rooks on my board without my permission. The hell if I allowed the underground to realize. "You tell Ray she's not a virgin because King's fucked her to kingdom come and will fuck him up if he dares tread on Nightshade territory ever again! No one touches *her*!" I shouted in his face, my personal feelings weaponizing toward him.

When I saw shock in Pat's eyes, in the eyes of my men, I knew my possessiveness over Kinsley shined like flames in my irises. He nodded, sweat colliding with tears on his face.

"I want you to think of her. Picture her fear of you in your mind and how you got off on it." He closed his eyes to close me out. "You have that pretty redhead in your mind yet?" I asked, a teasing whisper in his ear. "I'm thinking Ray didn't ask for the virgin or expect the package in Tallahassee yesterday. I'm thinking you did. When we took care of your partner in crime, you were pouting because you showed up for a product I stepped in the way of. You and your buddies staked out the bar and she showed. Scalpel, please, nurse?"

Joey snorted a laugh as he busied himself preparing a needle for stitches. He passed me a set of gloves I snapped over my hands, next came the scalpel I brandished with a delighted smile at the man on my operating table.

"At least you've already pissed yourself and gotten that out of the way," I offered, the tiny blade reflecting light over his face. "Now, this is going to hurt you a lot more than it hurts me."

"*No, King, NO! Please, don't do this to me, please, Klive, please, please, PLEASE! PLEASE!*" He begged over and over until his voice morphed into open sobs sucking in hysterical tears as I ran a scalpel down over his shrunken scrotum, watched the blood that came in the wake of the cut. I chuckled to myself since his balls retreated as though they knew.

"Sounds like the same dialog a sick fuck like you would get off on hearing from that pretty bartender trapped in your hotel room, am I right? Rather fitting." I reached inside the opened flesh. "Calm down, Pat. All you had to do was heed my warning, but you refused. As you can see, I am a man of my word."

Pat shouted, screamed, panted, pleaded while my gloves grew very messy. His head thrashed wildly, his eyes squeezed shut, his face screwed up in agony, his heels dug against the table to lift his body off the surface.

"Every time you move you only make things harder on yourself." I shook my head toward Joey as Pat's body bucked. "Can you believe this guy?" I grinned and gestured with the hand holding the scalpel while my fingers searched for the escapees. Joey looked away for a moment in a bit of amused shock at my cool demeanor with a disapproving shake of his head.

In truth, I saw his relief in my remembrance of myself. "In light of the release you're providing me right now, I'm feeling merciful. How so, you wonder? Since you seem to be a man of few coherent words right now, I'll take guesses from the audience."

I groaned when Patrick shrieked like a mad man as I took hold of the first runaway and made the cut. I pinched the testicle between my bloody gloved fingers and held the grotesque orb on display.

"There's a cherry for Kinsley."

His pallor drained and body fell limp; eyes rolled back and closed.

"That's too bad," I mused. "Takes the sport away like a deer feeder across from a blind. Where's the fun without the hunt?"

"You letting him live?" Gus's Creole accent spoke over my shoulder where he watched me cut the other testicle free.

"That's not the act of mercy, if you're guessing." My sarcastic kindness siphoned like the color in Pat's skin. "Shame he fell asleep before getting to the happy ending. I'm not in the mood for a banana split. I've had my fill of cherries on this Sunday. Now, he must brave the world as a eunuch. Doesn't get clearer or more emasculating than that."

Joey took Pat's pulse while I trashed the gloves and washed my hands. Jarrell and Gustav grumbled about how killing him removed the problem altogether, but Joey cleared his throat. "I agree, King. You've made your point beyond the easy way of body dumping. This is creative. A walking example. Let's just stitch him back up, shall we? I have a date later, and I'd really hate to show up late and make a bad impression."

"King?" Gustav asked. "You really bang Kinsley to kingdom come?"

"No. You really think she'd let me?" I grinned up at his somber expression. Funny he was more bothered by that than the limp man sucking his own teeth a few feet away.

"Nah, I don't. I'm glad we were there today."

"Believe me, mate, so am I. Try not to think of it or else you'll send me on an unintended spree."

"If I don't quit thinking of it, I'll talk you into one and help you along."

"You want to earn brownie points; you guys bring me the guys from that van. The guy who was in the bar when Pat assaulted Kinsley is in on this as much as the ones in the van. If he cowered to Pat in the bar, he may be the easiest one to crack. As it stands, I need you keeping a sharp eye on her and the others during work. Joey's on her detail, although according to Taylor, she's in the wind now. Hell, the guys in the van could've followed her."

"One thing at a time, man. Jarrell, help me get his ass outta here," Gustav said when he noticed Joey dabbing glue over the stitches on Pat's empty scrotum.

Joey washed his hands and drained the basin, cleansed the branding iron, milled while I stood and stared at the white walls long after the bouncers took the eunuch. The tools replaced in their designated locations, table stored back in the closet, floor spotless, evidence incinerated. Joe stood beside me and stared for a while, too. Probably to be sure not a speck of trace could be linked back to us, but we knew Pat was too spineless to go to the police. Inferno's own rivalry with the cops was enough to keep him away.

"You good?" Joey broke the silence.

"How can you even ask me that after the shit I just pulled here?" Conviction washed over me. "I should've left her alone. Should've waited till the contract was done, so I'd know which version of Cheatham I'd get before taking a step in her direction. Part of me feels vindicated now that someone else lost his balls over the same woman who took mine."

"Hey, King. Think of all the jobs you've pulled. The most impossible hits. The situations you've come up against with no way out. Yet you always land on your feet and each adds to the urban legend you've accidentally created for yourself. Doesn't matter how clumsy you know you were as long as they only know about the badass parts."

"No, I've got to put more distance between us. I can't have her finding out who I am. She'll loathe my existence."

He shrugged. "Suit yourself, but you're the one who said she might've been followed." Joey pulled his phone from his pocket and tapped an app. A map of Florida narrowed to a pin dropped in Clearwater Beach. "Good thing I always know where she is. Here, give me your phone. Don't tell Chris, and don't make me regret this. Klive, he specifically told me if I shared info, I'd need to find a new job. Because you've resisted stalking her every move the way Chris requested, and because you did an epic job today, I'm offering peace-of-mind the only way I can give for the moment."

Joey tapped my phone with his and we watched the same map and beacon flash onto my screen. "Looks like I'm taking my date to the beach."

12 | ♀

Monday morning traffic was always a mess. I was glad to be jogging downstairs from Constance's condo and walking the ten blocks to the building my father worked in rather than driving in the road-raging masses. Since she was studying cosmetology at a nearby institute, Constance masterfully braided and styled my hair in a way that forced tendrils to mask the bruise in my hairline. Gone was her blasé attitude toward Inferno after I'd confessed what happened.

She pressed at the tender flesh of my scalp to get a feel for the pained spots.

"I'm glad Jase shredded his face," she muttered when I winced at her fingers in my hair. "Tell me about this guy you and Bayleigh call Moonlight. What's his real name?"

"I don't know," I lied. I didn't want to talk about him too much yet.

"Well, Jase must be flipping out after all these years of lusting, now suddenly this other dude appears to rescue you when it's always been his specialty?"

"Rescuing me has always been his specialty? What am I? A trouble-magnet damsel-in-distress? How could he have anything to rescue me from when I keep to myself?" I shook my head. She was crazy. "You give Jase too much credit."

"Or you don't give him enough. You have no idea, do you?" She shook *her* head, now, disappointed. I rolled my eyes and sighed.

"Moonlight wasn't there when this happened to me. He was there on Friday night when I was harassed, but Jase was there after this guy hurt me. No matter what you say, Jase scared the hell out of me, Constance. I've never seen that side of him before. He almost scared me more than the biker, which is saying a lot. I don't want to run into Moonlight's arms because I'm afraid of Jase. I'm really just trying to take a breather where none of them would think to look for me, although Moonlight doesn't know me well enough to come after me yet. You should've seen the look on his face when he came in on Friday, though. He's scary to everyone but me. I don't even know how to describe the difference, it's just something you have to be there for, although I'm glad you weren't there for these incidents."

"You're babbling. You like this guy."

I winced as she pulled the hair back from my forehead to twist into a side fish bone braid.

"I know that hurts. I'm sorry. But we're gonna tease some of this out of the braid and curl the tendrils. Daddy will never even see a thing. But anyone can look at your eyes and tell something is bothering you."

"That's a good thing because normally I am crazy bothered if we've argued, and I am bothered by that, too." I bit my lip through another tug.

"It's sweet that your father matters this much to you. That you'd go out of your way to make peace. If you were anyone else, I'd accuse you of keeping the peace to keep the place you're living in, but since I've begged you on multiple occasions to come live with me here, well ... you must really love your father."

"I do. I can't stand thinking of what I must've put him through by skipping church yesterday without a note, then not coming home or calling? He has every right to gripe at me. Not because I'm his child, but because we are both humans who care for one another, and you just don't leave someone you care for in the dark."

"Oh?" she asked and leaned around to peer into my eyes. "You mean the way you care about Jase and left him worried? He's still worried and I wouldn't be surprised if he's looped your father into this mess. Maybe I should come have coffee with you as a buffer?"

I mulled her offer, then shook my head, mistakenly pulling my hair again as she worked. She chided me.

"I'm sorry."

"You're only hurting yourself, girl."

I sighed at the implied double meaning. "How about this? I'm gonna man-up after I have coffee with my father. I'll drive over to Jase's house, so I have to face him rather than having anything to do with my phone. How's that for bravery?"

"That'll do. I'd say you're on quite the streak. First, letting me draw henna tattoos on you, then letting me do your hair, now I get to play dress-up, right? This is like a real sleepover from high school or something!" she gushed. We both laughed. I had a group of henna stars she'd made into constellations on my ankle trailing over my foot, then she'd added three near my left temple to steal attention from my right side where the bruise was that she concealed with my hair.

When she'd painted them last night, I'd first watched her doodle on herself to show me how henna worked so I wouldn't freak out. "But yours are so cool because your skin is darker so you have to get close enough to see them. They're more subtle and classy versus trashy."

"I know, right?" She'd grinned in mischief while I'd tsked. "For real though, black guys with tattoos? Sexy."

"And black girls with tattoos?" she asked.

"Psh, Constance, as if you need anyone to tell you you're sexy. How often do you meet a black female rock star who can belt Lauren Hill and transition to Lzzy Hale like nothing?"

"White guys with tattoos are pretty sexy too, though. Especially the ones with dragon sleeves who can transition from Gary Clark Junior to Great White."

I'd huffed in frustration. "Touché."

"Speaking of singing, you been working on those scales I taught you?" she'd asked and told me to be very still as she'd painted my temple.

I didn't move, stared at the unused coffee pot on the counter.

"No. I'm not a singer, Constance. I'd much rather be in the audience appreciating your talent. Please?"

She'd sighed in mutual frustration. "Fine. Here's the mirror. Tell me what you think."

Now, I inspected my reflection in the mirrored windows of the high-rises I walked beside. This version of Kinsley Hayes said playful, light, fun and flirty. I didn't have any spare clothing in my car that didn't reek of sweat. Constance chose a tunic that fit me like a dress since I was shorter. Bright red, black belt cinching the waist, sleeveless. Simple makeup. Eyeliner and mascara like my normal self. Daddy's sweet little girl, she'd called the look.

I wore my flip-flops and felt like a hobbit walking through the fancy glass entry of the high-rise as the women around me trotted up the steps in heels of all heights. A few wore flats with their sharp pantsuits or pencil skirts.

I aimed for the ground floor coffee shop and pulled my phone to check the time.

"So, you've had your phone, just been ignoring me?"

I yelped. "Daddy!"

"Were you expecting someone else?"

"No, I came to see you. My phone died yesterday. I left it in the car to charge while I spent the night at Constance's so I could be here when you arrived. Looks like my timing was perfect."

"You know what timing is even more spot on? When I come to your apartment and see you any time I want."

"Please don't be mad, Daddy. I just needed some time to cool my head and think about what you said. Can we have coffee? Do you have time to chat?"

He looked at his watch. "I can always spare a few minutes for my baby. Are you really here for me, or for him?" My head turned in alarm while my father's laugh rang through the coffee shop. "Gotcha."

"Daddy, behave."

Klive wasn't here, but my father's co-worker, Ben, strode toward me in a killer suit with suave hair and eloquent manners as he took my elbow and leaned in to kiss my cheek after a warm, 'hello, beautiful'. I rolled my eyes before meeting my father's smiling gaze. Ben asked to buy me a cup of coffee. My father stole into his favorite booth. I agreed but frowned when Lucy greeted me from behind the counter. With everything on my mind, she'd been the furthest thing from my brain, as well as one of the last people I might tolerate in this climate. Ben complimented her hairstyle, then ordered my favorite. I grinned as he quirked his groomed brows like a quintessential player.

"See that? I pay attention," he said. Ben ordered his Venti mocha and my father's regular. Lucy took his cash. Ben tucked the change in the tip jar.

"Thanks, Ben. You go ahead and sit with my father. I'll wait for our order."

He nodded and gestured to the stars on my temple. I touched them, insecure and shy.

"Your father will kill me if I tell you how hot you look with tattoos, so I'll just tell you they're pretty."

"Ben, go on, mister." I grinned and turned to see Lucy gnawing her lower lip as she traded glances between my order and my face. "Yes, Lucy, is there something you need to say?"

She shook her head. I couldn't help how my irritation for her showed on my face. I've never gossiped about her behind her back. I wanted to say so, but I wasn't here to cause a scene, rather to mend the one my father caused on the track after Saturday's invitational.

"Then I told him, I don't think you appreciate the gravity of the situation with your company," a woman's voice said into a cell phone. She pulled the metal case down to demand, "Tall cappuccino with a double espresso shot. Hold the foam."

Um, wasn't a cappuccino all foam and espresso?

Poor Lucy. Now, I felt like asking aloud just to get a dig on this woman.

The lady's phone rose to her cheek again. "Yeah, he wanted to negotiate, but he's in no position after they discovered a roach infestation in his kitchen. I told Klive we need to go in for the kill ASAP."

A jolt rushed through my body at the mention of Klive's name. Part of me hated that *she* spoke so casually what he'd been mad at me for uttering. *What was she to him?*

"We're looking at a lucrative opportunity and this guy's back is against— oh, speak of the devil. I'll call you later. Bye."

"Do you need a carrier?" Lucy placed mine and Ben's cups on the counter, then my father's. I shook my head. Rather than my name scrawled on my cup the way *Ben* and *Andy* were on theirs, she'd written *sorry*.

"Sorry, eh? That an insult, Lucy?" a British accent asked. "She doesn't appear sorry for anything."

I gasped while Lucy stammered that she wasn't writing that her customer was sorry or bad in any way, she was apologizing for—

He chuckled with a hand up to stop her, ignoring me like I didn't exist. I hated how beautiful, powerful, charming and smug he came off.

The woman who'd been on the phone greeted him and offered to get him something. He brushed her off in annoyance, then spoke to Lucy, but I didn't hear his words because I didn't want to.

Like a good bartender, I triangled the cups in my hands and went to the booth my father and Ben tucked into. They chattered about some sort of medical device; a doctor giving Ben a hard time on believing this prototype could help his patients.

"Andy, I don't think this guy wants his patients to heal. As in, I'm gleaning he's afraid they won't need him if they permanently recover with the use of this device. He'd rather keep them addicted to pain killers and his prescription pad than see them free from pain. Makes me sick. Come with me? You have a better way with words when you're frustrated, and this guy, he's rubbing my nerves like sandpaper. Ah, thank you, Kinsley."

Ben took the cup I delivered and offered the seat beside him. I shook my head and sat beside my daddy instead.

"We should hire Kinsley to come with us. That doctor wouldn't stand a chance. Probably why he keeps a close relationship with his prescription pad. Have you seen the girls these pharmaceutical companies hire to talk doctors into pedaling their products to patients?"

"I have," my father said. "I think it's unethical. Kins can come with me if she likes, though. She knows I'd love nothing more than to hire her. Diabetics use devices, so technically ...."

"Not quite on the same scale as artificial knees and hips." I grinned. "I'm not instructing surgeons in the operating room when these diabetic devices are prescribed to a patient. Thank God. I don't think I could handle the stress."

"Nonsense. Once you've seen blood, you're okay." Ben grinned then cringed when my father reminded him of Ben's first surgery. "Yeah, you should take that as a good sign that I was green and came out with my job intact. Just look at me today."

We all laughed. Daddy's radiant smile soothed the tension Klive's words and presence injected through my body.

Klive stood at the counter for his order. The blonde by his side rambled on and on about some restaurant. My father and Ben resumed conversation about this problem physician. I stared at Lucy's handwriting on my cup so I wouldn't stare at Klive. Also, so Lucy wouldn't run away with more rumors. She was probably bursting to talk about how he'd treated me in front of her.

Why would he say I didn't appear sorry for anything? Was I supposed to feel sorry about something?

"—ticket if you'd like to bring Kinsley to the Polo tournament that weekend. What'dya say, Kins? Be my plus-one?"

"Kinsley," my father's voice jerked my attention. "Your mother and I are going. It's for charity."

"Uh, sure." *What was I agreeing to?*

All I knew was I needed to get out of here! Klive's voice was saying something charming to Lucy.

"I have to go, Daddy. I have class. I wanted to make sure you're okay? That we're okay?" Daddy inspected my sincerity. "I hate when you're mad at me."

"Honey, I'm not mad at you. Come here, kiddo." He tucked me under his arm with a big soothing squeeze. "I'm much better when I have my baby snuggled by my side reassuring me that she's okay. I'm sorry I hurt your feelings, Kins."

Sweet relief. There was no better place than his solace. I hated we weren't chatting on our porch swing, so I could've stayed put and worked through the thoughts churning rapids in my brain.

"I'm good, Daddy. Everything is good now that I know we're better. I'll see you later this evening." I kissed his cheek, then smiled at Ben. "Thanks for the pumpkin spice, Ben. Don't know how you pulled it off, but I'm glad you did. Y'all have a good day. If you need me to go with either of you to charm this doctor into doing the right thing, you have my number, but then that means in order to return the favor, I'd need to take one of you on my next interview for moral support, and how would that look?"

"Hey, are you calling me a coward?" Ben teased. "Because I don't mind coming along for moral support if you need."

My father laughed. "Kinsley, I think I can get this guy to come around, but it's common knowledge you have a knack with difficult men, so ...."

"Men like *you*, sir?" I bent to kiss his cheek again and ignored the pointed look he'd cast over my shoulder.

Klive was under my father's skin. Why? I had no idea. Especially when Ben was a chronic flirt anytime I came around, yet all Daddy did with him was laugh.

I grabbed my cup and hustled out of the coffee shop. *Was Klive watching?* I wasn't sure, but I needed to get away, needed space, air. *What was I thinking trying to be near him without being mad? He was the one who should've been sorry for insulting me. Screw him.* I pushed the door into stairwell, heading for the parking garage. *Just breathe.*

In ... two ... three ... out ... two ... three ... in ... two ... three ....

I counted my breaths as I jogged two flights down.

Bursting through the heavy metal door into the hollow concrete corridors, I barely took in the rows of luxury sedans, SUVs, trucks. Why couldn't I breathe? The memory of Klive capturing me to prevent our falling in this same area assaulted me with the charming smile he no longer gave me.

Why hadn't I taken my damn car? Stupid, Kinsley! You could've driven away now like you'd done then!

"Just breathe," I told myself and tossed the coffee in the nearby garbage can. My phone chimed several times. I looked at the display to see too many messages from Jase. *Did he deserve to say sorry?* Well, hell if I didn't feel like a hypocrite.

The door opened and closed a few moments later. I slinked into the shadows, suddenly aware of the fact that parking garages weren't the best places to be alone even in the light of day.

Italian oxfords invaded my view of the cement floor as they stopped before me.

"What are you doing?"

Klive King stood with his hands in his pockets.

"Checking messages," I said as my pulse thrummed, breath shallowed further. *Damn, he was all power in this capacity.* Something familiar itched in the back of my brain, but he interrupted my internal reach for that file in my memory.

"Try again," he said.

"For real." I displayed my phone to show him. Upon my first full glance at his eyes, I faltered. "Dammit, maybe I needed a moment to compose myself after you trashed me on Saturday. You did it again just now in front of the track manager so she can gossip to all her friends. I'm a little off."

His eyes flickered to the stars on my temple.

"They're henna. Not real," I stated.

"I like them. Now, tell me why you're here."

"To have coffee with my father after our fight on Saturday."

"The truth."

"He scared me, Klive!" I blurted. "The biker came back to the bar yesterday! He *really* scared me! I'm sorry I just said your name!

I forgot you don't like me saying it! But your name was the only thing I could think when he pulled my hair. I wanted you to come and make him go away!"

"Marcus filled me in." His jaw muscle jumped as he stared through me. "He also told me he suspended you from the bar because you weren't supposed to be there in the first place. You don't follow instructions well."

I gasped. "What the hell is the problem with every male around me? Don't victim shame me into apologizing like I was asking for it! Jase drove me to the bar so I could pick up my car. The keys were still inside the bar, so I had to grab them. I didn't do anything to provoke his outburst."

"Marcus also showed me the video."

"And?"

"And you were a bitch." Pride poked like a sunbeam through the gray clouds in his eyes. "I especially enjoyed the cherry on top of his Sunday. Clever pun on sundaes."

I rolled my eyes and huffed. "Okay, so maybe I provoked a little, but I did what you said."

"That's the problem." The pride in his eyes vanished. "I watched your boyfriend handle the situation the same way I would've. Instead of running into his arms to thank him, you ran away from him to find me."

"What? It's not like that. I came to have coffee with my father. This is coincidence."

"Bullshit." He sighed and rubbed the back of his neck before his palm rested against the concrete behind me. "Look, kid—"

"Hell no, you don't call me that. Not—"

"Listen to me, dammit." His hands cupped my biceps. Adrenaline lanced my veins as his kind veneer melted to reveal a cold steel. "It's not that I don't want you using my name, and I don't mean to insult you. Kinsley, I'm not good and you are. Jase is good. I know he scared you, but he's not who you should be afraid of. You need to give him the credit he deserves and quit running into the arms of anyone else. Including me."

"Stop."

"You do yourself a disservice and you're better than that. I'm bad, but I'm not *that* guy, either."

"Please, stop."

"I don't want to be used, I don't want to use you, and if we continue, I'll enjoy someone best left alone because we want different things. Jase wants what you want."

"Stop!" I shouted, my command bouncing off the hollows and pillars. I shoved against him. Klive stood like a wall. "I hate your words! The way you look at me! Why do you have to ruin everything?" I cried in overwhelming angst. This shouldn't hurt so bad, but my lungs strained for air harder than when I came off a relay race. I couldn't freaking breathe!

"Get a grip, Kinsley. You're stronger than this petulance."

"Oh, shut up with your effing wisdom and fatherly bullshit! I already have a daddy. I didn't run to him or you to make this better. Don't tell me to get a grip and accuse me of petulance when I'm pissed off. I can't believe you think I'm a using cheater! How insulting. You don't know me at all!"

I pressed hard against his chest and loathed how I looked up into his eyes because I needed to know their temperature during all this.

"Why did you send me flowers?" My voice cracked. "Take me to the fort? Pose as the good guy when you're a liar?" I sniffled. Tears drizzled down my cheeks. His hands cupped my face, thumbs swiped the tears in so much contrast to the words and cruelty. He made zero sense.

"Kinsley Hayes," he said my name like a pained curse.

I closed my eyes. Neither one of us made sense. What were we to each other, really? Strangers with chemistry.

"Don't close your eyes, Kinsley. Don't pretend you don't see me right in front of you. Or that you haven't seen me all along. Don't just see what you want to see. *Look* at me!"

I opened my eyes and hated how they traveled to his lips, his to mine, then we glared in matching anger and contempt. *For what?*

"Don't worry. I don't want to look at you ever again, Klive King. This was all a mistake. Thank you for opening my bloody eyes, asshole. I told you that you were all the same." I shoved out of his space, and he let me.

13 | ♀

Ten blocks back to Constance's condo offered plenty of time to gather myself, to correct smeared mascara, so that by the time I knocked on her door, I smiled easily. "Problem solved. Daddy's happy. Now onto Jase."

"Ready to man-up, as you say?" she asked. "Pretty sure he's on-duty at the beach right now." Her eyes bugged in the mirror while she applied magnetic eye lashes to her expertly decorated eyes.

"Yes, ma'am, I am." I grinned. She seemed to buy my relief. Truth was, I'd resolved that Klive only had the power to hurt me as long as I allowed. Therefore, I was done for the time being.

"Thanks for letting me crash here. We should do this again soon without the drama."

"Anytime, but I agree. Did he flip out about the henna?" she asked.

"Wow." My brows rose. "Come to think of it, no. He didn't say anything about that. Weird."

She nodded in agreement. I kissed her cheek and gathered my things to leave her place.

When I pulled into the nearly empty parking lot at the beach, the clock read 9:05. A thick haze blocked the sun that usually burned off after a bit. I parked but decided to come back for my bag and the little lounger in my trunk after a run. I needed to condition, especially since the angst and drama stacked like Lego blocks building a castle of complication. What to say to Jase after his scary side? After Klive's brush off due to my loyalty to Jase. The more I mulled the things he'd said, the more I hated his point; why run to him if Jase took care of the threat on the spot?

Because Klive is dangerous. What made Klive more dangerous than Jase, though? Something I couldn't place my finger to.

Jase was tough, scary, hell, downright barbaric yesterday. Why go to Klive? Think of Klive? Dream of Klive? *Why? Why? Why?*

Jase asked me to be his girlfriend ... defended me like a boyfriend would. How did one yesterday hold so many things?

Shop keepers unlocked their businesses along the boardwalk. Not technically a boardwalk since the walkway was by no means made of wood, nor right up against the shore, however, my parents dubbed the strip a boardwalk since before I existed. Family habit.

"Good morning," a man in a Hawaiian shirt said. He inserted a key into a lock and shoved a heavy bin of beach toys in front of the door to clear the path for shoppers.

"Morning," I replied. I checked for traffic, then jogged across the street to the sand. The flip flops kicked from my feet. I carried them between my fingers. The cool powder sifted over my toenails as I shuffled toward the shoreline until the chilly water washed the granules from my feet. Tiny holes prickled under the wet sand from burrowing periwinkles.

"Good morning."

I started at the voice. A handsome face smiled from a lifeguard stand. Well, well, well ... the same lifeguard who'd stolen my shoes when Jase was messing with me last week.

"A little overdressed for playing in the water, aren't ya?" He leaned on his elbows at the rail.

"I suppose, but that's not what I am here for."

"Oh? You came to see me, then?"

I snorted at the lame line. "Actually, maybe you could point me in the direction of Jase Taylor's post?" Last thing I needed was another guy complicating life.

"Aw, really?" He shook his head. "What is it about that guy? You know he has a legit girlfriend now, right?"

I raised my eyebrows and gaped. "Does he?" I waited, unsure how to feel at the thought. I had no right to be upset when Jase should be free to do as he wished with anyone. After all, if Klive were here, he'd say Jase was my loss or some bullshit like I deserved to lose what I refused. Ugh.

Unless....

"You mean Kinsley?" I tested.

"Yep. That's her name. And I'm Matt. You are?"

"Pleased to meet you." I grinned. Poor Matt probably thought I smiled because he came onto me. Inside, I happy danced that Jase claimed me when we weren't even *together* together. Jase mentioned me enough for his lifeguards to know and remember my name? Amazing! I wanted to press him about how long Jase and Kinsley had been a couple, but Matt asked my name again.

"Well, you already know my name."

"Huh?" He scratched the back of his head. "Wait. Are *you* Kinsley?"

I nodded like he was slow, though my smile grew to idiotic brightness.

"That lucky bastard. Just once I wish he'd fall into a bed of roses and come out smelling like shit." He laughed at his own joke while I shook my head and bit my lower lip. Matt grabbed his radio and said some code word.

"Yeah?" Jase's voice crackled with the rough texture of a pilot. Sexy. Flutters in my belly eased my anxiety. Damn, I was all over the map where Jase was concerned.

"Which post you at, man?" The lifeguard held the radio to his mouth as he looked at me. I shook my head and tapped my lips. He nodded.

Jase said, "Twenty-three."

"Copy. Triple take coming your way at three o'clock. Hot." He smiled down at me while I rolled my eyes.

"Come on, Matt, you know I'm trying to be good! You wanna get me in trouble?" Jase asked. I beamed down at my feet before looking back up at the lifeguard.

"What she doesn't know won't hurt her. Besides, what makes you think she isn't checking out some other guy right now?" He winked. I put my hands on my hips and shook my head with disapproval. Matt and Jase were very similar. "Trust me, Taylor."

"She'd better be friggin' *fine*, or I'll come down there, Matt. Over."

"Ten-four. Over-n-out." Matt lowered the radio and cast a mischievous grin. "Better get a move on, Kinsley. Run past my post anytime. I'm a great rebound if he screws up. Tell him I said so."

I waved a finger but thanked him before I jogged in that direction. I felt Matt watching me go. Sure enough, I looked over my shoulder and saw his binoculars over his eyes. Oh, hell. I'm not a fan of close-ups. Whatever. I had quite a few stands to go, so I paced myself and went into the zone. Constance's thin tunic whipped against my thighs and glued against my torso in the breeze. The sand flung behind every bare footfall. No obstacle course. No agenda. No schedule today. *No more thinking!*

A very fine physique wearing blue swim shorts, sunglasses, and earbuds jogged toward me. As he passed me, his head turned to openly stare. Maybe I did look a little silly in Constance's dress. I looked over my shoulder. Eh, Jase was about to check out some eye candy even though he shouldn't, right? Guess that should make me feel a little better about accidentally checking out a lollipop of my own. Had I not just shoved Klive out of my way in a parking garage, I'd have sworn he'd skipped work! Ah, but blue shorts guy was missing the huge stick up his ass.

As I pressed onward, I closed in on number twenty-two with a pretty brunette kicking her feet up on the rail. I gave a polite smile that she returned before I faintly saw stand twenty-three with Jase perched against the rail the same way Matt had been.

His arm rose to his face, then lowered while my anxiety ratcheted. What would he say after I'd abandoned him in pure panic yesterday? Was he mad I'd ignored him? What if Constance had finally texted him back with the truth?

Just breathe. In through the nose, out through the mouth, in ... two ... three ... out ... two ... three ....

Man-up and accept the consequences. Head on. No more running.

Braving a closer look, I saw now that he grinned while he watched through binoculars. How long he had seen me coming, I couldn't be sure.

"Damn, Kinsley, you're a sight for tired eyes!"

As I slowed below his tower, I heard the radio crackle before he spoke. "Nice try you bastard."

"But I was right," Matt said. "You gotta say it."

Jase laughed. "You're right, definitely a triple take, but no way she was checking you out when I'm her type. You don't even compare."

I chuckled at that one.

The radio crackled again, and Matt's voice came through. "If I'm on her radar, maybe you're not doing it for her. You should probably hit the gym or something, you friggin' pig." Jase laughed while Matt continued. "You're a lucky asshole."

Jase leaned on the railing and tilted his head with amusement as he studied me walking past.

"You win. I'ma lucky asshole. Now, do your job, over." At least Jase's voice was light and chipper.

"Over-n-out," Matt said.

"Hey! Kins! Where you going?" Jase shouted as I continued down the shoreline. The elderly, beach-combing couple I watched during my workouts scanned the sand with their metal detector. Aside from them, the beach sprawled wide and almost empty. Guess most tourists needed more heat and sunshine to don their suits and play in the sand ... or they were hungover.

While I watched the couple, Jase chirped his whistle. I jerked like a Girl Scout caught devouring her own Thin Mints as he climbed down his ladder and jogged after me. His strong arm came around my waist. I squealed while he spun me in a circle of ticklish laughter. Seconds later, he tripped me and rolled onto his back, taking the brunt of our fall like a football player making a tackle. He was out of breath while I regained my brain.

"Damn, baby, making me work. I wasn't even warmed up." He rolled me to my back in the loose sand, then held himself up as he looked down at me. I huffed several fake gasps, mocking his need to catch his breath. Mine was calm, though my heart pounded at our intimate position. Not to mention, that he assumed such in a public place with those little old people nearby.

"Hey, not all of us are constant runners."

"I should think a SEAL would stay in better shape. Maybe Matt was right," I teased.

He popped his lower lip pretending to be hurt.

"Tuck that lip away unless you want me to punish you," I chided, my voice too sweet.

"Ooh, what did you have in mind, sweet Kins? You shouldn't tease a hungry lion unless you're ready to feed him. I'm ravenous now that I know you're safe." His head tilted as he checked out my temple. "Henna looks good on you. Damn Constance." He shook his head and sat back on his heels. I sat up while my legs remained pinned between his knees.

"You should be saying, *'damn Kinsley'* because I'm the one who took her phone and ignored your texts. You have bros before hos. We have chicks before dicks."

He whistled. "Who knew you had such a potty mouth? If anyone needs punishment, I'm lookin' at her."

I scoffed. "I dare you. That little old couple is watching and ready to report you for slacking on the job." My eyebrow cocked.

"You're lucky they are. They can't protect you later. I've never once backed out of a dare. Careful what you ask for, Kinsley Hayes." His eyes narrowed as a sexy smolder heated his face. Ooh lala....

"Don't make promises you can't keep, Jase."

His expression morphed into one of pleasant surprise. I cursed my flirtatious stupidity.

"I don't."

"Good."

"Is it?" His lips twitched. Jase peered around, checking our surroundings to be sure there was still no reason to be up at his post. The old people stared with blatant disdain. Yikes! I wasn't some horny, no-good hoodlum, but if ever I read a mind! The old man shook his head and looked for more shells. The woman sighed as she drifted out of my periphery.

"If they're looking anyway, maybe you need a little mouth-to-mouth?"

"Perhaps I *am* having trouble breathing."

14 | ♀

JASE HELD HIMSELF IN **a plank over me** and descended in a pushup like a total show-off before his soft mouth tickled my lips with a tender kiss. Not what I expected, nor was the immediate wave of longing tugging at my mind as much as my body. So many aching needs! Jase's mouth infused life to my drowning soul, but the survivor breeching the surface was the duplicitous traitor of an alter ego who was so damn tired of being starved in the dark.

Jase pinned her to the sand beneath sunlight breaking through the clouds, even as my mind stormed at images he inspired of us doing this anywhere else. I wanted more. Maybe he shouldn't be throwing steak to the lioness in duress? She sure needed a distraction, and this seemed a perfect one.

His tongue snagged mine. I was going for more, but he pulled away. "You trying to get me fired for bringing you up to my tower to toss your dress and bend you over that railing up there?"

I gasped in scandalized shock and yanked backward in the sand. "Jase Taylor, you should be punished for such speech," I told him, aghast.

He chuckled and made adjustments to his shorts that lit my face on fire. I jumped off of the sand and pretended to need excessive dusting off.

"Can't say you weren't warned. There's a reason I didn't compare myself to one of those desperate seagulls. Gonna take more than a few crumbs of bread to satisfy what you've caused. I'll tell you straight, I'm in the mood for a buffet."

I gulped, looked down at how the chipped seashells near my feet matched the light coral nail polish on my toes, the henna climbing my foot and ankle. What did Jase's crass analogies mean for any relationship we may be starting? Or my sudden physical reaction to him? Was I somehow more attracted to him for beating the hell out of the biker, even as I feared the intensity I'd witnessed?

My mind flashed back to Friday night in his room. The argument we'd had about sex and his view on commitment. I chewed my lip with no one else to blame for leading him to this place; this new permission he felt to take the gloves and manners off his handling of me. How did I feel about this? Flattered. Nauseous. Conflicted.

His hand went to the small of my back as he guided us toward the old couple. They stood upright, eyeing us with suspicion as we approached. I was a bit uncertain while they gave us disapproving glances.

"'S'cuze us, we would like to apologize for our behavior."

Jase gave his most winning smile. The woman's tension melted into a pretty set of dimples and crinkling eyes. How funny, Jase's charm had no expiration. He extended his hand to the old man who hesitated before shaking Jase's hand.

"Allow me to explain," Jase offered. "I am home on leave, and we don't see each other too often. We were just caught up in the moment while the beach was empty."

The man's gaze softened and understanding crossed his haggard features. A hand rose in solute to Jase, and Jase returned the sentiment.

"Well, dear, if you don't have a long road ahead of you." The woman took my hand and goaded me away from the men while they put up that acronym-filled language barrier. She studied me in sharp contrast to the previous disapproval. Guess now I was no longer a common hussy because I was a soldier's hussy. Totally different, hee-hee.

"I see that look, missy. Let me tell you, it takes a special kind of woman to stay at home and wait on pins and needles, wondering if your soldier, well, in your case, sailor, will return to you."

Oh, hell. That remark stole all my musing, especially as tears filled her eyes while she recalled a sad memory.

"Is there a difference? Like between sailor and soldier? Aren't they all soldiers?"

"Oh, bless your little heart. Yes. Soldiers are Army. Navy are sailors. I've noticed the trident in his tattoo."

Now, I was officially out of my element. My cheeks lit on fire.

"Not only a sailor on your hands, dear, but a SEAL. Means that one's too stubborn or too stupid to quit and they're too proud to show their emotions. Men like ours bottle their emotions and reach for a pint. You'll be mistaken to ask him to let you into his mind. It's no place for a young lady like you. No, missy. You are the pretty sunshine, and don't you look nice all dolled up instead of sweating on the obstacle course. You *are* the young lady I've seen that young man staring at, aren't you? He sure has a shining on you."

I studied the sand through a shy smile. "Yes ma'am. Thank you for the insight. I've never dated anyone in the military before. This one ... well, it's surreal to be the one he has a crush on."

"You're welcome. Take what he gives when he gives and don't take it personally when he is stingy. He'll come around after he decompresses. They see the worst in humanity on a daily basis. We are their vacation destination. A place too pretty to live in without feeling guilty for those still on missions. These warriors can't help their loyalty to their cause, so do your best not to hold that loyalty against him and you'll find you've earned it for yourself. Loyalty is a golden attribute, my dear. That's how my husband and I are in our golden anniversary." Her blue eyes crinkled in the sun, her lips a thin smiling line.

"My goodness! What an amazing milestone! Congratulations," I gushed, genuinely impressed.

As we meandered back toward the men, Jase alternated between scanning the beach and appreciating this man's experience. I overheard the man saying his family had four generations of United States militia. A grandson currently enlisted. When we neared, they watched our approach, and the man turned to Jase and asked, "Now, why is a girl like her not wearing a ring? After all, you're gonna have to make her an honest woman before you behave the way you were about to ...." A kind eye winked at me and enjoyed Jase's squirming. Perhaps he enjoyed my own a bit, too.

My lips pursed before I gave into the huge grin he inspired.

Jase unleashed a bright smile, putting me on the spot. "This little lady is too honest for the likes of me, but I'm trying every day, sir."

The elderly man shook his head and said, "Son, you well know that *try* is a fail word, and with the men we've seen showing an interest while this young lady is exercising, you can't afford to fail."

My eyes bugged and rushed to the sand to avoid the depth of this conversation and the new look in Jase's face. I recognized that look, because I possessed that look anytime another girl dared threaten to take my victory on the track. *They tried*.

"Sir, yes, sir," I heard Jase heed his words like an order. Double crap!

"Young lady," the old lady said to me in a low, private tone. "You don't let this one slip through your fingers. Love doesn't wait forever and only comes around so many times. Snap him up before someone else does."

Her tone was one that I felt disrespectful not immediately saying, "Yes, ma'am" to, so I did, and flushed crimson wishing I had the sun to blame.

"Honey, I'm serious, just look at how handsome he is!" Her bony elbow jabbed my ribs. I giggled and grabbed the spot as if she'd tickled me, but her open appreciation for Jase's shirtless body made me gape with laughter. "If I were fifty years younger, he might be in trouble."

Oh, damn! "And if I were fifty years older, your husband might be in trouble," I teased. She chuckled while I gripped the old man's hand to thank him for his kindness as well as his service to our country. "Both of you, this has been enjoyable. Next time I hear your metal detector beeping, I may just drop what I'm doing to join your hunt for some of that Spanish gold they say litters the Florida coast."

"Now, that sounds like a plan. Pleasure talking to you both." The old man took his wife's hand. Jase and I watched them drift further down the shore, but the old lady turned and scanned Jase with a naughty wink.

Jase choked on a laugh, and I clapped a hand over my giggle.

"Shameless!" I gushed before my body shuddered with uncontrollable laughter. "Oh. My. Gosh! Epic!" I exclaimed. "Is there no one you can't woo with your body, sir?"

"As a matter-of-fact ..." he answered. All laughter seized in my constricted throat when he grabbed me around the waist so I crashed against his sun-warm skin. "Either you've just admitted that I've wooed you with my body and think there's no one immune, or you're counting yourself out and I've still got my work ahead of me."

The breath rushed between my lips at the way his tone had dropped. His hands cupped my hips.

"Which is it, Kins?"

He didn't give me a chance to answer before he plucked me from the sand and tossed me over his shoulder. As he walked to his tower, he landed a sound smack to my bottom.

"Jase Taylor! My gosh! What do you think you're doing?" I demanded as he grabbed the ladder with his free hand. "You can't do this!"

"Pretty sure I'm proving you wrong as you speak. Where's your faith?" He pulled us both up with his one arm, holding me with the other all the while.

"Unbelievable. You are such a Neanderthal."

He hoisted us up over the last step and walked onto the platform. The binoculars rose over his eyes to check our surroundings for signs of trouble. Seeing none, he laid them back down and set me on my feet.

"Take the chair." He gestured for me to sit. Now I felt kind of guilty. "What did you think I was going to do?"

"Psh! No one would ever buy your innocence, Jase Taylor."

"You're probably right, but just the same, no one would ever buy that you are a little temptress when that's exactly what you are. If you can look so innocent all the time while I know the truth, then maybe I, being so dangerously seductive, could, in fact, be innocent."

The wind off the waves carried my hearty laughter over the sand. "So humble. The ultimate player, an *admitted* player, innocent? That would mean that he would be no player at all. No one without an agenda should behave so scandalously natural. Not possible. Sorry. And I am not a temptress. For whatever reason you're admitting, I am just tempting for you, and maybe Rustin, but two men should not qualify for an entire generalization, wouldn't you agree?"

Jase studied the waves while leaning against the railing. We both squinted as the sun pierced the clouds.

"Let's not forget everyone's favorite British impostor and bikers who can't mind their damn manners." He sighed. "Kinsley, you confuse me. Always have. You are a chameleon. On one hand, you seem sweet and unaware. Then, you do something as simple as changing your clothes, and you rule me like a goddess who knows exactly how to flaunt her most tormenting assets. How am I not supposed to crave you? How can your God, sometimes my God, have created such creatures to help men when they hurt men so much in every way?"

"I've never deliberately set out to—" I broke off and bit my lip before squinting at him against the bright light. He pulled his shades over his eyes and angled his chin my way. "Jase, the only time I've ever set out to torment you was Saturday night after I caught you at the bar with another redhead. I wore that trashy outfit to rub salt from my wound into yours."

His head tilted. "And the Brit?"

"I believe you called him *Klive*?" I dared, although my heart pounded just saying his name in the light of day.

"Yeah. You using him to get to me as well?"

"Were you using the redhead? Because you didn't even know I'd be home Saturday night."

He shook his head, but I didn't give him an opportunity to hurt me with any fake excuse.

"Look, it's not in my nature to use anyone. You want me to pretend I don't have an attraction to Klive? I won't pretend. I'm attracted to him. Well, *was* attracted to him before he revealed what a prick he can be."

Jase jerked to his full height and yanked the glasses from his eyes. "What do you *mean* he revealed what a prick he can be? What did he do to you?"

"Whoa. Easy there. I already told you he told me I looked like a ho."

"Is that it?"

Something snapped at those words. "*Is that it?* Does there really need to be anything more? I find what he said very insulting even if he was telling the truth."

"If a woman wants to exercise her need to feel sexy, should she be judged for it?" he asked. "Because I'm all for a woman's right to express herself."

I stood back up. "I wasn't exercising any need to feel sexy. I was looking and acting like a ho in public because your slutty ass needed to see how it feels being on the other side!"

15 | ♀

HIS WARM HANDS CUPPED my cheeks before his lips branded mind like a hot iron melting my anger into pure desire. He hummed in a way that revealed a raw ache to run his fingers beneath my tunic as they ran down my shoulders, ribs, waist, hips, or at least that's what my wayward mind conjured while Jase changed angles to dive deeper into driving me crazy.

"You want the truth?" he mumbled as he took a breath against my lips. A few more loose pulls, a brush of his tongue against mine. "I want to see you lose control. I want you so mad with lust that you aren't thinking straight so I can see the real you. Every time I kissed a girl in front of you, I wanted you to hate it so much that you'd finally erupt before letting me have you. I want you right now so bad that my shorts feel like rubber bands around my balls."

I gasped but let him kiss me harder as my hands wove into his hair. When I bit ever-so-softly into his lower lip, Jase's fingers became claws in my flesh. He made the most lust-inducing sound of weak desire. "Jase," I mumbled, but one of his hands cupped my neck and tilted my head further. This felt romance novel cheesy and wonderfully inappropriate. Like the tunic should've been unbuttoned and hanging off my shoulders while my amplified cleavage swelled in his face.

This was bad! But damn did I feel like a real woman in his chiseled grasp. What was Jase like when he came undone with something other than anger? Was there a counterweight to the badass who'd made minced meat of that biker's face? Did he bang a woman with the same fervor, and if so, could my petite body handle him?

"Three o'clock," Matt's voice crackled over the radio. We ripped apart, me in startled alarm, Jase in relieved annoyance if his expression was any indication. His swollen lips barked into the radio way too harsh to sound casual. "Whoa," Matt said. "Easy, there, boy. Did I steer you wrong last time? Trust me."

"You bastard," Jase muttered back. He raised his binoculars to his eyes while I scanned for anyone who may have seen us misbehaving. *Should I climb back down before we get caught?* I didn't want him to get in trouble or fired. When I braved a sheepish glance at Jase once more, a huge smile played on his kissable lips. "Day-um!" he exclaimed.

"What the hell, Jase! Shame on you! Give me those!" I slapped his bare abs and stole the binoculars from him. Let's see ... who was Matt talking about? I focused the lenses. A pair of children played in the far distance with their mother. She was in conservative shorts and a tank. I shifted slowly to the right nearing the shore. I slapped him again, harder this time.

"Ow!" He grabbed his belly. "That stings. Come on, what was that for?"

I lowered the binoculars with an unamused glare. He winced. "Jase Michael Taylor, you should be ashamed. I know your mama raised you better. Don't you dare make me call her to whip your ass. You try that fake innocence again, I'll whip it myself and you won't like it." I shook my head. "You know better."

A woman in an itty-bitty bikini walked along the water as though she were God's gift. She had to be at least fifty pounds overweight.

"She shouldn't be wearing that," he said. "*She* should know better."

"Jase, if a woman wants to exercise her need to feel sexy, should she be judged for it? After all, you're all for a woman's right to expression...." I shook my head in disappointment with him but wanted to go cover myself up to not feel guilty for being in shape. A big part of me wondered how a woman like her managed to portray more self-confidence than me. Was confidence really such a choice? And should the opinions of others define whether we applied that confidence to our own carriage? *Ugh! Shut up, Kinsley Brain!*

"Jase, you should totally go work your magic. She looks like she could handle you."

"Nice ... maybe I should. Bet she would do a better job staying out of trouble than you do. Though, I am not sure who would be punishing who ... or would that be whom?"

"You are positively evil!" I ran my hands over my face.

"Attention all female passengers," Matt's voice crackled over the radio again. "We have another, three o'clock for your viewing pleasure. Kinsley, if you're listening, this one goes out to you."

I cackled while Jase cursed. He reached for his binoculars, but I jerked them up to my eyes.

"Helloooo, nurse!" I mocked an old cartoon and whistled.

"If he's not three-hundred pounds in a pair of grape smugglers, you'd better not be making cat calls." Jase tugged the binoculars and looked through the lenses. "Nice."

Rustin jogged toward us with no shirt, donning low-cut surf shorts. He waved at Jase and appeared surprised to see me as he slowed to a stop at the base of the ladder.

"Well, Miss Hayes, what a pleasant surprise." He sounded so respectful, if not a bit winded. "Looks like you're overdressed for the occasion." His eyebrows waggled as his lips split into a broad toothpaste commercial smile too wholesome to belong to such a flirt. Rustin stood clean shaven, hair gelled to perfection, a light sweat spanning his torso gleamed in the now sunny light of day.

I grinned over at Jase like I was justified in my catcall. He gave a smart ass look in response, then looked down at Rustin.

"How was your first shift?"

"Meh. Walkin' a beat like a newbie deputy ...." He looked down the beach and shook his head before re-focusing on us. "I spent more time imparting wisdom than seeing any real action.

Don't get me wrong, lots of fights, a few burglaries. The arms theft, that one piqued my interest, but the real dick on the force showed up and gave me a condescending finger when I tried to offer my insight. Gonna be fun making a name for myself, but you're worth it, Lacy Jasey."

Jase rolled his eyes while I laughed.

"You mind coming down, or can I come up?" Rustin asked.

"This area is reserved for our VIP guests only," I said. "Sorry, sir."

"Oh, shit, Rustin. Heads up, catch!"

"Huh?" I asked.

Jase scooped me up and threw me over the railing. Rustin caught me like they did this junk all the time! I struggled out of Rustin's arms and scrambled back, pissed off at Jase as I glared up at him.

"What the hell you were thinking?" I demanded.

To my dismay, Jase pursed his lips and leaned over the rail like a deaf man.

"You're just going to ignore me?"

The tirade welled up. Rustin grabbed my hand and yanked me into his arms. Before I could say another defiant, pissy word to either of them, Rustin threw me into a dip and used his mouth like a muzzle over mine. Rustin held me in a way I'd drop to the sand if I fought, so I clamped my lips into a tight line, though I considered biting.

"Taylor!" a man shouted. "Got some reports that someone was in your tower?"

"My post? Nah, you've got the wrong guy, sir. I've been watching the shore all morning and greeting friends as they trickle in from their hangovers." Jase cleared his throat, and Rustin eased me up. Fun times trying to erase the rage from the past sixty seconds of unpredictable bullshit so I could greet Jase's boss, especially when Rustin put his arm around my waist like we were a couple. "In fact, these two reported a person in the waves, but turned out to be dolphins. Thanks guys. Y'all have fun," Jase told us with a friendly wave.

Rustin waved and said, "No problem. Just wanted to be safe."

The boss eyed the two of us, so I relaxed my body language and leaned against Rustin's sticky skin like I enjoyed being gross in his sweat. Rustin smiled down at me and brushed a hand over my hair. His thumb dragged over the stars on my temple.

"Gonna take this little lady to buy a swimsuit since she came straight from the dorm," Rustin said. "You guys recommend one shop over another? There's so many to choose from."

Jase's tongue traveled over his teeth as he fought a smile. His boss gave Rustin the name of a shop I knew sold risqué suits. Jase must be enjoying the hell out of my having to pretend to be ignorant while his boss pretty much said without saying I belonged in a string bikini. Freaking perverts. How often did this man recommend that shop to tourists to get his fill?

Rustin held my hand as we turned to walk along the shoreline. If that old couple was watching from somewhere, I'd look like a cheater. Of which I am not.

"How are you feeling today, Kinsley?"

"What? Not Miss Hayes? I am feeling like a ho in public, thanks to your inappropriate kiss and this handholding."

"As opposed to hot and heavy making out in a lifeguard stand with another man entirely?"

My jaw dropped. He licked his index finger and drew an invisible tally. "I never go into a situation without recon."

I arched an eyebrow, but his smile remained in place while he swung my hand back and forth.

"Now, aside from your inappropriate public displays of affection, tell me how you're really feeling. Yesterday must've been pretty scary for you."

Whether I wanted to admit or not, my shoulders sagged in relief for an ear that may not be ready to commit murder if I admitted my fears.

"Off the record?" I asked.

He gave a more or less gesture with his head, then said, "Would you like it to be *on* the record? Because I can make that happen."

"I dunno. I kinda want to wish the whole thing away and pretend it never happened. I'm confused by some of the things that guy said to me, how he made all of his problems my fault. My scalp is sore where he ripped my hair out. Please, don't tell Jase, because I don't know ... maybe you're right about me not being able to handle him."

I watched our feet because this sucked to say aloud.

He paused our pace and looked over his shoulder. Jase was further down than I expected, which meant we'd covered a lot of ground while I'd been in my head.

The binoculars aimed toward the ocean, so Rustin reached up to brush the tendrils from my forehead and cursed. "This is why you have henna stars. Smart distraction. I'm impressed you had the forethought. If Jase saw this, he'd find wherever that jerk scampered off to and fuck up the other side of his face. I don't want that, so your secret is safe with me."

His hand dropped to his side. I swallowed, looking up into his tan face and brilliant blue eyes.

"I can't take credit for this. Constance was the clever one. I was just going to leave my hair down and let it fall over my eye." He raised his eyebrows. "You *do* remember who Constance is, right?" I couldn't help asking with an edge in my tone.

"Easy, there. Yes. Just because we had a one-night-stand doesn't mean I didn't learn her name or think any less of her somehow. In fact, she's like a delicious chocolate mousse. That what you wanted to hear? 'Cuz I can go into more detail if it helps." He waggled his eyebrows like a dork.

"No, thank you, Rustin."

I resumed walking. He fell in beside me.

"You're mad at me. Why?"

"Why would I be mad at you?" I asked. "That's dumb."

"Even if it's dumb, doesn't change anything. I want to know."

He rounded in front of me, so I had to stop. I tried moving past at either side, but he blocked.

I sighed. "Rustin, I know you're a chronic flirt. You don't mind screwing a stranger or kissing your best friend's crush right in front of him. I have no idea what you're even doing here—"

"Is that what's bothering you? That I flirt and sleep around? Or, that I did all those things and had the nerve to kiss you like it taints you somehow? I'm in Florida on a favor. Just so you know, to undermine Jase's feelings for you as a crush downright insults my best friend."

"So, you're not insulted by my assessment of your behavior, just that I demeaned Jase's definition of my significance? I'm not saying I'm tainted because you kissed me. But, maybe, yeah. I'm bothered by anyone who can just throw affections around to strangers with no meaning."

"The way you let Jase maul you in his stand any indication on how privileged he is? Or, hath the mighty fallen from her high tower of morality?" he asked. Somehow, even though I hated the words, he had a way of making them a joke. A flirtation. "I say, we put our swords away long enough to get you out of that dress and into a bikini. Then we can do some team-building exercises like making sandcastles or something."

I grinned, disarmed, though I rolled my eyes again.

"Come on, girl." He smacked my bottom and took off running. "Gimme a taste of that sprint you're so famous for! Giddy up!"

"Oh, hell no you didn't, sir!" I couldn't help my incredulous smile. He ran in zigzags over the powdery sand as I chased him. Every time I got close, he'd throw some playful insult, juke me, or even snag a touch here and there to keep me on my toes and fired up. I took a flip flop in each hand and threw one at his back. He cracked up laughing and grabbed for the shoe in the sand to throw the cheap foam back at me, but I spanked his ass with my other flip flop. His arm captured me around the waist, cupping me against his chest while his free hand wrested my slapping flip flop from my hand.

"Someone needs a spanking." He popped my bottom before releasing me. "Truce in exchange for your other shoe? Wha'd'ya say?" he offered while brandishing my flip flop.

I slipped my foot into the other and said, "Deal."

16 | ♀

Rustin and I jogged across the street to the shops. I aimed for one I liked while he faltered and pointed at the one Jase's boss recommended.

"Nuh, uh," I said. "This is the one I like."

"More reason for me to take the other guy's advice. No offense." He tugged my hand, but I tugged back. Rustin grinned. "If we're playing tug-of-war, I'm gonna bet I'll be the winner. Again, no offense, Mizz Hayes."

"How about you can buy yourself a suit from that shop and I'll go find one in this shop."

"I tell ya what, we go in my shop, I'll buy. If you don't find something you like, we'll come back to your shop and I'll still pay."

"I can't let you do that. My wallet is in the car and I'm parked just a couple blocks aw—"

"Damn, girl. C'mon. Why don't you give someone a chance to do something nice for you every now and then? No wonder Jase hasn't made headway."

I gaped in slapped silence searching for a retort. *Had Jase been trying to do nice things for me?*

Rustin gave my hand a gentle tug. My flip flops shuffled the whole way until Rustin rifled through racks and created stacks of his picks versus what he imagined would be my picks. I pulled a couple I loved and laughed at his Kinsley pile.

I lifted the top suit from that stack. "Rusty, this is a maternity suit."

"Ah, so it's Rusty now? Guess I can call you Kins. The hell I'm adding *sweet* to the front of it like Jase does. Love is blind." He winked and licked his fingertip before drawing that invisible tally. "Who knows, maybe you'll need one of them suits before long."

"Rus!" I slapped his stomach and threw the suit at him. He caught the black tent in a bout of laughter.

"Let's not get too carried away with the nicknames, Kins. Those piles are getting tall. Better get in that dressing room soon or else we'll lose daylight. Oh, and I need to see them in order to make an informed decision on my purchase."

I shook my head and carried both stacks into the dressing room.

The first one I loved, tan crochet one-piece with wooden beads. So retro and sexy, in my opinion, but I barely got the door open before Rustin's, "Nuh, uh. Next," stopped me. He sat on the bench surrounded by discarded suits lacking hangers. Rather than entertain my miffed expression, he rifled through the pieces of fabric as though searching for a diamond in the rough.

I crinkled my nose. "You know, for every suit no one bothered to hang up, that's a crotch that's touched those sticky strips."

"And that's bad?" He grinned and held up a pair of bottoms with no sticky protective strip.

"Gross!"

"Sooner we find a bikini, the less your crotch touches someone else's."

"That's repulsive."

"But my point is valid." His blue eyes flared in mischief while I glared in disgust. He chuckled. "You come outta that dressing room with another one-piece, I'm confiscating your dress and leaving the store."

"Fine." I skulked back inside and thumbed through the hangers. "I hate bikinis!" I shouted.

"The more for me to try on, huh, mama?" a woman joked from the corridor of dressing rooms. She shut herself inside the one beside mine.

"She can have all mine," I muttered to my reflection as I adjusted the top on a newsprint bikini with red sayings. I stepped out, and Rustin sat up with hungry eyes that shifted neutral, then disinterested.

"Oh, come on! I saw that look! It's cute. Don't you get it?" I asked and danced in a little circle.

"Cute don't cut the cake, little miss. Think about it. We're about to go on the beach where your boyfriend has a front row view of probably every bikini in this place. If you want to look plain beside them, that's fine by me, but I don't want to hear any fits or pouting."

"Black, white and *read* all over." I waved a sarcastic hand across my body like I was on *The Price Is Right*.

"Well, that *is* darling, isn't it, Angie?"

My breath caught in my throat like I'd swallowed a price tag.

No. No. No! Please don't be real. Please no!

I twisted to face none other than Jeannine Ansley. *Sonuvabitch! Ahem*, mother-*of-a-bitch*.

"Oh, my heavens, Kinsley Hayes!" Jeannine wrapped her arms around my neck before pulling back to look at me as if I'd grown. When you're this short, you haven't grown since Junior High.

Behind us, Rustin gave an appreciative whistle when Jeannine's daughter, my ultimate nemesis, left her dressing room in a bikini tailored for an assassin. Her fingers ran over her bottom to pull the scrap of spandex from her butt-crack. We swallowed mutual disdain in unison. Our smiles glued to our faces as we greeted each other for the first time since high school.

"I'll be damned. If it isn't my boss's daughter," Rustin said. "Angela Ansley, right?" His hand sliced the tension between us.

"That's right. You're the new officer." Angela's drawl nearly made Rustin's seem weak. Too bad her family hadn't gone back to Georgia.

"Deputy, actually, but—"

"Officer Keane, how do the two of you know one another?" Angela's mother asked as though blind to the awkward situation.

"Well, I'm friends with her boyfriend, and he'd like us to hang out to get to know one another better," Rustin supplied. I chewed the inside of my cheek while praying he didn't give Jase's name.

Angela choked on a giggle of absurdity, stepping back as if to see me better. "Kinsley, you didn't tell me you had a boyfriend. How cute. I figured you'd be married and having what's-his-name's babies while sporting a double belly in mom jeans. Shame. I guess some things don't work out the way we want them to." She shrugged and went back to inspecting her bikini. "You're still holding that spot on your ribs to cover that mark, huh? At least some things never change."

My eyes filled with hot pink hate for her reflection. Her eyes danced with mine in the mirror. She wrapped her arms beneath her hair, posed as she appreciated different angles of her figure.

"Now, Kinsley," Jeannine said, "didn't Claire say you were on scholarship here at the University? Track or something?"

Angela rolled her eyes and went back into her dressing room.

"Yes, ma'am," Rustin answered for me. "The newspaper just published a feature on her. I take it Angela doesn't read the paper?"

Jeannine scoffed. "Angelique doesn't read anything longer than two hundred characters on a screen." *Angelique?*

Rustin and I laughed before he filled her in on my sprinting career deeper than Chad had divulged in his article. How interesting.

Jeannine appeared genuinely impressed with my achievement, then slapped Rustin's arm with recollection. "So, *Kinsley* is Micro Machine? I remember reading something about that, but I confess I skimmed since I don't have a child in college...." She trailed with a saccharine bite in her tone.

Angela strode out of the dressing room in a copper one-piece like she just stepped onto a Victoria's Secret runway. My throat dried with no less than pure envy, because no man would look at this woman and not want sex on the spot. Even Rustin had to be faltering in all that Southern charm of his as she checked her reflection in the three-sided mirror.

"I simply don't have time for scholarships or reading anything longer than social media with all the pageants. Mama, what do you think about this one?" She lifted her bedazzled phone to pose for several selfies showcasing her body. "I think it sends a better message to the judges. Don't you? Like, I don't even have to bare it all to look sexy."

"Well, it's—"

"Look!" Angela shoved the phone screen in her mom's face. "I already have seven likes! Officer Keane, what do you think since you're already here to help Kinsley with swimsuit shopping? This is the perfect trial swimsuit competition." Angela came to stand beside me and gave a cutesy shrug that made the curled tips of her long hair bounce with her big boobs. "Should we pitch a selfie and create a poll?"

"No thanks," I told her, but she ignored me and pulled me under her arm to pose like we were besties. My smile had to be more like the bared teeth of a dog about to attack.

"Hashtag running into former competition when she's not competition anymore."

I will not slap her. I will not slap her. I will not slap her! Every molecule of restraint inside me deployed to play at polite rather than shoving her off me hard enough to smack her face into the mirror she wouldn't stop staring at.

Rustin started to say something when a group of girls holding handfuls of suits asked to squeeze past. One cringed in intimidation at Angela's sex factor, while another said, "Oooh, cute! Like that riddle! Where did you find this one?"

Then and there, I decided I shouldn't give a damn how brilliantly hot Angela was compared to everyone in the room. Next to her, I was the approachable one, and I'd take that in this moment.

"I didn't see anymore, sorry, but thank you," I told the girl. She pouted for half a second, then shoved inside a fitting room with her girlfriends. I almost busted out laughing since I knew girls changing together trumped Angela's existence in the presence of this pervert standing with his hands open.

"So, this is your pick?" he asked me. I nodded. He said, "Good. This suits you since I can practically read your mind in black and white."

I bit my lip through an expanding smile.

"Officer Keane, we would really like if you could come for dinner, say, this Thursday night as our way of welcoming you to the community?" Jeannine asked.

"Oh, I'd love to, ma'am, but I've got a gig on Thursday."

"A gig?" she asked. Angela turned to inspect him with more interest than before.

"Yeah," he said, and gave her the name of the bar.

"He performs there with Jase Taylor," I told her. "Didn't you have a thing for Jase in high school?" I asked like I had no idea.

Angela giggled like I was adorable. "Who didn't, Kinsley?"

"I hear Jase only got better looking during his time in the Navy. Is he still single?" Jeannine asked.

"Well, Mrs. Ansley," Rustin said. "He's sweet on someone but leaving his options open 'cuz she keeps shooting him down. A man can only take so much rejection."

I gave a tight smile. "You should come see them play," I offered.

"That's a great idea, Angie!" Jeannine gushed. "And you and Kinsley could catch up and mend the fences of your past. Things have a way of smoothing over when you've become adults. Forgive me, I'm assuming you'll be there to watch?" Jeannine asked me.

I nodded. "I never miss a performance."

"Yes, that does sound fun," Angela said. "I wouldn't dream of missing it, either. And Mr. Keane, we will see you for dinner Friday night. I simply won't take no for an answer."

17 | ♀

"**Well, that was fun,**" Rustin said.

We strolled out of the shop, me in my new swimsuit, a little red sarong tied around my hips. He carried a shopping bag with my tunic inside, my hand filled his other like I was a child needing protected while crossing the street.

"Oh yeah, delightful," I popped like a smart ass.

"I got myself a dinner date. You got yourself a boyfriend. Both are counterfeit to a certain extent. How are you gonna be at the bar for Thursday's performance if Marcus forbade it? Unless you're trying to test Jase when you're not even together?"

"Who knows, maybe a silver-tongued gentleman might throw in a good word for me?"

"Ha! You talking about me, or does this gentleman have silver eyes to match that foreign tongue of his?"

I sighed. "Rustin, I have no idea why you think I'd be talking about him. I was meaning you. What do you mean about testing Jase?" I asked and tugged him across the lanes.

"I see what you did there. I think the bar loses a very important big tipper when Little Red isn't on the menu. If Angela shows up without you there, you think she's gonna relegate her flirtation to me alone?" he asked. "Seemed like an old axe to grind in there. Kinda makes me wonder if you've had a thing for Jase for some time, too."

"Seriously?" I scoffed and shook my head. "I have it on good authority that he comes in more often when I'm not on the menu as you say. For the record, Angela Ansley has no scruples who or where her affections go. You've been forewarned. She's all about furthering herself," I told him. "Let's grab my beach bag." We aimed for the parking lot rather than the sand. "If she makes a move on Jase, yeah, maybe I'm daring the both of them. How better to test the man who claims to care about me?" I realized Rustin kept the grip on my hand. "Are you trying to make me look like I'm disloyal to my fake boyfriend by holding my hand in public?" I asked.

"Hey, if Jase's boss sees us, we have to be believable, right?"

I rolled my eyes.

"Okay, Kinsley, it's probably bad form to tell the best friend about the test. He might tell the pupil, and is that really fair?"

"It's honest." I shrugged.

"I'll tell you straight. I have no problem with her furthering her agenda so long as she doesn't get in the way of my own."

"Why am I not surprised, Offisah Keane?"

He chuckled at my mocking the officer bit Angela and Jeannine had just pulled in the shop.

"In the spirit of honesty, I'm starting to think you are a bit of a bitch, Mizz Hayes."

"Guess you don't pay attention to rumors, because any girl around would have told you that long ago." My car was now surrounded with a filled lot. "What is your agenda, sir?" I pulled my car key from the shopping bag.

"Nothing Jase doesn't okay first, all right?"

I took a full step back to survey this man's cock-sure arrogance. "Oh? And where do I fit into this?"

"Mmm ... why do you have to ask leading questions, Mizz Hayes?"

"Mister Keane, do you have a wish for a sexual harassment claim?" I asked with a charming smile.

"Wouldn't you much rather I be in my uniform for games like those?" he flirted.

My tongue traveled against my cheek. I lifted the trunk and plucked the shopping bag from his hand.

"Cuffing you might be fun. Here, you can carry the beach bag and the lounger as punishment."

"Mizz Hayes, I'm astonished at your impropriety. Maybe you *can* handle Jase after all. What's changed? You're different. Was it something I said? Maybe the silver eyes and tongue? Or 'bout you having a long-standing crush on Jase? Testing him with Angela?"

He adjusted his grasp on the stuff I piled into his arms. I slammed the trunk closed harder than necessary.

"Nope. I'm done letting you probe my mind to satisfy your curiosity or whatever angle you're working. May the best man win, ain't that right?"

"Touché," he said.

I glanced over my shoulder, unconcerned, for once, if he scoped my butt. In fact, let him enjoy the torment. He deserved every moment. Of course, he seemed to enjoy the pain. Perfect, since I was in a vindictive mood.

We stepped onto the now crowded sand. I kicked my flip flops to enjoy the granules like warm sugar on my feet. I held my shoes in my fingers and swiped tendrils behind my ear as the breeze picked up. Rustin tucked my lounger beneath the same arm he held my beach bag, all to free his fingers in order to snag mine and swing them up and down.

"Relax," he said. "You can be my safety. If I'm holding your hand, they think I'm taken. How else will I enjoy the beach without women coming onto me the whole time?"

"Rustin, anyone ever tell you how annoying you are?"

"Sexy, country-fried, corn-fed, but *annoying*? Nah."

My head fell back as I groaned.

"Now, *that* right there is a great look for you, Mizz Hayes."

I jerked my hand from his to smack his bare belly. He shrugged and teased the beach towel from the beach bag. We picked a spot close enough to Jase that he could see us from the corner of his eye, were he to look, that is. For the moment, Jase watched the waves like the dutiful lifeguard. While Rustin unfolded the lounge chair and extended the umbrella, I studied Jase. The professional set in his jaw, shoulders pulled back as he stood erect and alert. His sun-kissed locks tossed and tumbled over his forehead by the wind. *That* guy asked me to be his girlfriend. *That* guy cheese-grated an asshole's face for hurting me yesterday. *That* lifeguard guarded my life ....

I sat in the lounge chair while Rustin spread the towel, shuffled through my bag for a bottle of sunscreen, dabbed the tip of his nose and tapped some on mine.

"Rustin, you brat." I rubbed the dollop into my skin. He held the bottle and waggled his eyebrows. "Ha! I don't need no help, mister."

He sighed and watched me grease my own skin with lotion. After a minute of staring, he asked, "Why do you keep blocking that spot she pointed out in the store?"

"It's an ugly birthmark. I hate it. She's flawless. Everyone has something they don't like about themselves. Well, most of us do," I teased at the end, a little grin at him.

"Ugly, huh? Guess that's relative to the person doing the judging. She tell you it was ugly?" He pried at places I didn't want to go.

"Rustin, didn't I tell you no more psychological probing today?" I angled my face up to the sun with my eyes closed, relished the rays on my skin, fought the urge to cover the birthmark. He had to be staring. I practically felt his eyes.

"I just wonder how you are so insecure about that misshapen heart when if you look around, flaws are everywhere. Cellulite. Stretch marks. Scars. Fat rolls. Farmer's tans. Tramp stamps. Shitty tattoos. I don't see you holding them against these people. Maybe you should be nicer to yourself. Offer yourself the same courtesy, is all."

"Misshapen heart?"

"Yeah. That's what it reminds me of. Like the hearts little kids draw. You know, a little outside the lines? Maybe a scribble where they lost control of their marker? It's cute."

"Thank you." I sighed and tilted my head to look at him. He wasn't looking at me, though. He was watching Jase and the water. Back and forth. Finally, he chuckled to himself.

"What?" I asked.

"Are you blind?" he asked and gestured to the water. My mouth fell open in dawning, then closed in disappointment.

"Rustin, I am going to tell you just like I already told Jase, you should be ashamed of yourself. Especially after that spiel you just gave me about flaws."

"Oh, come on, Kins, you *have* to watch this, it's great stuff! Not to mention, the perfect example of what I was just saying. If she's not insecure, what the hell is your problem?" He was talking about the very same woman Jase and Matt had joked about earlier. The overweight bathing beauty. "I am going to have so much material to screw with Jase tonight." Rustin laughed again.

She rested on her elbows in the sand close to the shore, the water lapping at her hips. In direct view of Jase. Now, that I paid closer attention, I watched her glance back at Jase. She cast him a smile.

"Well, hell," I said to myself with a grin. I looked up to Jase. He politely smiled back while trying to avoid the attention at the same time.

"Damn." Rustin stared as the next wave washed onto the sand, over her body. "Can you imagine how ugly your birthmark would be under the same waves?" She put her hand into the water, ran her wet fingers over her breasts while she enticed Jase's attention. "Would just ruin the whole thing."

"Rustin, do I need to throw sand in your eyes, sir?" I asked.

"To get the image of your birthmark out of my mind, yeah," he said. "Please. It's killing me."

I fell back in my chair, a fit of giggles tickling my stomach. "How rich! I may join you in razzin' Jase. Say what you want about her. I *love* it! She's so bold!"

"I hope you're watching and learning, little girl. She may be overweight, but confidence is sexy, and *she* is sexy. More cushion for the pushin'. I applaud Jase for being a gentleman. By the way, she could look like Angela back there and he'd give the same cordiality. He's not the dog you treat him like."

"Right ... but what a damn cheater." I snickered.

He propped his head in hand, lying on his side, looking at me with a huge grin. "Speaking of cheaters ... you know what would make this epic?"

Whoa! What a wicked tone!

"What?" I sat forward in the lounger, intrigued.

"Why don't *you* go over there and play the jealous girlfriend card?" His grin was so devilish, how was I to resist? "Pretty please, Kinsley? You can have five tallies for this favor. I will love you forever."

"Oh, please, you're gonna love me forever anyway." I quirked my brows as I displayed a wicked grin, too.

He shrugged and nodded in agreement while I rolled my eyes and pushed off of the lounger, winking at him over my shoulder. Hell, here goes nothing. Every insecurity assaulting me with doubt drowned with each wave rolling over her body. I put on a persona

I hadn't used in years, imagining Angela standing on the shore with a number on her hip as she posed in my mind. That bitch. I threw sway into my hips as I sashayed toward the tower. I posed with one foot out in front of me, my hand gripping my hip, gesturing dramatically with the other.

"*Seriously?!*" I shouted loud enough to grab the attention of all bystanders. "I leave for an *hour*, and I come back to find you shamelessly checking out *another* woman?!" I flailed a hand toward the woman in the waves. She gaped back with slack-faced shock. "Am I not enough for you? I saw you smiling at her. Is she next on your list?" My expression soured; arms crossed under my breasts to make them bubble just enough to torment Jase as I berated him. "What the *hell* do you have to say for yourself, Jase Taylor? Was all that stuff about being *faithfully mine* a bunch of BS?!"

I didn't want to look up, didn't want to face him, but I knew I had to.

Oh, shit! I was most *definitely* in trouble now. Thrilling tingles traversed my body.

He leaned over the railing, working his hand across his mouth. I hoped to try and cover a smile, but I didn't think so. He was now the target of every woman in the vicinity, and they all glared at him like he was a cheating dog. Um, the good thing was, if he didn't fix this, he would have to deal with them. Ha! Maybe I'd also ruined any other play for a while.

Jase lifted his radio; said something I couldn't discern. Too late to undo this now. I glanced back at Rustin. He appeared ready to have a humor heart attack. His hand covered his mouth, sunglasses perched upon his head, eyes exploding with glee. He cupped his hands like he held a baseball bat and was hitting a ball. *Huh?* I looked at him, confused. He pretended to hit the ball, put his hand up to shade his eyes as he was watched his pretend ball fly out to the water.

Oh! Hit it home!

He saw realization dawn and nodded his head with an emphatic grin lighting his face. *Great, here goes nothin'….*

"Well, Jase, what do you have to say for yourself?" I placed a hand to my chest, biting my lower lip in anguish. "Should I just walk away from us? You going to let us go for someone *else*? Am I not *pretty* enough for you? Is that it, because I've been working out like you asked." The men around us scoffed and glared at Jase like he was crazy. But they had nothing on the gasps from the women, including the woman in the waves evidently rethinking her crush on this lifeguard.

Jase ran a palm over his face, threaded his fingers through his hair, then cupped his hands in prayer. *Ruh, ro ….*

"Baby, we've talked about this. Your therapist agrees, you must quit lying to yourself. True progress cannot be achieved until you admit you are an exercise addict and that you left me for another man." He gestured toward Rustin who was laughing his ass off on my towel. "Until then, yeah, I look at other women to pick myself back up from the hurt you've caused."

Smooth! Asshole!

Jase fought a smile while I pressed my lips tight and looked away, miffed. He shook his head like he pitied me.

"Kins, you're my girl. Sure, she's beautiful, but so are you. *So* beautiful, but you'll never believe what I say until you start believing it yourself! I'm sorry you're unhappy. That he isn't the man you thought he was, but I'm not him. That hole you tried to fill with him, I see he just wasn't enough."

Oh, hell. Nice innuendo! Don't smile! Don't smile!

"Maybe I wouldn't have left you for him if you weren't always flirting with other women," I reasoned and shot the poor woman a dirty look like I was inferior to her.

Jase glanced at her. "Baby, you want me, take me. Say it. In my life, it's *only* you." He made his face a mask of pain, swallowed dramatically. The woman was peeved now. I felt the crowd looking to me for a response while I recomposed myself under his turning my own shit around on me.

"You're just saying that because we're in public," I pouted.

Jase started climbing down the ladder. *Well, hell. Could I run away?*

He walked calmly over to me and unfolded my arms, grabbed my hands. "Will you please forgive me? I'm sorry if I made you feel like you weren't enough." He tipped my chin and made me look up into his eyes. He resumed the apologetic tone, but his eyes told me my ass might be served up on a platter later. "Please come back to me, Kins. We can work on your addiction together."

I looked down and ran my toe in a little arc in the sand. "You really mean that? You think I'm beautiful? That it's only me in your life?" I deployed the doe eyes I used on my daddy in desperate moments. His Adam's apple bobbed; lips twitched. "I used that other guy to make you jealous …."

He cupped my shoulders, squeezing just slightly so no one knew he was, but enough to warn me of impending doom. Movement in my periphery caught my eye. *Holy crap! Another lifeguard taking Jase's post! Rustin was so going to pay for this!*

"Baby, I swear, *you* are the only one I am *mad* about." His voice remained pleading and sweet, but I was close enough to hear his teeth grit on the word 'mad'. Sweet coos from some of the women sounded around us. Jase was off the hook, but was I?

"You want me back, Jase?" I shot the doe eyes once more. They flared on a silent laugh.

"I want nothing more." He tugged my chin and planted a sweet, lingering kiss on my mouth. His teeth snatched my lower lip and dragged. Yum! A couple men sent out cat calls. When he pulled away from me, the crowd clapped, happy that we had apparently made up.

The woman got up and frowned at Jase like he was a jerk, although now I suspected she wasn't upset he'd not wanted her, but that she no longer wanted him. She tossed her long hair and marched away. I kind of felt bad for ruining her play, but this was my lifeguard. *She could have Matt ....*

Rustin picked that moment to stand and fold the towel, shoved the terrycloth into my beach bag like he was throwing a fit for the audience. Bet that was fun hiding the huge grin he couldn't drop.

"What should we do about this other guy, Kinsley? Should I kick his ass?" Jase asked as he tucked me under his warm arm, steered me toward Rustin.

"Meh, why not?" I grinned up in adoration. The fingers of my left hand wound through his cupping my shoulder. This wasn't so bad. The closer to him, the further Klive was from my thoughts. How nifty.

"Think I should whip yours first, baby?" He inhaled as his eyes filled with lust. "You were a *very* bad girl."

"You were a very good boy." I grabbed his face for a lingering kiss. "I love that you said she was beautiful."

"Meh." He gave a sheepish smile. "You made a good point when you threw my words back at me. Now, if we could get her to teach you a few things ...."

"Damn, Jase," Rustin said. "I think you broke that poor woman's heart, and you damn near broke this one's, too."

I shook my head, smiling, and laid back in the lounger as Jase chased Rustin across the sand. I closed my eyes, releasing myself of the tension the past few weeks carried. I imagined for an indulgent moment what Jase's kisses on my lips and name on my heart might be like. This freedom felt good. My skin in a bikini. Not giving a damn about my mark. Or my conscience. I thought of Jase pinning me to the sand. The things he said in his stand this morning about how I changed with my clothes. Did this mean I changed without them too, like this bare moment in the sunshine with no shame? *Take that Angela!*

I squealed when I was suddenly plucked from my lounger and tossed over Jase's shoulder again. "I forgot to tell you I love your ass in this suit. First time I've been interested in reading the paper." He smacked my bottom. I yelped with a protest. "You want another one?"

"If I get one, so do you." I smacked Jase's flexing bottom as he walked. I forced my head up. Rustin displayed his hands in surrender, laughed, then sank into my lounger. "Ugh! Shouldn't a cop be responsible for defending the weak and innocent?"

"Weak and innocent?" Jase asked. "I suppose if you were, maybe."

"I am going to get a sunburn like this ... I didn't get to put any sunscreen on my butt."

"Baby, that was *very* foolish. I say if you burn, you *deserve* it."

18 | ♀

JASE RESISTED THE VERY powerful urge to give me some good ol' fashioned discipline; his words. He cursed when he pulled me off his shoulder because I grabbed his shorts. They jerked up his crack into a major wedgie. I giggled like a dang fool while he dug the material from his crack, a baffled grin on his face.

"Damn, Kins, who knew you were such a handful?" he asked. I stood grinning at the view. His hand grabbed mine. I was yanked in a way he could land his other in a sound smack to my bottom. "You're lucky. If I didn't have qualms about showing your ass off to the world, I'd have jerked your bottoms up your butt in retaliation."

I rubbed the heated palm print I'd swear he left over the whole right cheek of my bottom. We walked for a bit before I saw his Charger in a parallel parking spot.

"Are you leaving?" *Wonder why he still drove the car...?*

"Nah, gotta feed the meter. If I park here, I can see her from my tower with the binoculars. I don't like not having an eye on the special things in my life."

My eyes met his at the change in his tone. Guess a cute bikini and playing with him wasn't enough to take him out of the mood I'd caused.

"Wow, that must be quite a bitch where Tyndall's concerned, unless you have spies?"

"Quite a bitch, indeed," he muttered. "I'm not gonna apologize for what I did."

"I'm not gonna apologize for how I reacted." I gripped my hip.

He dug into his pocket, pulled a waterproof money holder he split open. Change fed from his fingers into the meter. Guess he still had another few hours of duty.

"I don't like you expecting me to, Kinsley."

I gasped. "I didn't—"

"You ran away from me. I didn't go home last night. Which is why I'm still driving my Black Beauty. She's fun, but a gas guzzler."

"Where did you go?"

"Right now, I'm going to the burger shack down the way for a bite to eat so my hangry doesn't cause the fight you want to provoke."

"I do not!"

"You need a burger too. See? You're already fighting with me."

My lips pressed closed in an irritated line for how I wasn't as irritated as I wished.

"If I eat a burger now, I'll have meat-coma at practice." I checked my invisible watch. "Only have a couple hours of beach time before I head to campus."

"You can have the lettuce from mine so the vegetables don't make me bloated in this sexy swimsuit." He blew an air kiss, quirked his brows. "I don't mind if *you* end up bloated. Makes my job easier."

"All right, mister, that's it." I backhanded his abs. He caught my hand and rubbed my fingers over the cut definition of each abdominal muscle. "Jase! Shame."

"What? I gotta get your hands on me for a little lesson in kindness. You're so violent and abusive, sweet Kins."

I laughed and struggled to pull my hand free. This felt weird. Familiar. Like the way my first boyfriend, Jack Carter, used to play with me in high school. Jase was far more complex, though, even if he pretended to be light in this moment. That brooding under the surface said he wasn't giving up on the lecture he wanted to unleash at whatever he felt about my behavior. How could I not be afraid of him yesterday, though? I didn't want to think of this because Klive's mean words during tender, contradictory actions jogged laps in my brain as looooong and slow as the laps coach forced me to run later for being late to practice.

Jase had offered to haul ass in his car to get me here, but lunch hadn't been my favorite because he'd launched into this story about Tyndall disrespecting his opinion on certain things and how she'd run headfirst into trouble from rebellion. He'd had to step in and do things he didn't want to, things he wouldn't have had to if she'd just followed his lead. I'd chewed my lip and looked around at everyone having fun on the beach, eating their lunches, chilling while I wasn't.

"Jase, I already have a father. How am I supposed to follow the lead of someone who has an attitude with Marcus over little things? If I work with shorts climbing my butt crack to make him happy—"

"Look, I see what you're saying. I may have an attitude on creative rights when we have different opinions on the sets I sing, but that's a far cry from capricious situations that put my life in danger. Maybe my parents want us together because they know I have to look in the mirror when I look at you." He shook his head, sun-kissed locks blowing in the breeze.

"Is that what this is? Your parents? Mine? Match-making because we've both been single for too long?" I'd asked.

"No, Kins, I didn't mean it like— where are you going?"

My banana peel hit the trash can before I strode back in the direction of my towel and beach bag. He'd tossed the foil wrapper of his burger in the can and jogged after me as he stuffed his mouth with the last few bites. At least he'd had the sense to stay quiet. He'd finished, swallowed and asked me to stop running away from him again.

"I'm not running away from you. If you ever came to a meet or practice maybe you'd know exactly what I look like when I'm *running*, Jase Taylor. I'm grabbing my things because this thing between us seems like one of those capricious situations that puts a life in danger. My heart isn't a game. I don't want a relationship with someone who's only making moves now because his parents want grandchildren."

"That's a heavy load of bullshit, Kinsley. I am not doing this because of our parents. Kins!" He'd grabbed my elbow, but before I was able to give him a piece of my mind, he'd reminded me of the piece of my heart he already held. His lips caressed my forehead over the henna stars. His muscular arms wrapped around me, bare skin-on-skin. Way more intimate than I could handle without something overwhelming settling like weight I couldn't shake.

My coach watched me, his hand scrubbing his mouth. "You got some pain," Walton said, "but the majority isn't in the ankle, Kinsley." He checked that the other girls were out of earshot. "What's going on, Kins? You hate when I'm right. Where's your bitchy determination to prove me wrong?"

"I don't know what you're talking about."

"You're running like shit. Your mind is cluttered and usually if a guy is on the brain, you can't stand letting me say I'm right."

"It's not like that," I protested. "Not exactly. Can we just focus on what you want to do about my ankle?"

"You aren't running this weekend. You need to condition through walking. No running. No wearing heels or those shoes with the cork—"

"Wedges?" I couldn't help my grin.

"Sure. Whatever. Nothing that you're clumsy in."

I rolled my eyes. "If you ground me, that chick from Gainesville is gonna take my medals! What about the relay team?"

"The relay team and I already discussed it. We wanted to discuss it with you, but you were late. Everyone agrees. We don't mind sacrificing a few wins for saving the big picture. Besides, the relay team may still win with Shay."

My eyes narrowed for a second in thought of her, *of all girls*, stepping into *my* place. "Walton, if you do this, dangle that carrot in front of her, you'd better make sure she doesn't hide in the shadows plotting a hired attack on me in order to keep that spot. Mark my words."

"Whoa. You know something I don't?" he asked, his hands on his hips.

"No. You're not blind. If you haven't seen her resentment, you're fooling yourself." I changed from tennis shoes back into flip flops, slung my bag over my shoulder. "These on my new dress code, or did you want me barefooted?"

"Kins. Don't be mad. I'm looking out for you, kid."

"What the hell do I do with myself? The assignments on my syllabuses are complete. Thesis written. I'm booted out of work. Now, no running? Guess I'll sign up for another trial elective with Miller to make up for all this extra time until finals."

"It's one week, drama mama. Though I'm sure Miller would be thrilled to have you. Says you have a good eye, and he likes your dorky movie references. He's probably happy to have someone who might get some of his jokes. He wasn't pleased you skipped his class today."

"K, I said I might take one of his courses, not go hang out with the guy. Glad he noticed my absence. It's your job as his friend to laugh at his jokes, Coach."

"Wait, why were you booted from work?" he asked like he just realized. "Did you get fired?"

"I caused a fight after a biker pulled my hair. My boss got mad and sent me away but didn't fire me."

"You were *assaulted*? Kinsley! Why didn't you tell me? Damn, I hate that job. No wonder your head's not in the game. Is this the same stuff Lucy was giving you crap about Saturday morning?"

Dammit. I didn't want to admit that I'd compounded the situation she'd given me crap about. "Yeah," I lied-ish. I mean they were related so did they count as the same? I hated fibbing.

"Figures you can't run now that your health and performance would enhance with normal sleep. I can't freaking win."

"No, *I* can't win because you grounded me from doing so. Maybe we should have a beer to commiserate together," I teased, but was so desperate for something.

"Actually, I have a date with the woman I gave your enormous bear to, so now is as good a time as any to thank you."

"Aww, Walton! That's great! Do I get to meet her?"

"I'm not introducing her to my kids till I know it's real. Don't want y'all getting confused if she goes away."

I busted out laughing and told him not to screw up.

"Only if you promise not to screw anything up while you're grounded, Kins. Tell me you're going to do your walks. No running, jogging, obstacle course, gym, high heels or wedgies. Whatever you called them. And stay away from the Pop-tarts and booze."

I laughed again and nodded.

"I want to hear it from your mouth, young lady."

I sighed. "Fine. I'll be good. The best I can be. Scout's honor."

"Had you ever been a scout, that might count for something. Why do I have a bad feeling about this? Maybe I should cancel my date with your future stepmom to keep you in line."

"Walton's got jokes," I said in a manly voice with my fist over my mouth like a dude. This time he grinned. I waved and went to my car.

19 | ♀

Constance cheered from her phone. "Twice in as many days? How did I get so lucky?"

"You're welcome," I teased.

"By the way," she said, "I'm back on the schedule with Rock-N-Awe on Thursday. He didn't say anything, but I have a feeling Jase would rather keep me closer now that he knows you seek refuge with me."

I laughed and walked down the sidewalk after parking several blocks away from her building, my phone to my ear.

"He is a mite perturbed." I recounted the stunt I'd pulled on Jase at the beach, how he'd turned things around on me, made me seem workout obsessed and psychologically challenged. She laughed and asked why I was bothered. "Because he isn't happy with me for having a problem with his attitude problem."

"You both have attitude problems," she said.

"You sure you don't mind me spending another night?"

"You never have to ask. I should make you a key," she told me. "You can't complain about me smoking on my balcony though."

"It's your place. I'm not gonna tell you what to do. Will you buzz me in? I'm downstairs now."

"Sure," she said. Wind whistled through her lips. She was smoking. The door was unlocked when I got upstairs to her unit. She stood on her balcony with her cigarette between her fingers.

Though we'd disconnected, she had her phone to her ear like she was listening to someone. "Tomorrow evening? Tuesdays are always the slow night, though. Uh, huh? Ah.... Sure. I'm off Hooters by then, no singing gigs till Thursday. Hey, I know someone who could chip in with me. She's a fantastic bartender and an even better server."

Oh, hell. My duffel fell off my shoulder onto her couch, hand met with my hip as she looked right at me.

"I know," Constance told the person. "Trust me, she's less than a six. The uniform will fit. No, she's not trashy. You'll be pleasantly surprised. Yeah, you've seen her at some of your jobs. Excellent reputation. Why would I bring someone who'd make a bad name for me? We keep our tips or split? Good. We are always down for extra cash and she's never available on short notice, so you're lucky I've caught her in an off period. I know someone else if you need one more. Yes, under a six, but she's a little trashy, great hustler though. Text me the address and schedule."

I went to use her restroom, so I didn't give her hell while she was on the phone. When I returned, she sat on the couch bent over a planner, scribbling things out and adding new ones. Her sliding door was open, her smoke in her hand while the cap to her pen stuck between her teeth. The ash on her cigarette was an inch long. I sighed and plucked the filter from her fingers to knock the ash off in the tray she had on the balcony. Her view was three stories up and overlooked a parking lot for a much nicer complex next door. Beyond, the main highway churned with noisy traffic near the airport. A plane dipped low to land, drowning what she said as she held her planner and walked outside with me.

She waited while we watched the 737 descend out of sight. Her pages ruffled in the breeze. She held them and reached for her barely-there cigarette to take a puff before pointing to the date for tomorrow.

"Since Jase put me back on Thursday, I canceled a smalltime gig planned for tomorrow. That opens us up to do a freelance cocktail waitressing job for a Spring Break party at a penthouse on the other side of the Bay. Some spoiled brat wants to toss all daddy's money off the balcony to feed the vagrants below while they worship her."

"You're joking right?"

"Not really. She's invited a bunch of rich people who have to agree to do the same to be invited. That was Chad. He's one of two deejays she's hired. This chick is throwing two different parties at once. One on the penthouse floor for all her rich friends and networking contacts. The big party is down below so people can catch their cash like the fireworks at the end of the show. Chad thinks she just enjoys having someone to look down on like subjects. Whatever. The pay is fantastic. Twenty-five an hour plus we keep whatever tips we earn. No splits."

"Why so much? How long is the party?"

"Chad says we need to arrive by four for training. Guests start arriving around six. Party starts at seven and money flows at midnight. The whole party is private, so I'm guessing they're paying for discretion, which means we may be asked to sign an NDA before picking up a uniform and tray. Her father owns the penthouse and the ground floor with a large pool overlooking their private beach area where she plans to make it rain."

"How did the 'vagrants' earn an invitation if they aren't her friends?"

"Great question, but the nature of this job is not to ask questions. Just show up and keep your mouth shut other than to smile and look sexy while you hustle drinks. You're the best I know. I'm gonna call Sara since she could probably use the cash and distraction. Not to mention, she trained you."

My mouth dropped. Constance gave me a smug smile while she exhaled a puff of smoke in a ring.

"You want to know why I'd invite her when I don't like her, don't you?" she asked. I nodded, dumbfounded. "Maybe I've been through my own abusive relationship in the past. Once you escape that ... I didn't know until you spilled her story. I don't have to like everything about her for my heart to go out to hers. I'm glad he's dead. After what the other biker did to you, I'd request Patrick Scott's killer pull another hit." My mouth dropped. She didn't look like she was kidding. Her cigarette stubbed in the ashtray. "I'll give you some more tattoos if you want to be a little more incognito. You'd look fantastic if you let me paint up one of your legs. You're not running, so it should come off by the next meet. We'll do your hair, so it hides your bald spot."

I scoffed. "I don't have a bald spot. He didn't rip an entire chunk, just enough to leave a red mark around the area."

"Uh, huh. If you had a bald spot, maybe some of the guys would back off barking down your door for a date."

I laughed and slapped her bottom as we walked back inside. She took in my track duffel and arched her eyebrow.

"Kinsley. Don't tell me this is all you brought. I don't suppose there are any shoes besides cross-trainers in that bag?"

"I didn't plan on working."

"We need to go shopping. I'm an eight-and-a-half and you need a great set of shoes to make that money. Jobs like these lead to more jobs like these. This is your chance to leave the bar in the dust or make Marcus give you a raise."

"Constance, I'm not gonna be a bartender forever. I'm about to graduate, remember?"

"At the very least, I bet Marcus gets wind of you working a higher scene, he'll be groveling to get you back before you change your mind."

"That does sound wonderfully vindictive. But you need to call Chad back and tell him you're one bartender short because I'm grounded from everything but flip flops and flats. Coach doesn't even want me wearing wedges." I laughed when I told her about how he called them wedgies. She chortled, too, but shook her head.

"I know you're gonna love working with kids, Kinsley, but this circuit might be exactly what you want to get into if you miss bartending but don't want to be a bartender, ya know? When you're just starting out in the field, you won't be making ends meet without a little extra, right? Surely, you aren't planning on staying in that garage apartment after graduation. Daddy paying the car note."

"I bought my own car. I paid it off myself, thank you very much."

"Because you didn't have groceries, rent or utilities to pay for. I bet you're still on daddy's health insurance, car insurance—"

"Okay, Constance! Gosh. They're called full-time student perks. Can we quit talking about this?"

"Tie getting too tight, as you like to say?"

I didn't feel like getting into all the specifics of salary and adulthood, but she had a point. I'd backed myself into a narrow field, but I'd go freelance consultant if I had to. I chewed my cheek at that thought because that bolstered her argument. Coach would freak out if I did this. Then again, if I got in with the rich and famous, maybe I'd not deal with bikers with bad intentions so often?

"No photos? I don't want anyone knowing I was there. Please tell me Jase wasn't invited."

"Not that I know of. If he was, he'd have to have serious clout. He's sexy, but I don't know if this chick even knows he exists. God help you if she does. Good thing Jase has no interest in scoring a record deal. She might talk her way into his pants to promise him the world through her father's connections."

"Ugh."

"Is that jealousy?" she asked with a little smirk. "We can talk rules with Chad when we show up for the run-down. If we make you hot enough, you might score penthouse, no singing boyfriend necessary."

"Are *you* wanting a record deal?" I tested. Not sure why the idea never occurred to me before. She had the pipes for a chart topper, that's for sure.

"You worried I'm aiming for her father's pants and connections? Give me more credit than that. I sleep with one sexy cowboy and break our marathon, well *my* marathon, of sexual fasting—"

"It's not like that. I didn't mean that. Maybe I really want to know what you want from life, Constance. Damn. Let's go shopping to get you out of here and out of your little funk."

"Finally." She stood and grabbed her keys. "We'll drive since your coach wants you off your feet."

I shook my head while she snickered to herself.

"How come you aren't with Rock-N-Awe tonight?" I asked as we stepped into the parking lot. Her nineties era 3000 GT baked red hot in the sun. The leather burned our thighs as we sat in the black bucket seats.

"I had to make Jase sweat it out. Told him I had company staying with me." Her pink lips spread wide over bright teeth. "I figure he might do the math on who all on his own."

"Rustin says you're like a delicious chocolate mousse, by the way."

Her stupid smile said everything. He may see her as a one-night stand, but she had reasons for going back to Rock-N-Awe that weren't only pertaining to networking. Freaking Rustin better tread carefully because you didn't burn Constance and walk away so easy. She gave vindictive a new name. Wonder how she'd handle Angela flirting her ass off with her cowboy on Thursday? That's if Angela unglued herself from Jase long enough to remember 'Offisah Keane' still existed.

I filled Constance in on my nemesis and bikini shopping as we drove to the mall. Wow, so much shopping on a single day. I never shopped. Mom loved to and asked if I'd go with her every chance she got. She filled my closet with things she was dying for me to wear that I never touched. Maybe I should go with her so I can pick what she buys? Hell, Constance was right about my parents providing for me. I chewed my cheek in guilt while Constance asked questions about Angela.

"Now we definitely have to pick the perfect shoes because we need Marcus to beg you back by Thursday. How we do that while you don't want this getting out will be tricky. I'm gonna have to whisper in Chad's ear so he'll whisper in all the right ones to get back to Marcus without anyone else giving you crap. Especially if you find you enjoy the Penthouse-style side jobs."

We parked and got out with red hot seat prints on the backs of our thighs.

"Constance, I'd much rather be with all the vagrants."

20 | ♀

Coach was going to murder me. That thought chimed in my brain so many times over the past few days, I may as well have slapped a marathon of snoozes on the various ways I slacked or disobeyed his orders.

I sat in the shoe section of a high-end department store. Constance sat beside me trying on shoes like she needed a new pair for every job she did. She leaned to the side to appraise her feet before she stood like a model to strut her sexy self to the full-length mirror, twisting and turning, making naughty eyes at herself before innocent eyes, all manner of expressions out in the open for anyone to see. She hadn't a care what another soul thought of her.

"Constance, I think this stiletto is too thin to remain balanced. Especially if I end up downstairs without falling to land there." I pulled the strap closed on the tallest, platform-free heels I'd ever dared testing. "Didn't you say there was a beach? My tennis shoes would be way better for that."

"Stand up and come here. Let's see if you can walk the walk first."

"Oh, girl, I can walk the walk no problem."

"Prove it. All I see you wear are wedgies, maybe because you can't walk in heels. It's okay, Kins. Not every girl can walk in them without looking like she's gonna tip over or stomping to marching orders."

"Wedgies?" I giggled.

"Yeah." She shrugged. "It's stuck now."

We grinned while I stood and kicked the boxes out of my way. My track shorts were way too short to be wearing with five-inch heels, gold straps decorating my open feet and wrapping my ankles up to my shins. Very Roman Empire. Constance wore the same pair.

"These look way better on your skin tone than mine. I'm not the biggest fan of gold, Constance. You look amazing, though." I stood beside her, considerably taller than norm, but still shorter than her.

"Thanks, but if that were true, I wouldn't have wanted you to try these on. I see you can stand, but let's test your skills."

"Game on."

We bent for our shoe boxes. She threw stuff inside them from around us, not caring about disorganizing displays for her own fun. We held the boxes over our shoulders and walked the aisle. An older, refined lady sneered at our legs in disapproval, but Constance asked her to pause.

"I have something for you," she told the lady. "These would make your whole package. Trust me. You should try them on." Constance passed the lady a kitten heel. Five minutes later the woman thanked Constance and walked out with a new pair of shoes. The manager asked Constance if she was looking for a job. "Meh, I already have four. But, if I get slow, I'll give you a call. Thank you." She always had a way of making everyone feel special and never allowed anyone's prejudice to remain without her trying to prove them wrong. In this case, the woman assumed we were two-bit hookers, so Constance let her walk away thinking we were two-bit hookers with an eye for style. I so loved her.

"Four jobs?" I asked her. "Hell, the manager was probably offering you a job, so you'd have to clean this back up and reorganize her displays."

She snorted a laugh. "You're probably right the way she's staring at us. Four because the one we are doing tomorrow counts since I'm aiming for more. Aspirations, Kins." She did the model walk and told me to judge whether these were a good fit. I smiled as I thought of Angela going up against Constance's wild makeup, flamboyant weave, henna tattoos and bright fingernails. Like a donkey beside a zebra. Angela would lose nine times out of ten. The more I thought of her, the more I got my head into this game to win my job back. *I had to be there Thursday!*

"Girl, you missed your calling with that strut! My turn," I said. Constance beamed with challenge and traded places with me. I pulled my shoulders back and thought of being on pointe in ballet. Just like walking on tip-toes without seeing the effort behind the strain. I also thought of Angela and ripped the old band-aid off that persona. I balanced the shoe box on my right palm, swung the other at my left side as I stalked toward a very pleased Constance, especially when two little kids ran out from a bunch of clothing racks. I whirled on one foot in an automatic pirouette to avoid crashing into them without tipping the shoe box.

"Damn, girl!" Constance clapped as I resumed undeterred. "What was that? *Ballet?* Looks like I'm not the only one who missed her true calling."

We gasped when we heard more clapping from the checkout counter in the shoe section.

"She's right, love. Very impressive. Little overstated with the ensemble, though." Grey eyes gleamed while he leaned against the counter with a box he paid for. My everything flushed. Constance had no way of knowing this was Moonlight. She thanked him, then looked at me, took a double take at my entire reaction. Great. "By all means," he said. "Don't stop. Are those the ones you're buying, or are you playing in the store?"

First, he calls me a kid, then he asks if I'm playing like I'm a child? I took a deep breath while he took in the mess of boxes and tissue paper we'd scattered over the floor; the various shoes we'd tried on that we hadn't yet put back.

"Perhaps a bit of indecision?" he mused.

"All right, killer. Let's see what you're buying." Constance flirted to dispel my discomfort while striding right for the counter. The salesclerk gave Klive a shy smile while Constance popped the lid off his shoe box. She whistled and pulled the prettiest pair of snakeskin strappy heels from inside. "Your wife has good taste or would these be for a lover?" she quizzed. "Six-and-a-half. Kins, you need to find these and try them on. They'd look great on you."

She held them up, so I had no choice but to wade back through our mess to look. Standing so close to Klive, smelling his cologne, seeing women's shoes in his possession; shit just welled up as Constance placed the shoe in my hand. Real snakeskin. Smooth scales and patterns like a rattler.

"You're welcome to try them on," Klive told me. "Only pair in this size."

My breathing changed. I felt like crying. Him accusing me of cheating on Jase, claiming he'd be using me, enjoying someone best left alone. He didn't have a ring on, but I don't know why I didn't think to ask if he was single. *Didn't he tell me he didn't date? Maybe he didn't date because he already had someone on the side?* This freaking sucked.

"That's very kind of you, sir, but I wouldn't dream of taking them from whoever they're for."

"Miranda, dear, you mind finding the same set in red? Gold is all wrong for her," he asked the clerk. "Six-and-a-half, did you say?" he asked Constance. She nodded. "What's the occasion?" he asked.

Constance spilled the private contents of our cocktail party while I worked to calm the heat in my cheeks and sting in my heart. He'd never answered who those shoes were for. I didn't want to think of him with anyone else, and *how awful was that? I didn't even know this guy!*

"I may have heard about that party," Klive said to Constance. She shot me a deeper look. This meant Klive was either penthouse or vagrant but invited either way. I swallowed in new trepidation. "This change everything," he said. My brows dipped while he called out to Miranda, the salesclerk, for a different set of shoes altogether. "She twisted her ankle last week. If she's wearing a stiletto, she needs strong ankle support."

Constance clucked her tongue. There ya had the writing on the wall, or rather, my forehead. Moonlight unveiled himself to her without my saying a word. Speaking of words, I couldn't seem to find any to stop this whole situation. Klive placed a hand to the small of my back, lighting everything at the touch. He was like a different person every time I met him. This morning I'm crying in his arms, now, I was guided back through my mess into the chair. Constance sat down in her own and took her heels off while Miranda placed two different styles of peep-toe lace-ups at my feet. One black with a thick leather strap that mimicked the look of a belt around the ankle. The other wrapped the ankle with a black cuff that laced like the corset I'd worn for Gasparilla.

Klive peered at Constance. "Place yours on top of the other box. I'm buying."

She squealed and thanked him. Didn't have to tell her twice. She'd once told me that if a man was offering to buy her something, she accepted without argument, and I should do the same, but hell if I could without wondering if he wanted more.

"Oh, they always want more, Kins, which is why they do it, but you control the P and his D. Shame on him for trying to buy his way into your pants. Make him pay for the presumption."

As vindictive as I wanted to be toward Klive, I wasn't as bold as Constance at accepting things.

"Kinsley," Klive stole my musing. "Try the ones with the leather first. They look stronger." He waited for Constance to head for the counter, then lowered his tone as he helped me pull the shoe from the paper. "This is a bad idea. You have one clumsy moment, one drunk bump, there goes your season finale. Not to mention the types that attend these parties. Is Jase going?"

"Types that attend these parties? Didn't you just say *you* were invited?" I barely felt him slide the shoe onto my foot for all the tingles. "I don't need Jase everywhere I go, dammit. I'm done with all you men telling me what to do. Bossing me around. Giving me your opinions on my actions. I've made it this long without any of you handling me like a fragile carton of eggs. Maybe you treat me like a child because I've been too nice and allowed you the courtesy of ordering me around. I'll pay for my own damn shoes, thank you."

"I offered to pay for hers, not yours." His eyes smiled at my glare. "Jesting. I already paid, Kinsley."

"Not for everything." I pushed off the chair and tested the heels. I hated to admit to myself they did offer a great amount of support. "I was right about you when I labeled you a damn psycho. You don't need to have a knife for it to be true. Your personality is all over the map. Make up your mind. I'm tired of whiplash. Thanks for the shoes. Guess I'll see your snobby ass tomorrow night. I'm assuming you're not one of us money-hungry vagrants, but one of her wealthy friends making it rain so we lowly may drink from your golden cup."

Klive had risen to stand but slumped in the chair I'd been sitting in. His hand went through the side of his hair before dragging down over his mouth. I hated how much I *hated* that look. Just like when he'd left the beach bar without me thinking I wasn't going to go with him. *No! I'm not apologizing for his ever-changing personality.*

Constance saved me from giving in by producing a card from her purse. "Hey, Moonlight," Constance called his attention.

"Moonlight?" he asked her like she was crazy. I slapped my forehead. They both ignored me.

"Take my card in case you and your friends in high places need a server, singer, bartender. Thanks a mill for the shoes. Tips should be great. Oh, and thanks for looking out for my girl's ankle. Very thoughtful of you. I promise I'll keep an eye on her tomorrow night."

"What if you get separated?" he asked her. No hiding his very genuine concern. Constance almost melted at his worry for me. She shot me a knowing look. He *did* have feelings for me. How to navigate Complicated Moonlight's thought process was another matter. *Maybe I quit letting him get to me? Quit telling him to stop bossing me around by taking action and getting over my own emotional fluctuations.* I cleared my throat and stood straight like Micro Machine on the track rather than Jase's bashful 'sweet Kins'. Klive looked up at me.

"I'll bring my Mace," I said and bent to kiss his cheek. I felt his surprised intake of air, the tension coiled through his shoulder I gripped. "Unless a protective, knife-wielding psycho decides to come keep an eye on me," I whispered. "I love the shoes. You mind unbuckling them for me?"

Jase had told me I was teasing a hungry lion earlier. Now, I toyed with a tiger as I may as well have grabbed his tail and told him to chase it just for me.

Klive bent and grabbed my bad ankle, but his thumb caressed the bare skin just above the strap. I swallowed, realizing this tiger wasn't chasing his own tail, but mine. He'd let me hold his tail like a leash, if only to have my hands on something of his. *How did his expression convey so much?* I whispered a curse when he lowered to his knees to work on my shoe. He was barely touching me, yet this felt more intimate than Jase's raunchy public display on the beach earlier. To make things worse, he used his hands by feel alone, his eyes remained connected with mine like we shared some sort of staring contest of communication. He was inches from my stomach, his view of me almost obstructed by my breasts.

"I'm thinking of painting a scrolling henna mandala on her thigh trailing down to her foot. What do you think?" Constance asked him and touched my thigh so close to Klive's proximity like she wanted to torment him further. His eyes lit as he told her he'd love to see that with these shoes when he makes it rain with the rich.

21 | ♀

We carried our bags away from the mall into the packed parking lot while Constance gushed about Moonlight and made me confirm.

"I can't believe you have any trepidation about him! Holy shit, Kinsley Hayes! No wonder Jase is losing screws over you all of a sudden. His dream girl isn't in the safe bubble he's counted on. What a delicious feeding-frenzy we have ahead of us. Can you imagine the connections!"

"Constance, have you no shame?" I asked with incredulous shock.

"Why would I? What's there to be ashamed of with Jase or Moonlight? The way he got on his knees like a willing slave to you, *ohhhh*! That was super sexy! You looked ready to fall to yours when he touched your ankle with his thumb. Please, just switch places with me for a night."

I grinned. "That would mean banging a cowboy with boots made for walking all over me. Not my type, babes."

She narrowed her eyes through a smile she couldn't fight. When we got home, she took out her henna kit and chose black henna this time. She turned on *Ghost Brothers* and said, "Sit like this in front of the TV and watch my future husband while I work my magic. Try not to fidget this time."

"I didn't mean to fidget last time. I have a hard time sitting still is all. Which one of these is your future husband? The one that's dressed well?"

She snickered. "Dalen is hot, but Juwan ... the tall one ..." She hummed and situated her tools. "I love a man brave enough to walk into the dark and face demons without fear." She had a point. Four hours and five episodes later, she'd covered my leg in what looked like scrolling torn lace with intricate mandala designs spreading away from the edges. She'd also painted my hands like I wore beaded fingerless gloves with hooks around my middle fingers. Of course, I didn't know all of this until I woke up the next morning laid out on her floor. The TV was on the local news. Constance talked on the phone while milling in her tiny kitchen.

"You're still a size six, right?" she asked the person on the line I assumed was Sara. "Our shoes are the same size, so I'll bring you some of mine unless you have— ah, life insurance kicked in already? Oh, still waiting. Donations for the funeral? Okay, well, do you still want— no big deal. Let me know if you change your mind. I'll have Little Red with me. Yeah, she's good. She's been worried about you. We all have. You think Inferno is still an issue?"

Constance waved and mouthed Sara's name, then pointed at the coffee pot she kept just for me. She took a mug from the cabinet beside her and passed the ceramic over. My hand trembled when I poured the coffee and mouthed a thanks. That's when I noticed my hands. I gasped and gaped at Constance. While she spoke of men I'd rather pretend didn't exist, I ran to her restroom to inspect my body.

The stars on my temple were retraced in black henna. The art on my hands up to my elbows was different on each arm. She'd erased the constellations from my right foot and ankle. I now had a single tiny heart on the ankle bone Klive had grabbed. She'd labeled the spot he'd touched while my other leg was damn near fully covered like I wore the coolest torn lace pants on only one leg and stayed naked on the other. Something about the contrast made my bare skin seem way too sexy and revealing.

When I walked out of the bathroom ready to lose my mouth on her, I stopped dead in my tracks at Klive's name. She gushed about him being on his knees in front of me, buying us these expensive ass heels for tonight. My jaw clenched. I thought of Klive's jaw muscle flinching in his cheek.

Constance talked to Sara like they got along the way she and I did. Jase beating the hell out of the biker came next. Unease expanded in my gut, though I couldn't peg why. Like we shouldn't be talking about any of these men or Inferno, the way we never said the words *Bloody Mary I killed your baby* three times while looking at the mirror in a dark restroom. Some villains seemed to have a supernatural ability to come out of their dark hiding places to attack anyone who mentioned their name.

"Okay, so we'll see you later? You think you can get your parents to watch Noah?" Constance asked. Sara's apparent change of mind after the mention of all this upped my bad feeling.

Again, I wasn't sure what instinct told me Klive was more dangerous than Jase, but I now looked forward to his personality whiplash if that meant he'd be at this party while Sara and I were in the same place at the same time.

Pat Connor implied he'd not killed Patrick Scott.

Someone else had that he was afraid of.

Should Sara still be afraid of the same?

"Sara's onboard," Constance cheered. "Now I don't have to find a replacement. She's super psyched to come out of hiding since she heard Jase shredded the biker's face for you. She also said you went on a date with Moonlight you never told me about. Someone's in trouble."

"Damn right someone's in trouble. You! Look at my body! My coach will kill me if I can't remove this before my next meet. My dad will flip his shit. I don't even want to imagine what my mom might say. I look like ... like ..."

"Me?"

My whole face dropped. "No. If I look like you then I'm flattered, Constance. Like I said, you look classy like this. Subtle, bad-ass, sexy all at once. This is *really* bold."

"And no one will mistake you for Sara in dim lighting, now, will they?"

My eyes lurched toward hers in sudden understanding. "Are you testing Inferno's motives?"

"Maybe. That, or throwing them off your scent. You don't look so much like you in this capacity, Kins. With that man on his knees for you and Jase willing to beat the hell out of any threat, I'm more worried about anyone who wants to harm you, than anyone coming up against them. Easy to see Moonlight is rich. Rich buys dangerous friends. Jase is part of the community. The community packs dangerous friends. Now get dressed. We'll bring our new shoes with us while we go meet Sweetness for hair and nails."

"How come you're not doing it?"

"I don't have time or the supplies for nails right now. A braid isn't good enough for tonight. We need you to look mysterious, not sweet. I need a new weave. Maybe I should do a wig. You know I only prefer Sweetness. He's the one who talked me into cosmetology. He's also part of the community, so we are in safe yet gifted hands. I bet he knows Jase."

We grabbed our shoe boxes. She stuffed my arms full of snacks to keep my metabolism up and commanded I eat while she drove to the salon Sweetness, whose real name was Antoine, worked in. When we arrived, and I'd downed enough snacks to make me feel heavy, she squealed in girly delight before running into his muscular arms. Clear as clean glass this man was part of Jase's *community*, as Constance referred to military with special skill sets. He was almost seven feet of stacked brick wall you'd need a wrecking ball to take down.

"*Mon cher!* You've brought white chocolate topped with the most delicious shade of strawberry I've ever seen." He introduced himself and ran his hands through my wavy hair after releasing the wispy fishbone braid. "Natural or colored?" he asked.

"Natural," I said.

"With that skin?" His head fell back on a groan of delight. "Constance, you shouldn't have." He bent cheek to cheek meeting my eyes in the mirror. "Mulatta?"

"Rare Italian trait that skips generations on my father's side."

"*Magnifique*. Do you trust me, *cher*?"

"The last person I trusted waited till I fell asleep and colored all over my body. Forgive me if I'm a little apprehensive." I shot Constance a look in the mirror. She smiled back, undaunted.

"Well, she did an amazing job. What's your name?"

"This is Kinsley. She's a sprinter at the university. We trust you to make her look hot," she told him. "New weave or wig for me? You got any new ones in the back?"

"Constance Marie Laveau. After the hours I spent last week sewing that in, you're wearing a damn wig, *mon cher*."

She chuckled.

When Sweetness left to grab wigs for her, I asked, "Marie Laveau?"

"My middle name is Marie. He teases me that I act like a voodoo queen, casting love spells on men both near and far. Locals and snowbirds, tourists, with my voice, beauty and charisma." She flipped the pages of a gossip magazine. "I must've dropped my latest love potion into your drink, though."

"Nice." I smiled. "Hope you don't expect me to pay for that."

She laughed while Sweetness brought her seven different wigs before he went to work on my hair like his fingers were made of scissors. I was afraid until he'd washed, dried, styled and layered everything in such a way that I looked like a go-go girl vixen. He asked Constance to pass him a jeweled comb. She handed him one crusted in black costume gems. He opened the wrapper and pushed the comb against the hair behind my temple, showcasing the stars. The tresses rose so that only one side of my hair fell free in classic movie-star glam. He'd gifted me with long, side swept bangs that reminded me of Jase as I flipped them out of my face. I coughed on the hairspray he applied before, during and after he teased and raised the crown of my hair.

He and Constance double-teamed my makeup while I listened to them gossip in broken French. She gushed about Jase being into me, then opened up to him about scary sexy Klive. Constance gasped when I told her, in French, that I agreed with her opinion of Klive. Sweetness said he was keeping me after that. They had slang I didn't know, so they laughed as they talked trash, then taught me the Creole trash they'd talked.

They stood side-by-side, almost cheek-to-cheek, as they ordered me to be very still while applying magnetic lashes to my already thick natural lashes. Each pulled tiny black jewels from an adhesive strip and lined my eyelashes by the tweezer full.

"You have the same hazel green eyes," I told them. "Same noses."

"We're cousins." The spearmint of her gum opened my sinuses. "Gustav is Antoine's brother, also my cousin."

"Wow, how did I not know this?"

"Never came up. Gus introduced me to Jase. Got me an audition with Rock-N-Awe. How do those feel?"

"Heavy. Hard to get used to feeling myself blinking like this."

"Let's see you give those big doe eyes to anyone in these lashes. Constance Marie Laveau has worked her voodoo love again!"

"Mmhmm, *mon cher. Tres belle.*" Sweetness walked away to tend to another client. She finished the lines she painted onto her own eyes, then settled on a black and pink wig with long spiral curls.

"You're so lucky. You can pull off anything you want."

"Yeah, but this one's not classy enough. You need just the right mixture of edge and class. Bad-ass versus trailer park, ya know?" She replaced that wig, her hair pulled back into a net thing that looked like pantyhose on her head. Amazing how she tucked so much weave beneath that tiny sleeve. She grabbed a glossy sun-kissed brunette wig with ombre tips. Angela Ansley hair. Ha! She should keep this wig for Thursday night. I told her so and she gave me a devilish smile.

"Kinsley Hayes, if I didn't know any better, I'd think you wanted your black friend to have your back in case you get into a cat fight. That, or you're trying to provoke *me* into one over a certain cowboy. You look so bad-ass, I look like I brought my mean white friend from the wrong side of the tracks to watch *my* back."

She swiveled the chair. I gasped at my reflection. My eyes were done so heavy but enhanced in such a way they looked like big baby doll eyes while the rest of me was exactly what she said. I looked like the girl you didn't mess with even as my eyes looked so sinful and innocent at the same time. Almost like having a sister who resembled me enough to know we were definitely related, but not identical. Interesting dichotomy.

"This is the girl that goes with the shoes Moonlight bought. Better bring your Mace."

We laughed in the mirror. My smile looked so wholesome like Rustin's next to my naughty appearance package. Constance kissed her cousin's cheeks. I took Sweetness's card with a promise to return as a loyal customer. Constance gave him a snarky thanks for stealing another future client. He kissed both my cheeks and shooed us out the door. She looked so beautiful. Her wig didn't look like a wig at all. She looked the exotic type natural with her eyes almost seeming to glow beneath her heavy makeup. Less bad-ass, more gorgeous.

"It's like we are reversed. You look sweet while I look tough."

"Correction. You look like Micro Machine is done playing on the track and wants to taste the rest of your world. Glad to bring her out to play. Now, let's head to our destination for training and uniforms. Oh, and we must leave our phones in the car. Not allowed."

"Will my Mace be allowed?"

She chewed her lower lip like she worried I was gonna ask. Her head shook. "Hope your guy shows. But this isn't the bar. We're serving the rich and famous, what's the worst that could happen?"

"Constance, do me a favor and never ask that question in my presence ever again."

She cringed in agreement.

22 | ♀

We drove through manicured hedges until we came to a wrought iron gate for an exclusive condo building on the other side of Tampa Bay. Guards stood ready to wave people through to their residencies or redirect to the valet down the street for a back entrance reserved for servants and staffers. The guard bent to look at us, took our IDs for reference, called them in. A voice came back and approved us to drive down to the back entrance. Far less prestigious than the main entrance. Valets jogged around as their boss gave directions for the evening.

Constance and I got out of the car and grabbed our shoe boxes while these guys practiced on the arriving staff.

"Oh my gosh. *Kinsley?*" a familiar face asked.

"Holy crap, Frat Toy!" I dug through files in my mind for his name. "Sorry, I mean Brayden, right?"

He nodded and stared like his jaw couldn't close.

"Take good care of my baby, Frat Toy," Constance told him and passed the keys before grabbing my hand to order me along with her. "Leave the dorm rooms behind, Kins. I need you in Spring Break bartender mode. You're not here as a guest. Professional."

"When did you get tattoos?" Brayden called after me, but Constance refused to allow me to answer him. I cast a helpless wave over my shoulder.

"Yeesh. Maybe I'm not cut out for this job if I can't even make polite conversation."

"You can make polite conversation with the guests who need something from you. If any of them try to buy you for a night, get away from them. If any of them start asking personal questions, you don't give them any truth. Be a different character for the night. Sometimes sex traffickers worm their way into these to shop for new girls. Sometimes they use other women our age to do the luring in. If you see anything suspicious, tell Chad or me. You don't leave without me. I don't leave without you. Understood?"

"Why didn't you tell me this trash yesterday before you told Chad I'd come with you?"

"Because you wouldn't have come. I need this. I meant what I said about this opening doors for you to make extra cash when you move out into the real world. Besides, the same bad people shop at the bar, grocery stores, playgrounds. I'd bet even some are on your campus."

"Omigosh! That's horrendous. How can you tell?" I asked.

"I'm street. I just know. We can talk more about this later. For now, let's get to our places and learn our tasks. Wipe the fear off your face."

"Damn, Constance. I'm sorry for upsetting you."

Several others trekked in the same direction across manicured grassy areas before we filed inside a back door up a flight of stairs that made me think of Klive chasing me in my father's building.

God, please let Klive show up. Please. Don't let anything bad happen to me for walking on the wild side for once in my life.

"Kins, I'm not upset with you. Ever think things like this make me tense, too? Safer in pairs. Buddy system. That sort of thing? Why do you think I made you so distinctive?" she hissed in a whisper. Her watchful eyes scanned everyone gathering to pick up uniforms in conference style room. "Same reason I make myself so flamboyant. Harder to do something bad to someone everyone will remember. At least that's my reasoning."

My mouth dried. "That is smart."

"Plus, tattoos help someone identify a body better."

"Constance!" I almost shouted.

She snickered to herself. "Damn, girl, you're so easy to vex."

"To vex? Since when do you use that word?"

"I heard a customer say it. I liked it. Anyways, Jase was right. Chill. I'm not worried. You'll know if I'm worried. We're good. Situations like this bring out rich men who think they can buy anyone for a night. Sometimes they're right, but I just wanted you to know so you can play it cool if you're propositioned. Look, there's Chad." She waved. He wove through the crowd to hold his arms open as he stood back to take me in before pulling me into a full hug.

"*You* are most definitely a pleasant surprise. Excellent work, Constance. The detailing of the lace is amazing! She's very striking."

"She's also right here," I said with a wry grin.

He released me and kept his arm around my waist as he pointed to the various tables where we collected information and instructions. "Uniforms are over here. Come on," he said and traded my waist for my hand. I grabbed Constance's hand. We formed a little train through the mayhem. I was glad Constance and Sweetness had worked their magic because sweet Kins wouldn't have been a contender with the servers I saw walking out of the dressing areas.

Chad waited for us like he appreciated familiar faces in this mix. I took a uniform from a very stuck-up man who did what Marcus did: eyeballed the size and handed me, you guessed it, an extra small. I sighed and went to change.

When I came out Chad was talking to Sara Scott. A very pretty, very freshly redheaded Sara Scott. She didn't look like a recent widow or even like the woman ringing her hands with worry about how to behave after Patrick's demise. She looked years younger and *expensive*. As in salon color versus bottle in a box like she normally used. Her makeup was as heavy as ever, but there was no dimming the bright and shiny exuberance she smiled with. Damn, if only Bayleigh were here to see this.

When Sara saw me walking up, she stood back the way Chad had and hugged me seconds later the same. As if I hadn't seen her days ago. Was that *two* days ago?

"You look amazing, Sara!" I gushed and fluffed her beautiful hair.

"Thank you," she said with a shy factor I'd never seen before, like *my* shy factor. *Was this real?* "Do you like it?" she asked. "I missed red. My grandma always told me redheads do things blondies only dream of. I only know I got tired of being brunette and didn't want to go blonde. You okay with this?" "Why wouldn't I be? It's your head, silly."

"Well, just, you know ... after everything. I'm glad you're okay. I'm sorry, I didn't realize. Did he attack you before or after I saw you on Sunday?" she asked. Chad's attention snapped, his whole face worried and angry.

"You were *attacked*?" He grabbed my hand and excused us from her, then ordered me to tell him what the hell happened.

"I don't want to end up in an article about Inferno," I told him as I looked around us. No one paid us mind.

"Inferno!" Not a question. "Please tell me as a worried friend, not a reporter, that you quit, dammit."

"I most certainly did not. I won't quit just because some jerk can't keep his hands to himself. I don't care what vest he's wearing. Marcus ousted me indefinitely. Why do you think I'm here? Besides, Jase kicked the Inferno's ass."

"About time he did something," Chad muttered with a shake of his head.

"Can I please sit down and put my shoes on now?" I asked. He snapped out of his crap. We moved toward a carpeted wall where I braced myself to step into the stilettos and bent to buckle the straps. The tiny heart showed just above the leather around my ankle.

I stood. Chad cursed as his eyes lingered on the shoes and slowly traveled up my legs. "Who are you and what have you done with my sweet bartender?" he asked. His foot braced against the wall, hands in his pockets, skinny tie around his neck, fedora on his head. He loved the old school style. He cleared his throat. "You made any headway on who may have gotten you roses for Valentine's Day? Heard someone gave you a rose at your last meet. Lucy seems to think it's the same guy."

"Chad, you're not getting any more gossip goodies from me tonight." I tested the heels and double-checked for hidden price tags. All clear. Damn, I hoped I didn't have blisters by the end of the night. Never break in new shoes when you have to do a ton of public walking. What an idiotic mistake.

Chad turned to face me, a flirty little smile on his lips. "Come on, not even a free sample? You look so delish tonight, *Kinsley*." I tossed my head back on a full laugh, then cupped my lips as I remembered where we were. "Saying my name in that sexy accent and flattering me isn't getting you anywhere. I don't care how handsome you are in that hat. Maybe I ought to steal it from you."

"You mean the way you stole King's hat from his head at the bar?"

I gasped and was glad I was already walking away so he didn't have to see my face. How did he know about that? He'd not been there. Instead of giving him a hint that he was right, I grinned over my shoulder while his eyes stuck on my tattooed leg and stilettos.

"No idea who you're talking about, Chaddy Cake. Eyes up here, sir."

He chuckled and walked after me with his hands in his pockets. Reminded me a bit of Klive's demeanor when he was in charm you out of your knickers mode. Chad was no Klive but seemed he may have ripped a page outta Klive's book.

"Chaddy Cake? You know I hate when you call me that in public."

Nice. Trying to seem like we had private times where I used that on him. "I'll keep that in mind, sir. See ya later." I fanned my fingers over my shoulder and watched him grab his tie and hold the red silk like a noose. I laughed and he seemed glad to make me happy.

I found Constance leaning against the wall adjusting her own heels. We stashed our stuff together in a cubby assigned to us with a number and ticket. Good thing I'd left my phone in her glove box because this wasn't very secure. Anyone could reach inside and steal my flip flops. By the end of this night those might be more valuable to me than my dang phone depending on how sore my feet might be.

"Marcus would be so jealous if he saw you voluntarily looking this way for another company," Sara said with a grin. She tossed her street clothes inside our clothing bin. We slid that bin in beside the shoe bin.

"Ready to play?"

"Damn right. Micro Machine doesn't have jack on this persona," I said and bit back my nervousness while we walked into the spaces we'd be manning. Chad was in a corner setting up his deejay booth. Club style music already pulsed heavy enough to vibrate the still water of the swimming pool. Chad's counterpart checked sound quality and speaker placement. A man took a group of us and gave us trays, pointed out the various drinks that were available at all times, instructions for those who requested special drinks, etcetera.

I found myself enthralled with the sleek white floor without a single visible seam. Neon blue and pink lights reflected off the pretty surface. White couches and chairs grouped in at least twenty different social areas. The view of the ocean beyond the infinite edge pool was unobstructed as the whole wall was nonexistent. A long bar ran from outside near the pool all the way inside. Four male bartenders dressed in tuxes with bow ties made standard mixed drinks and lined row upon row of glasses for us to grab and go. What appeared to be about a hundred crystal flutes grouped near the end. One of the bartenders poured bubbling champagne into each.

If we broke a glass, we bought a glass, alcohol and stemware.

El yay! Another reason I should've tested these dang shoes. *Thank God Klive had insisted on the ankle support!*

"Excuse me, young lady. You with the tattoos. Are you paying attention?" Took me several seconds and everyone looking at me to realize he meant *me*!

"Yes sir. I heard all of it." He wanted me to repeat everything. So, I did. He didn't look pleased that I'd been honest. "I'm watching you," he said to me once we were dispersed to grab glasses.

"Okay ... what exactly will you be watching about me?"

"This is a big deal and I'm not risking my catering reputation for your daydreams," he said too close to my face. I leaned away. "Get over your white trash awe and get to work without the stars in your eyes or else I'll make sure you never work for anyone." My jaw dropped on all of the above.

"Oh my gosh! Kinsley is that you?!" a woman's squealing voice gushed. The man turned with alarm as someone threw her arms around me before I had a chance to see. She pulled back. "Holy crap! Delia? You're kidding me! Were you invited?"

"She's the host," the man said with pure disdain. Delia shot him a *go to hell or get another job* glare. His face flushed before he excused himself to tend to the staff.

"This is your party?" I asked with insane dawning for all that meant. Constance eyed me in worry for her own job, but also a bit of surprise that I knew the hostess.

"This is my party. I came to the bar last night to invite you and your singer, but you weren't there. He was. I gave him your invitation, but how crazy that you're already here. Working no less. Come on! Let's go upstairs."

"Well, I came with my friends—"

"Grab them. I'll meet you over there by the elevator." She pointed and strode to the man who'd been rude to me. I waved Constance and Sara over to tell them Delia wanted us upstairs.

"You *know* her?" Constance asked like I was a creature she'd never seen. She wasn't sure whether this was good or made me a secret snob.

"Last year a guy was harassing her at the bar. I kicked his ass out and had Gustav ban him from the bar so she could drink in peace. Turns out I'd come through for a big fish with a stalker. I whispered in Gustav's ear once Delia confessed her misery. The guy was so psycho obsessed with her he followed her from New York to Florida. Gus says he knows friends in high places. Told me the problem was handled. Apparently, he was right. Delia's been down with me ever since."

"Wow," Sara said, chewed her lip with a far off look in her eyes for a second. She snapped out of the zone and smiled when Delia came to introduce herself to her and Constance. She asked them if they'd be her guests, not servers, upstairs in the penthouse.

"Any friend of Kinsley's is a friend of mine. We shall see if that sexy singer of hers shows as her plus-one. I hear he has a very sleek classic car. My father would be in heaven to see it,"

Delia chattered while we rode the double-sided elevator up to the penthouse. Her key hung in the number panel to lock all others from disturbing our ascent. She pulled the key when we got to the top. The doors opened on a different feel.

"Is she talking about Jase?" Constance whispered. I nodded with a worried look in my eyes. "Damn, this just got very interesting, Kins. I love that I'm a guest now, but how do I make a name for myself if I'm not working?" she asked. "Not to mention, we're in uniforms. We might be working even if we are guests."

Delia overheard that last bit and told us to follow her to her room. We gasped when we walked into her royal suite. Wall-towall windows looked over the Bay and the city glowing in the distance. Moon beams danced on the distant waves. I didn't have time to get caught up in the beauty of the view because Delia ordered us inside her closet. We all cursed as several lights flickered on to display the most gawdy pretty dresses, skirts, tops.

Constance was no longer a Delia down-looker. She was in love with a budding friendship with someone as flamboyant as herself. Sara went through various ensembles because her boobs were so big, they were popping out of the tops. Constance came out in a hot pink sequined mini dress. Sara a stretchy black cocktail dress with no frills because that was the only thing that stretched. I ended up in a one shoulder yellow dress that fell to my ankles, but Delia insisted because of the very high slit in the left leg she swore would be perfect for the art Constance created.

Delia begged Constance for a henna appointment and swore they needed to go shopping together before she went back to New York. Constance was thrilled. Soon Delia asked to know everything about her. Constance filled her in on Rock-N-Awe and her side job as vocals and guitar for Jase's band. I didn't see Jase anywhere. Delia grabbed Sara and Constance and told me to follow onto the enormous balcony overlooking the pool below, the beach beyond. I swallowed and stayed back while the girls rushed toward the glass banister. My heart pounded in my chest. I snapped up the first flute of champagne that passed by.

"I thought I'd have to take one of those off your tray as an excuse to say hello."

My eyes closed at the way my pounding heart increased in speed at Klive's voice over my shoulder. His body heat radiated close to my back. He came around to my front as I managed to open my eyes to a much better view than one that made me feel I would fall to my death. Wow, he looked good in a tuxedo! A single red rose pinned to his lapel. One hand in his pocket, the other held a glass of what looked like Crown. *Damn.*

He chuckled as I guess I accidentally said that aloud.

"The sentiment is mutual, love. I thought you were lethal in leather pants. I swear you are intent on killing me. The only thing missing is a gun strapped to your thigh in this dress. Who says you need a knife-wielding psycho to protect you?"

I smiled at all of the above. My breath hadn't quite caught up to my mouth just yet. Klive greeted Delia when she walked up with a very pleasant smile on her face.

"Mr. King, I'm honored you came. I hear you're kind of a big deal."

"You know what they say about believing everything you hear," he said with that smooth grace. "I'm honored to be invited. Thank you. Ladies, nice to see you," he told Constance and Sara. "I'm very impressed with your work, Constance."

She nearly fluttered when he'd said her name. This meant Klive had read her business card rather than just accepting her offering. He told Delia all about Constance's drive, motivation, pretty much solidifying her name in their circles for future reference. Not to mention, he'd not only read her card, but checked out her resume and portfolio on her website. Her hero worship couldn't be more evident, but my awe for his genuine care...just, wow.

Conversation flowed so well, I realized about half an hour later I was very close to Klive on the balcony, too close to the glass banister without noticing. About twelve others had joined us in talking about Rock-N-Awe mostly. Klive's hand settled at the base of my spine as he offered to grab me a fresh flute of champagne from the passing server. He traded my empty for a full in one motion. His hand never left my back. His fingers drew circles. I no longer heard a single word.

"Oh! Since we are on the subject!" Delia said and trotted away. We remained in a little confusion, but others chuckled and said that was Delia; traveled where the wind blew her thoughts. Constance was ready to join her wherever she went. Sara decided to bow out and go to the powder room. Klive and I remained while others drifted to different conversations. His hand lingered on my spine as he rounded in front of me once more. He removed the rose from his lapel and tucked the petals between my hair and ear. The fingers of his free hand brushed my bare shoulder.

"This seems remarkably naked without any henna."

My breath stuttered at the word *naked* from that accent.

"That's what I said, but I meant about my other leg because she left it blank except for this heart where—" I caught my words before they finished tumbling from my lips, but my ankle was already displayed, my fingers holding my dress to show the tiny heart.

His lips curled. "Where I touched you yesterday."

"You shouldn't touch me now, sir. I can't handle it. I can barely breathe as it is. You smell so good."

"So do you, love. You shouldn't reveal such things, or you'll tempt me to touch you further."

"Holy shit," I whispered as the backs of his fingers tested the bare skin of my shoulder again.

"If that's what happens with my fingers, I wonder what would happen if I kissed you there."

"Now it's you who shouldn't think such things, or you'll tempt me to let you." My voice was far too wispy and weak.

He looked around us. "Wherever has everyone trickled off to?"

I shook my head, unable to answer. He was right, we were alone.

"You know what I find fascinating, my sweet?" He ran his fingers up my shoulder, over my collar bone, up my throat. He stepped closer to seal the little space between us. My head tilted to look up at him. His eyes watched his fingertips prance over my pulse.

"What?"

"How afraid of heights you are, yet you don't even notice I have you against the railing of this balcony."

I gasped with a glance over my shoulder. "Klive!" My arms flew around his neck while his hand around my back pulled me flush against him.

"I'd never let you fall, but let you feel like it? Maybe. Are you afraid?"

"Should I be?" I asked, still too breathy, but also from fear robbing the strength from my voice.

His face dipped. My head fell back as his nose ran the length of my throat. His breath rushed against my skin. I no longer noticed how scary high up we were. My eyes closed because he never kissed my skin. Instead, he gave the smallest of laughs that sent thrills and chills all over my skin that prickled when the breeze lifted the tips of my hair over the edge of the balcony.

The elevator pinged Delia's arrival. We ripped apart when I heard Jase's laughter. I summoned a nearby server who'd been almost a statue for how I'd not noticed her in the shadows standing dutifully with her tray. She passed me a fresh flute of champagne. I downed that one and took a fresh one in seconds.

Klive cleared his throat and exchanged his dangerous seduction for the charmer. I turned to study the insanity of the view, pretending I hadn't noticed Jase. After all, Klive and I speaking to one another wouldn't be a surprise. However, being caught during the most fear-inducing seduction...yeah...not so good. I was grateful for the breeze to cool my heated skin and blood in my cheeks. When had everyone left to go downstairs together? How had we gone unnoticed? Or had we?

Delia chattered a mile a minute until she came onto the balcony.

"Kinsley, look! I found your plus-one! Isn't he sharp in a tux?" she asked while I spun. Jase took my breath away at how he cleaned up!

"Mr. Taylor, how nice to see you," Klive said.

"Likewise, Mr. King. Call me Jase, though. Kinsley, my gosh, you are ... *stunning* ... not sweet Kins tonight." His eyes roamed the slit in the dress, the tattooing. "Delia is there dancing, because I don't normally dance unless it's dirty, but how do I resist an opportunity to hold her close?" Jase finished with a look at her. I swallowed as I wondered if he was somehow calling mine and Klive's crap. No way he could've seen us.

"There is dancing on the first floor, though mostly dirty," Delia said with a naughty grin. "Now, Jase, what were you doing with that dyed redhead the other night when this one is way prettier?"

My eyes flared as I fought a huge smile. Jase coughed on his own surprise at her calling him out.

"Well, it wasn't what it looked like, because Kins and I aren't officially together. More a flirtationship." He faltered for words. "What I'm trying to say is I'm not with that other girl, and I wasn't with Kinsley when I was with her."

"But not *with her* with her?" Delia asked like she was confused just to torment him further.

Poor Jase. Constance grinned behind her back. I could tell she appreciated Delia's passive-aggressive vindictive side.

"Kinsley, care to join me downstairs, love?" Klive asked. "I was under the impression you were *together* together, but if you're not together ...." Klive mocked the confusion. Well, hell.

"Sure, I'll join you downstairs for now, but enjoy the little time you've got because this thing between Jase and I seems to be inevitable," I threw his own words back at him. His eyes lit with an amused challenge.

Jase looked downright flattered and conflicted at how I didn't blow him off yet took hold of Klive's arm. I looked over my shoulder before Klive and I boarded the elevator.

"Jase, you're coming, aren't you? I mean you're not going to let Klive keep me all to himself?"

"Let the games begin," Klive said with a private smile. His fingers stroked my right hand that held to his arm, always keeping me aware of his touch. We boarded while Jase came to stand at my other side. Jase grabbed my left hand dangling between us. Delia gave me huge eyes of excitement before looking at both men. Constance and Sara boarded with about three others. We all went down to mix into the vagrants.

23 | ♀

THE DOORS OPENED ON Tropkillaz *Mambo*. The beat seemed to set the pattern of the strobe lights. The others filed out of the elevator while I leaned back against the wall, disoriented from the dramatic change in atmosphere. A man stepped up and snapped a photo of us standing in the elevator. I managed to see him take several of Delia with her friends and mine.

"You alright, love?" Klive asked at my ear to be heard over the loud ass music.

"Did you spike her drink, King?" Jase asked in a pissy tone.

"I'm going to pretend you didn't say something so insultingly absurd, Jase. Here, you go first if you're going to act like a spoiled child." Klive kissed my temple and departed the elevator with both hands in his pockets.

"That was rude of you, Jase. Strobes always mess me up a bit. Chad knows this, but he also thinks I'm working upstairs," I told him and stabilized.

"Chad? Figures."

"He's the one who scored this job for Constance and me."

The doors closed us inside, but we didn't travel because no one had called for the elevator.

"I'm sorry. I'm a damn mess when you're so pretty. I don't even know what to do with myself. Can I touch your ink?" He asked in such a desperate tone I laughed and pulled my leg out of the slit.

He cursed and ran a hand through his slicked back hair, cursed again at maybe mussing his hard work.

He dropped into a squat to run both hands up my leg while taking in every fine detail of the designs that must've taken Constance hours. I gasped in stunned surprise when Jase's lips kissed my knee. "This is too beautiful not to kiss, Kins. Like you," he said and stood. His hands cupped my face as his lips kissed mine. I hummed when he did. "I can't blame Klive for losing his shit. I'm about to blow my wad in my tux. I have to get out of here and maybe jump into the pool to cool my jets."

"Klive hasn't lost his shit," I told him. He gave a short laugh and smacked the door-open button.

"Hold my hand while you get used to the lights." Jase led us out into the flashing laser lights shooting and reflecting off the white floor. "Acrylic flooring. I'll have to tell Tyndall about this. She'd be amazed. Seamless," he said as he appreciated our surroundings the way I had earlier. The seating areas filled with not a single vagrant. Jase and I mingled and met too many people to remember. Two couples spoke up about our scene on the beach yesterday.

"I knew that was you guys!" a guy said.

"Yeah, I couldn't tell since you have all this ink when you didn't in that bikini yesterday," his girlfriend said. "But him, I'd never forget," she told Jase. "That blond was hot, but this one is way hotter. You both are."

Um …. I swallowed as her boyfriend nodded at me before he and his girlfriend shared a look, little nod, then refocused on us.

"Do you swing?" he asked. *Holy shit! Is this what Klive meant about the types who attend? Surely, Delia wasn't into that?* I looked up at Jase in a bit of panic.

"Nope, we're monogamous," Jase said and excused us.

"Omigosh, Jase, did we stumble into an alternate universe?"

He chuckled and shook his head, squeezed my hand. "Nah. If this were that type of party, that pool would be full of sex already. Very few would be clothed. Don't worry, I'd rescue you from this place before allowing you to stay." From then on, Jase claimed me for both of our safety to discourage inappropriate advances.

Thank God he was right. After that, I couldn't help studying people a little closer. New money and old wealth dropped their disdain for one another. Locals mixed with visitors from other states, some from other countries. I counted seven different languages in passing. When we saw several we recognized from the bar, Jase and I seemed to sag together at once. His posture stiffened and hand gripped mine too hard when one regular begged me to dance with him.

"Easy, Jase. Damn. Is this a preview of being your real girlfriend?" I asked at his ear.

"Kinsley, come on, baby. Trust me. I don't like this guy."

"I'm trying to trust you, but this guy buys me a beer every Monday. You really scared me on Sunday and don't seem to care. I'm going to dance and hope it isn't your intention to shred his face."

"It's a bad idea, dammit." He yanked my hand when I pulled away. "Where's Klive?" he asked and looked around as if they would somehow team up against me.

"Oh, now I'm definitely dancing."

I accepted the regular's offer if only to get out of the clutches of all the testosterone flowing from Jase. I hadn't yet spied Klive, but I *felt* him. He was somewhere close enough that I looked around myself when I danced in the middle of a hundred others. Something passed from the regular's hand as he grabbed mine. That's when Klive stole my hand.

"Never again!" That's all Klive said to him. The guy's face went ashen, and he turned to fight through the dancers. Klive rushed me to the restroom.

"Klive, this is the men's area! I can't go in there!"

"Then close your damn eyes," he growled. Fear raced through my whole body at that tone. "Everyone out!" he shouted.

I closed my eyes when one man rushed to tuck himself away. Another washed his hands but fled without drying. I heard the lock flip a second later, then Klive had my hands beneath the water in the sink. I opened to see him squirting gobs of soap on my palms then he lathered them for the better part of a minute. I watched in silent stupefaction. Dumbfounded. *Had I drunk too much? Was this really happening?* A laugh burst from my lips while he scrubbed so hard.

He looked up at me and lifted one of my eyelids. I jerked back. He kept my hands so I couldn't go too far.

"Why are you laughing?" he asked. The water turned on and my hands shoved beneath the stream.

"Because one minute you have me leaning over a balcony while you seduce me with nothing but your nose, then next you're yelling at me, now washing my hands as if life depends on it. This night makes no sense. You make no sens—"

"He had drugs, Kinsley. He touched your hand. Transference."

"No!" Everything awesome melted down the drain with the suds. "Can that happen? From skin-contact?"

"Yes, if it's the right kind."

"Do it again! Wash them again! Oh, Klive! Please, this isn't happening!" I begged. "I have an internship interview coming. I have track! Holy shit! I don't do drugs! What if I'm tested?"

"Calm down. Do you feel weird?"

"How am I supposed to know?!" I cried. "You always make me feel weird!" I clawed my nails against my palms.

"What?!" he demanded, my hands under the stream again. "I make you feel weird? That's awful!"

"No, that's not what I meant. Not bad weird. You make me feel high, or what I guess high feels like, so how the hell am I supposed to know what high feels like if you're around? Shit! I need to shut up and I don't think I'm drugged up because without inhibitions I'd have taken your ass down on this bathroom floor."

"Fuck it," he said and grabbed my face. My tongue was in his mouth before I could pull a coherent breath. His hands were in my hair running down my back, waist, hips. My nails speared into his always perfect hair as he lifted me to sit on the countertop. "No!" He ripped himself away. "I shouldn't kiss you right now. If anything, it may confirm you're high."

"I'm drunk. Completely different," I said and grabbed his lapels to yank him back in. He caved. His hand yanked my hair to tilt my head back. Klive's mouth was all over my throat while his other hand ran up my thigh, beneath the slit in my dress. The white ceiling opened with blinding light as if the pleasure of his mouth on my skin made the world glow.

"No. Not like this."

He was torn away from me and pinned back against the tile wall by hands that came from the tiles. I hopped off the counter and wobbled as the room tilted. His image blurred with the geometric black and white tiles he leaned against. The shapes jumped off the wall with hands like they wanted to suck him inside.

"No! Klive! Get away from them! It's not safe! Come here!" He lunged away from the tile trap and caught me before I tipped over. "Klive. The black tiles are black holes. Don't step on the black. Don't let me touch them. Don't let them get you, they have hands. Please get me out of here. We will vanish and no one will know. What if they separate us?"

He threw the lid up on the stall toilet and held my hair before his fingers dipped too far back into my mouth. I gagged my guts up and tried to ignore the black walls of the stalls, the tile rising off the floor while I held to the white porcelain like a lifeline. The cold felt so good next to my cheek. My eyes burned as heavy mascara dripped into them. I heard someone else, felt Klive lift me off the floor.

A cold paper towel wiped at my mouth and eyes. "The black holes," I told the person. "Are you going to help us stay?"

"I am. My name is Doctor Duncan. I'm Delia's father. Look right here. Can you tell me your name, gorgeous?"

"I'm gorgeous? But I just threw up."

He and Klive chuckled, but their nervousness floated away from their skin like a crystal beaded aura. I reached for Klive's crystals, then watched my hand. The black henna patterns. I gasped in terror.

"You are gorgeous. Very pretty tattoos. Are those real?" he asked. A light blinded me. I squinted.

"Thank you. Kinsssleeee. Runner. I run. Fast. Not real tattooooos. Oh, gosh, they're alive from my skin and trying to take me away from you!" I gripped Klive so hard and pulled myself tighter to him. His crystals fell from where I knocked them. They shattered the black tile hole in glowing white light. Pretty.

"Shhh. Those tattoos aren't going to hurt you, Kinsley. We won't let them. Look at the light," the doctor said. "Any allergies?"

"It's pretty light. Shiny."

"No allergies," Klive said.

"She a user?"

"She's pure. Is she okay?" Klive asked.

"She's okay. Looks like a mild reaction, takes very little to upset a clean system. If he'd had a chance to make her hold to it long enough, we may have a real problem. Take her upstairs. Put her in the room across from Delia's. I'll deal with her friends. Here, take my key for the elevator. You'll find an IV bag of fluids in my master bathroom. Hook her up. I trust you know how?"

"I do. Keep holding on to my neck, Kinsley," Klive said.

I held onto his cologne, his voice, through so many blinding lights and patterns. I was floating up, up, up all while staring at the grayest eyes with yellow lightning strikes. Shapes caved and traveled close to my face. I slapped them away and tucked myself as close to Klive's neck as I could to block them from touching me. Delia. Constance. They were talking. Delia seemed to chant in my *Let's go Mi-cro* pattern as she repeated something over and over, but not my cheer. She was sad. Constance. Angel.

Singing angel.

"Constance Marie Laveau ... like voodoo everywhere ...."

I could hear but couldn't see. Couldn't respond. Just in and out sounds with images my mind conjured.

"Fluids are almost gone. Think she needs another bag?" Constance asked.

"Sedative seems to be working. We will let her sleep and give her another in a few hours. She doesn't have a catheter. I don't want her to cry about wetting the bed," the doctor said. "Poor girl. She's sweet. A definite affinity for you, Klive."

Constance snorted. "You should've seen her screaming before you came upstairs. When we tried to get her to let him go, she shouted the black was going to take him away. I'm trying not to be offended."

The doctor laughed. "She wasn't talking about you or any person. Hallucinations. The black tiles of the flooring and walls, her tattoos, the jackets of our tuxedos were all playing tricks on her like they were going to suck them up. She was afraid she'd lose him to the dark."

"Oh, gosh. I feel like the biggest dick," Constance said. "What if she's drug tested for track or for this second internship interview? She's wanted that position for the better part of a year. Everything will disappear. Her reputation ...."

"What is the internship she wants?"

"There's a diabetic counselor set to retire in two years who's taking applications for trainees to take her place. Nothing would make Kinsley happier than to be trained to take her reins. She looks up to this woman. Kinsley knows she's really young to hope for something that should go to someone with much more experience. She says reach for the moon, because if she misses, she still lands somewhere in the stars. She's a good girl. This is all my fault. She wouldn't have known what to look for. She never thinks ill of any of her patrons. That guy ... I hope Jase beat the shit out of him," Constance said.

"I will do a urinalysis and blood test on her. See what we need to take care of before it comes to that," the doctor said.

24 | ♂

Constance watched the doctor unscrew the empty fluid bag from the IV before taping the tube closed without removing the needle in case he ordered another round of fluids. He tied a tourniquet around Kinsley's other arm and tapped the veins on the inside of her elbow.

From the far side of the room, I leaned against the wall near the door staring with a dark anger Constance, I knew, sensed.

The guy who did this ....

I had claw marks from Kinsley's nails around my neck. My bow tie dangled from my unbuttoned over shirt where Kinsley had torn the silk away. Jase still hadn't made an appearance. Constance feared the two of us might end up fighting in our current frames of mind.

She was grateful for Delia's father being a doctor. He had a needle in Kinsley's arm, a vial filling with her blood. Another vial. He grabbed a cotton ball and pressed against her skin before removing the needle from her arm. Constance grabbed a bandaid and placed the adhesive around the cotton ball. The doctor labeled the tubes, tucked them into a baggie, then pulled his gloves off.

"A diabetic counselor huh?" the doctor asked.

"For children. She wants to coach them through the rough patches, keep them from getting depressed while they go through the ropes of learning how to use insulin or having to exercise. To help them cope with bullying from being overweight. She can't stand seeing any child suffer. You should see the free class she hosts once per month at the beach where she pretty much plays with all of the littles to help them enjoy movement."

"Sounds like a good woman." Dr. Duncan looked at me like he paid me the compliment.

While I agreed, I was unworthy. She was far too good for a man of my darkness.

The doctor got up and told us to get some rest. "Kinsley's fine, Klive. She's okay. He's been arrested. We had him taken off premises after the singer got to him. He left with the cops to give a statement."

Doctor Duncan closed the door behind himself. Constance and I sat in silence for a while. I finally pushed off the wall to sit on the bedside. Kinsley's hands were beautiful. I told Constance.

"Thank you, Klive. I'm a terrible friend for getting her into this. If her father ever found out, he'd never let her hang out with me ever again."

"No, you're not. You cannot control what other people do. That prick didn't tell her what he was doing. He knew better, though. I'd spied him the moment the lift—*elevator*— opened. I left Jase with her so I could watch this guy once Jase brought her out of the elevator. I've seen that prick watching her at the bar. He buys her a beer every Monday. Jase has noticed too. He once confided his fear the guy would spike her drink if she ever gave him a chance.

"She gave him a dance, *a single dance*, and look what the asshole managed to do. If something would've happened to her, Delia could've been charged. She needs to be more careful who she allows into her parties."

"I think he was valet or a server. I don't think he was Delia's guest. He wasn't dressed as nice as the other men," Constance said. "She'll be careful from now on. I guess since Jase seems to be gone for the night, I'm going to go crash on the couch. I think you should stay with her. She'd freak if she woke up and you weren't here, Klive. I won't let Jase do anything to disturb her."

"Thank you, Constance. You really are a good friend to her. Don't let the prick who did this make you feel you aren't. His actions. Not yours. You understand me?"

"Yes, Klive. Thank you. Good night."

"Good night."

I watched Constance close the door to the guest quarters in the Duncan's penthouse. Kinsley whimpered like the sedative was wearing off.

"Shhh ... sleep, love." I sat on the bed and worked on my cuff links. I tossed my bow tie and over shirt to the nearby chair. Kinsley's shoes remained on her feet. I went to the foot of the bed and worked the straps of her stilettos loose before shifting each from her foot. My hand lingered on her right ankle, my thumb stroking the tiny heart painted there. I stared at her in her pretty dress. That bloody man with bad intentions had stolen all her fun.

Even if Jase had shown up, I wasn't bothered. The challenge was fun. *This was not.* This was sobering reality that didn't belong in this young woman's world. That little prick was risking her entire career and reputation for what? A forced moment beneath her dress?

What the hell was with men making attempts on this young woman? Were these attempts anything to do with me? With Cheatham's threat?

"Oh, Kinsley, if I don't stop thinking of this, I'm going to kill him instead of lying here with you," I told her.

"Come lie here with me," she said. I flinched as she shifted to see me better. "What are you doing down there, silly?"

Had she not been so upset earlier, I'd have excused myself to give her privacy. Instead, I walked to her side. She didn't look bothered in the least. Her eyes opened like *Sleeping Beauty's* as she blinked several times. A pity no prince kissed her awake, rather a villainous King standing over her resisting his darkest longings in order to preserve her.

Was she sleep-talking to me like the other times?

"Will you help me to the bathroom, Klive?" *Not sleeping. Wide awake.* "I'm scared of what I saw earlier. What if I see it again?"

My jaw clenched. Something about her telling me she was scared shot through my entire being in too much of everything I couldn't even name.

"Dr. Duncan sedated you through the worst. The hallucinations should have passed by now, but I will help." I knelt for her to put her arms around my neck and helped her sit. One of her hands grabbed her forehead.

"The room is spinning." Her forehead fell against my shoulder. "I'm sorry. Give me a minute."

"Take your time." I caressed her hair. "The doctor left a cup. He wants a urine sample to test you. He doesn't think anything will show up, but he wants to be certain so he can detox you should he need to. If you hold on to my neck, I'll carry you in there."

"Oh, gosh. I can't let you do that. It's embarrassing."

"Please. Men piss in front of each other every day and we're forced to compare knobs every time. What do you have to be embarrassed about?"

She smiled the way I hoped she might. "When you put it that way, I'm so glad I'm not a guy. Can you imagine if women compared breasts every time we went to the bathroom together?"

I smiled this time. She seemed pleased like she'd tried for me, too.

"Blast." I snapped my fingers. "You mean to tell me they don't? You just ruined half my life's fantasies."

She chuckled. "Okay, you win, sir. I'll hold onto your neck, but I want to try walking."

I placed my hands beneath her arms as I stood and held her while she tested her feet. Her knees gave a bit.

"I'm sorry, I don't know what's wrong. Maybe the sedatives? I'm weak, dizzy."

"Does it help if you close your eyes?"

"No, but if I focus, you're like the still place after too long on a tire swing."

"Well, that's quite the compliment, love."

"Ha. You're welcome, sir." She held to me while we took each step slowly. She inhaled deeply. "My mama always told me that love isn't a moment of heat in a bed. She says it's a sick mate in a bed and the other helping without needing asked. The ugly moments. Not the raw lust. If I have to pee in front of you while I hold a cup, you'd better love me forever."

Though she teased, I saw the insecurity beneath her joke. She was modest.

"Don't worry. I won't look. You may have your dignity, Kinsley. I just want to make sure I'm on standby in case you fall in."

She giggled and turned when we got to the toilet. Her whole face morphed into a near meltdown.

"Whatever is the matter, love?" I asked of her sudden shift. Her chest rose and fell. Bloody hell. I remembered that look.

She burst into tears as though the enormity of everything crashed through her foggy mind at once. I managed to translate through another rain of emotion, only this time I wasn't an impatient dick.

"Oh, Klive! I need help lifting my dress and pulling my undies down, so I don't sit on my dress or pee in my panties." She wailed.

"I've had dreams of you doing this and *never* was *this* the way it happened!" The mascara began running. Oh, the irony of the entire situation.

I dipped to my knees and held to her waist, a big smile on my face.

"Forgive me for smiling while you lose control, I promise I'm not happy you are crying. I'm flattered. *I've* had many dreams of pulling the panties off the girl in the lift with the running mascara and attitude problem."

"Really?" She sniffled, smiling hope shining through unshed tears glossing her eyes. "You thought of me after? I mean even like that?" she asked what she shouldn't.

"If you must know, yes, and not a single dream is ruined by this being the circumstance, because I'll remove them any way you allow," I jested, half-serious. "Look at me, love." Look at me she did. I cleared my humor. "Kinsley, you are no less maddening this way than if we were to be in bed together for raw lust. I'll close my eyes. I won't look. This way you still get your fantasy when the time comes. It will. I promise."

"You are a good man." I closed my eyes under the best compliment I couldn't accept. "Klive, don't close your eyes," she told me. "Not yet."

I looked up from her stomach. She held my cheeks and bent down to kiss my lips. Dear, God. Kissing her in a raw moment of lust earlier was easier than this vulnerability.

A wise person once told me if you could explain a reason for loving someone, you weren't in love with them. You could *love* someone and dislike them, be *in love* with someone without necessarily loving them. You could *like* someone without either. To find yourself feeling all three was a bold sign. I liked her, feared I loved her, but the scariest was falling *in* love. The ultimate weakness. I wasn't ready to be so weak, but dammit if I didn't bend to her will in the most acute pliability when I kept a stiff distance between myself and most everyone. I was supposed to be driving her away, yet I pulled her closer. Which was worse?

She never opened her mouth. Her lips were so soft and plump. Her technique so sweet I had no choice but to reciprocate in the same *loving* manner. I'd never kissed a woman with affection in my entire life. This ... was like a great ballet. Serene. Hypnotic.

"And, now the ugly," she said as she straightened. I closed my eyes, relieved I didn't have to look at her after that, and lifted her dress from her ankles to her waist. She took the cloth from my hands, then held to my shoulder. Her breath caught as I pulled her panties down from each hip and guided them down to her ankles, unable to resist dragging my fingers over her skin the entire way. I was oh so close to tasting a whole other flavor of her body.

"You're doing so great, Klive. Don't get lax now, sir. Be strong for both of us and hand me that damn cup."

I smiled and walked on my knees, blind with my eyes closed in a bathroom foreign to me while she guided me with words broken by laughter as I knocked shit all around. I found the cup but knocked the bloody thing to the floor. No choice but to crawl on my hands and knees, I felt for anything round.

"Klive! Hurry! You're making me piddle because I can't hold it much longer and you're making me laugh!"

I chuckled. "Let's play hot and cold. Tell me. Hot or cold, am I close?" I crawled toward what I was sure was the door area.

"Cold. So cold."

I turned and felt around the base of the vanity.

"Warmer."

I crawled forward.

"Warmer. That's the trash can though." She giggled. "Nope. That's a toilet paper roll." Snickering. "Warmer. Nope. That's a stopper for the bathtub." She sighed in dramatic disappointment. "Cold."

"Damn." I turned back and explored all around the toilet.

"Hot! Hot! Hot!"

"Yes!" I raised what must be the cup while she laughed and chided me for making her lose more urine. I turned my back to her and sat on my knees while she filled the cup then the toilet in a way I needed to piss too. Can't hear a steam and not get the urge.

"K. I'm done. Filing paperwork now." She flushed and tapped my shoulder. I spun to face her. Her elbows perched on her clenched knees, chin cupped in her hands, panties stretched between her spread bare feet, pigeon toes. The stupidest grin took over my face. Dammit, Kinsley Hayes was adorable. We were eye-to-eye and hers were so bright and sweet.

"Yes, I'll love you forever. Happy now?" I leaned forward and kissed her, unable to resist.

She spoke against my smiling lips like her mouth was full. "Klive King, you can't tell me you love me for the first time while I'm on the potty." She cupped my cheeks and forced my face away, but I had the most heavenly high at her expression. "Sir, it's just bad form. You're supposed to save those words for the heat of the moment when I'm about to drop my panties in an uncontrollable frenzy. Seal the deal properly."

I grinned. "Noted. I'll only deploy the L-word when I need a convenient lie to make a home run. Anything else?"

"I need help."

"Clearly."

She bit her lip through a big smile.

"So, *this* is how love at first sight feels," I mused.

Her cackle echoed through the bathroom as she clapped her hands. "And just as absurd a concept, yes?" she asked.

"Absolutely. Now hold my shoulders and stand up before I accidentally propose while I'm down here." Was there a better sound than the full-bodied laughter from her lips? I closed my eyes as she did what I asked. I pulled her panties back up, but she asked if I'd take the dress all the way off because she wasn't comfortable sleeping in the material.

"Too tight," she said. "Scratchy."

I opened my eyes. "Do I have to keep my eyes closed for that?"

"No. But you do have to give me the shirt you wore earlier so I have something to sleep in. Do you think Delia has a spare toothbrush? My mouth feels gritty."

"Ah, think you can hold to the counter? I have a spare." I left her clinging to the granite while I dug a finger toothbrush from the inside pocket of my tuxedo jacket. "Here. Just wet it beneath the— *I'll* just wet this and standby for moral support." I handed her the package. She grasped the plastic as we made a team effort of breaking the brush through, placing the bristles beneath the water, my hand around her waist while she scrubbed and avoided my eyes in the mirror. Yeah. Intimate. *How did that work? Something so everyday innocent seeming too deep?*

I held her hair in one hand, her hip in my other when she bent to rinse and spit. I exhaled as quiet as possible at how this position went wayward in my devious mind.

"Hand towel, please, sir? Unless you wanted me to use your undershirt?" She grinned in the reflection as I realized she'd caught me checking her out. I pat her whole face with the hand towel to make her laugh. She plied the terrycloth from my fingers and slapped me, lost a bit of balance before surrendering to needing help back into the bedroom.

25 | ♂

SHE WORE HER HELPLESS frustration on her face as she tucked one arm around my waist, though she regained some strength by the time she stood beside the bed. Kinsley held to my shoulders once more as I peeled the dress up her body until she had to lift her arms. *Why did this have to happen this way? I wanted her in my bedroom! Beside my bed! Peeling her clothes away with my teeth, dammit!*

When the dress tossed to the same chair over my own clothing, she watched and looked back to me.

"I like the way that looks. Don't you?" she asked.

Son-of-a-bitch, I wasn't strong enough for this.

"Oh, Kinsley ...." I sighed and rubbed the back of my neck.

"Why can't we be together, Klive?" she asked what she shouldn't once more. "Why do you want me to be with Jase first?"

Such childlike, raw curiosity in her sudden sad sweetness. Every character she drove me mad with seemed to assault me in one long forty-eight-hour period.

"It's not like that, love."

"Then what *is* it like?" she asked, mirroring my words to her in the lift two years ago. She'd never forgotten. In fact, she seemed to recall that day with the same vivid clarity I had.

"It's ... it's ...."

"Complicated?" Her hands ran over my undershirt as if she imagined divesting me of the things separating our skin.

"More than you can ever imagine." I plied myself from her darkening eyes to retrieve my discarded shirt. When I offered the starched linen, she didn't pull the collar dangling from my fingertip, rather she held her arms in a way that she wanted me to dress her. I sighed again. "You're going to punish me, is that it?"

"Are you married, Klive?"

I burst out laughing at the absurd question.

"It's not funny, Klive. You bought shoes for a woman yesterday. You told me you didn't want to use me. That you'd enjoy someone best left alone. If you're not married, are you cheating with me while you lectured me about being loyal to Jase who isn't even my legit boyfriend?"

This woman ... she knew how to tear into me. I looked at her pretty eyes with so much sobering honesty, wishing to pour every awful secret that kept me from being with her into a burn bin and watch her light them on fire to destroy them until we were apart no more.

"I'm not married. Not dating. I told you I don't date. I meant that. I bought them for you. I was shopping after work when I just happened to stumble upon a mass of shoe boxes. Literally. I almost kicked them into the aisle. There I realized you, of all people, and a friend were testing high heels. Playing dress up. What a cruel joke. Couldn't get you off my mind and there you were like karma. I looked at the boxes on the floor and deduced you weren't the eight-and-a-half. You were so stunning. Gold looked amazing with your skin tone. I'd upset you that morning. I wanted to do something nice, but you got under my skin again, so I wanted back under yours."

"Mine? You bought me shoes before you bought the ones I wore tonight?" she asked, a flattered blush to her cheeks.

"Yes, yours."

"I'm under your skin?"

"Yes, love. Do you need a flashing neon sign?" I pulled the shirt closed and began buttoning the buttons over her pretty breasts in such a beautiful bra. Damn, I itched to touch second base. "Kinsley, you make my life so hard. Among other things."

Her eyes flared and so did mine when I realized I'd thought aloud.

"Klive King. Where are your manners, sir?" she asked me in my accent, but she loved the scandal. That much was written all over that pretty face.

"No bloody idea. Probably tucked behind this damn shirt." I gave in and tugged her against my body, so she was forced to feel the truth in my words stiff against her belly. "Maybe I left my manners in my pirate coat, or the hat you stole. You want my pants, next, love? Be the boss and command my every desire?" My palms traveled down to her bottom, filling with flesh against satin and lace panties climbing her ass crack. Her entire body released a silent invitation, eyelids fell a fraction, lips parted to compensate for heavier breathing. "You take souvenirs like a black widow killing my resolve at every meeting." She uttered a longing sigh. "Or perhaps I've left my manners in your mouth from the last time I kissed you and I need them back."

"Yes, I think so. Try there first. Then the shirt." She had such a bright look to her eyes, so much hope and excitement that I'd kiss her, obvious pleasure in how I dared touch her after contradicting my desire by tucking her away. Fact was, she was sexy as hell in my shirt and her panties, disheveled hair, tattoos creeping across the skin of her hands where she clung to me.

"I don't want you to be with Jase. I want to lay you down in this bed for sleepless hours until you're so depleted you sleep all day for recovery and become a slave to my command. But I have a job to do, you have school, and we need sleep."

"I'm not sleepy. Coach forbade me from running, and all my assignments are done except for the finals. I can play hooky."

"You'd so easily break Jase's heart and let me take you?" Grief struck a chord in her expression. I swallowed and nodded. "This is why I say what I do about Jase. You don't know what you want. I'm not monopolizing an indecisive woman and rushing to hurt an honest man."

"I don't need to have all life's plans figured out to know I want your mouth on mine in this moment, Klive. Please stop talking and kiss me."

If ever a line could hook a shark ... she reeled me in close with her hands behind my ears. My mouth opened on hers and Kinsley's tongue stroked mine like she wasn't going to let me walk away so easy. Every festering ache within my body welled to an explosive pain, desperate for a pressure release. She didn't attack the way she had in the downstairs lavatory during her high. She controlled our pace like the woman bitching at me in the store yesterday who was tired of men telling her what to do. My hands on her bottom gripped harder, everything harder, but none so much as the hardest moment of pulling away before I risked pushing her to the bed to tear her panties from her body and show her just how much I wanted to drive Jase out of her brain forever. *If he had her, would he be able to drive me out?* Fuck that. I kissed her harder, pressed back in closer to punish her for my idea, for maybe pushing me out when I couldn't get her out of my head.

"Mmhmmmm ...." She hummed into my mouth for more.

"Nmmummm ...." I argued back as we changed angles.

I felt her growl when I warred us apart.

"I'm not done, Klive!" she said as we lost contact.

"Oh, believe me, were this another time and place, situation different, I'd be just getting started. As it stands, how about we make a deal? I will kiss you again only if you get into bed and tuck yourself in while I use the facilities. When I come back, you have to behave."

"How do I behave, Klive?"

"Better than this, young lady. Take it or leave it. I will say no more on the matter." I whipped out the stern look reserved for the meanest of men under my charge. Her eyes flashed, but she wasn't afraid, she *wanted* my bad to play with a bad side she'd just hinted at. Her eyes narrowed as if she debated whether to respect my limits or provoke war to destroy them. I held to my best hard ass determination in fear that I'd met the one person I may have none against. I didn't want her to know or test power I refused to relinquish.

I wasn't ready!

She gave a defeated sigh and nearly fell as she wasn't one hundred percent just yet. I stabilized her and held the covers she pulled back so she climbed beneath them. While she nestled into pillows, throwing a minor fit I fought a smile against, I finally took the leak I needed, but jumped into the coldest shower hoping maybe she'd fall back asleep before I got in bed with her. *Was I really going to be able to handle that?* Everything that made me male was angry painful and bitching for relief when I dried off and redressed in underwear and the undershirt.

When I came around the bed to lift my side of the blankets, I started at her wide-open stare.

"I can't believe you're still awake," I said.

"No way I'm falling asleep without the promised kiss goodnight, sir." Her eyes lingered on my underwear loud and clear. If I wanted her, she was mine. *Take her!*

Not yet, dammit. Not yet!

Her gaze lifted to my eyes again like she'd been caught doing something awful. "Klive, I'm sorry if I upset you or broke your boundaries or something. I'll take what you give."

"That's what I like to hear." I chuckled as she rolled her eyes. The shirt went tight over her breasts when she turned to her back. *Shit!* My fingers fumbled in panic for the lamp to turn out the lights. I looked out at the darkness of the Bay and the faint lights across the skyline through the dark windows. The peak of my workplace lit like a bloody reminder of real life. I sighed and lifted the blanket.

"You are the only woman I've ever slept with. As in I've never gone to sleep with anyone I wanted to sleep with."

"Oh, Klive. You torment me."

"Only fair. You ready for more torment, love?" I rolled over to grant her lips the kiss I'd promised. She groaned and her whole body pressed in close against mine, rubbed against mine, desperate and aching. One of her legs wove around my waist to pin me against third base, ruining the effort of my cold shower in one hot moment. I couldn't help grinding against her.

Damn ... the guttural moan from her throat!

This was real! She was wide awake. This wasn't one of her dream states. I was in bed with the woman of my dreams while she kissed me in coherence! She wanted me!

"Please, Klive! *Please!*"

"Now, *that's* what I really like to hear. I was right about you, love," I mumbled against her delicious mouth. "You aren't very good at following directions."

"I could be," she flirted with danger.

"Dammit, woman." I kissed her lips several more times before I pulled back for air. "Kinsley, look at me." My voice and breathing were far from calm. "When I take you for mine, it will be right. It will be for only mine. Your body is ready. Your heart and mind I'm not certain yet. Let me make-out with you, maybe reach second base, but don't give yourself away just yet because I might not be selfless enough to refuse what I want so desperately. Please. Can you do that for me? Be strong for *me*, love?"

Her lower lip popped. "Only if you promise you're going to second base."

"No promises necessary, my sweet." She wasn't sweet at all. Maybe this *Sleeping Beauty* became a match for whomever awakened her first? *What a sinfully delicious fantasy!*

I went to second, toyed with third until I discovered new buttons to press and the way her various moans sounded.

She fell asleep contented to torment me for the remainder of the night until I became so weary, I finally caved into a deep nap with her resting in my arms.

26 | ♂

Two hours later, I strode into the police station with the authority of legal counsel.

"He in the back?" I asked.

"He is," a uniform told me and buzzed me through a door. "Wait. Gun."

I sighed and jerked the Sig from my back holster and set the pistol on the counter in front of the cop. He nodded I go on after he bagged my weapon. I strode into the corridor of cells. Taylor sat in the only chair, his mammoth arms crossed over his chest, dried blood on one of his knuckles. His stare bored into the bastard isolated from the over filled drunk tanks on either side. Taylor had those in his cell afraid to be near him. They watched him with wary caution as though he were unpredictable. He had his sights on one target, the very same one who'd landed him here. Kinsley's Monday night beer buyer.

When I leaned my shoulder against the bars, Jase didn't move his head, but his eyes shifted to mine. I smirked at the shitty expression on his face.

"She okay?" he asked, his jaw clenching and un-clenching.

"Yes. The strip didn't fully absorb. She's been sedated and taking IV fluids. Her trip's over." He nodded. I looked to the lonely soul inside the cell next door. "Guess who made bail?" I asked him like a friend, smile to match.

The guy, who appeared no older than twenty-five, shook his head. In fact, his whole body shook. I chuckled and told the bailiff I'd posted his bail. He left to double-check. Jase grinned with evil intent. The boy's eyes shifted back and forth between Jase and me, unsure who to be more afraid of.

"Your turn, Taylor. When you requested an underground earthquake, I threw in a volcano for free. Let's get you both out of here and see what you've got."

He stood and grabbed the bars like a prisoner wanting inside another's cage. After a deep breath, he snapped the meanest expression toward me rather than his prey. "King, I smell more than your fucking cologne."

"Did I forget to wash my hands?" I smiled, undaunted. Jase looked me up and down, noted the undershirt beneath my tux.

"Where's your real shirt?" he demanded.

"She needed something to sleep in. Where's yours?" I asked. His jacket was gone, maybe spattered in this guy's blood if the pulped cheek bone and bruises said anything. The wife-beater tank he wore was clean. "Don't worry, I only removed her panties to help her pee, but she begged me to do more. Whined when I turned her down. Good thing I possess superior selfcontrol. A lesser man may have taken what he wanted rather than satisfying her and tucking her in to sleep. She has *the best* moan. Does that make you jealous?" I wasn't asking Jase, though. I stared like death at the door of these bars to the man in the other cell.

Jase's knuckles glowed white, the tendons in his arms stretched tight, his breathing angry and fast. "I'm gonna kill you." He shoved away from the bars and forced himself to the furthest corner. The cell mates scattered to the other side of the tank. The bailiff returned to unlock the cell door next door to Taylor's.

"NO! No! I'm not going with him!" The guy inside pressed against the wall and shook his head.

"You're gonna die! You're gonna die!" an inmate chanted in sing song, pulling himself back and forth on the bars, high as a damn kite. "You're gonna die! You're gonna die!" Those beside him held to the bars like monkeys in a cage going nuts when one of their own got loose.

"Don't worry, I'm fairly certain the big guy was talking to me," I told the fearful boy. "Come with me and I won't let him hurt you."

The cokehead gave a dumb laugh. "That's 'cuz he's gonna do it himself. No one fucks with King and lives." He rocked against the bars and gave me a grin like a star-stricken kiss-ass.

"Quiet." I snapped my fingers. His smiling lips clamped shut. I refocused on the boy. "Don't listen to him. He's high. Come now."

The boy gaped at the coke-head's obedient reaction, shook his head as his eyes went wide. "Nuh, uh! I'm not going!" The boy flipped out when the deputy grabbed him by the arm to manhandle him toward the cell door. "I won't go near her again! I swear! I'll stay away from the bar and the girl! Please! I don't want to go!" He shouted, kicked, screamed, bit, punched. "I don't want out!"

"Come on!" Jase thundered and grabbed his bars again. "Let me out! I'll subdue his ass!"

"Jase, calm down," Rustin Keane barked. He strode down the corridor with angry authority, his gaze frosty toward me coming to his best mate's rescue before him. Jealousy was going around, was it not?

Jase fired a *fuck you* at his best friend. "You weren't there, Rustin! Don't tell me to calm down!"

Rustin entered the cell with the struggling bailiff and stunned us all when he evaluated for seconds, saw a vulnerability, reached in and sucker punched the boy so hard he went down in one fell swoop. The kid's head hit the concrete with a sick smack.

"Leave him," Rustin ordered. He flexed his hand as he exited the cell and locked the bars behind the battered bailiff. "Go to triage and send in your replacement. Don't let this perp out until the victim has had time to decide whether to press charges. Until then, we have just under twenty hours left to hold him," he said. The bailiff glared at Rustin, blood raining from his split lip and busted nose. Rustin smiled like a wholesome ray of sunshine. "It's hard when the new guy comes to your rescue."

When the bailiff left with his tail tucked, the cells went rampant with raging cursing and shouts to be released, shit about pigs holding them prisoner, I'm innocent, etcetera. Rustin held my eyes with another cold stare.

"You bailed *Jase* out. Why'd you do that?" His chin gestured to the bastard he'd knocked out.

"Couldn't resist screwing with him." I smiled and shifted to look at Jase. "Taylor, you're up. Let's go."

"I could've bailed him out for free," Rustin said. "You both belong behind these bars for your bullshit. We follow the law, not take matters into our own hands."

"Well, what a luxury, Deputy Keane. Ready to unlock the cell and free him? I didn't pay a penny, by the way. You're not the only one with clout among cops. In fact, you might find you earn clout way faster if we become friends rather than enemies." I shrugged. "Your choice. I just bailed out your best friend and kept the arrest from appearing on his record, but feel free to make me the bad guy."

Rustin's jaw fell as he jerked the keys to the cell and yanked the door open with the same animated irritation.

"Get your ass out here, Jase."

Jase stood and kicked the chair across the cell, scattering the group around him like panicked pigeons. He glared at Rustin as he came out of the cage. I stood back to give him room, but he walked right into my space like he wanted a quick entrance back into that cell. I smiled, hands in my pockets, my eyes holding his with zero intimidation. I won't deny he was scary. I saw what made Kinsley run from him, but I wasn't sorry for soothing Kinsley. Why apologize?

"Jase, back off," Rustin told him in new warning. "You don't want this. Especially if Kinsley has a soft spot for the prick. Imagine, you hit him, she sees damage, she's gonna keep running because you will establish yourself as the guy she can't date because he can't handle her around males. Big picture."

"I *hate* you right now!" he roared at Rustin, then turned his mean back my way. His hair unglued from the style he'd molded and now stuck to his forehead with the sweat beading from holding back. *Very good. Come on....* "Besides, I don't have to fuck with his face." I braced my stomach a fraction of a second before his fist slammed into my abs like a sledgehammer. *Yep. This was my guy.* Rustin chuckled as he kicked a trash can beneath me in time for me to throw-up. Only fair. I'd made Kinsley puke again; I wanted the same for absolution alone.

"She's *my* girl, King! Back the fuck off or next time, I'll break your neck before your security detail can come to your rescue. Invite him. I enjoy a challenge. One guy isn't even a fair fight."

Joey and Eric stood in the mouth of the corridor, but I held my hand up for them to stay put and straightened. Jase was smiling at them with his threat before I returned the favor with a knee to his balls.

"I've always wanted a friend to share everything with," I told him as he cupped his crown jewels and doubled over. "I'm not apologizing, because I'm not sorry for a damn thing. You lose her, it's on you. Better learn to keep your fucking hands to yourself. Don't make me get dirty, Taylor. Stand up!" I ordered and grabbed his hair, pulling more loose from the front.

Rustin tried to say something, but Jase knocked my hand away from his hair and we both shouted at Rustin in unison. "Stay out of this shit!"

Jase and I jerked our stares toward one another, pissed off, yet surprised.

"Know what I think?" Rustin said to both of us, disgust writ over his good boy facade. "I'm thinking maybe she deserves someone with higher moral character than either of you have put together. Like a cop on the right side of the law instead of hotheaded pricks aiming for her panties."

We both glared because neither of us could deny the truth in his words. I hated him for his honesty in every facet.

"Don't pretend you wouldn't aim for the same, *Keane*," Jase said through clenched teeth. His fist balled like he contemplated punching him, too.

"I don't have time for pissing contests," I said. "Some of us have adult lives to lead and can't spend every waking minute tanning on the beach and reading meters." Eric and Joey parted for me to pass. I pulled back to peer at Jase's raging expression, another smile warming my face. "By the way, you're welcome."

"For what? You just said you didn't pay a dime."

"For saving your girl from that prick and an overdose."

He and Rustin held my eyes with suddenly sobered respect. Jase swallowed, gave a little nod.

"Taylor, call me if you'd like to quit playing in the sand and make some real money." I jerked my chin and my guys fell in at my sides. The cop returned my gun and we left.

27 | ♀

MORNING CAME IN SUCH radiant brilliance I could no longer sleep for the joy that crossed my lips.

"Never seen someone so happy for intravenous fluids," a male said. *A male who* wasn't *British near my bed!* I freaked as I opened my eyes to see a stranger.

"Whoa, easy there, killer," Constance's voice said from my right. My face snapped her direction in confusion. Delia's hand patted my leg over the blanket I laid beneath. She sat where Klive had slept. *Tell me I hadn't dreamed him! If that was a dream, what the hell was he doing pulling my panties down to help me potty?!*

When I took a deep breath, I smelled Klive's cologne. I looked down. Klive's shirt. Not a dream. I sagged against the mattress in relief.

"Kinsley, this is my father, Avery Duncan. He's a doctor," Delia said. "He's giving you more fluids and wants you to stay and play with me today. One of your regulars from the bar dosed you with an LSD trip against your will. Thank goodness Mr. King was watching and got you cleaned up before the strip fully dissolved. I'm so sorry. I promise we didn't knowingly have drugs at my party." Shame colored her cheeks and dimmed the brilliance she'd had in her eyes last night. "Please don't sue us," she said. "We had the guy arrested, but cops can't hold him unless the victim presses charges. Jase didn't disclose your name, but he did go with his cop friend and his partner when they showed up. He's in the living room desperate to see you. I don't think he slept a wink all night."

"Klive left before Jase arrived," Constance said. "You are free to keep your night to yourself."

"Nothing happened, Constance. He helped me pee and brush my teeth. It was so romantic," I popped like a smart ass.

The doctor smiled and tapped the tube for air bubbles before I felt cold fluid travel through my arm.

"He left?" I asked. No use hiding my disappointment.

"He had to go to work, hun." Delia inhaled. "He sure smells good, doesn't he? This whole room smells like a man who makes money."

Her father chuckled. "That's because the man who makes the money to pay for this paradise is sitting right here, darling." They shared a smile. "Kinsley, if you feel up to it, I'd like you to get some food in your system. Anything sound good to you?"

My stomach rumbled then. "Anything sounds great to me."

He chuckled once more and stepped out. The girls looked at me.

"Will you let Jase in here? Or can I carry my fluids and sit with him, so he doesn't smell Klive all over?" I sat up to test my head and wits, my feet on the floor beside the bed near Constance. I held my temples. "I can't believe this really happened."

"Is your head still woozy?" She offered her hand to help me stand.

"Actually, no. Not at all. That's amazing. I feel so much better. My legs work again, my head is clear. The tiles aren't sucking any of you into hell. Why does anyone do that to themselves on purpose?"

"I've heard everyone reacts differently," Constance said. "Sees different things. I guess black scares you." She held my hand while

I walked into the bathroom. I stopped moving at the tone in her voice.

"Constance Marie, you'd better damn well not be accusing me of racism when you know better. I don't care if you are my tough black friend. I'm still rocking this henna, so that means I'm still your tough white friend from the wrong side of the tracks. We don't want those two to tussle over a lie in your head."

She snickered. "There's my girl. Now I know you're okay." She held my fluid bag while I pulled my panties down all by myself with no problems. Poor Klive. How embarrassing.

When I came back into the bedroom, Delia carried a comfy pair of shorts and an over-sized Daytona 500 tee.

"My dad loves racing; I love his racing souvenir t-shirts because they're super comfy. Enjoy."

She left us so Constance could help me out of Klive's shirt and into Delia's clothes.

"Kins, I'm gonna fold this one up and stuff it in my bag so you can snuggle in him whenever you want, sound good?"

I nodded; tears filled my eyes. Only another girl would understand that longing.

"I'm sorry for ruining your night, Constance. I'm sorry for so much. I feel too much. I've never done drugs, never slept with someone that way."

"I thought you said you didn't sleep with him."

"I didn't *sleep with him* sleep with him. I literally *slept* with him. I *wanted* to sleep with him. He wouldn't sleep with me. He says I'm not ready."

"He that big, huh?" she cracked and swiped at my eyes when tears spilled over. I blushed deep red in remembrance of him in his boxer briefs, pressed against me. My heart picked up, breathing changed.

"Whoa, Kinsley. As your purity partner, I'm sensing danger for your goals. Tell me, how bad is this? What do you want me to do? We never talked protocol; I didn't know we'd need to, but you're sweating!"

"Maybe it's residual side effects, Constance."

She arched an eyebrow, an unamused line across her lips. "Really? You gonna play like that? I told you the truth about Rustin even when I knew you'd lay into me."

"Let's just say, part of me is terrified I can't handle part of him. He's so intoxicating, I'm enthralled by the enigma. I can't stand the thought of wanting to be with him, but not being adequate to be with him in every sense. Does that make sense?"

"Sexy and equipped? Maybe that's why he carries himself so confidently. You trying to torture me?" Constance dabbed a tissue against my forehead and wiped beneath my eyes, the makeup creased there. "When we first made this pact, I didn't think you were serious. I took it on as a joke. Now, I'm realizing how...hell...I don't even know what word I'm looking for, but I've never met anyone like you at this age. Sheltered, maybe? Are you a *virgin*, Kins?"

"No. It's been almost six years. One guy. One love."

She blew a long breath like when she smokes. "Well, the body is an amazing thing, *cher*. Not saying there haven't been the few who were so big it wasn't pleasurable. They exist. Too much of a good thing isn't good. I am saying I'd find it hard to believe that if you saved yourself for love because of your commitment to God, that God would condemn you to misery by making the guy you want too big for you to handle. So...any idea what we're talking about?" She started naming produce and I lost my tears in exchange for laughter.

"I didn't see it, Constance. I felt it."

"With your hand! You little ho!"

"No! My gosh! Never! Against me. We kind of fooled around under the covers but over the clothes."

A wry grin crossed her lips. "And this is why you woke up with that huge smile on your face. Magic man, magic hands."

I groaned but nodded. "Magic mouth. On my *mouth*, woman. Like I said, nothing under the clothes."

"This is freaking adorable. You have a grown man acting like a horny teenager. Yet, you say he's the one who turned you down? As in he's forcing *you* to wait for *him*? Priceless."

"Yeah." I nodded and chewed my lower lip. "Bayleigh is gonna love the irony. I was worried about having to reject him. I've never been on this side before. In a way *I* feel rejected. Unwanted. Not desirable enough."

"You're kidding right? You woke up glowing because you fooled around. I'm pretty sure he wanted you. Says volumes about his level of self-control. I'm impressed. Besides, he didn't reject you the way you think. I saw him leaving your room this morning. He thought I was asleep on the couch. He pulled the door and held the knob; his head fell against it. He said, and I quote, 'I'm condemned to die by her hand'. Intense, right?" *Wow*. I nodded.

"Guess you and Jase have something in common now. This guy has you wanting him as bad as Jase wants you. Rebuffing you the way you rebuff Jase. Maybe you can forgive Jase for being pent-up and blowing his top while he tries to control himself with you? You haven't fooled around with *him*, have you?"

My eyes darted away while I wrung my hands.

"When?"

"Last Friday night."

"Good song," she joked. I managed a smile, but, gosh, the guilt. "Hey, up here," she said. "Do yourself a favor."

"Sure. What?" I asked, my eyes on hers now.

"Don't bang either of them until you know who you want to be with. Sex makes everything complicated. It's easier having meaningless sex if you never have to see someone again."

"You're nervous about tomorrow with Rock-N-Awe?" I realized.

"Yeah," she admitted. "I always worry about the afterthoughts. Or feeling like an afterthought. I'm not dead inside, but guys are so different, it's hard to tell. Do I pretend we never slept together? Do I walk in and take the bull by the horns? Pretend I had fun eating him up but now I'm full? So hard to pick who to be."

"As your friend, I say be yourself and let the chips fall where they may. Acting like someone else isn't your style. You're enough all on your own."

"Aw, Kins. Thank you. As *your* friend, I'm not upset with you for last night. Delia's awesome. Nothing like the rumors. I'm glad this worked out. However, as your tough black friend who has your back, I'd bribe a cop for five minutes alone with the guy who did this. I'm not upset with you; I'm upset you can't just go out and party like the rest of us seem to without attracting danger. It's not fair.

"Anyway, enough about him. You ready to brave the light of day?" she asked. "Delia's pool is wonderful, and she's got swimsuits galore. Even a one-piece she pulled just for you. We can make this fun. I'm taking the day off. Called in sick to Hooters to be with you."

"Thank you." I wrapped my arms around her. She caved into returning the hug though she hated them. "Let's do the damn thing."

"There's my girl." She held my bag of fluids while I shuffled into the bold and beautiful sunlight of the living area.

28 | ♀

JASE STOOD ON THE **balcony** with his elbows perched on the glass banister. His tuxedo pants and belt contrasted with the tucked wife beater tank he must've worn beneath the dress shirt last night. Part of his hair remained styled in place while the front pieces blew loose around his eyes and cheekbones.

"He's classic, isn't he?" Delia asked as she checked him out. "I tried to thank my father for this year's birthday present, but he told me that one was yours," she finished with a grin I shared. She held a tray with four pieces of toast, butter on the side with an array of different jams. "I'll carry this onto the balcony so you two can have the only breakfast I know how to make. Constance and I are going downstairs to swim. You're welcome to join when your fluids are finished. My dad can tape up the line in your arm. Let me bring you something to hang the bag from so the drip goes faster."

"Thank you for everything, Delia. I don't want you to worry. I wouldn't dream of holding you responsible for the actions of some predator. You and your father have been so kind to me. I'm grateful."

She kissed my cheek in passing, relief all over her.

Constance took the tray and set my fluid bag on top while we went outside. Jase twisted at the sound; his whole face warm when he saw me. Yup. Classic like he should have a cigarette tucked behind his ear, bad boy tired of dressing like a good boy handsome. Jase took the tray from Constance as I sat in a chair that hadn't been present last night. Delia brought a coat rack, gave a little shrug. We all laughed as she forced the fluid bag over one of the smaller hooks. Then Jase and I were alone. He set the tray down on the glass table in front of me and pulled a chair close to sit.

"Ja—"

His lips stole mine and drank my voice with the sweetest, softest kiss, his hand at my cheek, thumb caressing the stars on my temple. When he leaned back, he pushed his sunglasses on his head revealing eyes at peace. What in the world? This was the very last emotion I expected of him.

"Morning, beautiful. How you feeling?"

Flutters hit my belly. *Jase called me beautiful.* "I'm much better. Almost normal. Jase, I'm—"

"Kins, you don't have to say anything. I need to do the talking. I'm sorry. This whole thing made me realize the consequences of coming on too strong. Last night I spoke to you like I had some right to order you around. That wasn't fair. Rather than be mad at you, I'm choosing to be grateful King came to your rescue. How could I be mad about that? You're my girl. He kept my girl safe."

"He kissed me, Jase," the words tumbled from my guilty mouth. "I kissed him back."

"What's your aim, baby?"

"Honesty. Transparency." My hands went back to fidgeting.

"I let the redhead go down on me behind the bar before you showed up Saturday night."

I gasped louder than I should've, stunned, hurt. "We did more than kiss. We fooled around and shared a bed. No sex," I stammered in vindictive retaliation for the pain he'd stabbed in my back. So much for keeping my night to myself. "This sucks."

"Doesn't it? But if I told you Rustin was really who she gave head to, that doesn't hurt a bit, does it?"

I squinted at him in the sun like he was a dickhead moron. "No, why would it?"

"Good, because *that's* the truth. Now your conscience is clear and so are your feelings for me. I'm not insignificant to you, but maybe you might understand how I'd feel about another man fooling with my girl. What kind of jam would you like on this toast?"

What the hell? *The nerve!* I couldn't rip my glare from his cavalier demeanor. I'd been played like Tom Sawyer talking me into white washing his fence. This bastard.

"Orange marmalade."

He looked at all the bottles while I waited for him to realize.

"There isn't any," he said. He looked up at my face and leaned back in to kiss me again, a smile on his yummy lips, rather than giving into my angry moment. "You're a brat. I don't care how you look at me, I'm not leaving this balcony to buy you orange marmalade."

"Good, because I changed my mind," I said with a raise of my chin, crossed arms, careful not to mess with my IV.

"Is that going to be a regular occurrence?"

"Jase Michael Taylor, I'm not in the mood for your boyfriend bull. You just said you weren't going to be mad."

"I'm not mad. You are. I'm cool, baby."

"Shouldn't you be at work or something?"

He grinned at my agitation. I didn't *want* to want Jase at the same time as I wanted Klive. I wanted to be my simple self, dammit! He was right. Why be mad if he didn't matter? He freaking mattered. Klive was right to refuse me.

"Hate to disappoint, sweet Kins, but I'm off on Wednesdays. Sometimes I help on my dad's job sites, but only if he needs extra manpower. Delia offered to let me stay the day to live the lifestyles of the rich and famous with you guys."

"Wonderful."

"I agree. We might have to see if her dad has any shorts I can borrow. I didn't plan on staying."

"Well, *that's* a pleasant surprise," I said in bitterness.

"Uh, uh. We're not doing this. You had quite the experience last night, and the one you're upset about isn't worth the breath you waste on it. They said you hallucinated. That you thought the henna was coming off your skin to suck you and everyone else into the dark. Before we live it up, I need to know if you'd like to press charges. I told Rustin I'd find out. His partner doesn't know it happened to you. No names yet."

"If I press charges, that means what happened is public record, I can't hide what happened, or my name."

"If you press charges and your coach or anyone else drug tests you, you have public record of a crime committed against you. A reason for drugs to be in your system." Jase pulled his phone from his pocket to show me a photo. "You ever see this guy at any of your meets or practices? Maybe hanging out with any of the other girls? Courses?"

My brows dipped. I expected the regular who buys me beer on Mondays. "That's Brayden. He's a flirty idiot dating one of the girls on my team. I believe you labeled him Alpha Beta Asshat?" I arched an eyebrow. "What does he have to do with anything?"

"He's the one who got the guy into this place. He was working valet last night. Did you or Constance say anything to anyone about coming here?"

"No, well, she told Sara, but Sara was working with us, so she needed the info. She told Klive, but he was already invited and I kind of urged him to come keep an eye on me after he expressed trepidation because of people who sometimes attend these parties. Delia's good people, though. She wouldn't invite anyone bad."

Jase nodded. "Did you know the hostess before you arrived?"

"I've known Delia for a year."

"Let me rephrase." He chose a jam and spread mashed raspberries over a piece of toast. "Did you know who was hosting the party before you arrived?"

"No. I was pleasantly surprised to see her."

"Noted. Klive got you *out* of the situation. Alpha Beta Asshat got you *into* it. I'm interested in the perp, not the rescuer." He offered the toast. "You didn't say anything to any of your track friends or slip somewhere at school?"

"I don't want raspberry."

His lips twitched, his hand with the toast didn't pull back. "Sweet Kins, if you didn't want raspberry, you should've told me what you wanted when I asked. You didn't stop me from making a choice for you. If you don't like that, don't let it happen."

Jase's double talk pried my nerves like loose planks of a floor with rumored treasure hidden beneath. He might be disappointed when he found I was filled with more fury than gold. He gave another smug smirk at my stubborn stare, his chin tilting toward the toast like silent directions.

"Even if you showed to work the party," he continued, "still a pretty high-end gig. Might be something you bragged about in passing?"

"No, Jase. Bragging isn't my style." I took the toast with a bit of attitude. "Neither is talking to anyone from campus. I keep to myself. My sprint speaks for itself. I went to Constance's *after* I left school. She got the gig while I was at her place."

"Why do you keep to yourself?"

"What the hell? Is this an interrogation, Jase? You sound like a cop."

He smiled to himself and shook his head. "Kinsley Hayes, I asked you to be my girlfriend. Not sure if you know this, but I haven't offered anyone that role since high school. Judging by what you told King last night, you're going to be, it's just when that keeps me twisting in the wind. You also pretty much told me to get to know you outside my bedroom before I pull you back into it. I want to know what goes on in your life, your mind, why you don't talk to anyone from school. A girl like you must have a lot of friends."

I snorted in bitterness. "Fair point. Prepare to be disappointed." I looked away from his face to peer out at the white caps under the sun. The high-rises gleamed across the Bay. Daddy was probably so worried at my silence. "Apple butter," I told him. "On the next piece please. I love berries but hate seeds in my teeth. Guess I'll have to beg Delia for floss of a different type."

29 | ♀

"Thank you," I said.

He nodded then gestured he was listening. Dammit. This wasn't my favorite story to tell people like Jase.

"Jase, I thought things would be better after high school. You know, adults in an educational arena must be way more mature than the jerkoffs in public school. After all, we're all paying to be there. It has to matter more. Daddy used to tell me stories of his *Counting Crows* college years. The free thoughts and ideas, creativity and meshing of multitudes of personalities. I was excited to be around the growth, the sophistication, even the crap ideas for the different perspectives, not to mention I wanted to become something big so that Jack Carter would regret every mile he drove away from me when he left. I learned the hard way; this isn't the early nineties. You're no longer allowed to have a mind of your own in college without condemnation. I screwed up any hopes of being something to rub in that jerk's face. He's probably dancing on Broadway by now."

"Screw that guy. You are something big. I mean, damn, you told me you were courted by an Olympic scout. Did something bad happen?"

"I took a red shirt and sat on the sidelines my freshman year. I wasn't yet nicknamed, no one really knew me then. I kind of floated from course to course and flirted with the idea of joining a sorority. Daddy always told me to be careful joining anything that involved hazing, especially since I was on scholarship. I didn't want to risk it, though.

"Sophomore year the coach put me on the track, I drew attention, fans created my moniker. It was weird to have a spotlight. I'll be the first to tell you, I'm not good at it. The paper asked for an interview, and when I credited Jesus for the gift of speed, I inadvertently pissed off a group of atheists who wanted me booted from the team because I kissed my fingertip and held it up to the sky before I took to the blocks of each race. They didn't want to go to a meet and be subjected to my prayers. Even though it was perception on their part, I refused to stop because no way in hell I'm denying my faith to appease people who don't believe in anything. If they don't believe in anything, how could I harm them with my perceived public prayer?"

I realized I was talking with my mouth full, a big no-no and pet peeve of mine, but hell. I was getting mad all over again. Plus, Jase wasn't exempt from giving me shit about my faith. This was uncomfortable. I expected him to give me some smartass lip.

"Please, continue," he said, seeming interested.

"Daddy had to get me a lawyer. I was ready to walk away from all of it. I lost. I'm not allowed to point to the sky anymore before I take to my blocks. Thought about crossing myself like a Catholic to provoke their involvement and make a statement, but I couldn't disrespect someone else's faith and become a hypocrite. I'd be no better than those silencing me. I've never lost a race in college, but how do I feel like a winner when I lose something so open and shut as my first amendment right? It's all a sham."

"Hey, don't talk down on your achievements that way. They aren't a sham, they're impressive as hell. Not a single loss?" he asked in awe. "Really?"

"Not since high school. Twisted my ankle in my final relay and lost, same ankle I sprained in ballet. Same weakness you picked me up from at the course. Now I'm freaking grounded." I filled him in on Coach's lecture and rules. "So, you see, I'm like Achilles. There are several on the team who are salivating at severing that tendon so to speak."

"Kins, I may not always be on the same page as you concerning beliefs, but soldiers like myself are dying overseas to maintain your rights to freedom of expression and worship, so this pisses me off. I had no idea. I'm sorry. How did you lose? Seems an easy discrimination win."

"My lawyer got the school to agree to a deal; extend my scholarship from partial to full with the option to seek a master's degree in exchange for my keeping the whole issue on the down low if I kept my mouth shut. Neither of us wanted controversy. I wasn't as strong then as I have become now. Easily intimidated, unaware of the full scope of my rights. Trying not to rock the boat. I loved my moniker and the fans. I wanted to be liked so much. I was so grateful for the full ride, considering they'd signed me after I'd twisted that ankle in high school. I was a risk they'd gambled on. Guess Micro Machine had earned enough clout to be a winning bet."

"Did they do anything to the mob bullying you? Surely you weren't the only one with a slap on the wrist."

"The atheists were also bound to keep their mouths shut or else we'd go to trial. The university feared low enrollment of Christians or other prominent schools making me a public offer while shining in the press like the true indiscriminate institution. We were all bound by gag orders. Since the atheists couldn't brag about their victory over my rights, they set out to ruin my reputation. I tell ya, I didn't need a host of Psychology and Sociology courses to learn mob rule and human behavior patterns. Hate is contagious. People don't even need a reason. If someone else hates you and another really wants someone to hate, the enemy of my enemy is my friend. Same tactics, different faces, different causes, different aim, all drama fueled by the love of hate. Just like high school."

"Who bullied you in high school?" Jase asked, muscles and expression tight.

I nearly spit a sip of coffee. "You're kidding right?" He shook his head while I couldn't figure this man out. "Tyndall never told you?"

"No, baby. Nothing. Damn. Who?"

"You'll find out soon enough," I said, wondering how I was going to worm my way back in Marcus's good graces before tomorrow evening. "I don't want to talk about that while I'm pissed about this. You better feel special, Jase. I'm breaking the law by speaking to you."

"The gag-order?" he asked. I nodded. "Kins, you're giving me bad thoughts. Better behave because you look like a sexy outlaw with all this henna, messed up hair, smudged makeup. You're a pretty perp."

I smiled over the rim of my coffee cup.

He cleared his smile. "You still deal with harassment from that group all these years later? Mobs tend to find others after getting bored. You've kept my attention for years, but you're even more talented than I thought if you hold their rapt hate when these things shift where the wind blows."

Smart. As much as Jase wanted to figure out how my mind worked, I found myself enjoying prodding his thoughts to figure him out the same. He was more intelligent than he ever let on. Did he not want people to know? Had he made bad grades in school from sheer boredom?

He cleared his throat with a flattered grin, he licked his lips before biting the lower. *Attention Deficit Ooh Shiny* had nothing on those lips.

"You need another piece of toast? Seem hungry. Or maybe you're in the mood for meat. Steak, perhaps?" he teased, his eyebrows quirking like a naughty boy.

"Steak and eggs sound delish, actually," I said like a smart ass to buck his innuendo.

"My steak, your eggs. Sounds good to me."

I tilted my head on a laugh. My arm with the IV flicked a wrist against his bicep. He laughed and rubbed the spot.

"Shame, sir, but good job disarming me." I took a big, wonderful drink of coffee, swallowed the hot liquid contrasting the cool in my veins. "Most of that group graduated year before last, but rumors and legends remain. New ones started to keep the hate going like passing the torch in a fraternity.

"I don't hate all of it, still find glimpses of great in some courses. I really enjoy the Intro to Color Theory I'm taking to better appreciate Tyndall. I do have friends. I just don't enjoy school like I did when I went in with college rock angst wearing a beret with dreams of changing the world and being an educated adult with a title by my name.

"I'm bound to fulfill my scholarship or be on the hook for thousands of dollars I don't want my father to pay for. He wouldn't let me even if I told him I would pay. Track keeps me there, otherwise I'd probably be a bartender till I'm too old to hold a snifter. I'd rather deal with cantankerous drunks than small-minded crusaders pretending to stand for something as they tear everyone else down. On the track, there's something so vindicating about walking away the winner while their hatred for my success grows."

"Maybe I have something common with you," he said. "That bit about being the bartender. People freaking love you at the bar. I get it. Easier being that person. People love me as the singer of Rock-N-Awe, my body as a lifeguard, the flirtatious facade tourists want to screw like their Floridian fling. It's so much easier being that guy. Off American soil, I'm a different man. Hell, even you might hate me over there."

"Oh, Jase." I put my hand to his cheek. "You may bring out the bitch in me with your interrogation tactics, but I'd never hate you."

"You sure? Because you saw a hint of that guy come out on Sunday and you ran. You're still running. I have a feeling this is why you fooled around with Klive."

Well hell. "If you're hated over there, why keep going back?"

"I'm hated by the enemy because I'm an effective prick. I went back because of honor for my brothers. I'm here now, Kins. I'm done. Why do you think I finally asked you to be in a relationship with me? I got nothing holding me back."

"You're home? Not on leave?"

"As in discharged from duty, yes."

"You don't look happy about this, Jase." He had a haunted quality about his eyes.

"Okay, sweet Kins, let's not prod at my sore spots until you're mine to kiss them better?"

I nodded and chewed my toast. The heat and humidity felt so good against the cold guilt filling my heart. I hated the look I'd caused and how he pulled his glasses back down like blinds over a window he'd opened to me. Dammit. *Stupid Kins!*

"So ... those charges?" he asked, a little reluctant to prod once more at *my* sore spots.

"Jase, if Brayden has something to do with this, I might be inviting trouble by reporting his friend. I just told you about how I'm handled at school. I guarantee if I report this while I'm simultaneously absent from track, they'll victimize the bad actor and call me a drug addict, accuse me of doping because LSD will somehow become Human Growth Hormones. The NCAA will strip me of my record. The truth doesn't matter when enough people are shouting falsehoods too loud for others to fight against. I can't stand the thought." Then something occurred to me. "Jase, is this guy a student? Do you know?"

"We haven't looked that far into him just yet. He's got a few petty crimes on his sheet."

"Please look into that, or well, have Rustin find out. Whatever y'all do. If he is a student, he might tell people and screw me in any way he can since he lost out on his chance to physically do so, that bastard. I don't want the school to have any reason to drug test me."

Jase nodded, that mean look on his face for a flash. "Kins, do me a favor?"

"Name it."

"I need you to be very wary about who you allow to buy you drinks from now on. I understand you make your own, open your own, that sort of thing. I'm not implying you'd allow anyone the opportunity to sneak something in. Take it from a man, you don't know what goes on in a male's brain, baby. We think with the wrong head first, the heart last. You never know what might give him a false sense of hope."

I stared out at the waves again, swallowed against the dryness in my throat. "I hate this. Why can't I just mind my own business? Be myself like they get to be themselves? Run. Graduate. Move on and live life? Why can't people just be who they portray and allow me to be who I am? I don't want to hurt or upset anyone. Sometimes I'm so tired of everyone hating me. I'm so tired."

"Hey. Right here, Kins. Bring it in." Jase coaxed me into his big strong embrace as my throat thickened with unshed tears. "You have way too many who love you to think everyone hates you. Trust me."

"Jase." My voice cracked. "I'm sorry for leading you on for so long. I didn't know," I said against his shoulder, my voice muffled. "I really thought you were always sweet to me because of your love for Tyndall. I never meant to hurt you."

"Kinsley, I didn't mean you were leading *me* on. I meant that douche and any other like him. I'm sorry. If there's a contest for how many times a man can put his foot in his mouth around you, can I at least have one of your medals for winning?"

A hoarse laugh escaped my lips while tears dotted his shoulder, black with last night's mascara.

"How about we get your face washed, unhook these fluids, get you outta these clothes and into a swimsuit. That pool looks mighty inviting about now. Swimming is a great way to keep conditioned without running.... What do you say?"

"Yes, to all of the above."

30 | ♀

Constance took a sip from her umbrella drink. "Omigosh, Delia, how do you handle living this way?"

"Yeah, this is awful," Jase said from his lounger. He tipped a frosty beer bottle back to his smiling lips.

The Duncan's live-in staff supplied platters of finger foods, fruit trays, veggies, sandwiches and drinks galore while we laid in the sunshine.

Delia's metallic bikini reminded me of the one-piece Angela had worn out of the dressing room. All the talk with Jase about school bullies had Angela on my brain while I did a mental evaluation of her torment versus an entire group of torment. Whose was worse? Which was the bigger bad guy in my life? What did that say about Angela that I even had to ask? *I shouldn't have invited her to watch Jase!*

"You okay, Kins?" Delia asked, her face swiveled my direction.

"I'm okay. I hope you aren't doing all of this to appease me like you're afraid I'm going to do something stupid. I meant what I said. Plus, I'd hate to think of ruining our friendship. You don't have to woo me with finger sandwiches, but you could at least offer to put Jase in a loin cloth with a large fan while I eat my grapes."

They all chuckled. Jase rolled to his side, his beer passing to the concrete. He snagged my plate to steal a handful of grapes.

"Open wide." He grinned. My tongue ran across my teeth before I gave in to a big smile. I opened just for him to place a grape in my mouth. "One fantasy down, how many more to go?"

Delia lowered her shades to peer over the rims with big happy eyes. I tried to hide my amusement as Constance snickered to herself.

"Jase, you're not wearing a loin cloth or fanning me, so this doesn't count," I said.

"Next time I pass by the local loin cloth store, I'll be sure to pop in."

"Ha! I'm pretty sure that's the store your boss recommends to beach-goers." I filled the girls in on Jase's boss. "I tried on all colors of tiny scraps to cover my private parts. Should be easy for you to find something, if not in the men's, hit the women's section. They're on wholesale."

"Cheers to equality." Delia clinked her cocktail against Constance's.

"Ganging up on me now? Three on one. I like these odds." Jase grinned at all of us. We all slapped him while he laughed and guarded his stomach. "All right, I'll drop by that shop and see what I can find. Damn, ladies. You drive a hard bargain, baby."

"Damn straight," I said with a cluck of my tongue. "The harder the obstacle, the more gain for the pain." I quirked my brows, a little smile played on my teasing lips. Wow. Not sure if this was Klive's magic, but I didn't feel like myself. I felt relaxed, yet bold. Jase noticed, a little surprised by my flirtation. His lips lifted into a sexy smile like I'd asked for him to deploy those superpowers again. I shook my head at him and changed the subject. "So, Delia, your staff is fantastic. This place looks like nothing ever happened. I expected a few stray dollar bills or some trash, but nothing."

"Dollar bills?" she asked. "My staff? What do you mean?"

Constance and I pushed our borrowed sunglasses onto our heads and sat up in our borrowed bikinis. Yes, I'd even chosen a bikini over the one-piece. Delia looked back and forth between us. Jase sat confused.

"You know," Constance said, "the cash you were supposed to drop from the penthouse to the party people on your first-floor pool level?"

Delia jolted upright, ripped her sunglasses away, affronted. "What the hell are you guys talking about? The staff belongs to the whole building. So does this level. We just reserved it for private use for a couple days." She held to her chest. "Throw cash over the balcony? I'd never do something like that! I mean, we do charity work and fundraisers, but even if we did something like that, the wind would pick it up and toss the bills over the Bay or down to the other rich condo buildings. What good does that do other than make the rich richer or toss money into the ocean?" Her hands ran over her face. "Who told you this? Is that why people came?"

Not cool. I hated the idea of people only showing because of money. Especially when everyone here last night appeared to have plenty of their own.

"We heard it from the serving staff working for that guy who was bitching at Kinsley last night before you saved the day," Constance said. She swallowed. No way in hell she was flying Chad out on the flagpole. He wouldn't have crafted a rumor like that. Not his style. He did research to divide rumor from fact as part of journalism. Why didn't he divide rumor from fact in this instance? Seemed a pretty big mistake.

"Well, if you guys will excuse me, I have a call to make," Delia said. She pulled the bottoms out of her crack as she stood before storming inside and boarding the elevator. Guess the key was to get to the penthouse, not to keep others from using the elevator.

"Yikes," Constance said. We shared a look before Jase told me I'd just found a kindred spirit in high places. "What do you mean, Jase?" Constance asked, but her look wasn't pleased. She didn't want to share me. Aww!

"Easy, Constance. I meant with rumors. No one's taking Kins away from you. Damn, see, baby? You're loved," Jase muttered and looked at her like she was mean. Her whole face changed, and she hung an arm over his shoulders.

"Thanks, Jase." She kissed his cheek and ruffled his hair to draw a reluctant smile back out of him. "I feel so bad, but I don't about that catering guy. He was bad for business. Pretty sure she wanted to fire him last night but couldn't in the heat of the party. I'd like to know who started the rumor if only to scare them into never doing so again."

"If you want to scare anyone, maybe Kins should bring you to school for a day. Like a lesbian bodyguard. That's hot," Jase said about his own thoughts. Constance and I both reached out and slapped him in different areas. He stood and grabbed both of us under each arm while we squealed. The three of us plunged deep into the crystal blue water.

Delia sauntered back outside and stepped into the pool like the queen of everything flicking an ant from her arm. "Thank you for saying something. I hated that guy anyway. If you want jobs like the party I hosted last night, minus free-falling cash bonuses, I will recommend you both to the next company we use with a good review."

Constance thanked her. They conversed while Jase eased me slowly away from their space, his hand on my belly, his body at my back. Something about being in the water, his hand on my bare skin, I don't know, everything fired up like the moment we lost ourselves in the park on the blanket before the ranger had ruined everything.

"Jase, what are you doing?" I whispered and watched the girls drift further away as he pulled us toward a corner of the pool with a waterfall spilling off the edge of large rocks.

"What's wrong, Kins? Or is too much right with the way this feels?" he asked, his voice echoing beneath the heavy waterfall. He sat me on a small ledge. Jase ran water out of his face as he pushed his hair back.

"This is boyfriend behavior, sir."

"I know." He grinned like a smug smart ass. "Didn't someone say you should dress for the job you want or act like the man you want to be? Something like that."

My face surrendered on an indulgent smile at how adorable he was. "You're gonna get worse, aren't you?"

"Never give up, never surrender. The only easy day was yesterday. Face it, I'm programmed to succeed or to die trying. You want me to kiss you so bad, right now, admit it."

"Nope."

"That's right. Immune to my charm." He swam near, his face coming so close I backed away. He closed the space and ran his nose against mine.

"That's right." I breathed a little shallower. "Superpowers. Is it even safe to reveal all that badass in public, Jase?"

"Your voice betrays you, baby. You can make jokes, play your games, but you are seriously not playing about how I make you feel. I've studied this body for far too long not to know how you lean closer when you should back away."

I gasped, he pounced. Before long, my legs were wrapped around his waist while he held me and toyed with the string tying my top on.

"All right, I confess, you make my mind visit bad places, but even if I wanted to act on those with you, no way in hell I'm doing that here, so you need to chill. I'm not ready," I told him in thought of

Klive's words. Klive was right. My body was begging to get back in the sexual saddle. My heart and mind were at odds. A whole civil war raged inside my soul, no guys necessary.

"You win this round, sweet Kins." He nipped at my lips a couple lingering times until I whimpered in desperation. His lips stretched. "Never mind. I'm the winner."

"Haven't you heard I'm a sore loser?"

"I dare you to be and see what happens."

My eyebrow arched before I disengaged myself from his tempting body. Jase knew how to hold a woman too well to ignore his experience had trained him in the art of seduction.

Can't see the forest for all the trees.... Yeah, I was struggling to see clearly until Dr. Duncan came outside.

"Kinsley, time for another round of fluids," he called.

I swam out from under the waterfall as red-faced as a lobster.

He chuckled when Jase came out from hiding.

"You two keeping it clean?"

"On my honor as a soldier, sir." Jase gave a loose salute.

"Right. Because soldiers have a reputation for chastity," the doctor joked. I pushed up out of the pool and kicked water in Jase's face. Delia's father touched my forehead. "You seem to be feverish, young lady."

Yep, I blushed deeper because this man knew I'd shared a bed with Klive and now my lips swelled from kissing Jase. Delia's father offered me a towel and took me back inside.

"I'm not a bad girl," I told him as I followed. "I don't do drugs. I don't sleep with anyone. These two just came out of left field at the same time. You may want to examine my neck for whiplash."

He turned the light on inside the media room with movie theatre seating and red carpeting. A screen dominated the entire wall. The top row wasn't stadium recliners like the three lower rows. The top row he ushered me to consisted of a long, overstuffed sofa spanning wall-to-wall. Several blankets and pillows laid all over. The coat rack sat beside the far wall.

"Ms. Hayes, you don't need to explain to me. Please be seated." He gestured to the spot beside the coat rack. A new bag of fluids hung from the hook, a tube dangling from the end. "Your friends and my daughter have more than reassured me of your good name. If you were the things you just said you weren't, do you think I'd have invited you to stay in my house with my daughter? She doesn't have many genuine friends. Most are leeching off her. Something tells me she has found a good thing in you and your friend, Constance. Real people." He removed the tape from my arm, unscrewed the cap he'd placed over the IV line and inserted a fresh tube hooked to the full bag. The television remote placed in my hand while he told me to get comfortable and take a nap if I felt sleepy. "Ms. Hayes—"

"Kinsley, please."

"Kinsley, you don't seem to rest easy. I want you to sleep. Constance says you have no schedule at the moment. You're safe. Relax and let me and your fluids do our work."

"You have a good bedside manner, sir."

He thanked me and turned out the lights. The darkness and crisp cool air conditioning called the sandman from his daytime hiding place. Jase sneaked into the dark room with a little finger to his lips as he shut the door behind himself.

"I heard him tell you to take a nap. If you don't mind, I'd love to get in on that action because I didn't sleep last night. Tyndall says I make an excellent Teddy Bear."

I smiled and shifted so he could lie down on the deep cushions. He patted his chest and helped me get situated so my fluids weren't obstructed. Jase pulled a snuggly blanket over us.

"You're tense, Kins. Just relax. I'm not gonna make any moves until you tell me you're ready, but I might flirt with the line you've drawn. Just being honest."

"Thanks for the honesty." I grinned against his chest. His fingers found a rhythm of stroking my hair away from my face.

"Rustin told me about y'all running into Sheriff Ansley's spoiled daughter. I don't want you worrying that I'd screw this up for a trashy sex-tap. You have nothing to worry about in case you were worried about having eyes on me tomorrow."

I sighed. "It's not having eyes on *you* so much as on *her*."

"If I'm telling you there's nothing there, I mean it, baby. Let me see your eyes. I need to see that you understand." He tipped my chin and tilted his head for a better look, but the room was far too dark to see anything other than shadowed shapes. Thank God none of them had hands from hell.

He grumbled and reached over the edge of the couch. His phone lit and blinded us for a second. He used the display to see me. I gasped and stilled his phone. The wallpaper was a picture of us from the beach. He'd been kissing me after my fake tirade of jealousy.

"Rustin took it in between his fit of shits and giggles. See how cute you are with me, sweet Kins?"

"Come here, you." I cupped his cheeks and brought him to my lips for a few sweet pecks. "We do look pretty cute together. I can see it."

"What did I tell ya about dressing for the job you want?"

I gave him a light pat to the chest. How did I reconcile sleeping with two men in less than twenty-four-hours, no sex necessary to bring both to the point of wrapping me in their arms?

Maybe my mama was right about not giving away my ice cream for free.

31 | ♀

DELIA POUTED WHEN THE time came for Constance and me to leave her house.

"If we spend too much time together, we'll get tired of each other," Constance reasoned. "I get tired of Kins all the time."

We all chuckled. "Hence why we can't be roomies," I joked. Constance stuck her tongue out.

Delia shoved a sexy ensemble to Constance she insisted would make Rustin putty in her guitar-playing hands.

"Kinsley, for you," Delia said, "let's go little black dress so we don't steal from the henna. The bitch you told us about will probably be overcompensating. Let her. This dress is so simple it says you don't even have anything to compensate for. We get to play with your hair and makeup, though."

We played girl with an only child who'd always longed for siblings but whose mother had died when she was too little to remember. Delia had a chummy relationship with her father like I had with mine but bucked his rules all the time with her wardrobe.

When we got into Constance's lone vehicle in the large back lot, she sighed. "I'm a hypocrite. Here I am always removing people's prejudices when I was totally prejudiced against Delia and her family. How sad about her mom."

My throat was thick too. Delia was lonely and longing for real friends. "I'm glad we came even if that crap happened to me. Maybe God put us there for this reason. We both know we don't make friends with anyone easily. She fits like Bayleigh and Tyndall."

"She does," Constance admitted. "God didn't make that shit happen to you, though."

"Yeah, but He does use all things for good, turns the enemy's shit around on him."

"So, you're saying God is passive-aggressive too?" She chuckled.

"He has a sense-of-humor for sure. I don't think He's laughing at my behavior, though," I said, convicted, ashamed for lusting, let alone over both men.

"Ask for forgiveness, move on. Wallowing is like a rocking chair. Gives you something to do but gets you nowhere."

She put the car into drive while I took my phone out of the glove box to see the battery was dead. I'd have to charge when I got in my own car. Twenty minutes later, she dropped me off beside the Honda.

"Looks like you'll have to butter up a certain cowboy to deal with those parking tickets," Constance said. "I'm sorry. Who the hell knew we'd be gone this long? I'll see you at the bar in a bit. Don't worry about Gus. I'm gonna give him a call so he lets you inside. We'll deal with Marcus when we get there. You're gonna blow her ass out of the water."

"So are you, Constance. I'll see you later. Thanks!"

She honked before joining the city traffic. I tugged the tickets from beneath the windshield wiper. Guilt at being in trouble assaulted my courage. I'd never gotten a ticket before! Never taken drugs before! Never slept with anyone before! Never been in a love-triangle! I'd have a harder time playing *Never Have I Ever* next time....

When I walked up to the bar, our bouncer, Jarrell, did a double take, prepared to stop me.

"Whoa. Is this a good idea, Kins?" Interesting he didn't outright refuse the way I expected. Constance must've made good on that call to Gustav.

"I have no idea what you mean by that Jarrell, but if something bad happens will you do me a favor and take out the trash?" I fluttered my lashes to draw a chuckle outta him. "You should consider this a visual example of just how much faith I have in your ability."

He shook his head but opened the door. "You keep dressing up you're gonna cause me to up my game, Little Red."

"Oh, you mean this ol' thing?" The little black dress was as short as the leather mini I'd worn on Saturday, only the skirt had a slinky flare away from my legs. "What's the point in doing anything if you aren't doing it all the way? See, I'm helping." I waved and walked in, my shoulders back, telling myself not to lose my nerve. Jase's rough, sweet voice covered *All or Nothing* by Theory of a Deadman. His eyes closed as he sang into the mic and strummed his guitar alongside Rustin. White pocket tee, ripped jeans, unruly hair tamed and combed back, leather band wrapped around his right wrist as he gripped different places on the guitar. Too handsome. *Was Angela really so evil for wanting him?* Here I stood enthralled like the distance between Jase and me still existed in every sense. *That* was the same guy I'd fallen asleep on at Delia's? *Those* brawny arms held me, stroked my hair, hummed low and soft until I slept?

Ugh. Jase's voice wove a spell like the sirens in Homer's *Odyssey*.

Stay calm and don't go soft! She's in here somewhere and didn't come to play nicely. Guard up.

I walked to the bar feeling eyes following from the tables I passed. Wonder if they stared because I was me, or because I still bore the insane henna tattoos? I tried to ignore them, though my heart was in my throat, I was so nervous. Where was Micro Machine when I really needed a boost of bravery?

"Hey, Garrett, Tequila Sunrise, please?" I asked.

"I'll be damned." He leaned on the bar and smiled with no shame in looking me over. "Aren't you a sight, Kinsley." I looked down, tracing a knot in the wood with my thumb nail. There was something different about taking a compliment from a man who normally had no beef about busting my chops when we were on the clock together. Garrett scoped me differently too. I didn't know what to make of his inspection. He mixed my drink and pierced two cherries with a toothpick umbrella he set on the rim of my cup. "You're really quiet *and* quite sexy tonight, Little Red Running Hood."

"Well, thank you," I stammered through a smile. "I'm flattered, but are you saying I'm quite sexy *because* I'm quiet?"

He laughed and shook his head then took an order down the way without confirming or denying. Well, that was helpful.

I crossed my legs and swiveled with my drink in hand to face the band as they began a new song. Rock-N-Awe's drummer, Mel, looked over the crowd. His jet-black hair gelled in a fauxhawk. Tattoos covered his arms, neck, spreading down his fingers that clenched and opened as he beat different patterns of sound from a little box near his feet. Rustin stood before a keyboard and played notes as an electric guitar cut through the signature intro of *In the Air Tonight*. The single electric note hung over the crowd as the bar and I looked for where the sound came from. The only thing Jase held was that rain-shaker thing as he leaned forward to begin singing. Dan plucked a bass chord every now and again, but that missing electric guitar eluded the audience while the sounds played with Jase's voice, Rustin's voice joining on background. While Jase shook the instrument, I didn't miss the grin he cast my direction in knowing. Ha. So, Rustin must've told him. *What the hell was that thing called again?*

Mel jumped up to sit behind the drum kit, but the bar drowned the men singing as Constance came forward with her bright red electric guitar resting against her right hip. She donned a wireless mic and joined the guys singing while we all cheered. I held my drink up, my other hand in the air while I shouted her praise with everyone else. My life-size Christie Barbie doll was decked in red leather, bangles, and badass makeup. Henna tattoos covered her *cafe au lait* skin. She parted her red lips on a huge smile when Mel beat those iconic drumbeats and the whole bar joined their chorus. I was so caught up in the fun, I didn't see Angela until everyone sat back down while she was one of a few who remained standing.

My mouth dried. She was front and center but whirled before strolling toward the bar. Her pageant smile pinned me with a direct hit. She'd brought the shit. Her skirt looked so tight I wasn't sure she could sit without the material splitting, yet she cast that smile to the guy on the stool beside mine and sat in his willfully abdicated space without nary a tear to the straining fabric.

Jase and all of Rock-N-Awe watched like the whole band sensed trouble. Psh. *I could play nice. Really, I could.*

Heads snapped in our direction, curious as to what the band was staring at with the intensity they were. They sang another chorus like a foreboding omen.

Angela crossed her legs to further test the threads on that skirt. Men around us appeared to be waiting for, *praying for*, the same damage. Her red stiletto rested on the floor while I still wore the heels Klive bought me. She twisted her stool, so our knees almost knocked. Angela looked at my feet before her crystal eyes rose the length of my body, landing on my lips. Hers parted once more.

"Love them shoes. Never pegged you for tattoos. I thought you'd be workin' today," she said.

My glossed lips curled in genuine pleasure. "Nah, I decided I'd rather watch tonight."

Apparently, others were in the mood to watch as well because eyes darted between the bar and the stage unwilling to miss any impending action. Was our clash so obvious? I wasn't even being mean. I was in a good mood as this didn't seem to be as scary as my imagination had been.

"Uh, huh ... I bet. What's not to love about the view?" she asked.

We watched the band transition to a cover of Blacktop Mojo's version of *Dream On*. Constance took center, Jase stood beside her rather than sitting any longer. Rustin held an electric guitar now. No keyboard. Dan strummed chords on his bass like a harp player. Mel remained behind the drums. Constance cupped the mic while she sang with such a rough, bluesy scratch injected to her strong voice. Jase strummed an electric guitar here and there, sang her backup and harmonized on the chorus. Mel beat the hell out of the drums as if he were releasing steam. Like me on a run. *I could use a run.*

Angela had to shout over the patrons singing with the performers. I hated that I couldn't even focus on Constance because of Angela's axe to grind. Or was the axe mine since I'd invited her? I snorted to myself as the intensity of the song softened with the volume Constance sang. Angela's voice rose over all others and she cupped her mistake with a charming giggle. Patrons adored her while I was put in the bitch role when I laughed at her instead of with her. Ugh.

"I guess they like me," she simpered. I rolled my eyes. "Damn, listen to that voice. Reminds me of high school talent shows and when he sang the National Anthem before football games. That helmet tucked under his arm while he wore his pads. His ass was fine then, it's better now."

I swallowed my irritation as I remembered every account I'd forgotten. Then I thought of his ass. The scars all over his skin. Yeah, she saw the Floridian fling, I saw the raw ugliness of pain he must conceal behind songs like he sang now. She was exhibit A of the truth in the words he'd told me yesterday about playing roles people loved. He watched me while I watched him, our eyes holding long enough before he sang into a shared mic with Constance. Guess she'd disconnected the wireless mic for the theatrics of holding the mic well away from her face as she screamed the last chorus.

"Amazing, even *you* aren't immune to men anymore, huh, Kinsley? It's nice that you have tried so hard tonight. We're kindreds, you and I. Women of the *same* caliber. Like old times." *Old times? As in she's always viewed me as this brand of competition.* "If that's even possible," she finished and rolled her eyes.

I ran my tongue over my teeth before gritting them. Yup.

Maybe we both held axes.

32 | ♀

ANGELA LEANED ACROSS THE **bar.** "Garrett, honey. That is your name, I hope. Hard to read when you're so far away." He hooked his thumbs in his red suspenders as he came to stand before her. He pulled a suspender away from the embroidery over his chest. She traced the lettering with her glittered claw and covered over the 'Gar', so they only showed as rett. "Anyone ever call you Rhett?"

"Kins does," he lied and shot me a wink. Lord bless him!

"What are you drinking?" he asked her.

"Beer." She told him what kind, then, "Two tequila shots."

Crap. Drinking a Sunrise was one thing. Taking shots, quite another. Maybe they were both for her? Garrett set the glasses down before Angela, popped the cap from her brew then filled her shot glasses.

"Thank you, Rhett." She smiled at him as she pushed the second shot glass in front of me. 'Rhett' eyed me for good reason; Marcus never wanted trouble, yet here she was, throwing a damn gauntlet in my face!

I asked him for a beer, too. He nodded. "On the house, Little Red," he said.

He passed the beer, and I took the shot, chasing the liquor with the beer right away. This cheap tequila was awful. I downed a swig of the beer after spitting the shot into the bottle. Yuck! I held my poker face, though. At least the shot was diluted with the beer. Angela followed. I watched her throat move as she swallowed. She didn't seem to notice that I hadn't.

She licked her lips that lifted at the corner, her eyes holding mine without pause. "Rhett, be a doll and pour another round for both of us." She didn't even look at Garrett when she asked.

Unflinching. Shit.

Constance transitioned with the band into another song I didn't recognize. One of those bluesy alternative hipster type songs only uber cool music circuit peeps might know. Wish I did now so I had something to hang my hat on other than running really fast. Then, I remembered the reason I invited Angela. I met her smile with a smirk of my own. Marcus was gonna ground me for life, but alright, bitch, let's play. I knew how to take a shot.

"Rhett, care to spare some salt and lime wedges to help with the bargain basement brand she's buying?"

Angela scoffed. My smile grew. This was going to be fun. Garrett set the cup of limes between our shot glasses. Saltshaker next. I ignored the subtle shake of his head.

I licked slowly between two fingers, suggestively because I couldn't resist being that type of bitch. Can't fight like a lady if I'm not up against one. I sprinkled the salt on my wet skin, again licked slowly, glancing behind her as Jase's gaze was heating as he and Rustin walked up behind her. My eyes smiled at Jase, then at hers that smiled back, but also held intrigue, challenge, excitement. She fed off the reaction. Let her. I knocked the tequila to the back of my throat and sucked a lime wedge, never breaking eye contact with her.

"Hey, baby, will you sing *Fake It* next? For me?" I asked Jase behind her, still holding her eyes. Mine had a direct challenge in them. She glared at me, tossed her shot back and grabbed a lime wedge. My grin expanded to an all-out beam as she nearly gagged on the sour taste. I glanced at Jase. He looked at me like he wasn't sure what to do, though he had that lopsided grin across those lips. Rustin, too, looked dumbfounded, but I saw mischief in his eyes; the kind of guy who appreciated a good cat fight. Just like probably half the audience we'd garnered. I avoided looking around because I knew Marcus was pissed if he was watching.

Angela deployed her seductive smile, uncrossed and recrossed her long legs in her short pencil skirt, turning on her barstool. She ran a fingertip down Jase's chest. *Nope, I was no longer chill.*

"Baby, I didn't know you took requests ... I've been saving so many just for you, it'll take *all night* to recount each one." She turned to Rustin. "Hey, Officer Keane. I'm looking forward to that dinner date tomorrow." Her eyelashes fluttered while visions of plucking each fake one off her face dallied through my mind.

"Two shots of Patron for the ladies, please?" The accent snapped my attention like an owner calling his dog. I loved and hated my whirling emotions and immediate loyalty. My heart threatened to rip a hole straight through my dress. Hell if I could allow Angela to see. I prayed the flush in my cheeks may be from the alcohol. I looked down the bar. Klive King leaned against the wooden slab, smiling like a rogue in the mood for a little action, admiring the scene playing out before this group. *This man ... so eager to feed my fire.* Guys around him patted his back in appreciation. I nodded at him like Angela wasn't the only one battle resumed with. No use denying we had an inner war we each fought against the other. Eventually sexual frustration would morph back into a mutual attitude problem.

"Rhett, I need enough for the four of us," I told him. I shot Klive a look that dared him to buck my demand. "Go ahead and give big spender one as well."

Klive raised his eyebrows with a wry smile as he told Garrett, "By all means give her anything she wants."

Constance and Rock-N-Awe began Dorothy's *Gun in My Hand*. Garrett chuckled and nodded at Klive as he pulled top shelf. Damn, this was a bad combo. Klive and Angela amplifying everything at the same time? How could I play nicely with either of them? I swallowed at the recollection of the very last time I'd been with Klive. Magic hands, lips, words. Shit. I risked a glance down the bar at Klive. He looked past us to the stage, nodded with Constance belting the chorus, looked back at me like he'd requested that song himself. He held the shot glass up in toast to me, tossed the liquor back, slapped the glass face down on the wood, his eyes holding something I couldn't read. His head tilted toward Garrett pouring tequila in our glasses. I had to look away.

"Oh, Jase," I sang with a slow crook of my finger. He cursed and walked to my side. "Offisah Keane? Would you help me with somethin'?" My voice mocked Angela's southern drawl. She was very unimpressed.

Rustin's eyebrows quirked, unsure of where I was going. I stood so that Rustin could stand to my right. We were gathering a crowd now. Angie also seemed unsure of where I was going.

I licked my wrist, sprinkled salt onto my skin, though unnecessary with fine tequila. I handed the first shot to Rustin, then offered my wrist to his mouth.

"Oh, shit, man," he said to Jase before seizing my hand with a huge grin. His tongue ran indulgently over the salt, that naughty boy. He tossed the shot and smiled like an idiot while he grabbed the lime wedge. No hiding his glee. Angie was pissed. She moved to grab Jase, but I blocked her hand. I waved my finger and said, "Nuh, uh, uh .... It's not polite to touch things that aren't yours." Rustin wasn't mine, but how could I resist playing the player who could barely rip his eyes from my boobs to grin at me?

There was a collective 'Oooh!' from the guys watching. My pride gave a mental fist pump in triumph. I knew she was fuming now.

I also knew Klive hated 'Jase's sidekick' maybe making headway. The sidekick didn't mind taking one for the team, that much read loud and clear.

"You wish, Kinsley Hayes," Angela said, her smile replaced with incredulous anger. Her eyes dared me to put my money where my mouth was. Better still, I'd put Klive's money into my trash talking mouth.

I licked my left wrist and poured the salt. Jase stole the shot glass, seized my wrist and sucked without needing an invitation. Tingles shot to my toes as he played his tongue against my skin. He held my hand and tossed the shot back with his free hand before smiling triumphantly at my temerity while he sucked the lime.

"Well, Angie, it's just you and me. You first," I challenged.

She sat up straight, squaring her shoulders. She wasn't going down without a fight. To my ultimate dismay, she pushed Rustin aside to stand and walk down the bar like shopping the row of men. Klive gave her a neutral expression while I fought tooth and nail to calm my raging heart, the anger coloring my cheeks as she grabbed his tie. *Jesus. Please. I don't want to hate her so much. I hate her more than anything!*

The guys around him encouraged him to take her invitation. He held both hands up but shook his head at her. She twisted side to side with his tie in her hand. Multiple men stared at her ass.

"If that's the way you want to play," she said loud enough for me to hear, "you don't have to do anything."

I wasn't sure what to make of his expressions with her. He didn't seem pleased but wasn't mean. He avoided my face to an obvious extent as Angela grabbed his raised hand to lick his wrist, glancing up at him. I tried to appear unaffected, but I couldn't breathe. Klive had a dark look. Lust? Desire? Anger? *What was that look? I didn't know him well enough to know yet!* The only good I could draw was that he looked at me differently than any of this from day one.

She sprinkled the salt on his skin and licked again, then slammed her shot back. She looked at Klive, beamed that winning smile at him, suggestively sucked that lime in her mouth, keeping his gaze. She then looked over at me in triumph. Another collective sound, this time for the blow she'd dealt me. My, my, my, what a death blow if ever.

Jase seemed to have stopped breathing and his whooshed on a look at me. He appeared afraid for Klive, but his whole face morphed to something victorious. Nice.

"Bump it," I told Garrett. He was nervous as hell because he knew the ways Bayleigh and I had discussed Complicated Moonlight. He grabbed the tequila and doubled my shot. Screw them both. If that's how he wanted to play…. Micro Machine rose like the feminist bitch Klive urged me to be. I grinned at the spectators around us and waved my hands toward myself that they not hold back. I took worse shit than this when I came off every heat on the track in first place.

Angela arched a perfect eyebrow as she turned her glare on Constance. I loved when Constance covered male songs as well as the men who sang them. *Dangerous*. Shaman's Harvest. Jase held his hands open to her like he'd been screwed out of a set they'd agreed to do together. He was pretty fantastic at this song, but so was Constance. Who knows? Maybe after all her fear that he'd kick her out of Rock-N-Awe she had something to prove?

Angela resumed her place beside me. I shook my head and caught the absolutely dangerous, undaunted challenge glowing in the gray eyes watching me instead of Constance. Wow! His hand settled over his smirk as though curious what I was going to do about Angela. Klive's gaze wasn't what I'd expected in the least. He fed a superior faith that commanded I be worthy of him giving up the goods when he felt I was ready because he may have allowed her touch him, but no way was he cool about it. Intriguing. *Yes, sir*, my answering gaze said to him for the briefest of seconds.

"Your turn!" Angela shouted over Constance and her electric guitar.

Klive had a vindictive side that matched mine. He *was* dangerous, *I* felt dangerous as I settled back onto my barstool, grabbed Jase's shirt, and jerked him to me like I could take my anger out on him. He caught himself with either hand at my side against the bar. His lips parted, breathing heavy, eyes in awe and lust as he inspected a side of me he'd never seen. Hell, this felt like a new side I'd never met either. I held his shoulders and pressed him to his knees in front of me. He shot the dumbest smile at Rustin. I grinned and tapped Jase's nose so he'd pay attention. All in. Here goes.

I fisted Jase's white pocket tee and bent forward to taste the base of his throat between his collarbones, lingering just enough to see his chest rise. I sprinkled the salt, and Jase gave the weakest groan of longing when I licked him clean. My eyes shot to Angela's when I licked my lips. Priceless. I tossed the shot to the back of my throat and slammed my glass down, sucked that lime, then put my fist into the air triumphantly while the crowd roared along with my victory. I bent to chase my tequila with a fevered kiss to Jase's parted lips. His hand went right into my hair to hold my face to his while he stroked my tongue with his for as long as I'd allow. *Overindulgent much, sir?*

I gripped Jase's face to break our kiss. Angie gaped while Jase laid his head on my chest, his strong arms wrapping around my waist while he remained on his knees trying to catch his breath. I pushed Jase back a little and stood. I tossed a tip on the bar and quirked my brows at her, holding her gaze as I walked through the crowd that parted for me. I heard riotous laughter and looked over my shoulder just as Jase grabbed his shirt over his heart and let himself fall to the floor in my wake. He laughed and stood up to pass around high-fives and fist bumps.

Gimme a break. But how cool to see silly Jase behave the way he had in high school! Who'd have thought I'd ever be the girl causing silly stupidity in that man? Hell, who'd have thought I'd ever be the girl who did body shots with her arch nemesis?

33 | ♀

Klive turned on his stool when I walked by. "Why'd you go easy on her?" he teased. This man. I shook my head with a helpless smile. "Encore?" he asked and pointed at the spot just beneath the lobe of his ear. Well hell. I'd kissed him there the other night and earned the most intoxicating moan out of him.

"Sir, you need to behave," I told him over the music and mayhem.

"How do I behave, love?"

"Better than a few minutes ago," I shot with venom in my tone. My chin rose. He whistled and watched me walk away. I'd know the feel of those eyes like a brand anywhere. Just like I felt the death ray Angela shot at my back while I gave fist-bumps and high-fives to regulars as I made my way to the table near the stage. Constance shot me a grin through lyrics when I sat down to watch. My eyes wandered to the bar.

Jase clapped a hand on Rustin's back. They laughed about something a regular said, Klive in the mix of men around them as if they were all innocent friends. How did Jase know him? How did he know Jase?

Angela sat on her barstool and avoided looking at anyone. Probably plotting her revenge, even though she'd deserved every bit of what she'd just gotten and more for every day she turned my life to hell. But that was before I had a career on the horizon.

Talent too fast for her to take. A whole life that had nothing to do with her. This whole thing was stupid childish. I found myself waving her over to sit with me. She creased her brow but decided to hop off her stool and head my way.

Jase gave me a long kiss when he found me as if we functioned in such a natural capacity. His kisses *were* easier to accept.

"Damn, you ripped a page outta my dreams!" Jase said.

"To be fair, he stole my dreams before you ripped the page from his," Rustin joked.

Jase laughed and shoved him toward the stage. "Constance needs back-up," Jase called after him. He looked down at me. "I need a recharge for a very depleted battery. You sucked the life outta me back there."

"Who knew you were so cheesy?" I grinned up at his radiant face. *Wow! What a feeling!*

Jase's nose nuzzled mine before his lips pulled several delish times. "Alrighty, sweet Kins, I best be going back on stage before my own band kicks me out to make Constance the new lead." He shook his head but held my hand to draw me along with him as he went beside the stage cluttered with various cords, speakers, instruments.

He chose a blue and white electric guitar from a stand and tossed the strap over his head. From the corner of my eye, I saw Rustin waiting for a graceful moment to hop onstage with Constance. Angela said something to him. He grabbed Angela's hand and leaned toward her. She swallowed at whatever he said, nodded with a sobered expression. He caught me looking and winked before he stood in our space.

"Told her to mind her manners. That I'd hate to arrest her and see her behind bars in that skirt."

"You didn't," I gushed with a laugh.

"Nah, not the part about jail, but the minding her manners, yes, I did, Mizz Hayes. Least I can do after you so generously allowed me to lick the hand that feeds Jase."

I cackled and clapped my hands. "Don't get used to it, Deputy."

Jase kissed my lips before he relieved Constance. The bar had a different enthusiasm. Trouble in the air, and Jase stood before patrons like the conductor of a disorderly band who only listened to him. Rustin said something that made Constance laugh. No, wait, that woman *giggled* like a smitten fool. Hmm ... maybe the Perfect Pour was a good drink for that one after all. She wasn't easy to entertain.

"Kinsley?" Angela pulled my thoughts once I sat back down.

"Yeah? Was Rustin rude to you, because I swear, I didn't tell him to say whatever he must've said."

She snickered. "I wouldn't figure you for telling me I have a nice ass in this skirt that's too pretty for prison if I lay a finger on you."

I chuckled and shook my head.

Bitch server strolled up and wasn't rude to me for once. She took my order for another beer for myself and Angela, no lip or snarky remarks. Ha! Probably because I was paying tonight.

"Look, can we just put the BS behind us?" Angela asked. "Any woman who can make Jase Taylor fall at her feet is a woman I can respect, even if I'm an envious bitch. I'm sorry."

I gaped and pulled back for a better look at her. She held her hands up in surrender.

"Really, Kinsley. Deputy Keane cares for his best friend's girl. I could maybe care for Deputy Keane one day. So, you see, I'm not gonna lie and pretend I have no ulterior motives for making peace, but if I didn't, would you trust me?"

She had a point. "Well, I care about him, too. So, you'd better do right by him." I gave her a meaningful look.

"Truce?" she asked.

"You screw with him or my friend at the bar, the deal is off," I snapped.

"Rhett?" she asked.

"*No*," I said with no further explanation. Her brows rose while she nodded and offered her hand. "Truce." We shook on our agreement.

"Am I interrupting girl time?" Constance asked as she unscrewed the cap from a sweating water bottle. I rolled my eyes and shook my head. "Good," she said. "I'd hate to think you'd leave my ass for a white girl." She winked. Angela wasn't sure what to make of Constance's blatant assessment of her. "Hey, Miss Congeniality, whatever agreement you got between the two of you, I'm not afraid to throw down and lose weave over my girl, ya feel me?"

Angela cringed and nodded. I grinned at Constance, watching her dab away sweat with gobs of cocktail napkins. The guys tuned their guitars. To my surprise, Constance took her place beside Jase again rather than taking a break. The full band stayed this time.

"How's everyone doing out there tonight after those body shots?" Constance asked the bar. Angela and I shared a smile that held a private joke, then we busted out the pageant waves together like we'd be here all night. Bright and beautiful smiles we'd once weaponized for votes from judges. I heard hearty laughter from the bar. Klive laughed about something with a few guys around him, his gaze was glued to me, though. My smile morphed to a sharp inhale. Damn ... I held his gaze for just a moment, then looked back up at the stage.

Jase took the mic to warm the rowdy crowd. Rustin began playing the guitar. Marcus's gaze had finally found mine. My little stunt sold lots of shots. I knew that's why he was more watchful than warning.

The song began. Rise Against, *Savior*. Very quick pace. Jase now worked that guitar as he sang near that mic with fire in his breath. Sexy as hell every time he'd flip his hair from his eyes to stare out over the throngs of dancing patrons. Rustin went into garage band mode and rocked out, goading Constance to play with him. She sang backup into the same mic Rustin did. Their harmonizing together was pretty even if the song was hardcore. Constance held her guitar in a mirror of Rustin and they watched one another's hands like a contest to see who could chop notes faster. Jase didn't miss a lyric as he grinned and watched from the corner of his eye. The whole bar pulsed and crowded with Spring Breakers pouring in with Jase's music bleeding outside. The atmosphere was insane, fun, and I was kind of bummed I hadn't decided to work after all. Hmm ... maybe I would if the bar kept getting so crowded. Plus, I was sure that eventually I'd get tired of sitting in this woman's presence.

Mel obviously loved this song. He hit his cymbal and quieted the shimmery gold as the only sound was the guitar going back and forth between two notes. Jase sang in the somewhat silent air, my favorite part, his voice had that rough rasp while Constance and Rustin's guitars joined. The drums sounded loudly, and Rustin laid into that guitar, Jase weaving as he sang into the mic from different angles as Constance sang over hers. They did such a good job. So worth every penny Marcus paid for their performances, although I always felt biased about Constance adding something priceless Jase needed to keep.

Soon both Angela and I sang along with all the women in bar who were gaga for these hot musicians. How was I to rationalize that the lead was mine if I chose to stake that claim he'd spoken of. However, Angela was a new threat ... something inside told me not to trust her.

Perhaps the decade of hell? The beginning of *Letter from A Thief* by Chevelle wafted over the bar. How appropriate. I went along with her, deciding I would play along for now, but I was keeping my eye on her *and* her Klive grubbing hands. I don't care what she said about Rustin. Something was there.

Jase was singing his heart out, and Rustin and Constance came in on the background, harmonizing with the heavy music. I love this song, such a pained sound for such a heavy song. Jase grinned at me between breaths, through the pretty lyrics. He knew this was one of my favorites.

Their set included Seether, Shaman's Harvest, Metallica, Nirvana, Alice In Chains, and they were on a roll. There was no more room in the bar. I knew Marcus was thrilled, but where was his concern over the Fire Marshal now? I decided to go to the restroom, and Angie asked to come with me. Ha! Was she afraid of being left alone with Constance watching her from the stage? I caught the guys' faces as they sang into the mics together. Both sweaty, shirts plastered to their skin. Jase's hair stuck to his forehead. They didn't look happy about my going, but I dared Angela to do anything stupid in my realm. I sighed as the band called that they were taking five after their next song. *What did they think would happen?*

The line for the restroom was far too long, so I sneaked Angela in the hallway to use the employee's bathroom. This way I could gauge her without the shadow of dim lighting and chaos. Her lower lids smudged from sweat. On impulse I told her to be still and ran a sharp corner of a cocktail napkin beneath her eye. Both our mouths opened wide with our eyes. Automatic response. When I tossed the napkin in the trash, I caught her eyes in the mirror, trouble flickering from her irises the moment I turned back to the sink. She hadn't meant to look that way.

"It's hard getting along after not doing so for most of our lives, yeah?" I asked, leaning toward the mirror to check my own eyeliner.

"I'm sure we will piss one another off in some way before the night's over," she joked. We both nodded in the mirror. When I got to the end of the hallway, Marcus leaned against his perch, but he wasn't looking at the stage. He was turned toward us coming from the locker room.

"Who's your friend, Little Red?" He looked her over but wasn't checking her out. Interesting. He read her more like an animal with a sixth sense.

Angela offered her hand and a brilliant smile. "Angela Ansley. My father's the Sheriff of this precinct. Quite the crowd you pull to this little place," she said. He shook her hand and nodded.

"You a bouncer?" she asked.

"I'm the boss."

"I love a man in power," she purred, leaning closer. Marcus's lips twitched.

"I'm married," he told her. He wasn't married. "Kins, I have your check. Since you're here, come to the office and collect."

My checks were direct deposited, so I couldn't help feeling anxious when he shut us inside his office after Angela scampered back toward the stage. The band was already on break. Jase would wonder what happened to me.

"What's up, Marcus. I kept it clean earlier. Well, you know, I didn't pull hair and I wasn't on the clock. I'm not sorry for showing back up. Please don't call her father to have me arrested for trespassing."

"Slow your roll, Little Red." He held a hand up to me. "I'm not mad at you. I wanted to apologize for Sunday. I yelled at you in the heat of the moment. That prick put his hands on you, and I shouted at you like it was your fault. I was wrong to do that. Don't be mad at Taylor either. I'm proud of his quick reaction. Anything less with an Inferno is an invitation for more."

"Thank you. I'm trying to be chill about what happened, but the whole thing confuses me. The biker was so angry like I was responsible for everything. I could've sworn Sara was the problem child with them. That man didn't confuse me for her. No dim lighting. He knew exactly who I was."

"He why you're hanging out with the Sheriff's daughter?" he asked.

"No. I wanted to rub Jase in her face," I admitted. He chuckled.

"You more than nailed your target, Little Red. I don't think Moonlight, or whatever the hell you and Bayleigh named him, was too pleased with her antics, though."

"I know Klive's name now, Marcus. But I don't see how any man would be displeased with a woman like her—"

"King doesn't like anyone touching him, let alone an exchange of saliva? Nope. He's kind of a germaphobe. Just sayin', if what she did to him bothers you, I promise it bothers him more, in case you care."

My face melted into the sweetest smile while I threw my arms around his neck on impulse. He chuckled and held a hand to my back. "Dammit, girl. Stop making me miss you. I hate punishing my children."

"Who else did you punish?" I asked and pulled away.

"Bayleigh's not here, is she? Girl copped one hell of an attitude with me when I told her why you weren't at work on Monday. She is staging her own form of protest by refusing to come back to work until you get to come back. Think I should call her now or wait till tomorrow?"

"Wow, she's amazing and didn't even tell me! What a great friend."

"Uh huh. I'm glad you made the first move because my pride was getting weak." We both chuckled. "Here, Little Red. I got you a name tag. It's blank so you can make up any name you want. Pin it over your embroidery. You're free to order a larger pair of shorts, too. You win."

"Wait, can you repeat that?"

"Nope. You tell Bayleigh and I'll deny it. Now you have no reason to go looking for other jobs. The guy who drugged you is now on a watch list and no longer allowed in the bar. Get out of my office and behave yourself around that girl. I don't trust her. I *do* want you to trust Jase knows how to keep his hands to himself and her hands off him. Klive, too, whatever the hell is going on there," he muttered on the end there. "My point is, keep your claws retracted in the bar. I don't want the Sheriff knocking at my door."

"What about the Fire Marshal? Is he no longer a concern?"

"Kinsley Hayes, you need to learn to quit while you're ahead."

"Quitting doesn't compute in this brain, Marcus."

He sighed and shook his head, his long dreads and the beads at the ends shifted with the movement. He never wore them down.

"I like your hair tonight, sir."

"Right back atcha, kid. That's why you need to keep your claws retracted. Those men can't see anything but red when you're looking this pretty. I'd say you look better than when your mama plays dress up with you." He winked while I rolled my eyes.

"Thanks-ish." We walked out of the office. He locked the door behind himself. "You want me to clock-in for a minute? Help the others? I kinda miss my job since you so brutally grounded me." My bottom lip popped; Bambi eyes deployed. I earned the hearty laughter out of Marcus I'd aimed for.

"One hour, stage area so your man can keep his eye on you," he said. "Clock starts now, Cinderella."

34 | ♀

Marcus leaned against the wall at the mouth of the hallway once more. I trotted behind the bar to clock in. Garrett thanked me. So did the bitch server. Did she seem too nice tonight? Wait! Bayleigh wasn't here and neither was I, so she'd been covering both our absent asses. *No wonder!*

I caught Jase standing on the stage shaking hands that reached up to him, but his eyes aimed my way. I pulled taps for orders, so he'd get the message without my needing to wade through the mayhem to tell him I was working. I know Marcus said stage area, but I pumped out shots and mixed drinks for Garrett to show him gratitude for handling Angela earlier.

"It's all about loyalty, Red Running Hood," Garrett said with a grin.

"Well, *Rhett*." I paused to run a fingernail provocatively over his embroidery, mocking Angela. "Thanks for having my back."

"Damn. Poor Jase. That guy doesn't stand a chance," Garrett muttered as he looked down at my smiling eyes. "Neither does that poor Moonlight."

"Ha! The fault is all yours with Moonlight!" I called over my shoulder. I made the band's drinks and those I knew my table had been ordering while I'd hung out.

"What do you mean?" he asked.

"Remember the Gasparilla costume you picked for me? The leather pants and green corset?" I asked him. "It *was* my shit he was calling that night with the song because I'd run into him downtown and taken my temper out on him while dressed in that costume. Guess I should've busted those leathers back out instead of this dress, huh?"

"I'm too good at every job I do," Garrett said. We both laughed. "You know Bayleigh is gonna be so jealous you're telling me about this without her. She's hungry for every morsel on that man. Then again, so is your frenemy over there."

I lifted the tray over my shoulder and stabilized the weight with my free hand. "Can you blame her?" I grinned. "I only wish I knew whether she liked him for him or because he'd spoken to me. You be careful, she may aim at you just for pretending you were a smitten slave to me earlier."

"Who's pretending?" he called as I entered the crowds. My head tossed on a laugh while I shouted that he behave.

By the time I set the tray on the table, I had to readjust my bra and double check that my dress was still over my bottom. Too many touchy-feely drunks, clumsy idiots, inappropriate advances. Some of my shot glasses were missing. The band told me not to worry about replacing them.

About twelve others gathered around our table, including Klive. Angela was now feasting on attention from several men who hadn't seen our gauntlet throwing earlier. She still fixated on Klive every spare second. Why did that bother me? I should be happy, ecstatic even, that in a way she'd chosen to divert her attention away from Jase once I'd shown her we were togetherish. Dammit. I'd never been in this predicament in my life and was a shitty navigator at the moment. Too bad Bayleigh wasn't in. I could've used her advice or comic relief. Constance was too busy signing homemade albums and Rock-N-Awe tees for me to pick her brain.

Fortunately, Klive seemed dismissive, if not annoyed, by Angela's attention. I thought of Marcus's words: Germaphobe, hated people touching him.

When I passed him a Michelob, I gave him a flattered smile and watched his whole demeanor lighten, a little confused by my sudden kindness. That was the best feeling, even if we were bipolar in our dealings. He'd allowed me to touch him and never made me feel I couldn't. This germaphobe had swapped saliva with me.

"Thanks for remembering love." Klive pushed a ten-dollar bill across.

I pushed the cash back. "No. This one's on me as a thanks for the shots. If you don't keep the money, you'll ruin my blessing in the kindness."

His head tilted like he wasn't sure what to do with that. When I was close to him in order to reach a patron near the wall, I passed their drinks, then placed a hand to Klive's shoulder. "Do me a favor, Klive. Relax."

"What is this relaxation you speak of other than a cruel myth, my sweet?" He turned his face and our cheeks almost touched so his mouth could draw close to my ear. "I hated every bloody second."

"That makes two of us." I released his shoulder to pass out several other drinks. "Here Constance. Take these. Maybe you can drum up some more swag sales. I have enough drama in my life for three women." I handed her several business cards.

Constance made a lewd comment in my ear about Klive while she snatched the cards. We shared a naughty smile. *Tsk, tsk.* I also passed out numbers women had begged me to give to the band, but only to Dan, Mel and Rustin, not Jase. He gave me a pouty lip, so I handed him another stack out of my bra that men had passed out to me. "If you want some of those, I get to keep all of these!" I yelled over the rowdy crowd.

"I knew you stuffed your bra," Constance teased.

"Hey, Kinsley, your number isn't in my stack," Mel said, stealing my attention.

"Oh, silly me. Jase, do you have a pen I can borrow?"

Klive pulled an expensive pen out of his blazer, a naughty smile lighting his eyes as he passed the ink to me. I noticed his tie was gone like he didn't want any more access in that way. Jase laughed and pushed his hand away while Klive laughed and shrugged at Mel like he'd tried. Nice!

"This one's taken, Mel. Angela is free, though!" He nodded his head in her direction. Soon Mel stole her attention from all the other men gathered around the Scarlett O'Hara wannabe. Klive shot Jase a grateful smile, Jase nodded. He wrapped his arms around my waist and pulled me against his now bare chest, confirming that he hadn't disappointed those eager women. I let my hands roam over his pecs and up to his neck as I wrapped my hands just beneath his hair.

"Baby, I'm in love with your legs in those shoes, especially with the inked-up leg, but the lip gloss? I thought my whole face was gonna be a sticky mess when you mauled me in front of everyone," Jase said. "Not even a hint to brag about in the locker room, while your lips look so wet, I am thirstier by the second. You are the hottest girl in here tonight, you know that?"

"That's because I'm pressed up against the hottest guy in the place. Just look at your sweaty ass."

Jase laughed. "You are the best at accepting compliments, sweet Kins." He tapped the tip of his bottle against my nose, then tipped the glass against his lips for a full-on guzzle.

"Want water?" I asked. "I brought y'all a pitcher. I'm lucky it wasn't knocked on my head for how many bumped into me."

"Too bad. I wouldn't have minded a replay of you plastered."

"Mr. Taylor, you need to behave," I told him.

"You don't exactly inspire good behavior, Ms. Hayes, so what did you have in mind? I need to drench myself in salt and tequila to see some more action?"

My head tossed with a full laugh. I slapped his chest. "Don't tell me you've forgotten just who you're playing love games with, Jase. Need Angela to refresh your memory on the Virgin Mary here?"

Angela's head turned in shock. I smiled to myself. So maybe the tequila had me a tad tipsy and that's why I'd had to stabilize my tray?

"Picking right back up where you left me Senior year, I see," Jase said. He drained the rest of his beer and set the bottle on the table while the others in the band got back onstage. "I played your games then. You're in mine now, baby."

"Aw, Jase, that's cute."

I heard Klive chuckle and realized he watched with blatant enjoyment.

"What's cute? You know, aside from you in this dress," Jase flirted, the corner of his lips lifting into the signature smile.

"That you think you're close to a Super Bowl ring when you're barely off the sidelines. If you need me, I'll be doing touchdown dances in the end zone."

Jase's eyes narrowed a fraction as he realized I'd heard all of his locker talk with Rustin. I expected Jase to end his play with me there, that he'd get the point now that I'd laid the lines. He nodded and jumped onstage like a quarterback ready to create new plays.

The band began testing their instruments. Rustin ran onstage to grab his guitar once more. Jase took to his mic, Constance beside him on hers.

"Check. Check. One. Two. I have any football fans in the house?" Jase asked. I gasped and held to the edges of my empty tray. Lots of football fans in the house tonight. Several college players chanted their school cheers. If he wasn't careful, Jase was going to instigate a fight among rivalries. He laughed away from the mic and brought his hand out, lowering inch by inch, their volume decreasing in obedience. "Anyone a fan of track?"

I glared at him when only a fraction of the bar shouted. *What was this?* His way of showing me how his athletic talent was somehow superior to my own because his sport was more popular? Jase avoided my eyes, but I jolted out of my skin when a too loud whistle came from between Klive's fingers only feet from me.

Jase pointed at him. "We have a shared appreciation, boss." *Fascinating! What the hell was going on?* "I'm gonna use my band mates here for a little word problem. Pay attention, class."

I shook my head at how Jase's flirtation got the ladies going.

Little wink, crook of the lips, rock of the hips. He grabbed Constance's hand. "Let's pretend Constance is a renowned track star. She's got the speed, agility and drive that beats the competition."

Unable to resist, I glanced at Klive. He gestured to the only empty seat in the house like a barrier he'd maintained against those around him. A man sat beside Angela in what *was* my chair. I sighed and sat beside Klive, watching as Jase pulled Rustin beside Constance.

"Here, we have an All-American, Friday Night Lights MVP, Most Valuable Player, that is. He's not a bad singer either." Jase grinned at the audience and relished their ego-pumping cheers. Jase turned Rustin for a sec and landed a sound smack to his ass. I busted out laughing. Rustin howled and grabbed his butt cheek. The bar went crazy. "Looks pretty great in a tight pair of jeans, too. You agree?" Jase asked breathlessly through laughter. Rustin faced the crowd with a huge smile far too wholesome for the devil glowing behind blue eyes. That one didn't have me fooled. Like Angela, they had an undercurrent hard to define. So did several of my regular patrons. Just something hidden about them like the dick who'd dosed me. I didn't want to think about him.

"He's a humble man," I joked. Klive nodded.

"Back to our math problem. She's fast on her feet, but *oh-so-slow* in others that torment our MVP. He's used to gaining yards, making plays, taking hits. Knows how to go down *smooth* to avoid injury."

"Fabulous innuendo," I muttered. "That track runner's gonna have no problem leaving him in the dust."

"Should we place our bets here and now?" Klive pulled his wallet from an inside pocket of his blazer, a peek of his red tie balled up. When the lapel lifted, I caught sight of a pistol hanging from a shoulder holster. *Holy crap!* I swallowed whatever snarky response that died in my mouth.

"Nothing?" he asked. "You think you'll lose?"

"Do *you*?" I demanded, offended.

"He seems a pretty strong contender for the likes of any woman."

"Provocation indeed." I shook my head and stared straight at my brash singer.

Jase continued. "You throw the MVP onto her track, I'm not so sure he's gonna catch up. That's her turf. So, class, what happens when you take the track star off the track and throw her onto the field in a haze of men bent on knocking each other out of the game?"

"Klive." I stood and grabbed his shoulder. "I need you to do that painful whistle again." I held tight to his blazer while I stepped up onto the chair. Klive whistled. Jase and the rest looked at me.

"Jase Taylor! Is this rhetorical, or does it sound to me like you're throwing an open challenge?"

Jase's jaw dropped on a huge smile. "Baby, this whole thing is rhetorical. Did you think I was talking about you since you are the dominating force of this here track downtown?"

"Downtown? That's funny. Quite sure I can name a great many towns and states if you wanted to get technical." I grinned back and shined my nails on my dress as I took cheers and jeers at once. Angela had been so caught up in Jase's everything she just noticed my hand on Klive's shoulder, my legs so close to him. Were I a ditz rather than dominant I might fall on purpose so he'd have to catch me.

"Careful, someone's gonna see under your dress when you stand that way," Jase teased. I gasped and looked at Klive in accusation. His whole face morphed to shock at Jase. "He didn't look under there, but I bet he's thinking about it now." He laughed away from the mic and the commotion he caused.

"I see what you did there!" I shouted over the cat calls. "An MVP may be used to running plays geared to distract while he's coming in hot. Although, I guess it all depends on which position he plays that determines whether this track star can beat his ass at his own game."

There was a collective 'Oooh!' and everyone looked at Jase with grins on their curious faces.

"Damn, baby, who knew you had such a potty mouth beneath that innocent exterior?" Jase teased.

We all laughed, including Klive. I felt his hand grip my ankle to keep me stable. The same electricity from the department store engulfed my whole body at the charge from his fingers and warm palm. His thumb brushed the heart on my ankle.

"You saying you wanna play ball with the big boys?" Jase tested, so eager to call my bluff. Yeah, this man looked at me like the one used to women going down too easy. *Dream that dream, bud.* Constance shook her head with big eyes like I was insane. Rustin nodded and rubbed his hands together. "It's a dirty game," Jase said. "You might get hurt."

"What if I bring my own defense?" I squeezed Klive's shoulder. Jase's eyebrows rose and he glanced at Klive like he knew.

"Game on! Game on! Game on!" the crowd chanted. "Game on! Game on! Game on!"

Jase studied me in uncertain challenge and trepidation at once.

"See that look, Klive?" I shouted down to him in this mass.

"On Taylor's face?" he shouted back.

I nodded with a proud smile. "Yes, sir." I giggled like a drunken fool when I fell into his arms that rushed to capture my misbehavior. His eyes had such a smile in them. "Klive, that's my favorite look on a competitor's face before I put my feet on the blocks and the shot fires."

35 | ♀

JASE LICKED HIS SEXY lips like a man bent on playful revenge. He watched as I climbed out of Klive's arms and blew an air kiss at him.

"Y'all wanna know something about competition?" Jase asked the audience while he started picking at guitar strings. The chanting died down while they waited. "You save your toughest push for the greatest contenders. Greater the pain, the bigger the gain," he quoted me. "This one goes out to my one and only track star running laps around my heart."

The audience gave coos until he lit into the guitar and the band fell into a cover of Theory of a Deadman's *Bad Girlfriend.*

Jase laughed on the first few words when he took in my gaping jaw, hand on hip, narrowed eyes. The more he got into the song, he sang like he meant his dedication or at least fantasized about some of the lyrics being true. The bar didn't give a damn about the scandalous evaluation of my 'girlfriend' behavior. The patrons I served after that asked various questions about our relationship, whether I was wanting to put together a football game, some cheered me on and said I could totally outrun that quarterback.

Eliza and several of the track team grabbed my attention at a table outside my serving zone. I held a finger while I delivered a tray full of drinks before I went to say hi. Looney Lucy stood near Shay, both studying the changes Constance's art made to my body, the classic movie-star hair, pretty dress and makeup.

"What's wrong, ladies?" I shouted over the music and convo around us. "You surprised I'm not dressed like a ho?"

Eliza shot them both a glare. Lucy's whole night looked flushed with the defeated fall of her shoulders. Shay stood tall without a care for how this may affect Lucy. Poor girl. Lucy was just a pawn in Shay's game.

"We came to check on you," Eliza shouted and nodded toward the other two girls from our relay team. My real friends. "These toddlers decided to tag along." Shay's cocky gaze faltered as my team said loud and clear how they felt about her antics. "We don't want you to be mad at us for voting to bench you for a week to recoup. Walton would be so pissed if he saw you in these heels. I'm in love with them!"

Eliza beckoned Julie and Lindsay to see the shoes Klive had bought me.

"See, I have ankle support!" I grinned as they shook their disapproving heads.

"Well, that's kind of what we wanted to talk to you about."

"What do you mean?" I asked Lindsay. "Y'all about to ground me from shoes, too?"

They laughed and shook their heads.

"We should, though," Julie said.

Eliza spoke up. "We know you love working Fridays, but Walton told us we could bring you with us for support if you agreed to it."

"Why would you guys want me there? Wouldn't it be easier to make it seem like I was absent for family matters or vacation versus showing up to reveal this weakness?"

"Okay, I'm sorry, but we have to pause!" Julie shouted. "Is the guy singing the one coach is upset about?"

"If so, damn, I can see why ...." Lindsay said. "He's superhot. Makin' me thirsty."

"So are his backup singers," Lucy injected, desperate to get back in their good graces. "I know Shay's probably wishing she wasn't such a bitch to you, so you'd introduce her to the girl."

Shay gasped and slapped Lucy's arm.

"Shay has Brayden," I said, even as a cold rush went through me at his name and his friend.

"Oh, Shay's already slept with him. She's done," Lucy babbled. "She needs the D every now and then but goes back to chicks when she's had her fix." She shrugged her shoulders at Shay's anger like she was bucking her bully.

"Wow, that was fast," Eliza said. "Guess she already got what she wanted out of him, eh? Not sure what that says about him." Her elbow jabbed my ribs, a smile at her joke on hers and Julie's faces, but my breathing hollowed. My eyes bored into Shay's.

"Whoa, Kins, you okay?"

"Yeah," I forced. "I just have no respect for shameless users."

"No worries," Lucy said. "He used her too. Guess he only gave her a go because you told him to. He's really into you."

"Lucy!" Shay shouted and shook her head. Lucy shrugged again. Her face shifted as her eyes looked up over my shoulder.

Numb heat shot through my body before his hand even touched my waist, his breath behind me at my ear. "You okay, love? You seem bothered."

"Uh, huh," I managed. I swallowed as the girls all looked up at Klive standing at my back. I cleared my throat to find my voice as I turned my face to peer up at his so close to mine. His eyes held a smile like he knew exactly how I was affected. "I'm okay. A little pissed off, but okay. Seems Shay, here, was dumped by a guy with a crush on me, so now all her life's problems are somehow my fault." I smiled back at the girls; Shay's cheeks red even under the dim lighting. If she hadn't hated me before, she loathed me now. Did she loathe me enough to sleep with a guy for the sole reason of manipulating him to have me drugged and kicked off the team? Was I reaching?

"Girls, this is Klive. Klive you already know Lucy. My relay team: Eliza, Julie, Lindsay. Shay is my replacement while I'm grounded," I said. Klive nodded at each of them, a pretty smile for Lucy. They stared up at him with awed respect tinged with reverence.

"Great to meet you," he told them. "No matter Shay's positioning, you're irreplaceable, love."

All of our smiles, except Shay's, split with radiance.

"We were trying to convince Kinsley to come to the meet tomorrow for support from the stands. What's your opinion, Klive?" Eliza asked him. I raised my eyebrows at how she literally went over my head on that one. I looked over my shoulder again and reasoned my point-of-view in looking weak in front of the competition rather than them thinking I was merely absent.

Klive nodded. "Yeah, but isn't it more fun to let them think you're weak, that they have the upper hand on you, before you show them who's boss?"

"I love his style!" Lindsay gushed.

"If I go, I miss Friday night tips," I reasoned.

"Kinsley's never been involuntarily benched," Julie explained.

Add that to my list of Nevers.

"Ah," Klive said. "This is a pride issue?"

"Ugh! Not just a pride issue!" I argued.

Klive smiled. I bit my lip as I tried not to look at his mouth. This was such an intimate position in how if we'd been *together* together, we'd be natural. Simple. My parents had talked to me about sex, but mom never told me that the regular relationship things like standing close were so ... *tingly*.

COMPLICATED MOONLIGHT

"Right, I forgot about the ego as well. Forgive me," he said. He laughed when they did, too. I shook my head. His eyes strayed to my lips. Damn. His hand gripped my hip a fraction. "This the Gainesville meet?"

"Yes!" all of them said in unison, all flattered he knew or paid attention, me too. We were used to people like Jase getting all the attention. Football, Baseball, and Basketball reigned supreme in our kingdom.

The bitch server asked me for my empty tray and didn't glare at me for once. Well, there's a pleasant surprise considering the crap she'd given me about Jase and Klive before. She asked the group if we'd like something more to drink as I was now offduty. I guess Marcus had told her to relieve me.

"Can I have a beer, please?" I asked. She nodded and left.

"I think their strategy should be considered, Kinsley," Klive said. "Your steepest competitor is going to be on her home turf and hoping to stomp you out. What a sad disappointment for her when you're the cheerleader instead. Better she stomp-out your replacement while she thinks you're weak. The ultimate upper hand is yours, not hers."

"Oh, Klive, are you trying to talk me into kissing you, sir?" I teased.

"Or me?" Eliza asked with another elbow at my ribs. This time I laughed. "Kins, he's summing up what we were thinking. Buses leave at noon. Please, just think about it. Would mean so much if you came to support everyone even if you weren't running."

"Yeah!" Lindsay said. "Imagine how hyped the freshman team would be to have you cheering them on! They're so afraid of you. Hell, so are the JV."

"Wonderful opportunity!" Julie said. "If you end up angry, we can just go get some drinks and loosen you up. We're seriously flirting with heading up to St. Augustine to kick off our own Spring

Break right. Been forever since you partied with us. We'd love you to join."

"Yeah, when was the last time?" Lindsay asked with a finger to her lip, her brows drawn in thought as she did math in her head. "Damn! Like three years!"

Klive's hand tightened in warning. A thrill rushed through my belly. *What if I brought my own defense?* Would he come? Had he planned to attend the meet if he'd known our schedule?

"I'll be there," I said. "That sounds fun, and it's been way too long since I've had any." The girls clapped and thanked Klive for helping their cause and mind games. His hand hadn't loosened, and in fact seemed to have pulled me closer against him without anyone noticing. My lips twitched while butterflies fluttered even through my palms. Something about pushing Klive's buttons was so fun.

"What are we clapping about over here?"

Just like that, my private joy fell like a cinderblock to the wooden floor. Angela took my free arm as if we were besties. I know Klive felt me tense at her touch. His thumb stroked my hip bone. The girls filled her in while Angela intertwined her enemy fingers in mine. My palms tingled for new reasons.

"Okay, which of you is Shay?" she asked after they finished. Shay raised a smug hand as if Angela was one of my friends who might threaten her. Shay was a brave bitch, was she not? Then again, so was Angela. "Take it from me, Shay. If Kinsley leaves her shoes open to step into, snatch them while you can, but be sure your feet are the same size or else you might hurt yourself trying to be someone you are not." My chin jerked to look up at her in shock. "It's true. Those heels are killer, but your feet are way too small for me to wear your shoes." She took in how close Klive stood to me, his hand on my hip. "Looks like someone found Cinderella's glass slipper. Hope it doesn't shatter."

Whoa. Klive held me even tighter, but I wasn't certain he was holding *me* back. Was she threatening him or me?

"Better a wound from a friend than a kiss from an enemy," she said and bent to kiss my cheek before she left.

"Wow, what's her deal?" Eliza asked. "Couldn't tell if she was friend or foe."

"Bipolar," I said like what're ya gonna do? When Bitch server brought me my beer, I ordered a round of shots, but Klive spoke over my head and told her not to put that order in. I gaped in anger over my shoulder. "They were for all of my relay team, not just me."

"Ladies, if you wouldn't mind excusing us for a moment?" Klive asked them.

"Oh, no worries. We didn't come to party. We came for Kinsley. Our work here is done. No shots for us tonight." Eliza jostled my hand to get my attention off Klive. "Tomorrow night you can buy us a victory round. Good?"

"Yeah." I caved. "Sounds good."

"I think we know who Walton is worried about now," Lindsay said at my ear. She kissed my cheek. "Klive, it was wonderful meeting you."

"Likewise," he said. We waved good-bye to them.

Klive twisted me to face him. *Woo! Those eyes in this shade of conflict? Sexy. Dangerous.* I held the tiger's tail again but wanted to pet him to soothe the aggravation I'd created, even as I somewhat enjoyed the results. I knew the smile shined in my eyes as I tried to hide my amused victory.

"What are you doing, love?"

"The real question is, what are you going to do about it, Klive?

36 | ♀

ONCE AGAIN, MY CAR was left at the bar since I'd drank too much. Another effin' never that seemed to be common as of late. How the hell I hadn't tossed my tray, or my cookies earlier was beyond me. Maybe that was Complicated Moonlight's effect. Although how did someone make you feel drunk when sober and sober when drunk? *Is that what real lo—nope. Not going there Kinsley drunk brain!*

Jase and Rock-N-Awe had the bar so crazy by the end of their set, he'd had to take my hand and run with me out to the back parking lot. We'd rushed into the truck. He'd cracked up when the other band mates glared as he got out of there sooner than them. Klive had captured my plea for Constance; I didn't want anything to happen to her as the only female member. I also didn't want her rushing back into bed with Rustin if he took her home. I'd watched Klive take her hand to sneak her around the side of the bar. That was the last glimpse before Jase and me headed to my place.

Jase's hand went through his hair to pull loose strands out of his face. We now stood on my balcony outside my garage apartment. The milk in my fridge should be sour I'd been away so long, even if *so long* was only a few days.

I was certain I sensed Daddy's eyes from beyond the blinds in the parentals' house.

"You sure were pretty tonight. Hope you weren't offended by any of my songs," Jase said. He snagged one of my hands to kiss my palm.

"You mean the blatant sexual harassment in the form of song?" I grinned.

"Get over here, baby. I can't handle the distance anymore." He tugged me into his arms and wrapped them around me. "You have no idea how sexy you are when you twist men like King around your pretty little finger then flirt with me instead." His lips coaxed my smile apart.

"Mmmm ...." I hummed against his mouth and pulled back a fraction, urged him closer to the shadow of my doorway where Daddy's view would be obstructed. "And what of twisting you around my finger while I flirt with him, Mr. Friday Night Lights?"

"Maybe I love watching the carnage. Think you've got what it takes to run all over me on my own field?" Jase boldly ran a hand down over my bottom and gripped so hard I jumped against him. He held me there. His tongue ran across his lips before parting my lips once more.

When I sucked a deep breath through my nose at the feel of his desire pinned between us, he hummed and felt around for my doorknob. The door opened behind me. Jase urged me over the threshold, all the while tasting my tongue and lips with his flavored of vodka and beer.

"I'm in the mood to make a heavy tackle." He kicked the door closed behind us and took me down on the nearest couch in the living area. I moaned when he ran his hand up my dress.

"Nothing beneath the clothes, Jase. I mean it. My father was already watching from the window. I don't want guilt all over me from going too far. I'm also not ready," I rushed.

"I see how it is. You comparing notes, sweet Kins? Did Klive get under here?" His fingers ran over my panties between my thighs.

I bucked in overwhelming sensation, everything pulsing to life throughout my flesh while my mind went foggy and numb. "You thinking of him or me?" He pressed the most delicious spot and my body writhed against his. "Maybe we should spank you for that wayward mind."

Jase pulled back to flip me to my stomach in one swift motion. My dress flung against my back before his palm lit into my bottom. His hand traveled lower. I gasped for air at the pleasure pain combo he'd gifted.

"He's right. You do have *the best* moan," Jase said at my ear. When I gasped in anger and shifted to stop him, he spanked me again. "That's right, baby. Locker talk happens between more than Rustin and me."

"Screw both of you!" I fought against the haze of lust to kick him off my couch. My body was so pissed off at my mind in this moment. "Out!" I shouted, my chest heaving, body trembling from betrayal. I couldn't even imagine Klive stooping low enough to brag about getting places with me.

"What the hell?" he demanded like I'd stolen his steak. Damn right.

"Did I stutter, Jase Taylor? You and that player can take your games somewhere else. I told you once, my heart is not a toy, but I guess I should've included my body in that since you didn't put two and two together. How dare you guys talk about me like a football you keep tossing! This is so much worse than you just being cute for your parents like I'd thought. Y'all taking bets on who gets further faster? First one to sleep with me wins the Super Bowl ring rather than thinking of buying a ring to be with me?"

"No! Dammit, Kinsley! I *love* you!"

"Don't SAY that! Actions speak louder than your shallow words and songs, Jase."

"Actions? Kinsley Hayes, you have no idea what actions I've taken for you."

"I can't do this," I said. "Get. The. Hell. OUT! Call me when you've grown up."

"Sonuvabitch! Why the hell am I trying so hard for someone who only sees me as the same piece of ass every other fangirl does? Why did I even tell you that shit? You're just like them!"

I gasped like he'd slapped me. "How *dare* you! You get mad at your guitar when you hit the wrong note, too?"

"Wow, who the fuck are you?" he asked in pure disgust.

"Wish I was asking the same." *I shouldn't have said that.* I'd known before the words shot from my mouth, but I couldn't undo the damage, and I didn't know how to apologize to someone who had no qualms about using the L-word on his conquest of the moment exactly the way I'd joked about with Klive.

He grabbed the keys that had fallen from his pocket during our make-out session. The door slammed behind him a second later. The wall clock rattled against the texture. The chain above my deadbolts swung back and forth. Tears rained down my face.

When I opened the door to the hotel room I shared with Lucy and two other teammates, I wished to be anywhere else. I wasn't in the mood to party, or maybe I was, but not in a healthy way. I wanted to blow off all my friends to get drunk and drown the drama of men down the drain. These girls got drunk with each other on the regular. How did they get away with such a carefree or *careless* way of life? Had I ever enjoyed the same simplicity and not realized until all this baggage packed into my mind? I longed to be rid of the burden of thought as much as the duffel bag cutting a ribbon into my right shoulder. The bag bounced when dropped on the side of the bed that I claimed.

My father had offered to come to the meet, but for the first time in my recollection I didn't want to be around him. Besides, what was the point in coming if I wasn't running? He was mad at me for not contacting him and leaving my phone in Constance's car for days before texting him. Guess I'd been mere hours from a missing person's report had my friends not told him they'd seen me. Coach had to tell him man-to-man how he'd grounded me from flying across the finish line for at least a week.

"Why didn't you tell me yourself, Kinsley Fallon?" Daddy had demanded.

I couldn't recall the last time I'd been in real trouble like I was. Nor did I remember a time I didn't care, because for the first time I realized my age, even if I didn't always act twentyfour. Constance's offer of being roomies dangled in my head like a tempting carrot. Now, I must have been avoiding him, at least that's how he saw my misbehavior. He was concerned, but screw making more excuses for my contentious crush on a grown man or having who he called a 'boy' in my apartment. I was still so angry about Jase; I hadn't bothered arguing with Daddy or explaining what happened. My heart ached that Daddy assumed I was throwing all my rules and morals out the window. If I'd let Jase do anything with me in the short time I'd had him in my apartment, how sad to have finished so soon. Guess Daddy assumed Jase was a one-minute man.

Jase was not a boy, I'd told Daddy. When he'd brought up Klive, I'd told him I'd have figured he'd want me to want a man over a boy. Now I realized maybe he just wanted me to flirt with love, versus having the real thing for however long?

Then again, I wasn't being fair. My behavior changes did look worrisome. His daughter coming home from womanizer Jase

Taylor's house and taking a flower from another man on the same day? Vanishing for days afterward with no word, then the first time he sees me is with Jase sucking my face before pushing me into my apartment. Who could blame him?

But how could I explain the craziness taking a foothold in my blissfully bland life without freaking him out? All the damn men in my life were haywire. Jase's words haunted my heart, so did my reaction. Was he banging someone else while I sent him to do so with my bad attitude? I'd hit a sore spot, poured salt into the wound, then held my hand over top so he couldn't gain relief.

What a bitch. *Why spend so much time trying for me?* His words played over and over.

Then there was Klive. He hadn't shown for the Gainesville meet. I'd sat on the sidelines and cheered for my teammates, for every freshman and underclassman that my relay team desperately wanted me to. Hell, I even shouted my ass off for Shay when she was the first leg of the relay team. Eliza took the last leg, my true position. That, I did appreciate. They placed third. Shay had done well, and I wasn't above giving credit where credit was due, even if I didn't trust her.

All the while, I'd searched the stands with hope, wondering if I'd been wrong about those eyes like a brand on my skin. I'd swear I'd felt them, but he'd never showed. I'd chewed my cheek, bounced my knee in continuous wondering about when he and Jase could've possibly spoken to each other for him to say anything. I also couldn't help wondering if Jase was playing games with my head in retaliation the way he'd gotten me to confess to fooling around with Klive by twisting a few words. If I'd fooled with Klive, anyone would assume Klive might know the sound of my moan. Did Jase make that part up to see what I'd say or maybe admit to? What if Klive hadn't had locker talk at all?

Ugh! STFU Kinsley brain!

COMPLICATED MOONLIGHT

Lucy hustled to the other side of my bed to claim her role as bunk mate. Yay! Did I want to sleep in the same bed with a woman who'd had literal lesbian locker talk about copping a feel of my T&A last weekend? Damn, I wanted my own room, my own car, my own prerogatives, and no witnesses.

Lucy leaned across to offer me her extra pillow. This sucked. She was so kissing butt. Why not just come straight out and apologize instead?

I picked up my phone and sent a pic to Tyndall with a 'wish you were here'. She didn't text back. I wondered if Jase told her about my mean side. Why not? Everything else was effed up, may as well toss my best friend into that mix.

Lucy asked if I wanted to go to the liquor store to play a night of forgetting the safe way. Um ... I wasn't exactly great at the sleep-over girl-talk game. No painting nails and bragging about this week's lay for me. Adding booze to that mess? No thanks. Lucy stared like she was dying to ask if I'd slept with Klive. Was she into him, or was she upset that I wasn't into her? I was a tightrope-walker in addition to a track-runner, and I needed a breather; to be an outside the hotel alcohol-drinker. Wink, wink.

When I lifted the duffel and excused myself to go change, I heard the other two girls whispering with Lucy about what her life was like being in my company. *Ugh! Kill me now!*

Hey! Micro Machine wanna leave her prison to play? Eliza texted.

YES! I texted back.

I walked out in hip-hugging jeans and a snug tee that revealed my midriff like I could rebel against everyone if I allowed a peek at skin I didn't like showing. My bag cut into my shoulder again. Why did I bring this stupid bag if I wasn't running? Maybe I'd hoped deep down Coach would've changed his mind and put me in ...?

"Wow," Lucy observed. "You look hot, Kins. You're not partying, right? Don't you hate that? You can hang out with us if you want. We are about to order pizza. Or we could order something else? I know you don't like a bunch of grease sometimes."

I crinkled my nose and rubbed my belly, pretending I'd had way too much concession food. I was starving. A fruit chalk protein bar was preferable to pizza with Lucy tonight.

"I just want to be alone with my thoughts. Know what I mean?" I feigned soft crush heartache and waved my key card after I stole my license and credit card from my wallet. "I think I'm gonna go downstairs and have a minute."

All three cast empathetic looks that were sure to morph into wild gossip.

"Wait, don't you want to leave your b—"

The door clicked shut on Lucy's brown-nosing. I rolled my eyes and looked both ways down the walkway. Varsity runners loitered outside a few doors down and waved me on. Eliza threw my bag inside their dark room before we jogged in cautious silence down the stairwell together. Not hiding from Coach. He knew we were going out. We'd signed a waiver releasing the school of liability for our exploits. Eliza had brought her own car, so we'd also decided to ride home with her to stay the whole weekend while the rest of the team left tomorrow morning. We stayed quiet to hide from the others on the team we didn't want to babysit.

"You need some henna on your belly to complete the look," Lindsay said. "I want some on mine, too. You need to introduce me to your girl."

"I can do that. She'd like the business," I said of Constance.

"You ready to have some fun, girl? Where's your Klive? I'm surprised he wasn't at the meet earlier." Eliza held my hand while we jogged across four lanes of St. Augustine traffic after trekking across the dark parking lot of the Ramada Inn. Another reason I wanted to get drunk and escape. Pat Connor threatened to torture me in a room at the Ramada.

"Who's ready for a round of shots?" I asked them. "I know I am!"

We walked up to a bar with indoor and outdoor nightlife glowing as bright as the neon beckoning us inside.

"Ladies let's see some ID," the bouncer said at the steps to the outdoor area.

37 | ♀

We flashed our licenses at the bouncer and walked inside a moment later.

"Okay, *chicas*," Julie said, "if we get separated, we make sure to text on the group chat. If you leave with a guy, text name and location with code word. If in trouble, what's the word?"

"Fourth," I supplied. She nodded.

"If all is going well?" she asked.

"First," Lindsay said.

"Very good," Julie said. "We all meet back up at the Ramada by ten a.m., so Coach doesn't bitch at us for not showing. Now, bring on the shots."

We fist-bumped and headed for the bar.

A cover of Better Than Ezra's *In the Blood* was in full swing by a nineties throwback band wearing flannel shirts they had to be sweating in. The lead sang into the mic and tucked his wiry hair behind his ears. *Wonder what my singer is doing tonight?* Meh. Maybe I didn't want to ponder that too much.

While the girls found a space to hang, I squeezed between two groups at the bar to order. A hand on my waist caused me to turn and shove the fingers away like a fight was about to break out.

"Very good girl." Klive King grinned like a cocky asshole always two steps ahead.

"Whoa! Klive!" I gasped and hated how my smile betrayed any ill will I wanted to hold. I was so happy to see him. I threw my arms around his neck and loved his answering hand on my back. Everything tingled at his fingers on my bare skin from where the shirt rose. "Sorry, not sorry," I said. "I'm just glad you came. Safety net and all that."

"I appreciate your honesty, love. I'm happy to see you, too. Speaking of safety nets, here." He held two cups in his free hand like a pro and offered one to me. "This way you won't have to worry about someone putting something in it."

"Thanks! How did you know where we'd be?"

"How else? Or should I say *who* else?"

"Ugh. Looney Lucy?"

"The one and only. Say what you want. However annoying she may be to you she cares and keeps an eye on you."

"All right, you. Spare me the lectures. I'm trying to drown my cares, not add more."

Beyond him, Julie was laughing like an idiot with some guy. She already held a drink. I was nervous for her.

"Don't worry, I bought theirs, too. They found me first and directed me to you," Klive said like a mind reader.

"Klive, did you tell Jase I have the best moan?" I blurted.

"You think I'd need to?" Wow. Not the response I expected. He moved in closer so that I was tucked between the crowds at either side with the bar at my back. His breath brushed my lobe. All the cold anger I'd sworn to hold onto replaced with thawing heat.

I swallowed and found my voice. "Not unless you're implying he'd know because we'd done something together for him to know." I ignored his blatant advance and turned to flag the bartender. "Five Kamikaze shots, please."

The bartender tossed a towel over his shoulder and took my order with a grin like my mouth was bigger than my capacities. Maybe so, but I couldn't resist the urge to get a jab in at Klive.

"Nice," Klive muttered. "Told you I wouldn't need to. That drink worked for Taylor. Should I thank you now? Or wait till afterward?"

I reached for my card to pay so that I wouldn't punch him in the throat, but he reached over my head. The bartender took his cash instead. I yanked the glass to my lips and downed my shot. "Are you staying the night?" I asked, setting the glass on the bar.

"I grabbed a room at the hotel next to yours." He had the most beautiful array of teeth when he smiled. Even his smart-ass smile was gorgeous, and I envied him. "Hope I didn't scare you into thinking I'd just abandoned you. I had pressing matters to attend to earlier." He nipped a cherry then set his empty glass on the bar to help me carry the shots to my friends. Well, only two of my friends remained. Julie was already out the door with her hookup. *Damn! That was way too fast!* Lindsay flirted with a bouncer, and Eliza thanked me as we offered Klive Julie's shot.

"Normally I don't drink when I'm on guard," Klive said with his pretty accent. "But for you ladies, I'll make an exception. Cheers to third place. Not as good as first, but far better than last."

"I'll drink to that," Eliza said. We clinked our shots and tossed them back.

"Here, Klive. I got one for you, too," I told him.

"Thanks, but I came as your safety net." He offered the extra to Eliza. Turns out, you didn't have to ask her twice either.

"Eliza! Come here! Let them be so Kins can get laid! She needs the stress relief!" Lindsay called her away while I gaped. "Have my shot, Kins! Have fun!"

"Oh my gosh!" I shook my head like Lindsay was crazy, but she shook hers like *I* was and beamed at Klive. He chuckled while

I shrugged. "Just because I need the stress relief doesn't mean I'm partaking. Just so we're clear," I told him. My fingers wrapped Lindsay's shot glass. I held the Kamikaze up in toast. "When in Rome." I tossed back my third shot in less than thirty minutes. "Good thing you came, huh, Mr. King? You better hope I'm not pressing against you in a little bit begging for your brand of stress relief."

"Nuh, uh. I already laid down the law, my sweet, so let's hope you aren't, because you will be sorely disappointed and quite a bit more stressed for bucking my boundaries."

"Ooh lala! Klive, are you tempting me to be bad?" I bit my lip through a big smile. His eyes gleamed with amusement, but the steely resolve had gone nowhere. That was even sexier. Like the ultimate challenge.

"I never said I wouldn't be down for discipline, love. You may not respect me in the morning if I teach you new manners."

I just couldn't. "I'm feeling *mighty* disrespectful. Maybe I need another shot. Please?" I begged with a fluttering of eyelashes like a playful idiot. He laughed and trailed behind me as I towed him back to the bar. We squeezed back in, but when I went to flag the bartender, Klive pulled my hand down.

"Klive, what are you doing?" I almost whined.

"Turn around and look at me," he said in a new tone you didn't question. I did what he said. Our bodies nearly touching, I pressed my palm against him to gain enough distance to gauge his shift. His hand came over my fingers, guiding them around to his lower back. "Kinsley. Behave," he urged at my ear. Zero inside joke or double meaning. The humor gone, something in the sudden seriousness told me to go along with him. He didn't have to tell me. *The eyes I'd felt watching me earlier hadn't been Klive's!* Someone else paid attention, because as Klive nuzzled my neck, I felt a stare that obviously didn't belong to him. I gasped at the tingles that shot straight to my toes. I knew Klive was trying to hide our faces, but that didn't change the way his electric charge practically made the hair float away from my head in response to the cologne and our chemistry. The added danger amplified the intensity.

I ran my nose against his chin. "Who is it, Klive? Someone to do with Inferno? I pissed off the wrong people, didn't I?"

"Shhh, love. Don't panic. Follow my lead. Run your fingers over my hair and around to my face so your hand blocks enough that I may peer to my right without anyone noticing."

I nodded, nuzzling against him like some ho-bag in public, and did what he said. He released a heavy breath against my neck that made my eyes close. This was too easy. Too ... *familiar* ... in ways beyond the night we spent at Delia's.

"Excuse me, mate," Klive said over my shoulder. His hand wrapped around my back so that I pressed firm against his chest, face and all. Who the hell was he shielding me from? My gosh, was Pat here to take revenge for my slapping him and getting his ass kicked?

The bartender came behind me. Klive asked him if guns were permitted on premises because he'd just spied the two in the corner with one.

"It's illegal to carry where alcohol is served because drunks get stupid," he told Klive. "I'll have them taken care of."

"Very well. Do you have another door I can take her out of so that she's not freaked out? She's got a fear of guns. Don't want to cause a scene, you know? And after those Kamikazes?"

The bartender chuckled while I rolled my eyes since I was confident the object I felt beneath Klive's shirt was a concealed gun. To remain chill, I focused on Klive's delish cologne and how my lips brushed his Adam's apple with the breathing I was trying so hard to keep level. Were Lindsay and Eliza still here? I needed to text them if I was leaving.

Klive lifted up about thirty seconds later and urged me ahead of him as we headed in a direction opposite the one I'd come in. I didn't even see how there was any other way, but we squeezed past the tiny staging area the band performed from just as I heard the commotion of a fight beginning.

When I gasped and tried moving faster, Klive put his hand on my exposed belly button and eased my pace so that he controlled our speed. He slowed us to a casual stroll past the cooler and stock room. After that, I barely kept up with his strides as he took my hand and pulled me alongside him through the door around the back of the building.

38 | ♀

"**Are they bikers?**" I whined like the wuss I didn't want to sound like.

"Not sure. Could be an isolated incident. You're kind of cute tonight and revealing way too much."

I gasped, totally offended, and jerked to a stop.

He turned on me and gestured like a wise ass to the University shirt. "Uh! Giving away information, woman! Now, come on."

I began to half-jog beside him since he was so fast. "Is it Pat from last weekend? You said you saw the video. You know his face. Is it him, Klive?"

He laughed as though enjoying an inside joke. "No way. That bloke won't be chasing anything but his tail for a long while."

"What do you mean?" I demanded, Pat's words replaying. "Did something happen to him after I ran from Jase? Was there more on the video?"

"Jogging is a good idea," he said, ignoring my questions. We were now out in the open public once more. He picked up the pace till I was jogging beside him.

"Are you ignoring me?" I asked.

"Ask me no questions, I'll tell you no lies, and I will absolutely say *no more* on the matter." The look he gave made me swallow. "Want to play tag?" he asked out of nowhere. This time I laughed like this was ridiculous until I looked over my shoulder to see two forms run out of the bar onto the sidewalk.

"Okay." I nodded, realizing where he was going with this. "I'm gonna have to giggle like a girly moron, aren't I?"

His lips split into a full grin; a relief after the severe look he'd given seconds before. "Damn right, love. Try not to let me catch up. I'm counting on your speed. I know you're grounded, but there are times to use your talent for more than organized sport. You have to be dying to open up."

"I am," I agreed. *Especially if that meant not dying!* My hand tucked my phone deeper into my back pocket. I'd have to text the girls when we got to a safer place.

"Keep jogging so you're warm, Kinsley. We will run toward the fort. Cross the street and jog beyond the walls into the tourist area. Giggling is important so I don't look like I'm trying to attack you." I nodded and jogged beside him as he instructed. "When we get to the St. George Inn, I'll take point. Keep up. Watch out for cock-ups coming out of driveways and parking lots." He winked like this really was some stupid game. I tried telling myself I was just gearing up to beat the heat he wanted to bring. Just us. He said just that like he read my mind. "Just the two of us. Game time. You ready? It's about a mile up."

"I know. I've been here before. I can handle long distance. Can you?" I flirted and shoved him into the grass beside the sidewalk. He laughed, and I admired how well he pretended under pressure.

"Woman! Watch those hands. Payback's in order," he called as I jogged ahead of him. Sure enough, I giggled like a ditzy flirt. Give me a break. This was too bimbo cheesy and all my fault for wearing this crap. Meh, maybe the shots had flirtation flowing a little easier, too.

Oh, well. Who had time to rethink wardrobes when the time to run my ass off was now?

I shoved my mental energy into my legs like I could run from my screw-ups and everything that had clouded my mind back in the hotel. I glanced back at Klive. My laughter lifted over the sound of traffic driving beside us on the street. Behind us, the two tall forms loomed about half a block away walking too fast to seem casual. *Oh no!*

"Shame on you, sir!" I shouted like he'd just said something I wasn't really offended by.

"Oh, you want to play?" he called after me, closer than expected. "Faster," he huffed as he was too close. "The *real* sprint. Not this gentle crap. Go!"

Yikes! I floored the pedal on my speed as he'd commanded until we dodged couples and kids walking back to their hotels from the tourist town center.

"Hey, watch it!" a woman shouted as I side-stepped her, Klive dodging her on her other side. We laughed together for real. He shoved me through an intersection brandishing a flashing red hand signaling no walking. I shrieked and ran for my life before the cars across the street hit us as we launched through.

"Why'd you do that?" I demanded.

"So the stalkers had to stop. They're running, too. Dead giveaway."

New fear lanced into adrenaline and lit the heat beneath my feet. *This wasn't a game!* They were coming right out in the open with their pursuit! I wasn't sure how to get myself out of a situation he'd ordered me into with my attitude. *Was that fair?* No, I shouldn't blame him like he'd done something wrong when I agreed with his teaching. I hated this rabbit on the run feeling. Part of me wanted to screech to a dead halt and see what this man running beside me was really made of. What were two bikers to a guy with a gun defending a woman in peril? However, the more I thought about his power being tucked away, the more I realized he must've had a good reason to force us to flee rather than pull a gun on them to send a message.

I swallowed at the barrage of thought processes swimming through my head while the stone pillars and the wall around St. Augustine's fort came into view. About two more blocks. Thank God I'd trained all those miles in the sand, and I could say I was glad Klive did the same.

The view of the Castillo de San Marcos was almost as pretty as the beach at night and lit in the same blue sort of cast. I saw Klive calculating whether we should run inside of the fortress instead.

"Safety in numbers?" I sucked wind beside him and indicated we stick to the plan. I loved how in shape he was. "And the fort closed at dusk."

"Very good. Was there anything in particular your team had in mind when they picked this town? I'm a fan of the architecture myself."

I coughed an incredulous laugh at how casual he seemed. Like we weren't possibly running from someone connected to the biker gang, Inferno, who was looking for revenge for my role with Patrick Scott's early demise and my bucking up to Pat Connor before Jase grated his face.

Perhaps I was hyper-sensitive about the mounting situation in my head?

As we narrowed in on the final intersection, Klive glanced behind us while we caught our breath and waited for an opening in the cars to cross the street.

"Looks like we lost them, but let's get inside and take it from there, good?" His breathing was like mine.

"You're pretty quick on your toes," I offered. The cars were slowing.

COMPLICATED MOONLIGHT

"Oh, did I fail to mention that I was fast, too?" He quirked his brows, drawing an impossible smile through my panic. How insane.

"Race you!" I bolted through the crosswalk and hustled up the crowded sidewalk past the cemetery, finally clearing the street in front of the city gates. We slowed when we passed inside the walls. Tourists milled everywhere in every direction. *Praise the Lord!* While I praised the Lord, Klive praised me for doing such a good job following orders for once. "Brat." I slapped his belly, and he snatched my hand to pull me with him toward a crowded Inn.

"There's a great balcony. You want to be a spy for the night instead of sleeping in the roach motel your school picked back there?"

"Klive, they probably don't have any rooms available, and if they do, it'll cost a mini fortune! This is a bad idea."

"You have a better plan? What do you bet they saw you from the moment you and your friends left your room? They could have been sitting outside on the patio and watched you from there. You were saying?"

"Fine. If your smug ass wants to pay and they actually have a room, I'll bite, but I'm not giving any love. Understood, mister?" I pointed my finger in disapproval.

He winced. "Depends where you bite. I'm sensitive, love." I tipped my head and groaned.

"Not my fault you set yourself up for these things. Besides, I told you *I* wasn't giving love, glad we're on the same platonic page. Now, let's do business." He rubbed his hands together with mischief glowing in his eyes. Dammit. That was a look I'd never seen, and I loved playful Klive. His demeanor helped ease mine. I followed him to the counter.

"I'm sorry, sir. Before you even ask, we only have two rooms left and they come at a premium."

He stopped her right then and there. What followed was like a golden web woven by a beautifully scary spider about a couple in love and recently eloped against family's wishes longing for a single night of sanctuary to seal forever their act of love never to be undone. Holy crap. This timeless cliché was too pretty not to slip into, also clear warning that this man could have whatever he wanted, including my unplanned cooperation that should've been somewhat forced, but somehow wasn't in the least. The added bonus to her under the table for allowing us both rooms for the price of one was substantial. His reasoning: if family found us and wanted to try and spy, they couldn't because there were no more rooms at the inn. Who the hell was this guy to be carrying a wad of cash and natural charisma like this? That was just her sum! He paid for the rooms with his card! Hell, maybe those guys were after *him* for his money!

She handed the key cards over the counter, described each room and with a wry grin suggested, "Perhaps you could christen them both."

My eyes bugged. Klive's practically glowed in delight taking mine in. He jostled my hand and thanked her for the newlywed ideas.

That just happened!

She looked me in the eye when she listed the amenities, then wished us a great stay with free room service on the house to congratulate us.

The two rooms weren't just separate. They were in different buildings. Well, they were more so two-story cottages with boutiques on the first floor.

Klive took my hand, leading the way beyond the old schoolhouse to a shopping alley lined with loiters and local art leaning against the outer walls of little shops. An acoustic cover of *Hallelujah* crooned from a busker seated on the ground, his guitar case littered with greenbacks. Klive smiled and tossed a twenty into the case. His grip adjusted on my hand as we walked up the stairs I'd always wanted to when visiting in the past. How could I hide this from my mom when we always speculated about people-watching from the balcony? Or, having our morning coffee from the shop below with views of the fountain and cobble-stone street.

"Although christening sounds delicious, this room is yours. I'll sneak across the street into the other one. Look." He pointed back down the alleyway we'd walked. "See the second window from the right? That's the room I'll be in. Feel free to call me if you can't sleep or want company."

He opened the door for me to walk through but didn't follow.

"Wait. That's it? You're just going? After all that? With all of this?" I asked.

He stared with a myriad on his face, but a certain strain mingled, then mixed into my own. "I should leave," he said. "Kinsley, I did tell Jase you had the best moan. I meant it. You do, but I shouldn't have done that, and I'm sorry. Forgive me. I do not deserve another chance to hear pleasure from your lips. Good night, my sweet."

For a moment, I stood with no words. How did Jase piss me off so bad, but Klive comes clean and I...? I don't know.

I nodded, then the realistic side considered the rest. "Thank you for your honesty." That's what made the difference. Jase gossiped behind my back without apology. Klive had the class to ask forgiveness. Klive also turned his back to leave. "Wait! Klive, please, stay. I know I won't be able to sleep as long as they are out there and you aren't here," I confessed, my heart picking up at the impropriety, but the Lord knew my heart. "I barely feel comfortable enough for you to leave for the other room, and you going to do so will only prove me right when I'm alone."

His Adam's apple bobbed, then he cleared his throat as he stared down with the storm deepening in his eyes. "In all seriousness, Kinsley, after our last night together, I don't know that I can remain honorable."

I shifted close enough to run fingers down his arm to his hand. "I may not know you very well, but I have faith in you, Klive."

His eyes narrowed in confusion before closing. They opened clear and determined. He nodded, but instead of staying, he left the room without a look back. I understood the determination in his face was against me rather than for staying. Wow. Rejection sucked. *Was this one of his 'I'll say no moore on the mattah' moments? If so, why didn't he just say that?*

As I stood alone, I was right. Fear was like a person in the room breathing down my neck and checking all the exits, of which there was only one way in and out. That didn't comfort me. To dispel the lie expanding in my imagination, I threw the door open to lean on the balcony. Shoppers and tourists clustered together below. I searched for vests and scraggly ponytails, desperate to distract myself from the shock of Klive leaving and how the pain felt too physical.

My gaze drew toward the other buildings of the Inn where he'd pointed out the second room. I should worry more about Inferno than the head of dark hair striding through the throngs. Would I ever look out at a crowd without searching for his features ever again? In that moment, I realized I'd been doing that for so long without knowing, having no idea of my pirate's true features outside his gray eyes and delish cologne, height and the way he carried himself like the king of everything. Well, hell. This night was a revelatory blow to my subconscious.

While Klive looked for what I should have, I couldn't take my eyes off him.

39 | ♀

HIS HEAD DISAPPEARED BENEATH an awning, along with any hope that he'd change his mind.

Was he suffering inside the way I was? What the heck was wrong with my body, my emotions? My everything seemed different; distracted, attracted, discombobulated. My soul was tortured in ways that sappy poetry and songs with pained lyrics suddenly made sense. That man kissed me when I was sitting on a toilet, for goodness' sake. He'd pulled my panties down without making moves to get beneath them. *Shit*. He'd said he would love me forever. Even if we'd been playing, he'd not shied from playing with me with such a heavy word. *Gosh, this ache!*

Across the courtyard, I searched the upstairs window of the Inn for any sign of a sweet wave or something that said he hadn't rejected me. Like a cat with a laser dot, I spotted his head darting back into the crowd. He paused to speak to someone, then I saw him swap cash for the man's ball cap.

Leaning over the railing like the breathless Juliet, I grinned when he lifted the Crimson Tide hat in salute before blending into the crowds. He vanished to my right rather than coming back to me. My chest inflated. Was he going to look for the Inferno rather than playing safety?

"Ooh!" I cooed as he came back into the mix of people. *He was coming back! He hadn't rejected me!* I hurried to text the group chat. *First! Klive. St. George Inn.*

I chuckled at their responses. Eliza had chosen to head back to the room. The other two were partying in 'First' place; Julie at a bar a block up the cobble stone from me, Lindsay at the Hampton with the bouncer who'd gotten into a brawl. *Licking his wounds,* she'd texted.

Trotting feet on the wooden stairs carried Klive until he stood on the planks of the landing only feet from a place I'd sworn he'd abandoned. I tucked my phone back in my pocket. He held ice cream cones like a peace offering. How simple, childlike, adorable. How could I not smile like a smitten sap?

"You came back," I gushed then blushed and looked down. How embarrassing to wear my happiness so open to him all the time.

"Of course. I'd never leave you if you're afraid."

My eyes lifted at the sincerity in his voice and how I was able to hear his low tone in the deafening volume of rowdy crowds. He licked the swirled yellow and white ice cream and held the other one to me. Damn. Was this how men felt when women did provocative things without realizing?

"Thank you," I said, my voice small with the butterflies stealing the normal strength. I took his offering. My aching thoughts and memories of his sweetness at Delia's made me shy. He strolled slowly toward me with the most understated victorious smirk lighting his whole face. He loved the affect he had on me, my wretched poker face. I remained rooted to my spot and opened my lips for his as they landed on mine. His hand held to the spot just beneath the lobe of my left ear. Bloody hell, could I remember how to breathe? This kiss was different from the others we'd shared. Seemed I couldn't get enough oxygen with every soft pull and shift. I desperately gasped and gulped for any semblance of control during the greatest power surge I'd ever experienced. Every bulb in our vicinity should've burst for all of the energy sparking to vivid life.

He hummed something weak and weary and so deliriously real, I couldn't not wrap my free hand around his head to pull him tighter to prevent him from pulling away from this moment. His tongue tasted of pineapple and vanilla. He groaned. So did I, drunker than ten Kamikaze shots, spinning, spinning, spinning.

Several whistles and cat calls sounded off below. I gasped and smiled like a guilty fool when I pried away and realized we were on full display.

Klive's lips were the prettiest shade of puffy, his eyes heavy and hazy in the best way, a reflection of my own I was certain. His chest lifted and deflated more than when we'd run here. How flattering.

"If they're watching, others may be as well, dammit." Klive placed the enemy Alabama cap on my head and tugged the brim on a soft smile. "Here, hold my frozen custard." I took his cone, then squealed in happy surprise when he took my legs out from under me. "Gotta make this believable," he teased with a glorious smile. "You can't hold on, so try not to get that in my hair." He snickered in devious delight as he carried me over the threshold of the room before kicking the door closed behind us.

"How believable?" I said with wispy wanton in my tone. My breath was way too hot with lust, so I took a large lick from the cone he'd gifted. His eyes scanned me in the hat while I relished the feel of being carried to the bed. *Oh, how I wanted him to lay me down for restless hours as he'd spoken of at Delia's!*

"You're drunk, love." He laid me onto the heavenly comforter while I fought to keep the cones from tumbling.

"My friends get drunk and have sex all the time! One is doing it right now with one of the bouncers from the bar we came from."

"If your friends jumped off a bridge, would you?" he teased with a pretty grin. I loved how he didn't lift up yet. He leaned down over me, flirting with the dangerous temptation I longed to give into. He dipped his mouth to lick his frozen custard from the cone I still held.

"Brutal. If *you* jumped, I'd hold your hand," I told him, half-joking. Wow. There was truth in those words.

His eyes studied mine with deeper interest. "I'm flattered, love. I'm also a man of my word." He lifted away and took his cone from my fingers. My body wanted to throw a childish fit that my mind forced away. *How could he lick that ice cream and tease me so?!*

The air was much quieter by comparison to the chaotic fun outside, also crazy thick with unspoken desire. Klive grabbed the remote and turned on the TV.

"If you don't get to work, that's going to melt everywhere." He gestured to my frozen-not-frozen treat.

"Yeah, you're right. Gotta get my revenge somehow," I muttered.

He smiled as he opened a closet for a spare blanket and pillow. The sofa pulled out next. He set about making the bed like a diversion from said revenge but paused to stare at me. Heated color washed through my chest as I realized I'd been staring at him all the while licking the custard in a zoned-out longing. Too late, I averted my eyes to an episode of *Dateline*, thinking unfortunately of the episode I'd watched about a local woman from St. Augustine being murdered for being a good Samaritan staying too late in a bar. The same trepidation I'd felt when he'd left washed over me anew. He snagged the remote and found something else to watch.

Damn. The reminder of why I was in this room with him was colder than the tip of my tongue. I gnawed down the sugar cone and licked my fingertips.

"Too bad we don't have our bags," he said.

When things were calm like this, the TV not very loud, neither of us fleeing or fighting, his accent was very light and pretty.

I wrapped my arms around my exposed midriff and nodded.

"You don't have to be afraid of me taking advantage, love."

"Clearly." I shot a bitter look I couldn't help. "I'm cold after the frozen custard, that's all."

He chuckled with sympathy. "Right. Are you needing me to piss you off again to stop your pouting?"

"I'm not pouting," I looked down at the carpeting, pouting. The bed was the softest king with plush pillows. I crawled up to the headboard to pull back the luxe comforter. My tennis shoes hit the floor with little thuds before I nestled beneath the blankets wishing Klive wasn't afraid to share a bed with me again. I understood the allure of Las Vegas for the first time. No one but my relay team knew I was here with him. They damn sure wouldn't condemn me when they insisted that I bottled too much inside. Tyndall always said someone would come along, give me one good shake and I'd blow. Where was my determination and tenacity around Klive? Why did I seem opposite with him than I was with every other guy?

But where was the man who'd kissed me until my knees were sure to buckle on the balcony? What happened to the guy who'd tucked himself into the same bed and put me to sleep in such depleted pleasure without going beneath my clothes? Why didn't he want to play again? Maybe I was too much for him to deal with.

He tossed a pillow onto his freshly made-up couch, then gestured to the bed in askance. I blinked hard not fully understanding what he was doing. He reached across and snatched a pillow off of the bunch I had on the bed, then tossed the tiny cloud beside his other.

Did he snore? Fart in his sleep? Holy crap what if I did stuff like that without knowing? What if I'd done that stuff after he'd put me to sleep the last time? What if I accidentally slept walked? Shit! Was this maybe why he'd wanted to stay across the street in the other room? I should've let him stay there! Which was scarier? A couple bikers with bad intentions or humiliating myself in front of this always suave asshole?

My worries were interrupted by a hard knock on our door that made me lunge out of bed in his direction. I gripped his arms from behind without realizing.

"Room service."

His body tense, he edged out of my grip. "Kinsley, go to the loo and lock the door."

Could my heart beat any harder? I nodded. He nudged me on my way, waited till the door lock clicked into place. I heard the door to the room opening.

"May I see some identification?" his accent asked.

"Certainly, sir." A pause. "Your order is ready. As requested, a valet brought your car to our lot. Here is your luggage. Also, that other matter you requested ...." The voice dropped to a tone too low to hear.

"Excellent, thank you." The door closed. A moment later he tapped on the door with an all clear. I opened to see him holding my track duffel. The fragrance of charred beef made my stomach growl.

"You are a life saver."

"Not something I hear very often," he said more to himself with a small chuckle. "I ordered cheeseburgers and fries. Salads in case you'd rather—"

"Cheeseburgers sound amazing right now. Thank you. How did you get my bag?" I asked.

"Your friend, Eliza. She was only too pleased to pass it over to the bellhop when she heard you were staying the night with me. You have naughty friends, love."

"I told you. You've made me the black sheep of the group ...."

"Woman, behave. Eat. I'm taking the shower first."

"What? No chivalry?" I teased and moved toward the bed so I could rest the duffel on the mattress and rifle through the contents to be sure no one else had.

"Chivalry doesn't go very far where you're concerned."

"Great to see you only whip it out in case of emergencies."

I grinned over my shoulder at the look in his eyes. That look said he was turning the water to cold. Good. Misery loves company.

40 | ♀

I waited for him to lock the bathroom door and turn on the shower before I was outside gulping air that wasn't thick with forbidden desire. Maybe, I should call a cab and go to the Ramada while I had the chance. Was I strong enough for this? *I can do all things through Christ which strengthens me ...* I repeated that verse in my head several times and prayed about whether this was the Lord's provision or not. How was this guy in the right place at the right time so many times?

I backed into the rocking chair, content to people-watch as I tore into my burger. Tension released in favor of watching teens egg one another on in a frozen custard-eating contest. Whoever had brain freeze first had to pay for the next round of competitors. Boys were so dumb sometimes, but I admit antics such as these made me smile. The girlfriend of the first loser began massaging his temples while he whined against her chest, then she caught on that he was just copping a feel and she pushed him away.

The busker's voice sang a song I didn't know over the playful bantering, his guitar strings strumming in time to the rocking of my chair. Orders came and went through the busy coffee shop. Life bustled all around. These people weren't having drunken fun. They were interacting with each other. The only phones I saw were for taking pictures and posting to social media. Refreshing.

My phone was in the room, having been tossed inside with all of my effects so I didn't have to read the texts from my father or Tyndall right now. Had Jase texted? Was he sorry the way Klive was? Would Jase ever apologize even if he was wrong? Everyone could accuse me of ghosting them, but I didn't want to ponder real life right now. I wanted to disappear inside this realm and pretend not to be Kinsley Hayes track star with high expectations. I wanted to play and cuddle, make-out like those teens down there, like Klive had done with me last time. Since when was I not grossed out and disapproving of public displays like that? Since I learned how amazing such affection felt only what? Maybe fifteen minutes ago? Klive had the best technique with his lips and tongue like he knew exactly how to kiss me, what I liked, what I didn't, the right amount of restraint and need at once. My eyes closed to savor the memory that made every part of my body staticky.

I swallowed the final bite before the door yanked open so fast, I gasped and gripped the armrests. Klive's hand stole my arm, his eyes panicked.

"What is it?" I asked, my heart in my throat. He didn't give me an answer, but hauled me up and into the room, slamming the door and throwing the lock. "What the hell!" I ripped my elbow away, my mood immediately pissed for him having touched my pet peeve.

"Exactly, Kinsley. What the hell are you doing? We're supposed to be keeping a low profile. After our mistake, we can't afford another."

I gasped and tears welled in my eyes before I could stop them.

He sighed and rubbed the back of his neck. "That came out wrong."

"No, you're right. We made a mistake. It won't happen again," I said, sobered and somber.

He wanted to argue but threw a neutral expression that tormented me to the core. Not fair how guys could shut off while my pain was so red and wounded anyone with eyes saw the hurt. I hated the expanding silence. This something in the air stifled more than the previous desire.

"I'm sorry, Klive, but life is happening out there, and I wanted to see it!" I threw my empty hands. "No. I don't want to just *see* it. I want to be part of it. I'm so tired of watching!"

Crap. I'd just thrown a mini fit in front of a grown ass man who was wrapped in a towel with a couple of droplets traveling over his abs. My throat dried. Jase popped into my head. My singer in my apartment, kneeling before me offering a towel while looking up at my coffee covered bra and panties. Was this how he'd felt? No way. Jase was desensitized to this type of intensity. I wasn't and Complicated Moonlight glared by the time I looked back at his eyes.

"Did you lie to me then? Pretend to be afraid to lure me once more into this miserable predicament, because I'll tell you right now, Ms. Hayes, I am not one to be trifled or toyed with."

I swallowed at what his current attitude did to me. Maybe I should've felt afraid. Some of me was, but I wasn't scared. I couldn't breathe. He was too sexy when he looked like that. Like the tiger again, but instead of holding his tail, I held the whip and felt an instinct to drop the discipline and coax this creature to peace again.

"I didn't lie to you." My voice was weak, hoarse, lacking conviction but conveying guilt. No. I *should've* conveyed guilt or felt guilty. He felt tricked. *Had I tricked him?* I wouldn't do that on purpose.

"Forgive me, but you don't seem so afraid anymore, and I feel I've been had."

"Mr. King, tell me you look at me and don't see fear."

His brows knit as he stared. "I see fear in you, too, but it isn't a bloody thing to do with Inferno. It's us in this room and what happened at Delia's. The kiss on the balcony back there. I feel I need to be tied inside a sheet with my hands cuffed to behave with you. I can't endure another sleep over."

That anger fell with the bob of his Adam's apple. The man walked close to take my hand and turn my palm to plant several slow kisses to skin that seemed attached to different parts of my body. The pads of my fingertips came next. My breath panted from my parted lips. His free hand drew around mine. In a flash of unexpected movement, my wrists were pinned behind my back, then released but ordered to remain.

"We aren't playing anymore bases. No touching. Kinsley, if you respect me, you will keep your hands to yourself, and if I respect you, I'll do the same." He pulled his hands behind his back. "As I indicated last time, when at last I wrap you in a sheet, it won't be to behave. I know your conviction. I refuse to be the one who compromises your morals. But I will kiss you again if you promise to keep the layer of respect between us."

"Dammit. How do I behave, Mr. King?" I gave the most wicked grin like dangling feathers in front of a kitty on catnip. Or was that the other way around?

"Better than last time. You need to quit asking that question, love."

"You keep inspiring misbehavior, though," I whined.

His eyebrows rose in authority. "Kinsley, if you don't behave, I refuse to kiss you." *Oh, damn, he had the most seductive drop in his tone.* My eyes closed. His lips brushed my jaw line, my ear, my forehead, dragged in all the places in between like the ultimate tease. I gasped when they landed on mine, but rather than kiss me, he spoke much the way he had when dropping me off at Sara's condo.

"I think you're worth waiting for. Am I, love?"

I whispered a closed-eyed curse against his plush mouth, defeated, but determined. "It must suck to be a guy." I grinned feeling every bit on the opposite side of the scale. I mean, c'mon, the man was naked beneath a towel, the backs of my knees pretty much up against the mattress of a bed we could share in secrecy. Was there anything more tempting? And yet, he was asking me to wait for him now? Constance was so right. No wonder Jase was so sexually frustrated with me. I should apologize to him ....

Klive chuckled and captured my mouth for one kiss, a couple of tantalizing pulls, a stroke of tongue, and pulled away to vanish inside the bathroom. I stayed where I was, locked in position praying away every warring, pained emotion until he re-emerged in boxer briefs and a tee shirt.

"Oh, come on! If you want me to behave, why prance around in lingerie?"

His head tossed back on a hearty laugh. My soul took flight at the sight and sound. On a deep breath, I hauled my duffel bag into the bathroom to change into the only clothing options I had inside, but he knocked a moment later and shoved his hand into the space, a tee shirt dangling off of his finger. How'd he know?

"I thought we agreed I'd take your pants next time," I teased, enjoyed another laugh from his lips. "Thank you, sir."

When I emerged, I'd tamed the girly bliss of wearing another of his shirts down to a casual contentment. However, he had that heavy look again when he saw me come out. The fry in his hand paused on the way to his mouth. His shirt almost hit my knees, way too big, nothing sexual, but that was what I learned that night about sex. For some reason, I'd had this commercial notion that sexual feelings were coaxed to the surface by lingerie and intentional sensuality. Klive was different. He studied my thighs like imagining pulling me onto his lap and pushing the shirt up to my waist. How crazy when my track uniform showed almost one hundred percent of my legs, but Klive, I realized, was driven by mystery. He wanted and needed the pain and thrill of the hunt. The chase. He was who Bayleigh surmised, and I had a long road ahead of myself if I wanted to tame this one. We matched. Constance was going to love the irony of him confirming her suspicions.

"If you like this, just wait till you see me in a muumuu." I snickered at Klive's continued stare. He grinned and snagged my hand on my way past the couch where he laid.

"All play aside, are you okay?" Gray eyes searched mine for cracks in my calm, but there were none to be found.

"I am. Thank you for coming back."

"Anything you want, love."

I raised my eyebrows and he chuckled and said, "*Almost* anything."

"You're a tease, Mr. King." I released his hand and crawled into bed, snuggling up and building a nest with the pillows while I felt him watching.

"Ditto, my sweet."

"I hate that word." I shot a play glare his way.

He gave a playful pout. "Which one?"

My turn to smile, but the look on his face was so serene, all my lust took a backseat to absorb what I somehow knew to be a rare moment of calm in someone who was always calculating or on guard.

"I'd never hate the endearment. Good night, Klive. As my daddy always says, 'sweet dreams and say your prayers'."

He nodded and aimed the remote at the TV for an instrumental music channel. "For the record, Kinsley, I find myself praying the entire time we're together. For what, I haven't yet worked out."

COMPLICATED MOONLIGHT

If I were honest, I did the same thing when I was with him and had no idea what I was asking God for when Klive was the subject matter.

"Ditto," I whispered and said another aimless prayer in my head.

Continue onto Mad Love

VOLUME 3 OF THE DON'T CLOSE YOUR EYES SERIES

MAD LOVE

Lynessa Layne

USA TODAY BESTSELLING AUTHOR

1 | ♀ - Mad Love

I STIRRED AT THE sound of Klive's accent.

"Fifteen minutes, please. Keep a low profile. I'm about to rouse my wife. We will meet you down the street outside the gate. Thank you."

My heavy eyes unglued when Klive's finger traced my profile and tapped my nose. I blinked several times as his face took form before me.

"I heard you talking, I think," I mumbled, my voice distorted as half my face pressed into the pillow. "Was I dreaming?" Suddenly, I jerked up in alarm. "Did I wake you up? Was I sleepwalking?"

He shook his head. "I wasn't aware I needed to worry about you walking out the door in the middle of the night."

I fell back into the nest of pillows with relief, then looked at him. "Something wrong? It's still dark."

"Love, nothing is wrong, aside from what brought us together in this room. We've shaken our tail for now, but if we don't get back to Tampa before they know we're gone, we may lose our edge. I'll drive. You sleep."

"Bummer. I was so hoping to trick you into wearing a banana hammock on the beach to torture my friends."

Klive laughed out loud and shook his head in disapproval. "All right, naughty girl. Your friends have the luxury of drinking their days away on the beach. You and I operate under different circumstances. Here, I pulled your track pants from your duffel and packed the few personal effects you took from it. I'll give you a moment to dress and use the restroom, then meet me on the balcony."

I nodded and shoved the heavenly cloud of blankets aside. In a stupor I did as he said, then pulled the door to the room closed at my back once I stepped onto the balcony. Klive leaned over the railing and peered down at the deserted cobble stone streets below. I couldn't help memorizing him this way and wanting to somehow preserve the man before me. Instinctively, I knew he was to vaporize with the responsibility life doled. I replayed what I could recall from the phone call he'd made before he'd awakened me. Klive called me his *wife*.

What would that be like? To see him this way and run my nails over his back the way my mother did to my father? I'd never pondered the intimacy and permission of such gestures until this moment when I wasn't allowed to without being weird. *Did Klive even like to be touched that way? How did he like his back scratched if at all? Hard, soft? Barely grazing?*

"Oh, good. You're ready?" he asked as he turned to find me watching him. I nodded and chewed my lower lip. "What's wrong, love?"

"Klive, if I wrap my hands behind my back, will you kiss me one more time before this all vanishes? Is that too inappropriate to ask?"

He smiled though the look in his eyes was strained and sad, aching like my own. His hands wrapped behind his back as he dipped his face to mine. My hands clasped tight behind my back, as tight as I wished to hold to him. *Oh, Klive King... what you do to me*, I thought as his kiss was so ... *consuming.* The world around us melted under the warmth of his mouth and brush of five o'clock shadow.

He pulled away, kissed the tip of my nose, my forehead for a lingering moment, then unclasped his hands to offer one to me. I took his fingers and allowed him to lead the way downstairs around the corner to the gates of the city. A white Tesla idled silent with an obedient bellhop standing beside a valet. Klive tipped them both, walked me around to the passenger side, opened the door, and helped me inside. The door closed. He got into the driver's seat a moment later.

"I was right about your car, sir. I deserve another kiss."

He leaned across the console to peck my lips the way a normal couple does. Sigh....

Klive decided to take the A1A back to the I-4 so I could enjoy the scenery of moonbeams against the East coast waves along with the beautiful mansions that dotted the beach front properties. To be honest, I thought he was prettier. So was his hand he held my fingers in. The thumb brushed my knuckles every so often. My heart clenched so hard, a lump of emotion constricted the air in my throat. I looked out the passenger side until I fell asleep. When the car stopped, Klive opened the door and lifted me from the seat. My hands wrapped around his neck, but I was too sleepy to care about walking. He carried me until I heard the beep of a key card in a door, the slam a moment later. More beeps. Another door. Another soft bed with heavenly blankets.

"Sweet dreams, say your prayers, love." Klive kissed my forehead, and I whimpered in protest. I reached up and pulled him down until he kissed me the way I wanted.

"You are the dream, Klive. I want you."

"So are you, Kinsley, and I want nothing more."

Hours later, harsh beeping of an unfamiliar alarm clock jerked me from my dreams. My eyes opened to bright light outlining heavy curtains above a humming air conditioning unit. The jarring sound had my fingers fumbling around the unfamiliar nightstand until the damn thing silenced. The red digits blurred and focused.

Holy crap! Ten-thirty!

I jumped out of the bed and yanked the curtains back. Blinding sunlight glittered against the white caps of Tampa Bay from about ten stories up. At the shock of light, I squinted while blinking back spots as I peered into the dark cave of the hotel room I'd slept in. A note rested on the nightstand. Took me a few moments before the words appeared without green glowing orbs blocking them.

Morning, love.
Brunch downstairs before parting ways to look like we crossed paths by chance. St. Augustine our little secret.
X-Complicated.

He had very elegant handwriting. Mom would've appreciated his technique. I wasn't sure how I felt about him not signing the note. Eh, at least he'd more than confirmed he'd sent all those roses. I folded the note to keep and went into the bathroom.

"Our little secret?" I asked my reflection while unwrapping a toothbrush and the travel sized toothpaste offered by the hotel. Damn. *Why hadn't I considered this?*

My eyes didn't look offended, nor did the glow of my skin. I wasn't offended at all. Intrigued was more apt. If I went home like this, my parents would think I'd gotten laid for all the natural flush in my cheeks and light in my eyes. Bayleigh always had this glow after a good romp. So, what did that say about Klive and my magnetism toward him if he didn't touch me and lit me up this way?

I found my duffel bag on top of the chest of drawers. A billowy sun dress with a strapless fitted bodice hung on a hanger in the tiny closet. Well, hell. Klive was a passive brat. I tapped my chin.

I couldn't wear a bra with this dress, nor was I packing pasties in my track duffel. Loved how he refused to get me out of my clothes when I begged yet chose this to enjoy my lack of certain clothes in his own mind. Wicked man. I smiled with a little chuckle when I looked at the floor and noticed a brand-new pair of heels to go with the dress. The same ones I'd tested with Constance, but they were in red rather than gold. Guess Miranda, the salesclerk, had gotten his other request after all.

"Of course, heels and a dress, Mr. King." I had half a mind to wear my jeans and tacky tee outta this refined establishment to blow a hole in his plans. Crazy, though; how had this man managed this when he'd been up all night? Or had he brought these things to St. Augustine when he'd packed his own bag? Maybe he'd planned to take me out today but had to shift his plans when those guys chased me? My heart ached at the mystery and stolen potential date.

I freshened up and dressed, finger-combed my hair since I didn't have my brush. *Thank God for a modest padding!* I adjusted the bodice firmly over the girls, stepped inches taller into the heels. *Remarkable how well everything fit,* I thought, as I buckled the straps. In the full-length mirror in the room, I whistled at what these heels did for my calves. No wonder Constance was in love with them. For good measure, I took a few laps around the room to get my balance right. No public fails for me today, thank you.

I tucked Klive's shirt and my track pants inside my duffel. "Holy shit!" My keys tumbled in the bag! The Honda key was gone from my Civic's key chain, a neon tag with a number and the name of the hotel in its place.

"What the hell?" I left my car at the bar because Jase had taken me home Thursday night. *Do I even want to know how the magic man performs his tricks?*

"No," I answered my thoughts as I checked the room to be sure nothing was left. Did Klive not want to be seen taking me home if he went out of his way to have my car brought here? Klive hadn't slept in here. Had he gotten himself a room, or gone home with plans of running into me here? Should I stay or go? If I stay, was that a silent agreement to creating secret rendezvous? If I left, would he come looking or wonder where I was? Maybe feel stiffed the way I'd made Jase feel after standing him up?

My mean girl conscious popped up and said the only fair option to Jase was that I leave Klive. How could I be so offended at Jase's desire when I'd felt the same toward the man rejecting me last night? Yeah. I needed to leave. Just because I wanted Klive didn't mean I was giving away my self-esteem.

I stepped into a long hallway, counted the paisleys on the carpet as I walked with my track duffel slung over my shoulder. A little awkward with my heels and the weight of the bag, but I worked the look with more confidence in each determined step to leave this foolishness behind. I exited the elevator downstairs while studying the valet tag. Outside, I passed the ticket over and waited for the valet to bring my car. There, like a perfectly directed play I had no idea I starred in, Klive appeared from the corner of my eye with two other men. All of them wore light colored suits and spoke of fishing. Klive was laughing at something one of his company was saying when he faltered as though genuine at the sight of me. Maybe he realized I was leaving?

"Upon my word, gentlemen. You've seen the runner from the paper, yes?" he asked. "It is you, is it not?" he asked me as though barely acquainted with me.

I swallowed and nodded, then remembered to smile. The valet parked my vehicle at the curb while I pretended I wasn't stupefied as to how my Civic got here.

"I am the runner, yes, sir. Glad to know someone read the article," I said. "In fact, I just came off a meet last night." I gestured to the heavy bag resting against my hip.

"Kinsley!" My father's colleague, Ben, jogged out from the parking garage. "What a pleasure running into you here," he said with a great smile. Ben took me by the hands and kissed my cheek. Klive wore surprise in his eyes. Before any of the men said anything, Ben turned and greeted them, then asked if they minded whether I joined them for brunch. *So Klive and Ben knew one another? Had brunch together? Small world.*

"Oh, Kinsley, I guess I should've asked if you were free first. I hope you will join us," Ben said. "It's delightful and my friend, here, is buying. I'm almost positive he wouldn't mind one more."

Klive said, "By all means. Would be our pleasure to have you join."

"What do you say? Hungry?" Ben asked. "You look beautiful, by the way. Those are killer heels."

"Thank you," I said. "I suppose I could join as long as it really isn't too much trouble. Y'all can be my alibi for missing family yard work," I teased. The valet placed the bag in the backseat of the car when I told him I'd be back after brunch.

"Kinsley is Andrew Hayes' daughter." Ben filled the others in while we headed back into the hotel. Apparently, all of these men worked in the same building. I couldn't help my fascination with Klive in this capacity. He was way too distracting in a white suit like the hero rather than the dangerous rogue I sensed. Funny thing was, in this capacity, with these men, he was like another personality altogether. If I'd worn white, I'd be a magnet for strawberry jam mishaps. I bet Klive would walk out of here looking as spotless as he did walking in.

I ripped my eyes from his smooth complexion as he pulled the door open for me, gestured I go ahead of them much the way he had when we'd been enemies in the elevator. He switched characters between last night and this morning just as he had two years ago after asking me out then doling an insult for my refusal.

"Thank you, sir." I walked through, Ben and the others behind me while Klive fell in back. I pulled the door for the restaurant. Each man tried to refuse my hospitality, but I arched an eyebrow and told them to go on. Until I came to Klive, that is. I didn't give him the chance to insist I go ahead of him. I released the handle and followed the others before he caught the door and stepped through. He chuckled to himself at my back while flutters filled my belly, more so as I fought to look like we didn't know each other.

"Her father's been going crazy with worry over her," Ben was saying. "She didn't make things easy at the office this past week. Just for that, Kins, you owe me a lunch date to pay for your mistake."

I laughed too loud and slapped Ben's arm. "Not a chance. You can have brunch, but I'm dating another man, Ben."

Klive swallowed and appeared ruffled. He said his name to the hostess before she led the way. Klive motioned I go before them. I noticed the hostess glanced back at me, then looked beyond at him.

"Dating another man, huh?" Ben asked. "No wonder your dad is up in arms," Ben muttered. "Is that why you were MIA? By the way, you look badass with all these designs on your leg and hands. I bet he'd flip his lid if he saw you, though."

"Thank you. I've been MIA because I was with friends doing college things that college girls do before I grow up and graduate. One of my friends painted this on my body. Yes, I'm sure he'll flip when I see him."

"Graduation?" one of the men asked. Ben filled in the blanks while he ushered me into a chair he pulled away from a table for me.

"Thank you." I scooted closer to the white tablecloth and unfolded the linen napkin to lay across my lap. Suddenly, all my mother's drills on table manners rushed through my mind as I tried to pretend to belong with these men. *Elbows off the table. Work from the outside in. Crossed ankles, not legs. Sit up straight.*

"Very impressive," one of the men stated. I blinked up at him and took a sec to realize he was speaking about my major, not my manners, hee-hee. "I hear diabetes is the silent crisis growing bigger than global warming and at a faster pace."

"Yes," I said with a bright smile. *Someone knew!*

"Well, Kinsley, it's a shame your father couldn't join us. Although he may give us all grief for stealing a moment to have mimosas with his daughter." One winked.

Ben chuckled. "I promise this moment is more pleasant than what you go home to."

"Yikes. I believe you are right, Ben." I couldn't help my genuine smile, even if I worried about my father the more Ben seemed to. "Bring on the champagne and orange juice, STAT!"

We all laughed while Ben signaled the waiter to order our drinks. The waiter rushed like a man on a mission. *Good.*

"Where are my manners?" Ben asked and introduced the others, in one ear out the other, before landing on their very quiet host. "Kinsley, this is Klive King. Don't be offended by his silence. He's really not as rude as he comes off. Girls scare him," Ben teased. "Klive meet Kinsley Hayes."

"Hi, Klive," I said with a blush and placed my hand in his. No different than the way I had the others, but Klive's touch was charged.

The waiter returned with crystal glasses filled with our pretty cocktails. When he left, I picked back up. "Nice to meet you. All of you. And thank you for inviting me to brunch. I've not had the pleasure. To be honest, I never considered coming into a hotel to eat without having slept in it the night before." *Shit. Stop talking.*

"Ms. Hayes, the pleasure's all mine," Klive said. He unfolded his linen napkin with deft grace and laid the cloth over his lap. His fingers wrapped the stem of his crystal glass. "Girls don't scare me. I find most women think I'm off-putting for not putting up with their bullshit. The ones that don't find me off-putting, I'm put off by." Klive's eyes lit while his lips smirked. His company gaped at his audacity while I chuckled. No way *I* put him off. That much was evident by our back-and-forth liaisons. I wouldn't be surprised if half his smirk was due to the fact that he knew I wore no bra.

"I'll gladly drink to that." I lifted my mimosa. His brows shot up in pleasant surprise to clink glasses with me. The others, not expecting my reaction, lifted their glasses in agreement.

"I'd never fault you for your honesty, Mr. King. We share a common thread. Most women find *me* off-putting, which works since I'm put off by most of them as well. Perhaps we should hang out to keep them at bay?"

The group laughed as I took a sip of my orange juice and champagne. The men asked about my sprint, my average times, what events I ran, then surmised why other women probably found me off-putting.

Klive's foot bumped mine beneath the table. I swallowed the thrill with more mimosa.

"So, gentlemen, do we order from a menu, or partake of the buffet?" I asked, looking around.

"Anything you want, love," Klive said. "I prefer the menu. Not a fan of the shared serving spoons and others breathing on my food." *Ah, the germaphobe.*

"You don't mince words, do you, Mr. King?" I grinned and opened the menu.

"Ms. Hayes, please, call me Klive."

"Well, Klive, you may call me Ms. Hayes." I fought a flirty smile as Klive pulled the menu down so his eyes grinned over the edge. I lifted my chin, shoulders back like a proper lady. I cleared my throat. "Having been in the food service industry for some years, should I spoil everything with wondering when the last time they disinfected their menus was? Or whether they used a dirty cloth to do so?"

"Oh, ma'am, we wouldn't dare," the waiter rushed in alarm, giving his eavesdropping away. "All of our facilities are given the utmost care and attention for maximum customer satisfaction."

I quirked my eyebrows while his very defensiveness and guilty blush confirmed my theory. Ben chuckled to himself, the other men seemed amused as well.

I turned my faux snobby charm on the ruffled waiter. "In that case, may I have the Eggs Benedict with the Hollandaise on the side, please?" I handed my menu over. The waiter nodded and took Klive's order. The others said they weren't afraid of germs and willing to brave the buffet. Klive rolled his eyes and produced his phone. I grabbed my mimosa and took a long drink to hide my contempt at this ultimate dating pet-peeve.

"Pull yours too, love. If I ignored my phone for you, these gossip whores would have a field day. We are being studied. If I don't look at my phone, one may accuse me of infatuation for being unable to rip my eyes from your shoulders and collarbones in that dress. The way your pulse beats in your throat. The dry swallow that belies my effect on you ...."

"Holy shit," I whispered. "My phone is in my duffel bag. What the hell do you want me to look at instead of the way your jaw muscle jumps when I get under your skin? That little twitch in your lips when you try not to smile?"

His eyes shot to mine, stunned that I paid him as much mind as he apparently did me. "Seems we are both wretched poker players," he mused and texted like I didn't exist.

"Indeed. Know what my father taught me about poker?" I asked.

"What's that?" he asked without looking at me.

"Be willing to quit while you're ahead. No sense losing everything you've gained to bluff on a hand you can't win with." I stood, downed the last of my mimosa, set the glass back down.

"Give my meal to a homeless person."

Klive's phone laid on the table. "What are you saying?"

"I'm saying there are safer bets I'm willing to make. No bluffs or secrecy necessary. Thanks for everything, Mr. King."

His jaw muscle jumped while his eyes turned to stone. I strode toward Ben to kiss his cheek and tell him I got a call from a friend and needed to leave.

"May I walk you to the valet?" Ben asked.

"I'd like that. Thank you." I took the arm he held out as if we were together. Ben told the guys he'd be back. I smiled over my shoulder and waved at them, but my eyes flared at Klive before shifting to neutral. There was a difference in secret rendezvous together in a hotel room versus shame in public with others.

Klive needed to learn the distinction. I was no one's girl coming or going by the back door.

When I handed the valet my ticket, Ben studied me in a different way than I ever recalled in all the years he and my father worked together.

"What is it, Ben?"

He shrugged. "I don't know exactly. Something seemed ... *there*."

"With?"

"I've never seen him check anyone out. He skimmed you. *Twice*."

"Who?"

"Klive. Then again, I've never seen him approach someone in passing. He read about you and approached you like he was a fan."

"It happens on occasion," I told him.

"He called you *love*. I've never heard him call any woman that. *Dear*, maybe. *Miss*. *Ma'am*, but of course it sounds like *mom*, which is pretty funny, but never *love*."

"Oookay ...." I trailed like Ben was crazy. "I'm pretty sure Brits say that often. Easy endearment," I offered.

"He shook your hand, Kins. He'll shake hands if he has to, but he hates contact."

"Ben, maybe he just didn't want to make me feel uncomfortable. You're reading too much into that back there. Trust me, as a bartender I come across all types. People do strange things sometimes."

Ben laughed and shook his head. "Kinsley, Klive King does *not* go out of his way to make women feel more comfortable. You heard him. He's put off by them, therefore he never does anything to draw anyone. As long as I've known him, he actively repels them. I guess I thought he was a closet gay. I just— hell, I don't know. The way he looked at you. *Not gay*. But he didn't only look at you like you're hot in the heels, the way normal men do. He ..." Ben tilted his head like the right word might fall from his ear.

My car came down the ramp of the parking garage into the bright sun. The light glared off the windshield into our eyes. We squinted at one another.

"Ben, I'm flattered. He's attractive, but like I said, I'm dating someone. So, if you're trying to set us up or someth—"

"Admiration!" His fingers snapped. "Kinsley, he *admires* you. That's what it is." Ben dismissed me altogether, shook his head at his own thoughts. "Damn, girl, you've got the magic touch. I've never had more respect for you or him. Enviable, Kinsley. His respect is hard to earn."

I thanked the valet as he passed me my keys. Ben gave a tiny wave and walked back inside as if he'd had an epiphany.

"He okay?" the valet asked.

"I guess." I shrugged, tipped him, and drove away from an odd experience more confused about Klive's enigma than before.

Continue Mad Love

Acknowledgments

Thank you to TK Cassidy and AJ Layne for your time, patience and constructive criticism of this project. I appreciate your attention to detail and holding me to a higher standard than I sometimes want to set for myself when I'm exhausted.

Thank you to the servers at my favorite dive bar, Pratt Pub. You fill my mind with inspiration with every drink you serve and the kindness you show your patrons.

Thank you, readers, for enduring the ride along with all the changes and shifts I've made to this series as I find what works.

About Lynessa Layne

Lynessa Layne is a native Texan from the small town of Plantersville. She's a fan of exploration, history, the beach (though she's photosensitive), Jesus, and America too (RIP Tom). Besides being an avid reader, she's obsessed with music of all types (hence her reference to Tom Petty). As a child, she created music videos in her mind and played Barbies perhaps a little longer than most with her little sister, not yet realizing she was writing and enacting stories all along.

Though she's put away the dolls, she now uses her novels as an updated, grown-up version of the same play.

Lynessa is also a certified copy editor and a member of Mystery Writers of America, with work featured by Writer's Digest and Mystery and Suspense Magazine. She has also graced the cover of GEMS (Godly Entrepreneurs & Marketers) Magazine and was a finalist for Killer Nashville's 2022 Silver Falchion Awards for Best Suspense and Reader's Choice.

For more visit lynessalayne.com and sign up for her newsletter, Lit with Lynnie and follow on social media:

https://www.facebook.com/authorlynessalayne

https://www.instagram.com/lynessalayne/

https://twitter.com/LynessaLayne

> Writers like me depend on readers like you.
> Please leave a positive review.
> Thanks
> ♡ - *Lynessa*

Made in the USA
Middletown, DE
27 July 2024